# VOLUME ONE

## EDITED BY B.K. BASS

KYANITE
Publishing

ISBN
Paperback: 978-1-952152-53-5
eBook: 978-1-952152-52-8

Editor-in-Chief: B.K. Bass
Associate Editors: Sam Hendricks and Crystal L. Kirkham
Cover & interior design by B.K. Bass

www.kyanitepublishing.com

# CONTENTS

Preface iii

Fall, Sacred Apple 3
by *Emory Glass*

The Seven Curses 53
by *Alan G. Provance*

Call of the Void 84
by *Crystal L. Kirkham*

Mist Shroud 129
by *Melissa Matos*

Curse of the Dark Lake 155
by *Michael D. Nadeau*

The Jaws of the Deep 198
by *Elizabeth Carlyon*

Tree Crypt 229
by *Sam Claussen*

Protector of the Realm 270
by *Brett Venter*

# PREFACE

Anybody familiar with my preferences in literature, either personally or professionally, will be aware that I'm a man of varied tastes. From the sunlit fae knolls of fairy tales to the sleek lines of an interstellar battlecruiser, I feel there's a lot to be discovered across the breadth of speculative fiction. I'll even dive into a contemporary thriller, mystery, or historical fiction from time to time.

There's one very specific genre, though, that has been at the heart of my love of fantasy for well over a quarter of a century. Bringing together all my favorite elements of sword and sorcery, gothic horror, and weird fiction; dark fantasy has long been and shall likely long remain my favorite genre of speculative fiction.

What is it about dark fantasy that creates such a draw for me? It's hard to say. I'm a sucker for sword-swinging adventures like Tolkien's *Lord of the Rings* or Brooks' *Sword of Shannara*, but at the same time there's a primal appeal to the atmosphere of gothic horror tales like Stoker's *Dracula* or Shelley's *Frankenstein*. When aspects of all these stories are mashed together, something magical happens.

I hope you find the same sort of magic in the eight novelettes we've collected within these pages. Each of them approaches the genre from a different perspective.

But, no matter their approach, I hope all of them bring you some thrilling Visions of Darkness.

— *B.K. Bass*

# VOLUME ONE

# FALL, SACRED APPLE
## *Emory Glass*

The Catechism of Birth ended in the silence of a child born with a veil. Six hands peeled the fleshy sac away from the newborn's fragile skin. Rid of the caul, he cried.

Corbha exhaled a weak laugh. He was alive: their first new spirit-sibling in twenty-four years. Trembling, she spread the caul on a ceramic plate painted with holy words, never looking away from her newborn brother. Unaid, the last formal nursemaid at their abbey, held him against his mother's heaving chest.

He was bald. Like most of her spirit-siblings, his skin was grey as the sea. His ears, deaf for now, pointed skyward. Faint wisps of crow-black hair tufted from their tips. Though all newborns' eyes remained closed for at least a week, Corbha already knew their ice-like glint.

Her gaze settled on his mother—the first and only Wife she had ever seen. The Wife bled into the cloudy birthing pool waters, face pale as the triplet moons. Her blood, once pure white, gradually reddened until it was as rich a scarlet as an apple. It mesmerized Corbha, though it was not a unique occurrence. It happened to every Wife who birthed a blood-spirit's child; the same act had pigmented Corbha's own mother's blood and that of her spirit-sibling's mothers. This was the Covenant of Blood fulfilled. Such peace cloaked Corbha that her heart ached. Magnificent things were to come.

"It's the omen," Sabha whispered through her surgery beak. Everyone at the abbey wore them when exposed to viscera: an owl-like leather mask stuffed with a medley of powerful herbs. Sabha rubbed the Wife's shoulders. She was catatonic. Rivulets of sweat trickled down her twilight-blue skin that now withered into the misty grays of dawn.

Nobody here could keep her alive. The abbey's infirmarers isolated themselves days ago to protect everyone from the agony of bloodrust. The blood-freezing disease would consume the abbey if allowed to spread. This Wife would die, but it was no cause for sorrow. The Blood Mother had heard the Divine Orchard's appeal. Between the birth of a healthy new spirit-sibling, the caul, and the Wife's passage...

"Corbha," Sabha said. "She's fading."

Corbha drew a razor-sharp knife from her tool satchel and sliced one small, square wafer from the caul. "Blessed is the Blood Mother, Red Goddess of the Eightfold Orchard," she recited.

"In Her name, thou art commended for thy deeds, Wife of the Sacred Apple," replied Sabha and Unaid.

"Go forth from this Fold unto the Orchard, knowing thy covenant is fulfilled."

"In Her name, thou art blessed."

"Let the sacred fruit of Her Orchard fall upon thy tongue." Corbha slipped the wafer into the Wife's mouth.

4

"In Her name, thou art loved."

"Prithee know peace in Her Orchard, where all things grow yet none grow old."

"In Her name, thou art extolled."

"Cross now the honeyed sea—"

The Wife's breaths moistened and crackled. Corbha glanced at Sabha, who mouthed, "Go on."

Brow furrowed, she continued, "Cross now the honeyed sea and moor at the harbor of Her love, for here thou art ever young."

"In Her name, thou art absolved."

Corbha watched for the Wife to accept her absolution. Her eyes were glass and her heartbeats silent. A new soul had crossed into the Orchard.

Strangely, Corbha's stomach turned. Death came rarely to the abbey. Clammy-palmed, she set the cauls' remains in a tightly sealed box, pocketing the knife. She watched Sabha for guidance.

"Take it to the Abbot," she instructed. "You did well. We will prepare the body for you."

Corbha bowed her head and stood. "Yes, sister." She lifted the caul-box and hastened through a wood-walled passage to the dorter where everyone slept. Woolen wall hangings depicting scenes from the Exodus and Settlement swung on the breeze she left behind.

The box pulsated with divine energy. After so many weeks waiting for an answer, the Blood Mother finally offered her blessing. Delivering the caul was a tremendous responsibility, but one Corbha gladly mantled. Now that there was a spirit-sibling younger than her, her siblings had cause to let her perform more significant duties. This was her chance to prove she deserved it.

She strained to inhale, but not from fatigue. The cloyingly ripe odor of the herbs within her beak made drawing breath almost painful. Yet she dared not unfasten it until the caul could no longer tempt her. To work with flesh and blood without the beak's nullifying effects was a cardinal sin for her kind. Without it, sanguiren may give in to temptation: temptation to consume. Sanguiren like herself occupied a singular and sacred position of trust between their fathers—the blood-spirits—and the full mortals with whom they made covenant. They were the conduit by which the white blood of full mortals became red. To let predatory desire overwhelm their senses was to abuse their privilege in the most blasphemous way. There was no greater sin.

Corbha arrived at the dorter and banged on the tarnished kickplate. The reinforced door opened, revealing her mentor, Fhucan, a thin old man carrying a cresset lantern. Sleep crusted his wrinkled eyes.

"It's the omen." She held out the box.

Fhucan stepped aside. She went straight to the Abbot's cot at the opposite end of the dorter. Erchid was the eldest abbey monastic at eighty-six years old. Despite his imposing rank, she admired his kindness and piety. She shook his shoulder gently and whispered his name.

He sat bolt-upright. "Huh?" his coarse voice softened once he saw her. "What?"

"The Wife passed. Her son is healthy."

"Is that?" the Abbot pointed a twisted finger at the box. "Was he?"

She nodded, beaming.

He let his head drop back on the cot. "Praised be the Blood Mother, for she has given us a sign!" Laughing, he waved her away. "Go. Sleep. You've earned it. The Prioress and I will announce our stratagem at the chapterhouse in the morning. Be prepared for important company in the coming days."

*     *     *

Sunrise trickled in through the dorter window as Corbha put on a pair of dull brown trousers cinched at the ankle. This morning was so tranquil, she mused, that it would be criminal to let the crisp autumn day pass by without enjoying it. She stepped into her wide paneled skirt and knotted it around her hips, tucking the strings behind the waistband, before donning a long-sleeved, pale red lèine. The hem and sleeves had frayed. *Good,* she thought. Mending clothes created a fine excuse to slip away for a while—once today's duties were complete, of course. Already she had been up at dawn to stretch and practice the flexibility exercises Martial Master Tairad assigned for the week. Although the Wife's funeral meant no formal weapons or hand-to-hand training today, she expected she'd have a chance to self-study: another way to appreciate the pleasant weather.

Over her head she drew a currant-red tunic, pinching both sets of sleeves together before turning out the cuffs three-quarters of the way up each forearm. Satisfied, she bound the habit around her waist with a broad woven cincture. Neat red embroidery at its tail displayed her name, abbey, and profession: Corbha, Abbey of the Sacred Apple, Sacrist mentee. It was nice to have something of her own when everything else was communal property.

She admired the morning a little longer as she bundled her thick black hair under a crimson cap. A turndun buzzed loud and low near the temple. The chapterhouse meeting was about to begin. Corbha yanked the strings taut and snatched her rose-colored veil from the cot. Then, she nimbly pinned veil to cap, buttoning the loose ends at her throat with an apple-shaped closure, snagged her apron, tool satchel, and red folded cap off the bed, and flung them on as she scurried toward the chapterhouse.

She sailed down a short corridor that paralleled the great cloister, passing the pungent reredorter without drawing breath.

When she reached the chapterhouse door, she straightened her habit and awaited her mentor. Two of her spirit-siblings—Bursar Berugni and Refectorer Teghor—greeted her with bowed heads as they entered. Finally, Fhucan ambled toward her, supported by a sturdy cane. He was not quite as ancient as the Abbot or Prioress, but his once-black beard was now light grey and his bare head splotched with liver spots. She took his arm to ease him over the threshold.

"Good morning, sister," Fhucan said, fighting tremors to nod his head. "Is the day treating you well so far?"

"*Very*," she responded with a grin. "The Blood Mother received the Divine Orchard's petition, we have a new baby brother, *and* it's the start of a gorgeous day. Truly, we're blessed."

The corners of his lips lingered somewhere between a grin and a grimace. "Let's have a seat."

They sat on a bench at the head of two neat rows of four before the Abbot's office along the northern wall. The chapterhouse was a sizeable room with a low, thatched ceiling braced by limestone bricks and beams: the sole place aside from the warming house and temple built of stone. Lector Ridrag and Chamberlain Sebnall entered via the scriptorium to the east. Kitchener Serbhica and Cellarer Rulidh came in from the cloister, no doubt having just finished taking stock of provisions. Corbha's leg bounced against the wooden floor. The Abbot was almost certainly inside his office, although there was a chance he may emerge from the passage that led to the temple and sacristy. Again, the cloister door opened. Sabha held it wide for Unaid, who carried the baby in a white sling. She smiled at Corbha as they sat on the bench behind her and Fhucan.

Unaid tapped her on the shoulder. "Isn't this so exciting?"

Corbha turned. "How are Mhleca and Đusca? Will they be here?"

"I expect not. They're out of the woods, but any lingering bloodrust could prove devastating. They'll sequester in the infirmary until sometime next week, I think."

Their whispers ceased when the Abbot's office door opened. Prioress Lubhyll stepped into the chapterhouse, pausing in front of the benches with folded hands. The Abbot, emanating such verve that ten years melted right off him, started talking the moment he crossed the threshold.

"We gather here today under the auspices of the Blood Mother, for She has given us a sign: the caul of the first child born to our Father the Sacred Apple in twenty-four years to the day." He glanced at Corbha, consciously avoiding eye contact but making his gaze known. She blushed. Yes, she turned twenty-four yesterday, and she was by far the youngest spirit-sibling—at least, until now. With any luck, the baby's birth meant her siblings may treat her less like one. Now she had a younger brother, too. She intended to raise him alongside her elders.

The Abbot continued, "Prioress Lubhyll and I, with our Father's guidance, asked the Divine Orchard to petition the Blood Mother's consent to the stratagem devised to bring our detractors back into good graces. Unaid." He gestured for her to rise. "This child is a gift from the Red Goddess herself. The Blood Mother has answered our prayers. Praised be the Blood Mother!"

Corbha and her spirit-siblings repeated praises.

Prioress Lubhyll cleared her throat and strode forward. She was a slim, severe old woman with papery grey skin and more creases than a linen shift. "Because of this blessing, I gather you to announce a plan of action for a matter of utmost gravity. As a select few of you already know, the Divine Orchard of the Sacred Covenant of Our Mother of Blood extended a letters patent to the Senate. This order required them to publicly confirm their faith by the last day of summer this year." She exhaled with grievous incense. "Of one-hundred-twenty-five senators, three from our very own province of Sris Nimach-Lovach delayed this demonstration until early autumn."

Corbha blinked. One did not ignore a letters patent, least of all from the Divine Orchard itself. There was no higher religious authority in Ren Drocha. It was tantamount to the mortal domicile of the Blood Mother herself.

The Abbot said, "These three senators, Silnaid Arcadhec, Godabhor Simicic, and Draghor Gabhrit, have decided themselves above the need for deadlines. Why do they assume the rules do not apply to them?" He shrugged deeply, mockingly. "That is something we do not know."

Prioress Lubhyll waited for the snickering to abate. "Because winter fast approaches, these senators rather erroneously assume their tardiness is unnoticed and our abbey will write it off as a lapse of communication."

The temperature in the chapterhouse plunged.

The Prioress' eyes blackened, mottled with starlight. A thousand whispering voices spoke with hers: "Let it be known the Red Goddess does not *mince* Her *words*."

Gooseflesh raised the hairs on Corbha's arms and neck. Speaking through the Void could strike fear even in other sanguiren. She thanked the Blood Mother she had not been born a full mortal.

The Void faded from the Prioress' eyes. She rasped, "As sanguiren fade from popular interest, so too dull the doctrines of the Red Pact. This cannot stand. They will lead Ren Drocha to ruin."

The Abbot raised his arms. "But! Just as we made this child known to the world by tearing his caul away, so too shall we reveal these senators' endangerment of every redblood. Without trust between *sanguire*—" he motioned at something that wasn't there. The blood-spirits never left their secluded groves. There, they were protected from most anything that wished them harm. Immortal though they may be, they could yet suffer pain and dispelling. "And mortals—" the Abbot pointed southeast toward the Widow's Convent, "society will collapse. Our blood will be forever blighted, and we will have turned our backs on the Blood Mother who so selflessly delivered our ancestors from oppression and slaughter. Thus, the Divine Orchard has entrusted us with correcting those who would create a mockery of our solemn duties."

Corbha flicked her ears. Obviously, the Divine Orchard intended to sacrifice the senators as they would a sanguiren guilty of the same crime. The only question was their manner of death.

The Prioress withdrew a scroll from her sleeves and held it out. In her usual unaffected tone, she said, "Since they are from our province, we have invited the senators to sup on the morrow with our abbey to celebrate our brother's birth. They will receive holy orders to 'live out their remaining days in contemplation of their actions' within our sacred walls."

"What?" The word escaped Corbha's lips before she could stop herself. She bit the insides of her cheeks and looked at the dusty floor. That couldn't be true. Holy orders? Granted to disloyal conspirators and cowards? And to send them here? To *this* abbey?

This was a ridiculous punishment. Not one that was her place to challenge, but even as her face scorched with self-consciousness she heard her siblings whisper amongst themselves. What could the senators learn from this? That the Divine Orchard rewarded insolence with duty? That a life of devotion was a *penalty*? A sour taste filled her mouth. Were she not bound to decorum, she would spit.

Sacrist Fhucan tugged her sleeve. "The Divine Orchard must gain some edge from this," he mumbled. "Stowing the senators here will keep them under close watch. They cannot poison the public against religious obligations if they cannot reach them at all."

"Something so unholy does not belong in this hallowed place," Corbha hissed.

"If I may continue," the Prioress warned, "There is more. If they refuse holy orders, the Divine Orchard will interpret it as treason. The senators 'shall be relieved of their duties in this Fold of the Void. Otherwise, they will remain intact and free to go about their daily lives at the abbey.'" She re-rolled the scroll and tucked it inside her sleeve. "Either option they choose, we will spend today preparing for their arrival. Martial Master Tairad shall retrieve the senators from their encampment and lead them here. Three of you will tidy the temple and guest house with the help of Chamberlain Seþnall. Two others will clean and decorate the refectory under the direction of Refectorer Teghor. Cellarer Rulidh and Kitchener Serbhica will establish a menu for preparation in the morning, cooking which will require assistance from as many hands as possible. The rest of you, please perform your usual duties for the day. Sacrist Fhucan and Unaid," she added. "Please stay."

Everyone else left. Serbhica and Sabha hovered near the door, no doubt waiting for Unaid. The three grew up together, thick as thieves. They were rarely apart for long.

"You and Unaid will prepare the temple for communion," the Prioress stated, moving closer to their bench along with the Abbot.

Corbha raised an eyebrow, not daring to talk out of turn again. She was the Sacrist mentee, not Unaid. Surely minding their brother while helping with, say, the refectory would prove simpler. But, she waited for Fhucan to speak.

"There is the matter of preparing the Wife's body for said communion," Fhucan reminded the Prioress. "Would I not be of better help in the sepulcher and Corbha at the temple?"

The Abbot put a hand on his shoulder. "I think it's time, with your permission, to allow Corbha this opportunity to practice the rites associated with her profession. I know you've taught her well."

Her chest buzzed with the joyous light of millions of fireflies. Funerary ministries were seldom needed. Until now, she had only observed Fhucan's work. This was splendid news. They trusted her—had confidence in her, even. She bowed her head, cracking a smile. "Thank you, Abbot. I won't disappoint you or Sacrist Fhucan, if he allows me this opportunity." She cast a hopeful peek at him.

"I'm confident you won't," Fhucan said. "You have me for a tutor, after all."

The Prioress turned to Corbha. "When you finish, fetch the Widows so they may perform consecrations. Attend your daily chores afterward. Tomorrow morning, report to the kitchen."

Corbha blanched. The last time they'd asked her help with that, she had charred the bread beyond edibility. It wasn't fit to feed the ducks. She followed Serbhica out the southern door, saying, "I'll do the washing if you like. I... understand if you would rather I not cook."

Serbhica waved her away. "That was ages ago. I'm sure we'll find something you can manage."

Corbha overtook her. Heading outside toward the Wives' Sepulcher, her heart beat in her throat. The Blood Mother may have heard the Divine Orchard's pleas, but She had answered Corbha's prayers, too. This responsibility was her personal blessing. She prayed it was the first of many to come.

\*　　　\*　　　\*

The Wife's body rested on a stone table inside the sepulcher. Three score stone ossuaries packed with the bones of earlier Wives filled the slotted walls. Fifteen empty spaces waited for further ossuaries to occupy them.

Corbha set the two wooden pails she hauled on the floor near the Wife's head. One held plain water, the other suds. A red sheet of fine linen covered the Wife's body for modesty. Red, not white, though the latter was the shade of death. Red for honor and highest esteem. Red for the blood the Wife so selflessly sacrificed so vermillion might flow through her family's veins.

Corbha soaked her rag in the sudsy water. The soap was unscented; not that it mattered since her senses were deadened by the herbs in her surgery beak. Light filtered in through the slatted windows, illuminating her face against the water's surface. Hand laid on the Wife's in reassurance, she asked, "May I cleanse you?"

Of course, the Wife wouldn't respond. Asking was a matter of respect. After waiting a moment in silence, Corbha said, "Thank you."

They sent few Wives to the Abbey of Sacred Apples anymore—or any abbey, if Corbha was forthright with herself. Almost every Ren Drochan gained red blood decades ago. Other whitebloods existed, but the Promise of Blood did not extend to them. Only Ren Drochans.

Corbha washed the Wife's limbs in slow, gentle circles, taking care to cover her cold and papery flesh with the sheet. Though her soul had long since shattered, her body was the most sacrosanct part of her able to be reached in this Fold. It merited as much reverence in death as it had in life.

She clipped and buffered the Wife's fingernails. Her hands were smooth and lissome—not unusual for a woman of her status. Darkly, Corbha wondered how holding her newborn for the first and last time all at once must have felt.

She moved to the Wife's feet and raised the linen to bare them. The Wife's soles were raw and soil-blackened. She had labored for two days in agony before giving birth. By the time the baby crowned, she had trudged so many moiled laps around the cloister there remained a muddy rut where she tread. Corbha took a heel in her hand. "Don't fear," she said as she grabbed a pumice stone from her tool satchel. "It won't hurt."

At the sound of coarse skin sloughing off, Corbha's chest fluttered. She tried to think of the baby. The Abbot would not name him until Mhleca and Đusca were well enough to meet him. Unsure of what to say yet drawn to speak, she said, "Your baby is perfect. He's as cheerful and calm as can be. Very gentle and sweet."

When he wasn't with Unaid, he was with the Widows. For as long as Corbha could remember, there had been only seven. Last month, the Divine Orchard sent a Widow from the Orchard of the Sacred Fig in apprehension of this very situation. Sanguiren were barren and made no milk. If a Wife died in childbirth, someone had to feed their baby: ideally, a Wife recently made a Widow. Even when they served as a wet nurse, it was rare to encounter a Widow. They sequestered themselves in the confines of their convent at all times, only emerging to sanctify their dead.

Though raising a child laid outside her realm of knowledge, Corbha hoped Unaid would allow her to mind him often. Despite sharing a father, she felt closer to the baby than their older siblings. Her own mother died to bear her, never to become a Widow and see their hallowed halls. But, even if she had survived, they never would have met. After giving birth, wives of the Sacred Apple were sent to one of their sister fruit's convents: the Abbey of Sacred Figs or the Abbey of Sacred Pears. Only sanguiren were fit to raise sanguiren when a single one of their kind could slaughter whole villages if improperly disciplined.

The Red Pact mandated strict temperance and meticulous training for all sanguiren. It was wholly imperative, in Corbha's opinion. Here at the abbey, surrounded by his own kind, she and her spirit-siblings could inundate their newborn brother with every holy duty of their kind: keeping the Mysteries of the Blood Mother; learning to manipulate blood, souls, and bones with anatomancy, if capable; studying Ren Drochan history, sacred literature, and the old Moþbyll traditions; and mastering blade, blunt, and bow to serve as the sword and shield of the faith.

Satisfied with her effort, Corbha replaced the linen sheet. She rinsed her rag in plain water and continued to the Wife's head. Two apple-wood discs engraved with blood tongue weighed shut her eyelids. Two words noted her identity: "apple" and "wife".

This Wife was young. Although Corbha wouldn't suggest she was pretty, there was a certain quaint charm to the roundness of her face and twilight-grey skin. She wiped the Wife's cheeks. Sanguire never chose Wives for beauty but for the number of veins they could redden by birthing a sanguiren.

Nowadays most any woman who was white-blooded, fertile, and had no children may be chosen as a Wife, regardless of whether she had any living white-blooded relatives left. A surge of guilt heated Corbha's cheeks. She would never dare say it aloud, but so few white-blooded Ren Drochans existed, let alone eligible women, that it threatened the stability of the Pact. In centuries past, no senator would have dared to flout a letters patent. She wrung out the rag and wet it once again. Three defiances, all at once, did not bode well for the future. That was why the Divine Orchard should — *needed* to — sacrifice the senators.

With great care, Corbha dabbed away the dried mucus and congealed blood on the Wife's aubergine nose leather. She swabbed her cleft and nostrils, dredged the sleep from the corners of her catlike eyes, scraped the wax from her ears, and packed her mouth with salt.

Now came shearing her hair. If there was one step susceptible to catastrophic failure, this was it. Cutting the scalp would be disrespectful, but the hair had to stay with the bones. Corbha pulled out an arched, narrow blade.

"Before I do this…" Corbha brushed her fingers through the Wife's bone-white hair. A shallow pan built into the ground beneath the table waited to catch the clippings. "I wanted to thank you for delivering a new spirit-brother to us. I'm sure it was difficult to leave him so soon. Please know we love him terribly and will take excellent care of him." She drew a deep breath and bundled the Wife's hair in her free hand. Trying her hardest to align the knife perfectly, she positioned it at the nape of the Wife's neck. "Again—thank you."

The gossamer hair severed with a fizzing noise all too delightful to Corbha's ears. She let the bundle fall into the pan. Once the rest was shorter than her little finger, she lifted the Wife's head. With great care, she cropped close enough to remove everything without scraping her. When the bald spot reflected the sunlight, free of wounds, Corbha breathed a sigh of relief. She lowered the Wife's head and sheared the rest with many fewer pent-up breaths.

When the Abbot chose her to become a Sacrist, Corbha worried the requirement of attending corpses would be too macabre to weather. Although working with the dead was not something from which she derived enjoyment, it was easier than she had expected. Besides, the Widows handled the *truly* grisly rite: the Consecration of Flesh. Though she could never be a Widow and therefore would never learn the ritual, she hoped to witness it at least once. Most of the Widows were elderly. Every one of her siblings was ancient. One day, it might be necessary knowledge.

Regardless, it would never transpire. Temptation to consume prohibited sanguiren from performing such rites, even if there was no one else to conduct them. The dictums of the Red Pact encoded such boundaries. Disregarding its scriptures violated the fundamental doctrines of civilization.

Her thoughts soured as she oiled the Wife's body. The Divine Orchard would sacrifice a sanguiren for disobeying the Pact, yet they saw fit to *reward* full mortals for their transgressions. Not once in her life had she argued against their word. It may as well have been the Blood Mother's own voice. But this was such a… a *feeble* response to a severe act of dissent that it felt wrong to remain silent.

But now was not the time for such opinions. She finished oiling the Wife and crouched to wet her hands in the suds. When clean, Corbha stood. Focused entirely on the Wife's body before her, she let the mortal Fold melt away. Naught but a star-strung sky against the fabric of the Void remained. She bid it whisper through her.

"Aloud I sing thy praises so She mayst know thy benevolence. Thus I lift mine own hands and intone her name: gaze toward this woman loved as a Wife of thy Sacred Fruit and the mother of His nameless child. With mine own mouth, I beseech Thee; listen. Red Goddess, Mother of Blood, heed mine own evocation! Thou art her merciful Mother. Let thine adoration embrace this woman who hath perished for the blood of Thy blood. Satisfy her soul with the fruits of Thine Orchard. Discard the afflictions of her mortal life; stay her woe and suffering so she mayst rejoice and be fearless in the refuge of Thine Orchard, surrounded by her ancestors who exalted Thee. Hear me, Blood Mother, yond she mayst witness Thy magnificence. Aloud I sing this woman's praises so she mayst know Thy compassion and enter Thy Orchard as a testament of Thine endearment. Thou art her Mother whom I venerate. Mine own love clings fast to Thee. I pray Thy grace shall glorify her."

She paused in silence, letting the whispers echo and vanish while her eyesight returned. The heaviness in her throat became too onerous to bear as the herbs worked to overwhelm her senses.

"Thank you for letting me cleanse you. I'll send for the Widows now."

Corbha exited the sepulcher without the buckets. On her way to the Widow's Convent, she loosened her beak. At the convent gate, eight Widows shrouded head-to-toe in red waited for her. Corbha pointed open-handed to the Sepulcher. It took her a moment to realize their veils were so complete they could not see her.

"She's ready for you," Corbha said.

The Widows filed ahead toward the sepulcher. Corbha watched in place until the door latched behind them. Her breaths quickened. If their veils prevented them from seeing her, maybe...

Absolutely not. The Consecration was not for her to witness. And, if they caught her, the Abbot would quite literally skin her alive. Worse, if she somehow, despite their heavy veils, found their gaze, there would be no saving their souls from shattering if her self-control failed.

She took a timid step. She had to pass by the sepulcher return to the abbey, anyway. Another step. The Abbot before Erchid died when she was three. There had been other deaths since then, mostly travelers or sick villagers, but never had she been so close to the Consecration. Three steps forward. Mere sights or smells wouldn't overpower the surgery beak—or else why would the Red Pact dictate their use? She had attended a childbirth and caul-tearing without smelling as much as a *hint* of viscera. She strode halfway across the curtilage. Her siblings endowed her with restraint and plenty of respect for full mortals; mere temptation couldn't goad her into doing something so horrific.

She was silent, a blur, faster than any full mortal could hope to match speed with. Pressed flat against the mossy sepulcher wall, she listened, holding her surgery beak against her nose with one hand while tying it around her veil with the other. The Widows murmured in Blood Tongue. Nothing loud enough to make out.

Her chest was a beehive, hand still fumbling with the tie. Impatient, she pressed her nose against the wall to free her other hand to tighten the beak.

Without warning, the Widows shouted, "Praised be the Blood Mother!"

Corbha jumped, knocking the mask askew.

As soon as she smelled it, she knew.

The sweetness of raw flesh dulled her senses. Her mouth watered. No amount of discipline could shield her from this craving, this *lust*. She peeled herself off the ground, clawing at moist soil and grass until her palms were grass-stained and blackened. Dirt and weeds lodged underneath her fingernails. Her hunger screamed for her to look, to know, to eat. She crumpled. This was the sanguire within all sanguiren. The blood spirit howling for its due. She rammed the beak over her nose. It was too late. Nothing was more potent than the sweet perfume of death. On hands and knees, she crawled away. Her eyes watered and blurred. Every movement was to turn a lead wheel. Blood. Flesh. Organs. Entrails. Every scrap of marrow within the Wife's bones. All of it abandoned.

*Blood Mother*, she begged when she yearned to turn back and ravage the sepulchre. *Help me. Please.*

Corbha half-stumbled, half-ran across the abbey grounds, not stopping until she came to the apple orchard at the northwestern-most reaches. It was the farthest place from the sepulcher, and a shrine with an icon depicting the Blood Mother sheltered there. She'd beg mercy.

Barely able to support herself, Corbha forced open the heavy wooden gate, shuffled inside and collapsed on her knees. The gate creaked shut behind her. Staggered breaths left the bite of copper on her tongue. She huddled against the shrine like a wounded dog. Half-rotten apples fermented around her, hidden under red-orange foliage that coated the ground like gold leaf. She buried her head in her skirts and inhaled slowly, deeply, praying the scent would diffuse. With a hooked finger, she scooped out the herbs and rolled them between her palms. Their juices wet her hands. She smeared them over her nose leather until her nostrils seared and her head split like a log. It was too much. Far too much.

Quietly, fervently, she recited the Catechism of the Wheel, murmuring to herself as if it were her sole salvation. "A seed becomes a sapling; its flowers bear sweet fruit. Four spokes on a wheel. In Autumn it withers unto the barren ground, decaying, blessed by fate. Eight spokes on a wheel."

It soothed her. She wiped her nose on the back of her hand. Muddled herbs fell from her skirt onto the orchard floor. She bent down to sweep them into her palm and crammed them back inside the beak. If someone discovered their remnants, it would raise questions. No one would return here until winter ended, but it was better to be certain.

She dared not cast her eyes to the Blood Mother and confront her piercing gaze. She watched the fruit-laden trees instead—another sign of her ineptitude. Most of her spirit-siblings were much too frail and ailing to help with the harvest. This year, she, Unaid, Sabha, and Mhleca were the only ones healthy enough to handle the arduous task. Her stomach twisted at the thought of years to come.

The icon wheeled inside her mind's eye. She bowed her head to the Blood Mother's image: a shapeless red shroud not unsimilar to the Widow's garb. "I betrayed You," she admitted. "I'll never overstep my bounds again. It was thoughtless and greedy. I'll fast all week and burn a wreath for You."

Like the Wife, the icon remained mute. Slate did not speak.

Sometime later, a turndun buzzed in the distance, heightening in pitch as it spun round and round on its cord. Communion. Had she been out here so long?

Corbha rushed toward the temple. It would be obvious she had slunk off somewhere if she didn't arrive soon, if not the reason for her tardiness. Her thoughts flew.

Someone would notice.

\*　　\*　　\*

The temple's eight stone apses encircled a central dome. Exquisite bas-reliefs on each ceiling depicted a story from Ren Drocha's history: the Exodus, the Settlement, signing the Red Pact; the First Wife of the Sacred Apple; the Divine Orchard's temple in Les Opisac; the first sanguiren's birth; and on the final apse, a portrait of the original Senate. A stunning high-relief of the veiled Blood Mother looking into the temple filled the central dome. Her eight children, the sanguire, circled her in the form of eight sacred fruits: apple, apricot, cherry, date, fig, pear, plum, and pomegranate. A slate icon of each rested under the small apses.

Paint once brought the reliefs to life. By now, most of it had peeled and flaked away. A pang of guilt turned Corbha's stomach. She stepped between the pews, which spiraled out from the central altar. Harvesting apples and taking care of the most strenuous chores was one matter. She was no painter. The Divine Orchard was unlikely to send artists out to the middle of nowhere, and that stung her heart in a way she didn't know how to articulate.

She sat next to Unaid at the spiral's end. The baby slept in her arms. Her heart ached for him. His life would be bleaker than most.

Thirty-two spirit-siblings once kept the abbey in immaculate condition. Everyone except herself, Unaid, and their brother was older than fifty; the heaviest upkeep depended on what the two of them could manage. She and Unaid may be closest in age, but Unaid was still forty-eight. Sooner or later, she'd lose vigor, too. Even if they were healthy and younger, fifteen monastics and a baby still could not sustain an abbey this large.

Her foot bounced against the floor. Unaid bumped her shoulder.

"Would you like to hold him?" she asked.

Without hesitation, Corbha took him from her. He was a soft and warm little bundle swaddled up in a red wool blanket.

"I remember your first communion," Unaid said. "You were so little—just three. It's not often a baby gets to hold a baby, is it?" Immediately, her face fell. "I'm sorry. That was insensitive of me."

"I forgive you," Corbha said.

She had no business denying anyone forgiveness after what transpired at the sepulcher.

The baby groaned like a barred owl as their siblings filled in nearby pews. Corbha studied his face. He was still blind and deaf. A sanguiren's eyes were their deadliest weapon and most dazzling feature. For now, he looked the same as any full mortal child. Until his eyes opened, he may as well have been.

Unaid glanced at the floor. She gasped. "Corbha? You're covered in dirt."

Panic shot through her chest. Muddy soil caked her apron. A bit of dried squashed apple hung off the hem. "Oh," she stammered. "I guess I am."

"Well, why?"

Before Corbha could respond, Lector Ridrag arrived through the sacristy door clad in liturgical garb: red robes, white cincture, head crowned with a flat white cap. Everyone rose as he positioned himself at the altar. The Prioress followed, carrying a painted ewer and chalice, and stood by the first pew. Abbot Erchid came not far behind with a covered ceramic offering plate. He waited beside the Prioress.

The sweet scent of funerary communion filled Corbha's lungs. Her mouth watered despite her pleas for temperance. She wasn't worthy of this. Not after this morning. Had Unaid seen? Would she tell the Abbot? Her knees felt much too frail to hold her brother safely. When she tried to hand him to Unaid, she whispered, "Keep him. You'll remember this longer than I will."

The Lector raised his arms. "Be seated at Her table wrought of bone and blood."

Everyone responded, "Blood of Her blood and soul of Her soul, the Ancestor and Architect of the Covenant of Blood."

Thoughts raced through Corbha's mind. Was she too loud? Too quiet? Did they hear her voice quaver with dread?

The Lector rang a bell. "Six hundred years and twenty more, She gifts us the Wine of the Body and bids us drink of her blood."

Prioress Lubhyll held up the chalice and ewer as if to offer their contents to the Blood Mother's relief. "Enlightened is the Mother, Ark of Blood."

"Now we pass this gift from hand to hand and wet the lips of Her devotees," the Lector read.

The Prioress offered everyone a sip of the Wife's blood: Fhucan, Rulidh, Teghor, Berugni, Seþnall, Sabha, Serbhica, and Unaid. Anticipation welled within Corbha as the chalice drew nearer. The mere scent tormented her; they wore no surgery beaks. Communion was one of the few times the Red Pact permitted sanguiren to go without.

When the Prioress reached her, Corbha bit her tongue to stifle her excruciating thirst. She prayed the Prioress didn't notice her filthy apron. Before letting Corbha drink, the Prioress left a droplet on their brother's lips.

Warm. Bitter. A marriage of iron and sea salt. Delicious, light-bodied blood. It tasted just as transcendent as it smelled. The Prioress returned to the dais and let the Abbot and Lector drink before taking her sip. She rested both ewer and chalice on the altar.

Everyone's voices swelled in unison: "Noble is the Daughter, Bearer of Blood."

Corbha eyed the ewer. Mhleca and Đusca needed communion, too. No doubt there was more blood stored in the cellar for tomorrow's supper as well. It cried out to her. She resisted the urge to vomit. To hold this woman's son after disrespecting her so—

Someone coughed. She jumped. Her heart was a war drum. Each beat pounded in her throat.

The Lector continued, "Divided are the cuts of flesh and shared amongst our table to honor the woman gone to Her Orchard."

The Abbot lifted his plate. "Divine is the Sister, Promise of Blood."

"Rejoice with me, for this is the gift of her body," the Lector said.

The Abbot placed a wafer of flesh on each waiting tongue. Before conferring it to Corbha, he crushed a piece over their brother's lips. The tender heart meat melted against her tongue. She forced herself to keep it in her mouth. The Prioress and Abbot showed no sign of unhinged hunger, nor anyone else in the temple. She could control it. She had to. Unaid was already asking questions. How could she lie to Unaid? Corbha swallowed. Her stomach ached for more. This was wrong. So very wrong.

Next came lung, liver, kidney, marrow, tongue, and sweetbread. Each wafer was a leaden weight upon her heart until she had to force herself to swallow the final offering.

When the Abbot returned the plate to the altar, everyone said, "Remembered is the Wife, Marriage of Blood."

The Lector said, "Availed now of the blessings set before thee, this meal draws to a close."

"Ageless is the Widow, Fulfillment of Blood."

"Silent now, the table cleared, but never shalt thou hunger for her, for she is ever within thee."

"Shadowed is the Crone, Keeper of blood."

"In time, Her daughters and sons will be seated at Her table again."

"Immortal is the Goddess, Mystery of Blood."

The Lector threw his head back and addressed the Blood Mother's relief. "Be thee now satiated, sweet children, for the bounty of Her body is filling and sweet."

"In Her name, we eat."

"In Her name, we eat," the Lector repeated.

As everyone left, Corbha stood to give her brother back to Unaid. "Thank you for letting me hold him," she said, hoping Unaid had forgotten her earlier query.

"You're very welcome." The crow's feet at the corners of Unaid's catlike eyes pinched her midnight skin when she smiled. "But honestly—are you alright? Did you fall?"

"Yes," she said before thinking. "I... I fell. In the orchard. Martial Master Tairad wanted me to practice some of this week's techniques after I finished cleansing the Wife, since the weather is so nice. I just wanted fresh air after working in that musty old sepulcher. I thought it might be pleasant to feel some sun on my skin, too, before the winter makes the air too cold, you know, so I went to the orchard shrine. And... I tripped over a rotten apple, stupid me. Honestly, I forgot all about it. Since I'm not hurt or anything," she added.

Unaid looked no less concerned. "Well, I hope you have a lovely time. I'm surprised you walked that far just to practice, since you would have had to cut across the martial field. Anyway, the Abbot asked me to remind you to spruce up the sacristy before afternoon orisons, but you'd better wash yourself first."

Corbha nodded. "Oh, and—" she said as Unaid was leaving. "Any news about the senators? Are they still coming tomorrow?"

"As far as I know, they'll be here next afternoon. Sabha says they're encamped at the ruins of Madhcha and have been for a while. Martial Master Tairad went to fetch them this morning."

"Oh? Town is that close?" Corbha asked. She had lived her entire life within the confines of the abbey. It never bothered her, and she didn't intend to let it. Here, they were safe from harm and prying eyes. Full mortals played by different rules at the abbey; the rules of the Blood Mother, not their twisted misinterpretations wrought by years of distorting the Red Pact.

Unaid's look of confusion deepened. "Well, New Madhcha is three days away over the Vacant Hills, but the ruins are much closer. Perhaps when Serbhica goes to sell cider, I can convince her to let you tag along."

"I'd love that." Corbha smiled. "Well, best get to tidying the sacristy now. Go with grace," she said.

"And you," Unaid replied.

She found herself alone in the temple. Biting her nails with sharp teeth, she headed for the sacristy. It was a compact room which housed the abbey's valuables and temple items and connected the temple to the chapterhouse. On opening the heavy wooden door, she swallowed the lump in her throat. Liars deserved no respect or trust. Yet, it came so easily. All it cost was feeling like a fake, a fraud, and a blasphemer. She undid her apron, balled it, and tossed it near the chapterhouse passage door.

She worked in silence. In her head, she sang hymns, but she didn't let herself speak lest more false words tumble out.

While organizing cinctures, Fhucan stepped in through the chapterhouse passage. "And how are you this afternoon?" he inquired.

She drove back the cold sweat that threatened to expose her terror. "Not well. I might be sick with something."

Something like a lying habit and a sullied soul.

He looked concerned. "Not with bloodrust, I hope. I don't know what we'd do without you."

"No, nothing like that. Just... unwell, like I ate too many sweets." That was closer to the truth. Not by much, but not too far.

Fhucan finished folding the cinctures while Corbha rinsed the ewer, plate, and chalice in a wide-brimmed bucket of sudsy water. It would need to be dumped and replaced soon. That meant dragging the entire thing outside to drain it before filling it again, jugful by jugful, from the well on the other side of the martial field. She passed him day-old dishes to dry.

"Thank you," Corbha said while she grabbed the broom.

"Everyone needs a little help sometimes," Fhucan said. "Even old coots. Especially old coots, no matter how much they resist."

She pretended the statement didn't trouble her while sweeping the floor. He must have overheard Unaid's remarks.

He spoke with measured words. "If I may, Corbha, I came here to express my admiration of how you've taken charge. Not just since our brother's birth; you've helped maintain our little abbey since you were very young."

She opened her mouth to protest, but he brought a finger to his chapped lips.

"I remember being your age—can you imagine that? Me not being a wrinkled old bag of skin and bones? I recall how my elders treated me, and because of that I want you to know how proud I

28

am of you. We all are. I hope you can forgive any slip-ups from these old coots here at the abbey. You've been the youngest sister for so long it's—" He stooped to retrieve the rag he dropped. Corbha swooped in first and returned it. "Thank you. You're no longer the youngest. Though it's tough to see you as anyone other than bold little Corbha tottering about in awe of the world, you have grown." He held out his arms. "I bid you remember this: since the moment of your birth, you have *always* been our equal."

She bit back tears with a smile and leaned in to embrace him. His ribcage protruded like a washboard, even underneath three layers of robes. If she hugged him any tighter, she feared he'd snap.

"But," he playfully grinned, "You'll always be my little sister."

"And you, my big brother," she asserted, letting a single tear fall from her cheek. She wiped her nose with the side of her hand. Lying to Unaid was terrible enough. There was no way she could lie to Fhucan. He had invested more time and patience into her than anyone else. Anything she needed, he provided. Any accident, mistake or lapse in judgment, he helped her correct and learn to be better. But this shame... the penalties for endangering mortals the way she had were harsh—just as harsh as she thought the senators deserved.

She coughed to hide her tears. It frightened her to her very core that what he said was true: she didn't know what they'd do without her, either.

"I'll see you at orisons." he twiddled his fingers at her and left.

Alone in silence again, Corbha knelt on the sacristy floor, holding her head while she wept.

*     *     *

Forty peeled apples later, Corbha's hands were sore and sticky. Beside her, seven of her spirit-siblings worked in the kitchen, all preparing a different dish: herbed grape brandy and candied figs, sweetbread, fried pâté, drob, brain salad, blood sausage, grilled heart. To her surprise, Serbhica had charged her with preparing dessert—walnut-stuffed, honeyed apples—instead of tidying up behind everyone.

Not ruining dessert was the least she could do to make up for her lies. Groggy though it was well past dawn, she rubbed sleep from her eyes. All night she had tossed and turned, dreading the punishments she knew she deserved: whipped feet, flaying, having an eye or tongue plucked out—or both. That was if exhaustion didn't kill her first. After tidying the sacristy yesterday afternoon, Rulidh and Serbhica called on her to help move the heaviest things from the cellar to the kitchen. Then came the matter of attending orisons—which the Lector allowed to continue well beyond suppertime—not to mention meditating, doing her daily reading from the Red Pact, laundering a small mountain of robes, and minding the baby for Unaid so she could wash herself and rest.

She stirred the pot of honey syrup boiling alongside her. Cellarer Rulidh permitted her to use the juice of a single lemon in the syrup: a strange little fruit from Blood-Mother-knew-where, brilliant yellow and plump, that puckered her lips after its sour juice exploded out when she squeezed each half over the pot. Before now, she had never laid eyes on such a fruit. She doubted it even came from a tree, as Rulidh insisted.

Still stirring, she plopped the apples in one, two, three at a time. Once they all sank to the bottom, she covered the pot and went to fetch the jug of sheep's milk from Berugni's workstation. On her way, she passed Serbhica, who was chopping vegetables for the drob.

"Looks delicious." Corbha peeked over her spirit-sister's shoulder to glimpse the tabletop. Scallions, sweet red peppers, mushrooms, dill, parsley, garlic, lovage. Despite how delectable everything looked, she meant it when she told the Blood Mother that she would fast for a week. "Too bad I can't smell anything." She tapped her surgery beak.

"You know why." Serbhica transferred the vegetables to a giant wooden bowl. "I'd offer you a bite, but Rulidh might beat me with my own spoon."

Corbha stifled a laugh and grabbed the milk. When she returned to her workstation, she poured it into a pot packed with crushed walnuts. Now to let it soak.

"Clean as you go," Rulidh instructed as she made her rounds. Since grape brandy and figs required little more than plating, her work was long finished.

"Yes, Cellarer." Corbha gathered the apple skins in a tightly woven basket. There was a compost pile just outside, near the vegetable garden. She took the scraps to it and dumped them, pausing near the door to wipe her brow. This was the most boring part of cooking: clean-up. Nothing was less interesting than waiting around for food to moisten and tidying behind herself in the meantime—even worse if there were dishes to rinse. Besides, it was only getting colder. She hung around the kitchen door a moment longer, picking at a hangnail.

Though outdoors and away from any kitchen smells, she re-tightened her surgery beak firmly against her nose. No mishaps today. No mishaps ever. She'd wear the beak day and night if meant never feeling so out-of-control again. The thought of losing herself in front of everybody curdled her bile. Such high concentrations of the herbs festering near her nose would ruin her keen sense of smell eventually, though she didn't see why she needed it. Caravans were uncommon, and many never stopped to barter. Only a handful of visitors came this year. Most did not tarry. Travelers, whether in groups or alone, barely acknowledged the abbey anymore.

She yawned and stretched, returning inside with the basket on her hip. As she strained the walnuts into another bowl with a slotted spoon, Cellarer Rulidh meandered to her workstation.

"Corbha," she asked. "Would you like to lead us in the Catechism of the Promise?"

She grimaced. Her outdoor break had gone on too long. "Yes, Cellarer." She began, "What is the promise of blood?"

Pots and utensils clacked as everyone continued preparing their dish. Without interrupting their work, her spirit-siblings answered, "That white shall turn red as the bloodflowers where our ancestors fell."

Corbha added butter and honey to the bowl of walnuts, mixing it with the syrup-spoon until she couldn't tell what was butter and what was honey anymore. "What is the sacrament of blood?"

"That life shall bring life, and unto each other we have conferred what the other cannot unto themselves."

She lifted the pot lid to check the apples, poking one with a paring knife. The tip slid through its flesh. She began scooping them out onto the tabletop with the slotted spoon. "What is the vessel of blood?"

"The sacrality given to the sanguire, for mortals they are not."

The kitchen door creaked open. Refectorer Teghor stepped in and, hearing their recitation, remained where he stood in silence.

"What is the evidence of blood?" Corbha asked.

"The hope brought to our ancestors, for sanguire they are not."

Cellarer Rulidh gave her a firm, laudatory shake of the shoulder before moving on. Out from under her gaze, Corbha cored the apples. With any luck, the recipe wouldn't be an utter failure. If only she could concentrate.

Quiet as a dormouse, the Refectorer approached her workstation. "The Abbot sent me to summon you to the chapterhouse," he said.

Her stomach dropped. This was it. He'd found out. They would never let her out of the dorter cells again, if they let her live. Her knees weakened. Wiping her quivering hands on her apron, she asked, "Why?"

"He didn't say. Only to hurry. Best go now."

"But who will finish the apples?" she asked, not realizing how desperate she sounded until he gave her a strange look.

"I... suppose I can. The refectory is in a decent state." He glanced at her workstation. "What am I making?"

"Just finish coring the apples, fill them with the walnut mixture, and drizzle with the honey syrup in that pot when they're done," she said. "Thank you, brother."

"You're welcome."

By the Blood Mother, this would be the last time she ever saw any of them and nobody knew it yet. Her breaths quickened as she lurched toward the chapterhouse. Fhucan's words reverberated in her mind: what would they do without her? Her heart beat in her ears. She hadn't allowed herself to think this, but it exploded from her, acrid and caustic, as if the thought were a squeezed lemon. What would she do without *them*?

*   *   *

Corbha entered the chapterhouse half-expecting the Abbot to be standing there holding a rope to hang her with. Every scrap of flesh and blood in her stomach rollicked and roiled. It was foolish of her to have done what she did.

To her surprise, the Abbot stood near his office door. Three senators and six bodyguards between them waited at his side. The churning of her bile only quickened.

She cast her eyes away to avoid their fascinated gaze. Given their abject stupidity in ignoring an order from the Divine Orchard,

33

she doubted they'd respect the simple fact that making eye contact would wrench their stained-glass souls into the Void and shatter them with not a single care for their rank.

The senators looked wildly out of place: plump-bodied, clad in sumptuous robes trimmed with gold and fur, their hair knotted in ornate updos. The only thing that might make them look *more* absurd would be if their outfits dripped with jewels. Corbha didn't doubt they'd stitch them on, given the chance.

"Corbha!" The Abbot chirped. "Thank you for arriving so soon. I was just speaking with our guests about you. They are very interested in observing the martial techniques we learn here at the abbey." Gesturing at the female senator first, he said, "This is Senator Silnaid Arcadhec."

A fleshy woman, greedy-eyed with smoky grey hair and plum-colored robes, whose guards bore an apple crowned with flames on their golden shields.

"Senator Godabhor Simicic," the Abbot said.

A rotund and middle-aged man who seemed restless. Behind him, his guards wielded shields emblazoned with a vermillion heart overlaid on an apple tree leaf.

"And Senator Draghor Gabhrit," the Abbot finished.

This one was thin and tall as a beanpole. His guards' red shields displayed three golden apples arranged in a triangle. A black stripe cut across it, sinister to dexter.

Corbha asked, "When will Martial Master Tairad arrive?"

The Abbot hesitated. "The Martial Master is receiving funeral communion. He missed it to guide the senators here."

Senator Arcadhec pointed at one of her bodyguards; a sharp-faced recruit not much older than Corbha. It was strange to see a man so young. "This is Dobhnic, my newest recruit. If any display of your abilities requires help, I am *certain* he would be *honored* to accommodate."

Corbha cast a cursory glance at the boy. Given his cocksure grin and exaggerated stance, she knew that if they sparred, she would break him. "I'm sorry, Senator, but I don't want to hurt him."

Dobhnic guffawed. "Trust me, you won't. Looks like you'd need about ten meals a day to put enough muscle on you to come close."

Corbha turned to the Abbot. "I would prefer to wait for Tairad—or Unaid, if possible. My apologies for the disappointment, but I think it would be *irresponsible* of me to spar this..." she searched for a polite word. "Man."

The Abbot nodded. "Perhaps the senators would prefer a demonstration of agility and speed in the meantime?"

Senator Gabhrit huffed. "We didn't fuss about traveling all this way only to have this *lay sister* deny us a chance to witness the raw power of your kind. I, for one, want to know if the rumors are true. I've heard a lot about sanguiren's abilities and I want to see it for myself. Get a read on your methods. It's not fair to hoard our ancestors' knowledge away in these empty ruins of yours. Fhilesc," he called. An older bodyguard wearing thin mail and a bronze torc stepped out from behind the Senator. "If you're so certain you'll defeat the Lady Senator's boy, fight mine, too. I doubt *that* will prove so easy."

Sensing this was not a battle she could win, Corbha turned to the Abbot. "So long as they understand the infirmarers are presently afflicted with bloodrust, and if *you* insist, I suppose I have no choice."

The Abbot bowed his head. "Thank you, sister. Now, let's all go to the martial field."

Corbha left first via the temple passageway. This was a terrible idea. So many things could go wrong, many of them irreparably so. She ducked through the side door a few paces before the sacristy. In earlier times, everyone had stretched and worked on balance in the mornings and practiced blade, blunt, and bow in the afternoons, on occasion coming out again at night. Now that everyone ailed with myriad aches and pains, including Martial Master Tairad, she did most afternoon training alone. He instructed her, of course, and if it was a good day for Unaid, Mhleca, Serbhica, and Sabha, they joined. Rarely did anyone feel well enough to spar.

She marched across the field. When she found a level spot she liked, she took off her folded hat, veil, and cap, knotted her hair in a bun, stripped off her cincture, tunic, and her middle skirt. She contemplated untying her surgery beak while tucking the lèine into her trousers. No, she decided. It was too much of a risk. She took a few deep breaths for focus and stretched under the late autumn sun. If the guards were sanguiren, she would have enjoyed testing her mettle against someone near her age. As things stood, the senators' guards had approximately zero chances of winning. She prayed the senators soon realized why this was an exercise in foolishness for their sake.

She watched the Abbot, senators, and their guards file out of the side door. A crumb of pity settled within her as she watched Dobhnic and Fhilesc strut with the pomp of twin roosters to square on either side of her.

"What counts as a win?" she asked.

"Whoever draws first blood," Dobhnic said.

"Absolutely not. It is against the tenets of my vows."

"Well, there has to be some way to figure out a victor."

"Easy. Whoever falls first," Fhilesc asserted.

Corbha grounded herself in the soil. She kept her joints loose yet firm. "If you say so."

The Abbot and senators, along with their entourage, stayed some fifteen paces back. One of Senator Arcadhec's guards called, "Three, two, one, square!"

Time slowed for her. Dobhnic swung from the right, Fhilesc hooking left. She effortlessly dodged them and whirled around, striking Dobhnic on the back before sweeping down to kick Fhilesc's legs out from under him. Both landed with a thud.

"Shit," Dobhnic scrambled up, brushing dirt and grass off his tunic. "That wasn't fair. I didn't even have time to hit."

Fhilesc picked himself up without a peep.

Corbha shrugged. "I was unaware you were meant to let the other party strike you."

"You won't get that lucky this time. Again."

The easier choice was to let him triumph. It made no actual difference whether she "won," but the little wretch was so smug she couldn't stand the thought. Corbha took her stance.

Dobhnic swung left and Fhilesc right. She laid them both out with even breaths. They were far too slow and uncertain. Once re-centered, Dobhnic sneered at her. "So you're fast and have creepy eyes. And? Your hits don't hurt at all. Why don't you show us what you can *really* do?"

Corbha stiffened. "I don't have to justify myself to you."

"What will you do, then? Pray at him until he goes away? You'll have to knock him cold or dead," Fhilesc said.

Dobhnic smirked. "You do spend all day praying, so I imagine you're pretty good on your knees."

Corbha didn't know what that meant, but it sounded as if it was supposed to be an insult. She called to the Abbot, "If this has satisfied the senators, I would like to return to my duties preparing for the feast."

Nodding at her, the Abbot turned to speak to the senators.

"Coward," Dobhnic spit at her feet. As he turned away, almost mocking in posture, she sensed him shift his weight onto his other foot. As he pivoted to strike, she caught his fist, bent it back until his knuckles brushed his wrist, and declared, "You will not provoke me. Go now. I am tired of this."

His face turned violet as he strained to keep his composure. "Fine then," he forced out. "I'll make you show us."

Blood. It flowed from the corner of his indigo lips, glistening against night-blue skin. He spit. Blood sprayed her in the face. The idiot had bit his tongue.

No. She couldn't lose herself in front of the Abbot. There was only one way to avoid frenzy. She looked Dobhnic right in the eyes and let the Void envelop them.

The mortal world melted away, leaving naught but star-strung sky against the fabric of the Void. His misty silhouette materialized before her spirit. Every shard of his multicolored soul brightened and dimmed with his pulse, each crack, every flaw made known. The temperature was an ever-descending lead weight. She put a glasslike hand against his freezing cheek.

"Fool," spoke a voice that wasn't quite hers yet flowed from her mouth. "You know not the danger you are in."

She kissed him on the lips just to taste the ichor, savoring every tasteless drop upon her tongue.

Cracks made hairline fractures in his soul where her hand touched him. She could kill him with impunity in the Void. No one could reach them here. He'd never realize his mistake.

A soul shard splintered near his eye socket. It might blind his mortal body. A pit grew in her stomach. Yesterday, she could have killed the Widows this way. Her veins flooded with shame. Again, she had lost control—in front of the Abbot, no less. She had made a vow to the Blood Mother to never betray her Pact again, yet here she courted that very thing.

Every shard of her being roared at her to shatter Dobhnic's soul.

She prepared her mortal self to smell his blood. Straining, aching, she withdrew her hand and pushed him away.

The Void evaporated. She balled up her lèine and held it against her face, backing away from Dobhnic's crumpled body as his screams rang out across the martial field. He was pale as moonlight and frozen to the ground in a heap. He tried to speak. No sound but coughing gasps choked out. His eyes searched for something that wasn't there; the Void, Corbha assumed. Perhaps for the Blood Mother within it to beg forgiveness for testing her child's patience and goodwill.

At once, the Abbot had thrust himself between them, chased at length by the senator's guards. "Corbha. Return to the kitchen." the Abbot said.

She brushed past him, the guards, and the senators to fetch her habit. Senator Gabhrit muttered as she passed, "What a cursed child."

Digging her nails into her palm to keep from wheeling around and striking him, she swept off toward the side door. A demonstration they wanted, and a demonstration they received. Asking for such an exhibition in the first place was a grave misunderstanding of what a sanguiren's gifts were meant for. It was not a toy, nor an oddity, nor a fetishistic display of power or might. It was to protect the Divine Orchard, the assets of the Blood Mother, and the sanguiren here in the mortal Fold. She tore the door open and let it slam shut behind her. Dark thoughts fueled her already fuming mind as she stormed down the corridor. How dare they treat her like an oddity? This was not some tyrant's menagerie of exoticism and wonder. It was *sacred*. It was *holy*. It was *firmly* out of the grasp of primitive mortals to understand.

She went straight to the dorter to change. If this was what she was in for with the senators' holy orders to the abbey, she would petition the Abbot to take vows to become a hermit. She threw on her skirt, tightened the strings, and yanked on her tunic in one ragged motion. Damn this. May they never see Her Orchard. May their souls fester between Folds until the end of time. She'd be a hermit before living with them, even if it meant never seeing Fhucan or Unaid or the baby until the senators were dead. What entitlement. What nerve. She knotted her cincture, flung on her cap, veil, and folded hat, then snatched a fresh apron. Storming out of the dorter, she tromped through the east cloister hall and into the southern, passing the warming house and refectory. When she reached the kitchen, she took a deep breath and smoothed her skirts before entering.

Serbhica noticed her at once. "What happened to you?" she asked. "Your face is purple."

"Nothing!" Corbha said louder than she intended. Her spirit-siblings all glanced at her, not stopping their cooking but slowing enough it was clear they were paying attention. Cellarer Rulidh and the Prioress came to her.

"Are you okay?" Rulidh asked. "What did the Abbot want?"

She struggled to hold back tears, flinging her hands about as she spoke. "The senators wanted some *demonstration* of what Brother Tairad teaches us, so the Abbot asked me to spar with two of their guards. One made himself bleed, and we made eye contact and—"

"You *what*?" Rulidh put a hand over her mouth. "Why would you *do* such a thing? Have you no self-control? You could have killed him," she hissed.

"*He* bit his tongue, so I'd smell his blood," Corbha snapped. "He *forced* me to."

Rulidh scoffed. "Well you need not be rude to me. I had nothing to do with this. You said the Abbot requested this of you? Why?"

"I know why," the Prioress said. "Corbha, please come with me. I'd like to speak with you about something."

Not this again. Her stomach couldn't take another wretched moment of uncertainty. Tight-lipped, hands squeezed into fists at her sides, Corbha followed the Prioress to the Abbot's office: a tiny, closet-like room stuffed with scroll shelves and a dozen half-melted candles and empty cresset lanterns.

The Prioress sat behind the Abbot's desk and gestured for Corbha to take a seat. "The senators are here on holy orders. You know this," the Prioress stated.

Corbha stayed silent. Her fingernails cut into the skin on her palms. She knew this, but knowing it didn't make their presence any better. They deserved death. *She* deserved death.

Lightning struck her heart. She could confess what she did to the Prioress right here, right now. Maybe that would end this misery. What she had done to Dobhnic was orders of magnitudes worse than what had happened at the sepulcher. Senator Arcadhec would be well within her rights to call for her execution. Corbha wrung her hands.

The Prioress spoke gently. "Are you aware of what those orders are?"

Through gritted teeth, Corbha replied, "To spend their remaining days at the Abbey in contemplation of their faults."

"To *live out* their days," the Prioress emphasized. "Tell me, after a transgression such as they committed, how many days do you believe they have remaining?"

Corbha blinked. Her foot bounced. She hadn't considered that.

"The senators, in all their bumbling stupidity, will not be long for this Fold. They violated a letters patent from the Divine Orchard. Only one fate could befall them."

"But *when?*"

"When the Blood Mother deems it advisable." The Prioress folded her hands atop the desk. "There is another matter I would like to discuss with you."

Her stomach dropped. "Yes?"

"You've been acting strangely. Sister Unaid said you hurt yourself in the orchard yesterday."

Corbha bowed her head. "I…"

A deluge of everything that had happened flooded her mind. The smell of the Wife's blood, how rich and wrong her body tasted as she held her only son in her arms, Fhucan's admission that without her, they wouldn't know what to do. She bit her tongue hard enough to draw tears into her eyes. Confessing her transgression carried the weight of such punishment she was certain the burden would crush her. But how could she lie to the Prioress? How could she lie *again*?

A tiny voice inside her whispered that this was a test, that the Prioress already knew why she went to the orchard. Another lie might seal her fate. If they sacrificed her, perhaps the Divine Orchard would see the need to send fresh, young, able-bodied lay brothers and lay sisters to rebuild the abbey. Perhaps her death would be a good thing.

Another thought cut through her like a heated blade. More likely they wouldn't. It would be simpler to send her spirit-siblings away.

She swallowed. "I was just overwhelmed by the Wife's… everything. Her death, the rites, her consecration. The communion. Everything happened so fast. It was…" she searched for a word. "Dizzying. I wanted time alone with the Blood Mother to contemplate."

The Prioress nodded. "As is understandable. Death comes for us all; you aren't wrong to be wary, but I urge you to never succumb to the fear of it. There are far worse things in this life than death. Some right here at this abbey," she said.

A long pause. Was this it? Would her spirit-siblings soon taste her flesh and blood?

"It's no secret that our way of life is dying," the Prioress said.

Corbha sat on her hands, gaze locked on the edge of the Abbot's desk. This was not the discussion she expected. It wasn't anything she had thought about at all.

"It is. Dying. I will not lie about it. The public sees no use for the Red Pact anymore, let alone the Covenant. They do not understand what it is our shared ancestors did for us, or how immense a sacrifice it was." The Prioress' eyes grew watery. "Wives, Widows, Sisters, Daughters—all of this the natural order of things, but in the most unnatural of ways. Some may think these designations are a relic of ancients long since passed, but it is the very precarious foundation upon which our society totters."

Corbha's foot bounced against the floor. Her skin was warm and numb, like the Prioress had draped her in a blanket soaked with oil. Choosing this path had been no choice at all for their ancestors, sanguiren or full mortal, but it was because everyone *chose* to sacrifice their wants for the needs of their neighbors that their society had become so great. It was no minor thing to alter the shade of one's blood. In comparison, the Blood Mother and Her sanguire asked for little in return.

The Prioress sniffed. "Our apples rot on the orchard floor, too many for our gnarled hands to pick. Our brewery stagnates without enough able limbs to make cider. We bring in less money each year, starving our bodies of the barest sustenance. We are old, most of us; the Abbot may make a wonderful show of pretending otherwise, but his health is failing him. Two of us are stricken with bloodrust." She exhaled. "No. Things are not well here, and they have not been in years. Unless something changes soon, it is likely that in your lifetime our abbey will shutter for good." She paused; eyes locked on her clasped hands. "But: you, the child, Unaid, Serbhica, Sabha—you must find solace in each other. We all are born of the same blood: our father, the Sanguire of the Sacred

Apple. Our spiritual bonds transcend mortal vows. It is important to me, Corbha, that you remember your siblings when any of this causes you despair. Do not think you are alone. Our problems are plenty and our solutions few, but a seedling will sprout from ashes even if the grove has gone up in flames. *You* are the future of this abbey. Our way of life is vested within you, and it is a burden I wish with all my heart I could wrest from your hands." She brushed tears from her crooked, wrinkled eyes with the back of her hand. "Well. That's enough melodrama for the day. You may return to the dorter to rest. I'll send Unaid to retrieve you for the feast, unless you feel well enough to return to the kitchen."

Standing, Corbha said with eyes trained on the dusty tile floor, "Thank you, sister. I will take my leave."

Her head spun. This was far more than she had ever wanted to learn in one day. At least the Prioress still trusted her, whether or not she deserved it. As Corbha placed a hand on the coarse wooden door to open it, the Prioress said, "Sister."

She stopped.

"Do not believe this is a punishment," the Prioress said. "If you're up to it, we could still use your help in the kitchen, but I care more for your wellbeing. I love you as I love all my siblings. Trust me, if you can, that the senators will face divine retribution at the earliest juncture."

Corbha thought for a moment, but no words were enough to stymie the despair in every word the Prioress had said. Bowing her head, Corbha replied, "Thank you, sister. I love you too."

*     *     *

The dorter door creaked open. Groggy, Corbha rolled over in bed to see Unaid creeping toward her with the swaddled newborn crying in her arms.

"Corbha?" She asked over his high-pitched shrieks. "I'm so sorry to wake you like this—we're almost ready to eat."

"Supper?" Corbha sat up, rubbing her eyes. Early evening light illuminated the dorter. "I slept that long?"

"Are you coming?" Unaid asked.

She wanted to say no, but then she'd have to explain why. So, she got up and opened her chest of drawers to find a fresh habit. "I just need a moment to freshen up."

The baby screamed and wailed through her words. Unaid asked her to repeat herself. As Unaid turned to leave, Corbha said, "Wait. Leave him. I'll see if I can calm him down and bring him to the refectory when we're ready. You deserve a break."

Unaid looked as if she'd been handed a bar of solid gold. She laid the baby on Corbha's cot. "The Widow from the Orchard of Sacred Figs fed him just before I came to get you. I've tried everything—changing, burping, rocking, rubbing his back, singing—it must be colic. If you can calm him, I'll sneak you an extra dessert. It looks delicious, by the way."

"I appreciate it," Corbha said with a smile. "Thank you, Unaid. You're so sweet."

"Oh, please, you'll ruin me with flattery." She giggled. "I'll see you two later."

Corbha dressed herself, stopping every so often to stroke the baby's face and shush him. Once she donned her veil and folded cap, she picked him up and bounced him around a little, shushing him again. Whyever it seemed to help, she didn't know, but it was too good a solution to risk him starting up again. Besides—the longer she kept away from the senators, the better.

She walked with him up and down the eastern cloister hall, once in a while pointing at a door or passage to tell him where it led. Slowly, she made her way around the cloister: east to south to west to north. He seemed calm enough while moving, but the moment she paused he started crying again.

On their fourth or fifth lap, the unmistakable scent of burning wood wafted into the cloister.

Her heart fluttered. She made her way back to check the warming house a little quicker than before. Heat emanated from within, thawing her icy hands. It was the only place in the abbey wherein fire could be kept, aside from the kitchen. She passed the refectory to check that Serbhica and Rulidh had put out the fires. The hearth and ovens were cold.

The smell only deepened.

Corbha stepped out of the kitchen to see two shadowy figures dart across the cloister. Both carried shields embellished with an apple crowned in flames.

She jumped back over the threshold and shut the door as quietly as she could, heart thumping. Those were Senator Arcadhec's bodyguards. Clutching the baby close to her chest, she cracked the door.

A thick, black blanket of smoke poured into the kitchen. Gasping, she yanked off her cap and held it over her brother's face. Hot, acrid air enveloped them. Holding him close, Corbha tore across the cloister. When she reached the door that led outside, she threw it open.

Her heart stopped.

The orchard.

It was aflame.

She screamed for help, but there came only the sound of battleaxes struck against shields and chain mail jingling in the distance. Corbha bolted toward the refectory. No, no, no, no. This couldn't happen. Not like this.

Corbha pounded on the refectory door. "Erchid!" She screamed. "Erchid! They're attacking the abbey!"

Muffled clanks and crashes answered her. She tried with all her might to yank open the door, sobbing, abandoning her place when she looked behind her to see a glut of soldiers flooding the cloister. Flaming apples blazed across their shields.

The refectory door exploded open with enough force to knock her backward. Scrambling to right herself, she looked inside with teary eyes. The Abbot came tumbling out, run through with a spear. Death screamed back at her as the air left her lungs. The bodies of her spirit-siblings sprawled out dead on the ground: an ocean of red so deep it soaked her bare feet. She felt one hand behind her, then another—Unaid and the Prioress, glistening red and coated in sweat.

"Run!" the Prioress commanded.

Her feet carried her away.

Three places in the abbey were fireproof: the warming house, the chapterhouse, and the temple. Only the temple doors led outside and away from the orchard. They fled through the cloister, all of them faster than the senators' soldiers but Corbha the swiftest of all. They ran across the southern cloister hall, hooked left to run up the eastern, and found the door to the chapterhouse.

"I'll block the doors. You go!" The Prioress overturned benches and shelves.

Corbha ran into the temple passage, Unaid not far behind. Inside the sacristy, they halted.

"What's going on?" Unaid sobbed. "What's happened?"

"They're attacking the abbey," Corbha whispered. Fear stabbed her gut when she heard shouts and clatters on the other side of the door. "Shh. Listen. Listen."

The cacophony of looting and destruction pierced her ears. Their soldiers must have broken into the temple. Shaking, Corbha looked between the baby and Unaid. "What should I do?"

"Leave," Unaid urged. "Get out of here. Take him. I won't make it as far as you. We'll meet—"

The temple door cracked open, knocking Unaid to the ground. Corbha screamed as a bronze ax cleaved through her head, painting the walls with blood and tissue.

Sobbing, Corbha stumbled back into the passageway, heart and soul shattering as she ran with the baby in her arms. She shouldered through the side door and out onto the martial field. Soldiers with shields bearing three golden apples upon a black stripe surrounded the temple—and the north gate.

Only one safe place remained: the infirmary. From there she could reach the south gate and escape. The baby shrieked like a wounded bird. Corbha ran so fast the world blurred and her lungs seared. Unaid. Her head split so easily. An apple divided by a sharp knife. The Prioress, no doubt dead by now. The soldiers' war cries bleated in her mind. Her breaths came so shallow and rapid she feared she'd faint.

Corbha kicked the infirmary door until her foot numbed. "Please, let me in, please," Corbha begged. "It's me, it's Corbha. I have the child. I have the child, please, open the door."

"Unaid?" Mhleca's muffled voice asked from the other side.

"Corbha!" She screamed.

The lock jiggled. Mhleca and Đusca stood behind it, both pale as ice. "Touch nothing," Mhleca cautioned. "Where's the Abbot?"

"Dead!" Corbha wailed. "And the Prioress and Unaid and the orchard—everyone—the senators, it's—"

"Corbha. Listen. You must escape with this child. You *will*." Đusca said in a stern voice. "Go through the Widow's Convent. There's another gate there. Escape into the hills and don't stop until you reach the Namach River. Follow it and you'll find New Madhcha. Do you understand?"

Through gasps made by searing lungs, Corbha sobbed. There was no escape. Not from this. Nothing escaped death. Voice cracking and stuttering, she wailed, "I can't abandon you to die. There's too many. Please, let me help."

Đusca shooed her toward the back door. "You can help. Take the baby. Don't abandon his life. Go. We'll follow you out. Go. Quickly! We're right behind you."

Unaid had been, too, and now she was dead. Corbha ran out of the infirmary into the night, followed by Mhleca and Đusca. They swept across the sepulcher's curtilage. Corbha stumbled, holding her crying brother ever closer to her chest, gagged by smoke and tears. More soldiers—on their shields a vermillion heart over an apple tree—poured in through the south gate.

"Go! Through the Widows' Convent!" Mhleca shouted in blood tongue. Her voice was rough and strained.

The sound of a wet thump struck Corbha's heart like lightning. Đusca collapsed. An arrow stuck out of her chest, staining her habit a darker shade of red. Mhelca went down beside her.

Corbha peeled through the Widows' Convent, fueled by the sight of their bodies laid out in clumps along the paths, too mangled to count, silently slain with no mercy. She ran and ran, heart thumping, head pounding, until she saw nothing around her but empty, windblown hills.

*     *     *

Corbha barreled across the Vacant Hills. Run. Hide. Keep the baby alive. Those were her sole commandments until they could reach safety. She saw Unaid—poor and lovely Unaid, head split like a melon—and sobbed.

She tore blindly through the night, not caring that her feet were bloodied and lacerated by all manner of broken glass and rubble. A slick film of sweat formed between her breast and the baby's swaddle.

Unaid said town was three days away. Three days was too long to go without feeding him. He'd die just like everyone else, and herself not long after. Was it kinder to let him starve or throw him into the river to drown? The Wife of the Sacred Fig was almost certainly dead. But what then? What of herself? Where would she go?

She stumbled on a dip in the ground, catching herself, bleating like a wounded auroch. The baby had long ago stopped howling, just twisted his face and balled-up hands into a painful knot. She ran until her knees gave out and her arms could carry her brother no longer. Blurry-eyed, she dragged herself and the child toward a lone tree on a hillside.

No one had ever suspected the senators might do such a thing. How could anyone have? Who in the Blood Mother's graces attacked an abbey? But it seemed obvious, now. This betrayal was planned. The sparring match was an experiment, not a show. One question burned in her mind: how had Tairad not seen their cohorts?

She collapsed against the tree trunk with the baby atop her stomach, staring up into the starry sky. She begged the Blood Mother to answer one faint whisper: "Why?"

Why her? Why now? To what end? Visions of a pike jammed through the Abbot, the Prioress swarmed and stung by bronze swords, Unaid's skull split in two, Mhleca and Đusca pierced by arrows—visions of all their corpses cycled through her mind, ensnaring her in an unending torrent of carnage and death. Fourteen sanguiren. Fourteen children of the Sacred Apple, gone. Their faces flashed in her mind's eye. Gory-faced, bloody-mouthed, heads severed and bleeding red. Red. So much red it could fill an ocean.

All that remained at her abbey would be charred flesh and bones. She knew this, yet she yearned to walk into that plume of thick black smoke in the distance with every shard of her soul. Erchid. Lubhyll. Unaid. Mhleca. She whispered their names over and over. Đusca. Serbhica. Sabha. Fhucan. All dead. All dead. Teghor. Ridrag. Rulidh. Berugni. What were their last moments like? Seþnall. Tairad. Gone. All of them, dead.

"Blood Mother," Corbha croaked. "Blood Mother, I need you. I cannot bear this—" she coughed. "I can't. I can't. I can't!" Her voice was air, though she tried to shout. The baby cried anew. No more tears streamed from either of them, just grief, and she lay there in the dark letting the chilly autumn air caress them. Echoing screams carried on the wind, melding with the baby's mournful keen.

*Do not think you are alone*, the Prioress' voice rang inside her head. It cut Corbha to her marrow. How long would it take to forget their faces? Their voices? Their names?

*Do not think you are alone.* But she was. Any other children of the Sacred Apple were bound to be at the Temple of the Divine Orchard. The baby would starve before they reached halfway. Exhaustion would be what killed her.

Corbha buried her face in her knees. It didn't matter that she couldn't breathe through all the mucus and fabric. She and the baby were doomed to die. She knew it.

*This is my fault*, she told herself. *Mine. If I hadn't tried to watch the Wife's consecration this wouldn't have happened. I'm stupid. So stupid. Irresponsible, disgusting, wretched. I should have died with my siblings.*

If not for her brother, she'd go back and walk into the flames. Let her ashes fertilize the field where the orchard once grew. For once, she'd do some good. Her thoughts overflowed.

The baby wouldn't live long. Not without milk and warmth. But until he drew his last breath, they were all each other had left. He didn't even have a name.

She rubbed his back through the swaddle to soothe his mews.

"Oh child of blood, sleep thou peaceful here." It was just a fragment of a hymn, but she remembered no other children's songs. She rubbed his back in gentle circles, singing nonsense words and prayer fragments to calm him.

By now, the scent of smoke had reached them. With her luck, if they slept out here, the senators' soldiers would find them before sunrise.

Exhausted, she closed her eyes. Could she weep, she would. She failed her spirit-siblings. If she couldn't figure out how to keep him alive, she would fail their baby brother, too. Another betrayal with which to dishonor his mother.

Her breaths were ragged. She tried to smooth them for the baby's sake. The Wife gave so much to bring him into the world. The wicked, cruel, foul world. She dragged air into her lungs. Her siblings sacrificed everything to keep both of them in it. Was her promise to escape with him a lie, too? Would it be another falsehood spit out to soothe her own worries?

No. They couldn't be. Above all else, she would protect their brother. She had to. This responsibility was hers alone to bear. As long as she lived, so would he. This would be her sacrifice.

Safety. Shelter. Milk.

She had until dawn.

# THE SEVEN CURSES
## Alan G. Provance

Before she swept two invading armies from her lands and long before her own kin betrayed her and stole her crown, the Shining Queen travelled with a band of warriors, serving various landed lords and ladies in the winter and living off the land during the summer as custom dictated. The band consisted of Anja, the Covenant Breaker, late of the imperial army from the east and still bearing its tattoo, alongside her sister Aria Báirseach, the brothers Somrael and Sirius, Arctos the Mighty, Salen Alfwine, and Fiabhras the Swift. All of the companions bore the mark of the gods, a gift and curse in equal measure for each, for even the gods themselves could not alter the fate of those who vexed them but they most certainly plagued those mortals audacious enough to win the gods' power. Bound by the trials put upon them, these seven made their way in the world for long years before the fullness of their destinies were revealed.

One autumn, a month before the wheel turned and the seven companions would seek the castle of a lord or lady to stay in for the winter, Fiabhras took up her bow and went to get dinner for her companions. In no time at all, she'd found the tracks of a magnificent stag, and set herself to the hunt, running swiftly without losing the trail. Three times she startled her prey without seeing it, and three times it leapt away to run through the forest, but Fiabhras patiently followed and at last the stag's energy was spent. It lay down in a glade, panting with exhaustion and overheating, but when Fiabhras parted the undergrowth to finally see her prey she cursed. The stag had pure white fur and red eyes, marking it as a sacred beast of Arawn, the god of death. To kill such a magnificent creature would earn Arawn's wrath, yet Fiabhras' curse would give her no respite if she didn't finish a hunt once started, and to let this stag go would mean that Fiabhras could neither sleep nor eat until she felled the magnificent deer. With a heavy heart, she nocked an arrow and whispered words of power to it, asking for the quickest death it could bestow, and loosed it into the stag's breast. The mighty beast ceased breathing immediately and lay still, allowing Fiabhras to dress it. She sang prayers to the spirit of the stag and to Arawn as she worked, though these would not be enough to avert the god's wrath, and she left the entrails in the woods for ravens or hungry wolves. Within minutes Fiabhras had hoisted most of the stag onto her shoulders, and made her way back to camp.

"What have you done?" hissed Anja, the first to see Arawn's stag draped over Fiabhral's shoulders. Fiabhral stared at her own feet, and Anja knew enough about her curse that nothing more needed to be said. The other companions gathered around, and though the white stag meant trouble ahead, no one chastised Fiabhral. Space was made for the huntress as she skinned the stag and began preparing the meat. All agreed that to let such a magnificent animal go to waste would only further enrage Arawn, and Fiabhral took great care to prepare that night's dinner as well as she could, while preserving the rest. Aria and Salen saw the potential in the stag's hide and began quietly discussing which spells to weave into it, and the other four ate without mirth, wondering how to apologize to a god of death for this act.

After some time, Arctos broke the silence. "I know a druidess nearby," he rumbled. "In matters of the divine, we'll get more help from her than we will sitting around waiting for Arawn to devise some doom for us."

"Not all of us are on great terms with the gods as is," muttered Anja, looking at the legion tattoo on her arm. "Will that complicate things?" The tattoo had been a covenant between Anja and the gods of the empire, and upon breaking it she'd been cursed to forever have a measure of her companions' strengths and curses each.

Arctos shrugged. "I'm not a druid myself, so I couldn't say. Honestly, the lot of us should probably talk to them more often, but that's a conversation for another time; let's head out in the morning to meet with her about our immediate predicament." The others nodded in agreement, and retired to their tents or slept out under the stars. Autumn's first early chill wound its way into the evening air, hinting at a bitter winter to come. Arctos assumed the form of a great bear in his sleep, for he could assume the form of a powerful bear whenever it pleased him, though he sometimes changed unintentionally, and could lose himself for a while. Sirius dreamt of battle, and his dreams were enough to stir the Warp-Frenzy that was his curse, though mercifully he wasn't fully consumed and needed no intervention to come out of it. The bite of cold could not kill Somrael anymore than the bite of a beast, so he lay in discomfort but knew the dawn would find him alive, for no wound would kill him and he would heal all within a day, though he felt everything keenly. Anja and Fiabhras lay together to warm each other, while

Salen and Aria did the same. Salen could wear the forms of men and women from around the world easily, and wove illusion and words so powerfully that even his companions weren't sure what he actually looked like, if he even had a fixed form. He could also ensnare the hearts of men and women with ease, though his own heart became ensnared as well, and this is why he curled up next to Aria, for her mind always dwelt half in the Otherworld, to which she could travel with ease.

Dawn came slowly, as fog poured out over the world and the seven companions woke to damp, muffling grey. Aria and Arctos made signs of warding against ill omens, while Salen wrapped himself in the skin of the stag to ward off Arawn's influence. The Otherworld was said to host the dead as they waited for their next life, and it appeared like this, reminding all of the burden from Arawn that they needed to lift. They broke camp quickly, wolfing down cold venison with hard bread and the last of their mead. Arctos had resumed the form of a man and led the others out toward the highway. A small village lay nestled in the foothills of the dark mountains dominating the horizon, and today as it wallowed in damp fog, the villagers felt too keenly the wild and the weird pressing down upon them from the outside world, and had nothing but cold stares for the seven companions as they ambled in shortly after noon. Undaunted, Arctos walked up to a small house in the town square, festooned with oak leaves and ribbons. After a few sharp knocks, the door swung open to reveal an old woman clothed in a pure white robe.

"Arctos! What a pleasant surprise. Who have you brought to darken my doorstep?"

"Rhiannon, these are my companions, and we seek your assistance with a grave matter. May we impose upon you to honor the law of hospitality?"

Rhiannon grumbled something under her breath but bade the seven to enter nonetheless. Druids could no more defy the laws of the gods than stout warriors could fall to their knees and grovel; it simply wasn't done. After the companions were seated comfortably and Rhiannon had given them meat and mead, Arctos related the story of what had befallen them while Rhiannon listened carefully. At length, she drained her mug of mead and laughed. "Seems to me that Fiabhras here is the only one likely to catch Arawn's fury. You others borrow trouble; simply eating the meat of Arawn's stag will not incur his wrath."

"Fiabhras is not the only one among us cursed by the gods" Anja whispered.

Rhiannon examined each companion closely. "The gods of the empire have no influence here, my dear. I can see the afflictions plaguing the rest of you though. This matter demands a consultation, and for that I need entrails. Come." Their dinner had concluded so the companions joined Rhiannon as she left her abode and walked to the town center. The sun hadn't quite set behind the foggy mountains, but darkness rushed into the village all the same. Lamps illuminated houses and spilled a little light into the center, where three iron cages stood with slumped figures in each. Rhiannon approached each cage and held out lots, which the prisoners numbly accepted. A disheveled woman, likely imprisoned for stealing, drew the short lot. Rhiannon opened the cage and before the woman could resist or even scream, Rhiannon drove the point of a sickle into her belly, ripping upward and gutting the woman to let her entrails spill out onto the ground. The woman's body knew its end had come and rattled with its last breath shortly after, and as soon as the woman went still, Rhiannon kneeled down to examine the guts in the last light of day. The seven companions watched patiently as the other two prisoners thanked the gods and ancestors for sparing them this grisly fate. After the sun finally slipped behind the mountain peaks, Rhiannon stood up, wiping the sweat from her brow. "A castle sits on top of a mountain nearby, made all of black marble. Here is the hall of Arawn's mortal son, and you must speak with him directly to absolve yourselves of this sin against Arawn. His castle will be difficult to reach, and you will face trials without and within. Family will betray family. Some curses must remain, yet if you choose to ignore what happened, all of you will be called to Arawn's court in the Otherworld by winter's end." All seven stood silently for a moment, before Anja cleared her throat.

"We shall set out for the castle tomorrow. Thank you, Rhiannon," she said. The old druidess nodded, and returned to her house with the seven companions, offering them a warm place to sleep as was custom. Also by custom, the companions didn't tarry in the morning, setting out before midday for a black castle atop a mountain peak. Fiabhras had smoked the venison well, and Arctos would assume his bear form to find berries and mushrooms and honey to supplement the companions' food. The first night that the companions stopped to make camp, all seven could hear the howling of wolves. Arctos sniffed the air and shook his head.

"These wolves are sent by Arawn himself. They will strive to mangle us, but if we slay them, we will only compound our curse." As Arctos spoke, keen eyed Fiabhras spied white furred shapes moving through the trees in the twilight.

"You all set your tents and sleep within. They may chew upon me and not be satisfied, and I will survive the night," declared Somrael grimly. The others nodded in agreement, though none wished to see their friend suffer. The other six companions slept in their tents as their campfire went out, and when the white furred wolves with their red eyes entered the camp, Somrael taunted and goaded them, kicking dirt in their faces and jeering until all seven wolves leapt upon him and tore into his flesh. Somrael's growls of defiance turned into roars of pain, and his companions slept uneasily that night, though the wolves could never finish dismembering their meal and as the sun rose opposite the mountains they scattered into the woods, leaving Somrael in peace. Somrael lay wounded still, for the wolves had torn him mercilessly and despite how swiftly he healed, for the rest of that day Arctos carried him. When the companions prepared to make camp for their second night of travel, the howls of wolves sounded through the woods once again.

Looking at his brother, Sirius spoke up. "I will not allow my brother to be torn apart again. Tonight I shall divert the wolves, though we must set our camp near a stream that I may come down from the Warp Frenzy in the morning. Take my spear and my sword so that I do not kill them in my rage; surely the hounds of Arawn are sufficiently strong to endure my fists." The others nodded, and Somrael gratefully lay down in his tent to finish healing and sleep properly. The rest of the companions followed suit as the fire died and twilight brought the wolves of Arawn yet again. This time they found Sirius waiting for them, and, thinking that they would actually be able to finish off one of the companions, they leapt at him in earnest. Sirius had prepared himself however, and the Warp Frenzy had already taken hold. The first wolf tried to bite down on his arm and howled in pain as Sirius' flesh burned the inside of its mouth. Steam hissed from Sirius' skin as the wolves' slavering evaporated, and the same heated fist crashed into the wolf's head, sending it sprawling. Another wolf tried nipping at Sirius' heels but received a burn as well, and in the throes of his Warp Frenzy, Sirius began yanking off his clothes to prevent them from going up in flames. His body grew into a monstrous shape, hideous to behold and impossible to clearly define, seeming to shift as the wolves tried to focus upon it. Despite being the hounds of Arawn, lord of the Otherworld, the wolves became frightened and ceased their attacks as Sirius roared and began chasing them through the woods. Ever mindful of his companions, Sirius had the presence of mind to stay near the tents while also avoiding them, though in his rage he could concentrate on little else. One by one he caught the wolves and smote them with his burning fists before flinging them down the mountain, and though the wolves were indeed hardy enough to survive this assault, none returned to the camp that night. Sirius stumbled into the spring near the camp letting the cool water wash over him, calming the Warp Frenzy and sending up a wall of mist so thick that even if the wolves had returned they would not have found the camp. Sirius looked up from the stream in time to see the sun rising over the distant horizon, and shook his head wearily, for he knew he'd get no sleep. The other companions had slept uneasily as well, with Sirius's roars and the howls of pained wolves keeping them up. Arctos now carried Sirius because of how weary he was.

As the companions prepared for their final night in the wild before reaching the castle, Salen spoke up. "My friends, it's clear that neither Somrael nor Sirius can avert the wolves this night, for we have slept poorly both evenings and we can neither have Somrael wounded again before we arrive, nor is there a spring for Sirius to come out of his Warp Frenzy. I can weave an illusion over fallen logs such that the wolves will bite into wood, thinking it is us. They will no doubt see through this illusion shortly, and would have smelled the falsehood on the first two nights, but now I suspect that their pride goads them and they will be too hasty to fulfill Arawn's command." The others nodded, and set their tents away from the campfire. Salen wove his illusion, and where there had been seven fallen logs collected by the companions, now it looked like the seven themselves, sleeping peacefully by the fire. The companions then returned to their tents to sleep, as Salen wove another illusion to mask the tents from sight. All seven slept well that night, only interrupted once as the wolves bit into wood and howled in disgust and anger. If they tried smelling their prey, they would have been overpowered by the scent of Arctos' bear form, and the wolves had been instructed to hunt seven humans. The ban against killing the animals of Arawn did not apply to wild creatures, and the seven wolves had no desire to test a bear in the wild, so they slunk away back to their master.

After three nights in the wild, the companions at last neared the castle spoken of by the druidess, and such an awesome spectacle hadn't been seen by any of them hitherto. Black marble had indeed been used for every wall, and the massive keep was surrounded by a curtain wall that ringed the whole peak on which the castle sat. One tower touched the sky itself, and treetops could be seen peeking above the wall from within, indicating an orchard within the castle itself. No moat or crevasse barred entry, but the cobbled road to the gate rose steeply enough that any army foolish enough to challenge the son of Arawn wouldn't be able to bring horses or engines to bear. All the land around the castle had been cleared of trees and brush, and the companions stood at the edge of the forest, pondering their next course of action.

"It would be best if we knew more about the castle and our prospective host," Salen said. "Surely no manner of lord would deny succor to a woman in the wild. Let us send one among us to assess the situation and return with a report." Aria and Anja looked at one another, while Fiabhras shook her head.

"I have no proficiency with courtly customs and manners," the huntress said. "I fear I would glean little within."

"Though I am cursed by foreign gods, their mark upon me is palpable to all gods everywhere. I would not risk arousing ire or suspicion," said Anja.

"And I will be using the stag's hide to scout in my own way," answered Aria. Salen shrugged his shoulders and began rifling through his satchel, pulling out exotic looking clothing and shoes.

"No need to explain yourselves, my friends," he said cheerfully. "I had no intention of letting any of you carry out my plan. I trust in the laws of hospitality being carried out by the son of a god, and I shall adopt one of my other forms." Showing no modesty whatsoever, Salen disrobed before his companions, and before their eyes began to shift and change. The companions had known Salen to alter his form of course, though none had witnessed the actual transformation before. Salen's prior form had been perfect for a mysterious minstrel from any of a hundred local towns, with pale skin and blue-black hair the color of midnight. Now, as the others watched, his body became feminine and shapely. Pale skin darkened to appear kissed by the sun, like the peoples from the south, and straight black hair changed and twisted itself into small braids mixed with ochre. The wandering minstrel had become the adventurous merchant, and the transformation had even imparted the scent of exotic spices to complete the appearance. "You may call me Natasha as you usually do, for I don't wish to hear anyone in these lands stumble over my actual name," she said with a wink. Gathering her things, Natasha set out for the castle, promising to return in the evening with tidings of what the companions could expect. No one wished to try the wolves again, and all hoped for a swift resolution.

As Natasha left, Aria began gathering toadstools and herbs from the woods around the companions, and set up stones to hide a small fire. When her preparations were complete, Aria lit the fire and let it catch thoroughly, before throwing the stag hide over both her and the flame, reducing the fire to smoldering embers and trapping the smoke inside with her. The other companions busied themselves with the sharpening of their weapons or playing cards or, in Arctos' case, procuring food, but Aria had said she would scout their opponent as well and that's precisely what she did.

Just as Aria began her ritual, Natasha reached the gate of the castle, having been spotted by the guards as soon as she left the trees. They said nothing, though they clearly wished to know her intent. Natasha flashed them both a smile. "I am called Natasha Alfwine, and I beg the law of hospitality from the lord or lady of this castle," she called. The guards exchanged glances but soon raised the gate, still saying nothing. As Natasha entered, four other guards approached to escort her to the keep, though these men also were silent. Their lord had appointed them well, granting each man and woman in his retinue beautiful blue steel cuirasses over matching mail, with elaborate designs of stags, wolves, and boars on the guards' vambraces and greaves. Each had a steel shield and short sword with sturdy spears, and their helmets bore black plumes of feathers. Natasha had thought these impressive, but as she was led into the main hall the opulence of this lord overwhelmed her. Mounted upon the walls were heads from beasts she'd never heard of, and winding about the whole of the hall was gold filigree spelling out a story in letters from far to the east. Silken carpets covered the smooth floor and ebony chandeliers hung from the ceiling, carrying dozens of fat beeswax candles. A massive oaken table sat in the center of the room, large enough for a score of men or more to sit comfortably, and this table looked as though it was merely a section of one great tree; its chairs were also oak, but chased with silver and ivory. At the end of the hall, the lord sat in a throne carved from a single large bone, and he wore the white robe of a druid. Behind and above him on a pedestal sat a massive iron cauldron that seemed at odds with the decorations in the hall, but was clearly important all the same. The lord of the castle rose from his throne upon seeing Natasha and bade her approach, though so massive was the hall this took some time.

"Greetings, wanderer. I am Gwydyon, the lord of this castle, and I bid you be my guest and enjoy my hospitality. Will you sit with me and enjoy some refreshment? You must have wandered for some time to find a castle as out of the way as mine."

Natasha nodded as a servant brought a chair for her to sit on. Gwydyon returned to his throne, and gave the order for mead and bread to be produced. After drinking and eating, Natasha turned to her host. "My lord, your offer of hospitality is gracious. I have been chased by brigands for several days, and even leaving them the bulk of my wares did not satisfy them. I fear that a farmhouse or inn upon the road would have offered me the same, but the brigands would have overrun it."

Gwydyon laughed. "My lady, this castle is impregnable, and one hundred men-at-arms stand ready to defend it. Were these brigands an army, they could not molest you here."

Natasha smiled, relief playing across her face. "That is wondrous news! I can't believe you're able to maintain such a host, here on top of a lonely mountain." Her words were woven carefully, and already a snare formed around Gwydyon's heart.

"Surely you saw the orchards even from outside the castle. I have ample fruits and an apiary, a modest garden, and my father gifted me with wondrous pigs, who are slain each day only to rise whole once again the next morning. We want for nothing within these walls."

Natasha looked impressed, and feigned ignorance as she continued the conversation. "Your father must be a powerful wizard to have procured such magnificent beasts!" she exclaimed.

Gwydyon grinned. "Nay, he is far more than that. My father is none other than Arawn, the god who gifted the world with swine. These special pigs are unique, but you've never had a meal so good, I assure you."

Now is when Aria arrived, for her magic allowed her to send out her soul into the veil between worlds, and while her body lay beneath the skin of the white stag she travelled as a cat up to the castle gate. The guards couldn't see her, and to Aria the guards shimmered and looked faded, as though she observed them through a fog. The castle itself remained remarkably solid, even here, since the structures of men and women often cast pale faded reflections upon the veil between worlds, but Aria had little difficulty entering. In addition to the guards, the small spirits of the castle and its orchard flitted about at the edge of her vision. Focusing on the task at hand, Aria entered the hall and saw the ghostly image of Natasha conversing with Gwydyon, and could see that even as Natasha drew Gwydyon in, her own heart had been captured by the handsome lord. Gwydyon appeared lively and whole even from the veil, leaving no doubt that he was indeed the son of Arawn. After the two concluded their conversation, Aria followed Natasha as she was led to a guest room to relax and bathe, which is when she revealed herself by stepping from the veil into the world. Natasha jumped a bit at seeing a cat materialize from nothing, but recognized Aria even in another form. "We are lucky indeed, Aria. Gwydyon is a good man, I can tell. He is also a druid, and surely he will be able to remove any curse upon us from Arawn. Winter is nearly upon us, and Gwydyon wants for nothing; tell the others to request that we spend the season here."

Aria shook her head, and spoke with the voice of a woman despite being in the form of a cat. "You were supposed to tell them yourself, Natasha. Has your heart been smitten by this lord so easily?"

Natasha laughed. "Truly, he is handsome and generous, and possesses a wise air about him. Even you would succumb to his charms given time. Regardless, I can't leave after requesting hospitality, it would look suspicious. Finish your work and bring the others." Having said this, Natasha concentrated on bathing, luxuriating in the warm water. Aria sighed and slipped back into the veil before padding away to see the rest of the castle.

Even between worlds, Aria needed to be careful, for potent sorcerers and nefarious spirits could ensnare her. She quietly scoured the castle, taking much of the afternoon to do so, and could not shake the nagging feeling of something being out of place. By long tradition, no castle was built without someone interred within the foundation, and as Aria travelled to the bowels of the castle to speak with the castle's tribute it dawned on her that she hadn't seen a single other ghost. The ghostly man sitting calmly in the castle's lowest cellars was the first, Aria stepped fully into the Otherworld then, noting the chain around the solemn spirit. "Gentle ghost, greetings! How fare you today?"

The ghost looked up at her in surprise, and moved his mouth as if he'd forgotten how to speak. It took him some time to answer. "Spring has nearly ended here, and I look forward to the summer. Who are you, wanderer? I've not spoken with another since the day I was buried beneath the castle. I trust the keep is strong, for I have not been reborn."

Aria nodded. "The castle is strong indeed, a testament to your strength, gentle ghost. You must have been a mighty man indeed. I am Aria, a seer. I have come to ask why the castle is empty of ghosts, for surely not all who have died here were prepared to enter the Otherworld."

"I am Amaethon, brother to Gwydyon, and son of Arawn himself. There are no ghosts because none who die within the castle remain dead; my brother's most prized possession is a cauldron without equal in the world. Any who die are placed within, and the cauldron may hold a vast host. When the sun rises on the following morning, all of those within the cauldron are reborn, though they may never speak a word again."

"Are you not driven mad by loneliness, Amaethon? How many years have you stayed here with none to converse with?" Aria asked. The Otherworld provided an unusually beautiful vista from the mountaintop, with only Amaethon's chains to serve as a reminder that a castle sat here in the world of the living.

"Truly, it has been a blessing, even though I initially came to rest here under protest. My father and brother both had so many demands of me in life that the solitude here is respite. Nothing is expected of me, and I have no duties to fulfill other than remaining here for the castle to endure. This peace I wish upon all souls. I am grateful that you visited me, Aria; there is something about you that fills me with joy. I wish you luck on your journeys."

"You did not choose to be interred? I am sorry to hear, but grateful for the peace you have found. Fare thee well, Amaethon."

Satisfied with her investigations, Aria slipped back into the veil, hurrying now to find the rest of her companions. Returning to her body just as the sun started to slip below the horizon, Aria cast off the stag skin, startling her companions. Imparting all she'd seen and all she'd heard from Natasha, Aria bade her companions approach the gate and request hospitality. The guards were silent for them just as they had been before, and Aria whispered that they must have been brought back with the cauldron at some point. Nevertheless, the gate opened, and a well-appointed retinue guided the companions to the great hall of Gwydyon, who sat in his throne as before, though now Natasha sat at his side. "Welcome guests!" said Gwydyon, his voice loud with enthusiasm. "You arrive on a most wondrous evening, though please assure me that you are not the brigands who pursue my beloved Natasha? If you are bent on mischief while under my roof, speak now that we may resolve this with steel before I waste bread and mead."

"Nay lord, these are my boon companions! I found your castle before they could find me, please make them welcome." Natasha's words instantly swayed Gwydyon, and he called for bread and mead to be served.

"I do not doubt your words, Natasha, but your companions do not appear to be from the same kingdom as you. Whence do you six come?" Gwydyon asked, as his mute servants brought refreshment.

Anja spoke up. "My sister Aria and I are daughters of the Witch Queen Ceridwen, though we have been without a kingdom since the empire invaded. Our friend Arctos wandered up from the lands to the south, by the sea that separates our continent from Natasha's. The brothers Somrael and Sirius bear imperial names but were born in the north, and earned their freedom from the imperial arenas."

Fiabhras cut in before Anja could introduce her. "I am Fiabhras, lord, a huntress born in these lands though my parents come from the grassy plains far to the east. My mother pleaded with the goddess Epona to make me a huntress without equal who needed no horse, for my parents lost theirs on the journey to these lands. I became that huntress, though that is the reason I seek your counsel. My companions have stayed by my side on this quest, and it is a happy accident that we find our seventh companion here with you already." Fiabhras added the last part hastily.

\*     \*     \*

Her words rang false with Gwydyon, who stayed silent as he pondered everything she'd said. Though jovial and generous, Gwydyon's heart burned with passion, and such were Natasha's charms that jealousy wormed its way through Gwydyon's thoughts as he regarded her companions. The name Ceridwen also troubled him, though he couldn't quite recall why; still, Gwydyon remained bound by the laws of hospitality, and graciously invited the companions to sit with him at the large table in his hall, where the swine of Arawn were served with all manner of other food and drink. His silent servants brought forth fresh honeycomb and soft cheeses, numerous fruits and vegetables, spiced bread with pounds of butter, and a whole barrel each of ale and mead. It appeared that these companions hadn't enjoyed such a banquet as he had prepared any time recently as they all ate ravenously, nearly consuming the whole of the meal and drink. Their appetites sated, Gwydyon and his guests spoke at length of inconsequential matters, swapping tales of the petty gods who lived in the mountains or the fearsome engines of the empire who took the shape of men to wage war. Gwydyon assured his guests that they would be able to speak of their plight in detail at dinner the following evening, and bade them all goodnight, except for Natasha who retired with him.

Gwydyon slept peacefully next to Natasha after they'd spent hours acquainting themselves, but jealousy festered in his heart and blossomed fully when he awoke. Convinced that the other companions sought Natasha's hand, he devised means of eliminating them, confident that they would forget to request hospitality a second time, as they would assuredly want to winter here and one simply didn't make such requests too close together. The time for wintering would begin in a week, and Gwydyon owed at most two more days of hospitality before his duty was discharged. That day passed easily, and he heard from the companions about their curse, declaring that he would confer with his father about the best course of action. The second night he spent with Natasha as well, and if he was more jealous of her time and attention that evening, she didn't appear to notice. If anything, she felt just as enamored of him for his charms and wit, deepening his affection for her further still. The third day he declined to give an answer on the companions' dilemma, stating that he required the right phase of the moon and a proper sacrifice in order to speak with Arawn, and there were no druids among the companions so they trusted his words on the matter. At last the third dawn came, and the companions expected assistance so they did not leave the castle, but Gwydyon's ban had now been lifted. He'd kept his intentions close to his heart, and not even Natasha suspected any ill will from him.

Calling the companions together, Gwydyon offered bread and mead, before suggesting a hunt. "A great boar has roamed these woods for a long time my friends, and I would have him for the feast at the turning of the wheel," he declared, and the companions nodded agreeably. Gwydyon had horses brought forth, though Fiabhras needed none, and the party set out to find the tracks. Sure enough, within minutes, Fiabhras found the tracks of the largest boar she'd seen.

*    *    *

"Lord Gwydyon, may I assume that this boar is not favored by your father? I do not wish to compound my crimes against him," Fiabhras whispered.

Gwydyon shook his head. "Nay, good lady, hunt at your leisure; this is no pale beast consecrated to Arawn, but a mighty brute of the largest stock in this world." With this assurance, Fiabhras sped forth, following the tracks so quickly that the horses of the others had difficulty keeping up. The chase took a long time, as the boar was wily and led them through the difficult woods of the mountain for hours. At last, after the sun had passed its zenith, Gwydyon and the companions found the boar in a large thicket. All the companions, save Fiabhras, dismounted and advanced on the boar with spears. Fiabhras nocked an arrow, whispering words to it as she'd done with the stag. Loosing the arrow, Fiabhras shot the boar in the eye, but so great was the beast that the magic didn't take right away, and in its death throes the boar threw itself at the companions. Somrael stepped in front of his brother Sirius to take the brunt of the boar's charge, and Arctos dropped his spear to grapple with the mighty creature while the others wetted their spears in an effort to further weaken the boar. At last Fiabhras' magic took hold, and the boar breathed its last. Gwydyon clapped the companions on their backs and assisted Fiabhras with dressing the animal, placing it on his horse for the trip back.

As Gwydyon and the companions approached the castle, Anja noticed that no guards stood upon the parapets or at the gates. "My lord, where are your men-at-arms?" she asked, and Gwydyon simply stated that they were performing drills elsewhere, and that because of the castle's location they didn't need to staff the gate all that often. Once within the walls, a stablehand took their horses, and Gwydyon escorted the companions to his hall without any retinue coming for them. "Are all your men-at-arms drilling at once? Curious that you wouldn't even have a small detachment ready should brigands think to try a castle with empty walls," Anja asked, but Gwydyon merely waved dismissively. When the companions entered the great hall, they were stunned to see that magnificent decorations had been set up in their absence. Brightly colored lamps of stained glass adorned the walls and wreaths of flowers wound around the pillars in the room, while colored ribbons had been tied to the many heads mounting the walls. Five score sacks of grain hung from pillars and rafters in anticipation of the harvest festival that marked the turning of the year, and old oak leaves hung precariously from the chandeliers, ready to fall to the floor and make way for the flowering holly. "We shall feast tonight and all the nights until winter begins in earnest, my friends, to celebrate the turning of the season as well as my great fortune in meeting my beloved," Gwydyon declared, punctuating his statement by kissing Natasha. "Please, make use of the baths and your rooms as you see fit, and I shall dine with you all shortly."

As Gwydyon left for his chambers, the companions made as if to go to their separate rooms, but all converged on Anja's. Natasha spoke first. "There is something wrong, my friends. Gwydyon is lying, and though he bears me no ill will, I sense malice in his words."

Anja nodded. "He is acting strangely, though I can't determine what he plans. We have scant hours before the feast; Aria, do you have enough time to walk the veil? I fear any other snooping about would make our host too suspicious."

Aria produced the half-burned remains of her fire from before. "I saved these just in case. Leave me the stag hide, and Natasha, try to keep Gwydyon busy until sunset." Natasha nodded in agreement as Aria rekindled the ashes in a brazier and covered herself with the stag skin. The others went to their rooms to prepare and avoid suspicion.

Assuming the form of a cat once again, Aria slipped into the veil between worlds and began prowling around the castle. The first thing she noticed was that all the mice in the castle, and there were many in a large castle like this, were moving toward the basement. Following closely behind, Aria followed the trickle of mice from her wing and watched it become a veritable river of the small creatures, and when she entered the cellars the reason became clear. A massive mound of grain stood out in the open, as though sack after sack had been dumped out. The mice ate this grain freely, and Aria turned to head back, for following the mice had taken some time in the large castle and she needed to hurry. Finding herself again, Aria rolled up the skin and covered the brazier before walking over to the room where Somrael stayed. Knocking softly on the door, Aria waited until Somrael opened it, fresh from the bath and still dripping water. "Somrael, someone dumped the sacks of grain out in the cellar," she whispered, and Somrael's face twisted in puzzlement.

"What hangs in the main room, then?" he asked, for no lord could have enough grain for a hundred sacks and still more to waste in the cellar.

Aria shook her head. "I don't know, but aside from Fiabhras, you are the most cunning in our number. I doubt she would wear the stag's hide, but Natasha wove magics into it that shield the wearer from Arawn's gaze, and if you don this skin no artifice or magic of Arawn's son will see you. Please, continue the investigation while I prepare myself for the feast."

Somrael nodded grimly and took the stag skin and his short sword, a blade curved in the style of the continent to the south, and padded softly toward the main hall. He wore naught but the hide for fear of clanking or the squeak of leather, and so passed unseen and unheard despite the servants preparing food in the kitchen. The main hall was empty, but Somrael kept the skin tight around him as he shimmied up a pillar and squeezed the bag nearest him. Inside he felt an arm, and from within a hand tapped on the bag, as if asking for a signal. Somrael took his blade and slid it slowly through the bag where he guessed the soldier's throat would be, and when nary a gurgle escaped but warm blood pooled at the bottom of the bag and there was no further tapping, Somrael assumed that the silent soldiers had been bound up in the hall for some nefarious purpose. Moving swiftly from bag to bag, Somrael squeezed each one, and each one tapped a question before Somrael's blade found a throat. So skilled was he that no outward sign was left that every one of the hundred men-at-arms had been slain, unless one looked down on the bags from the rafters, and Somrael completed his grisly work with enough time to steal back to his room and hastily ready himself for the feast. Natasha had done her job well, and no servant came to call the companions to dinner until the sun had nearly disappeared behind the horizon.

All seven companions entered the great hall to see Gwydyon beaming with pride, and the feast brought out to meet them far exceeded that of the first evening. The pigs had been prepared with honey and sweet spices, while capons simmered in wine and the boar from the day's hunt were also produced. Savory vegetable stews fragrant with exotic aromatics joined the fruits, breads, and cheeses the companions had come to expect, and the servants poured rich dark ale alongside mead, wine, and even distilled spirits. Somrael especially enjoyed said spirits, and though they went to his head, he alone harbored no trepidation about that evening. He had not been able to tell the others, who could not feast with abandon as they waited for something to happen. Once even the most reserved of the companions had drunk some quantity and was in their cups, Gwydyon stood to address them all. "My dear friends, I am grateful to host you as we prepare for the coming of winter. When that day arrives, I sincerely hope you request to winter with me, that we may spend the cold months together in good cheer." With this proclamation, Gwydyon clapped his hands twice, and paused as if waiting for something to occur. Seconds of silence threatened to stretch into a full minute, and though Gwydyon was clearly flustered he made a good show of playing off the clap as a request for more drink. When the spirits arrived he clapped twice again, even louder, but this too he had to play off as a request for a spectacular sweetmeat, brought to the table in flames for him to extinguish. He clapped twice one more time, though this only because the desert delighted him so, he said. The companions heard Somrael chuckle darkly, and took this as a cue to indulge themselves further, and the first night of feasting passed without incident. At the feast's conclusion, Natasha asked Gwydyon if he would enjoy her company that evening, but for the first time since she'd arrived he politely declined and excused himself to attend to druidic matters. Once he'd gone, Somrael shared the story of his deeds with the others, and they resolved to sleep well that night before Gwydyon had a chance to pour his soldiers into the cauldron. They would need their wits about them the following day.

As dawn broke, Gwydyon's silent soldiers climbed from the cauldron in the main hall, and mutely resumed their duties for the time being. The companions had all woken prior and prepared themselves for the second day after Gwydyon's hospitality had been discharged. Enmity blossomed between the guards and the companions, but Somrael had not had any way of preventing Gwydyon from retrieving his servants while remaining subtle. Servants came to invite the companions to the great hall, and Gwydion greeted them as food was brought to break their fast. Soldiers silently patrolled outside and within the hall, dressed in their splendid armor. "My friends, how did you sleep? I know that the turning of the season to winter won't be upon us for two more nights." Gwydyon let this last statement hang in the air, sowing discomfort among the companions in their precarious status.

Fiabhras spoke up. "When first we arrived, we told you of our plight, and within the time allotted for the law of hospitality. The turning of the season brings the first night of winter, when the veil is thin and Arawn has greater reach into this world, yet we are no closer to absolving our sins in his eyes. What say you to that?"

"I am a druid, huntress. Do not presume to lecture me on the laws of the gods, nor should you be concerned, for by reciting the ancient lore passed down among our order I may prevent any from the Otherworld from crossing the veil."

Now Sirius spoke. "You understand our position here, lord Gwydyon. We have no assurance that you will intervene on our behalf, and regrettably we are still at your mercy until it is proper to request wintering in your castle."

Gwydyon looked longingly at Natasha, who returned his affectionate gaze. "You do not wish to be discourteous guests, I understand. You have my promise that no ill will befall Natasha, and of course, I would do nothing to bring her distress. In the meantime, I still have plenty of food and many rooms. My servants have been busy heating water for baths; please refresh yourselves for the evening to come." Anja watched Gwydyon and Natasha exchange glances, and knew the curse of her companion intimately. The flame of jealousy burning in Gwydyon's heart was obvious to her, and as the companions walked to their rooms, she whispered a warning to each of them. Upon returning to her room, Aria threw the last of her herbs into the hot water of the tub, and sank into the water with the stag hide stretched over her. The others disrobed and stepped into the baths, but each kept a weapon nearby.

The silent soldiers wasted no time, and the companions had scarcely entered their respective tubs when Arctos, Sirius, Somrael, Fiabhras, and Anja were stormed by a score of soldiers each. Arctos swung a mighty hammer, crushing the chests of those soldiers sent against him, and when all laid bleeding upon the floor Arctos took his bear form and hurled the soldiers out through his window to prevent Gwydyon from returning their bodies to the cauldron. Sirius entered the Warp Frenzy, and the soldiers sent against him were so overcome with terror they trampled each other trying to escape as Sirius hewed them to pieces. He flung the gobbets of flesh and bones through his window before he ran howling back to his bath, which evaporated with the heat of his rage but sufficed to draw him out of it. Somrael slipped like a shadow between his assailants, tricking them into slicing each other, and when he took a wound he let his blood spray in the face of his adversaries. Eventually all of his well-armored opponents lay dead, and

Somrael hid them within the castle, where Gwydyon could not find them. Fiabhras sent twenty arrows into the narrow slits of twenty helmets, felling her opponents the fastest, and these she hung like coneys high in the rafters. Anja produced a sword when her opponents arrived and performed a dance of steel that called upon the many gifts she'd been bestowed: a portion of Arctos' strength and a sliver of Somrael's fortitude, with a small measure of Sirius' fury and a whisper of Fiabhras' prowess. Unlike the others, she did nothing with the bodies, and finished preparing for the feast.

Under the hide of the stag, Aria witnessed Arawn's wolves being let into the castle. They clearly searched for her in particular, but the hide shielded her from their noses. Anticipating a battle on the other side of the veil, for Gwydyon was a druid as well as the son of Arawn, Aria took the form of a dragon within the veil. Unlike her cat form this dragon would have towered over any mortals in the veil, and her long teeth and claws were matched in strength by thick black scales, glossy like a still ocean on a moonless night. The wolves could peer into the veil, being creatures of Arawn, and the mighty dragon appearing before them sent every wolf running in fear. Her wings unfolded and she took off into the veil itself, searching for Gwydyon. Her affect was so great that her shadow appeared in both worlds on either side of the veil, and Amaethon looked up from his stupor at the base of the castle and wondered at the shadow that looked so familiar.

Aria didn't need to wait long before an alabaster white dragon with red eyes rose to meet her. The two spared no words, and Gwydyon drove upward for an attack, catching Aria off-guard. He wrapped his teeth around her neck but couldn't bite down; Aria took the opportunity to buffet him with her wings. The two tangled in the air, falling and splitting up to begin again on high. No matter how he tried, Gwydyon could not injure Aria, though he received many gruesome wounds; he eventually quit the field in shame to return to his body. Aria followed suit.

Of the companions, Natasha alone had no battles to endure. Her love for Gwydyon burned hotly, but so did her love for the companions, and she knew that Gwydyon had succumbed to jealousy. She prepared herself and checked on the others, ensuring that they could amply prepare themselves as well after fighting off all the men-at-arms of the castle. All seven arrived at the feast early, and Anja stacked the bodies of the men she'd slain in the hall as a challenge, but Gwydyon never emerged from his chamber. The companions enjoyed the food brought out by the servants and boasted merrily of their deeds that day. The servants wondered where their lord was, but did not wish to anger the companions after Anja's display in the main hall. The evening passed without further event, though all seven companions slept in one room, while taking turns on watch against any further treachery.

The third day dawned and the companions entered the main hall to break their fast. Anja's display remained unmolested, and no other guards had been reborn by the cauldron's magic, leaving the castle empty except for a few fearful servants. In defiance of Gwydyon for his vile behavior, the companions all took advantage of his absence and made the castle grounds their own. Some played hurling in the orchard, others took horses and rode about the grounds, and Aria in particular explored the castle to divine its secrets. Though fully awake and armed lest the wolves had returned, the companions didn't see them, for Aria had terrified them sufficiently. Their sport abated as the sun touched the horizon on its downward descent, and all seven returned to the main hall. Anja regarded her sister as Aria came up from the cellars. "Did you find anything interesting?" she asked.

Aria shook her head. "Precious little, I'm afraid. Druids are forbidden from preserving the bulk of their lore and magic in writing, so the books and mosaics were merely cautionary tales about kinslayers or those who ignore hospitality or those who fail to honor the gods at their appointed times. Gwydyon has vast stores of food and drink, but nothing else of note that we haven't already seen." As if on cue, Gwydyon himself emerged into the hall, appearing pale and sickly. No visible wounds plagued him, yet he had the appearance of one who had narrowly survived a harrowing battle. He carried a bow made from yew, and a quiver of arrows sat at his hip. So great was the hall that Gwydyon could shoot every companion before they closed the distance, if he so chose.

"I fear not death, for I shall be welcome in the hall of my father when I go to the Otherworld," Gwydyon intoned, knocking an arrow. "And I can neither abide your coming between me and Natasha, nor your insolence in my house." He raised his bow and aimed at Anja, but his fingers would not release. Gwydyon grunted in frustration, eventually roaring at Aria. "Damn you, witch! Why can't I loose this arrow toward you?"

Natasha ran forward to plead with him, but in a fit of jealous rage, Gwydyon loosed his arrow upon her. Fiabhras had nocked her own arrow and this she loosed with such surety that it collided with Gwydyon's missile and knocked it to the side. Gwydyon nocked another arrow, but Natasha had drawn too close to him, and with tears in her eyes she pierced his heart with the long, slender sword she carried. Red blossomed on Gwydyon's snow-white robe, and within seconds he breathed his last.

The feast that night was a solemn affair, with no boasting or merriment. The companions had known that Gwydyon would be the only one who could lift Arawn's curse from them, and he had not done so, nor had the prophecy been fulfilled; no kin had betrayed kin. After all seven had eaten their fill, Anja picked up Gwydyon's body and approached the cauldron, reverently placing him within. With no men-at-arms walking the palace and Gwydyon awaiting rebirth, the seven companions slept long and undisturbed, though the curse hung over their heads.

Morning arrived to herald the day of transition, the time when winter began and the veil between this world and the Otherworld thinned. Anja woke before sunrise and waited in the great hall to see Gwydyon climb from the cauldron. Though he looked confused at first, understanding dawned on Gwydyon, and he opened his mouth to scream yet no sound issued from him. Fixing his gaze on Anja, he tried hurling curses and invectives at her, but it was to no avail. After trying in vain for some time, Gwydyon sank to his knees in tears, and this is how the other companions found him when they joined Anja. Natasha sat next to him and took his head in her lap. "My lord, all is forgiven. Will you honor your word to grant us this place to stay over the winter?" Gwydyon nodded his assent, comforted by Natasha's presence. Natasha wept as well, for her power to take other shapes did not always obey her will, and the time of transition was likely to remake her as she slept. Should she take a new form, the love between her and Gwydyon would be erased, and she did not think it could be rebuilt anew, as it never had with any of her other lovers.

Aria approached now, and gently asked if there was anything she could do, though she had no formal training as a druid. Gwydyon shook his head, and regarded Aria and Anja both curiously. Anja returned his gaze, a smile playing across her face. "Your inability to harm either my sister or me is puzzling," she said with a laugh, "but it hardly makes for a sporting resolution. Whom among my companions will fight with you?"

Gwydyon pointed at Arctos, and discarded his weapons, indicating a desire to grapple. Arctos agreed, and to give Gwydyon a chance declined to take his bear form. Gwydyon was still the son of Arawn, and he gripped Arctos so tightly he drew blood, though

Arctos remained the stronger and easily threw him. More puzzled now than despondent, Gwydyon excused himself to prepare for the evening, as the time of transition demanded that the dead be appeased as well as the living. The companions now had hospitality's protection for the rest of the winter, and spent the day collecting the men-at-arms they'd scattered and placing them all in the cauldron. Then each bathed and dressed, preparing for the final feast that would herald winter. Natasha felt a change coming upon her as the year pivoted, and though she left the hall as the woman Gwydyon had fallen in love with, it was Salen who returned, bearing the visage of one who had long journeyed the steppes far to the east. His love for Gwydyon didn't falter, but the lord of the castle regarded him coldly, as Salen's curse dictated.

By tradition, Gwydyon and his hall waited until the sun had fully set before beginning the feast, and it truly exceeded all the previous feasts in opulence. Added to the dishes from before were fresh salmon, poached quail's eggs, honeycakes, and a great ox which the servants had been cooking since sundown the previous day. To Aria's surprise, a seat was reserved for the dead, though she knew that no ghosts tarried near this castle as all who died were reborn quickly. She was surprised again as Amaethon, free of his chains, entered the hall. Gwydyon would have gasped at the sight of his brother had he the ability to speak still, and the other companions looked at their new guest in puzzlement. Amaethon walked to Aria and bade her stand, at which point he embraced her and kissed her forehead. "Aria, are you and your sister the daughters of the Witch Queen Ceridwen?" he asked. When Aria nodded, Amaethon embraced her and kissed her again. "Then you are my daughters, for Ceridwen and I married ere I formed the foundation of this castle."

Gwydyon stared in shock, but of course could say nothing. Aria reasoned that his spells had kept Amaethon from disrupting the castle, and he could no longer perform them. "Mother had said that she'd married the son of a god, but we never knew you, father. When were you at mother's castle?"

Amaethon bowed his head. "I'm sorry my daughter, I never arrived there. Like my brother, I can take the form of a dragon and travel the veil, and that is where I met your mother, for she has those powers, too. Such was her beauty, with scales of glinting ruby and wings that could blot out the sun! You look very much like her, you know. That is how I recognized you as you battled my brother above."

"And that is why Gwydyon could not strike me or Anja, for the children of gods may not break their laws," Anja whispered. All in attendance now understood, and Gwydyon scowled at his bad fortune. "Tell me father, would Gwydyon have been well received in your father's hall?"

"Indeed," said Amaethon, "and because the veil is thin this night I daresay he may have returned more powerful than he is here to cause untold trouble for your companions. Your sister prevented this and also stripped him of most of his power by placing him within the cauldron." Aria and Anja shared a look then, and realized that kin had betrayed kin after all.

"Father, I have one more question; if one of our companions had slain a stag sacred to Arawn, how would we cleanse ourselves of that wrongdoing? Gwydyon never told us, and now he never will. How can we avert Arawn's wrath?"

Amaethon looked up then, and a shadow fell over his face. "You may ask him yourself," he whispered. Turning to look in the direction of Amaethon's gaze, all seven companions, and Gwydyon as well, beheld a towering figure, taller even than Arctos, dressed in robes of bone white and pale corpse green. A rack of stag antlers grew from his head and through a hood that cloaked his face in shadows, but an unearthly chill flowed from this man, and all who stared at him caught a fleeting glimpse of their own demise in the mind's eye, leaving no doubt that this was indeed Arawn, king of the Otherworld. Gwydyon stood immediately and offered his chair, the very throne he sat upon, and Arawn silently accepted.

Aria and Anja approached, the former holding the rolled up stag skin she'd carried and used so often. "Lord Arawn, how may we atone for the killing of this stag?" Anja asked.

Arawn regarded both for a while before speaking, and his voice was a low, faintly echoing rumble. "You have returned my son to me for this one night in the year. I consider your debt to me repaid."

"What of Gwydyon, my lord? Need we atone for what has befallen him?" Aria asked.

"No. The cauldron is a powerful relic, and all such things will turn on their owners in time. He had mastered the druid's path before, but now he may master the warrior's path. Do not concern yourself." Arawn finished speaking, and bade Gwydyon sit at his left hand and Amaethon at his right. The feast then began in earnest, and much storytelling and boasting and singing accompanied platters of food and barrels of drink.

This is how the seven companions came to spend winter in Gwydyon's keep, and they would use this castle a great deal in the years to come, though those are stories for another time.

KINGDOM OF BROKEN SHADOWS:
# CALL OF THE VOID
*Crystal L. Kirkham*

## CHAPTER ONE

*Jump.*

Aleyna jerked at the soft voice that breathed the word into her ear. Eroding rock crumbled beneath her toes. She stumbled backwards, flailing to keep her balance. "What?"

*Jump.*

She looked around at the barren, windswept landscape. Only curious gophers and wary birds met her gaze. Giving her head a shake, she walked back to the edge. Jumping wasn't her intention; she was here to clear her head. Release her sorrow and grief into the wind so that she could move on.

She stared down at the river far below, it looked more like a photograph than something real. Distance made the white water look as though it were frozen in time. If anything moved down there, she had no way of knowing. This was the perfect spot. A place where time didn't exist.

Aleyna leaned further over the edge. Scrub grass and stunted trees clung desperately to the sides of the canyon as if they too were afraid of the distance between them and the ground. She couldn't blame them, her stomach flipped at the thought of how precarious her position was.

*You want to jump.*

"Oh hell, no!" she shouted and pushed back from the edge.

*Jump.*

"I am not hearing voices. This is not possible." Aleyna pressed her lips together and shook her head. Her hands wrapped around the locket that hung from a delicate chain on her neck. It had been a gift from Grandma before she'd passed. *Everything you need*, she'd said, *lays inside*. Pity the latch was stuck on it, but simply grasping the ornate metal managed to soothe her frayed nerves.

It was one of two items that had been left with her in the basket where she'd been found, screaming and abandoned in an alley. Thankfully, Grandma was a kind enough soul to take her in. From her pocket, she pulled out an envelope. The other token of her past. It might even tell her where she came from, but she wasn't sure she wanted to know what it said.

Grandma had never even bothered to tell her about it until she was dying. *You'll understand when you read it.* She'd pushed those words out through parched lips; it had taken almost all her remaining strength to do so. Although, her last words were even more cryptic: *No matter what you choose, I'll always love you.* Aleyna squeezed the locket harder as tears stung her eyes at the memory.

She stared at the letter, not wanting to let go of the locket long enough to open it. The wind attempted to steal it from her, but she held tight. If she let go, it would simply disappear as if it had never been. The thought was tempting and one of the reasons she'd chosen this spot.

Every time something bad happened, she'd come here with a photo or letter—something that represented her pain—and she would let the wind take it away. It always made her feel better. This letter, she was sure, wouldn't leave her happy, but it might give her the answers she had once longed to have.

Answers that she had given up ever knowing when she'd passed into adulthood.

Taking another deep breath to steady herself, Aleyna let go of the locket and opened the envelope. Carefully, she removed a thin, single sheet of paper. Trying not to be disappointed at how little there was, she unfolded it.

JUMP.

That was all it said. Aleyna flipped it over and back. That was it. One word. The wind surged around her, pushing her towards the cliff's edge; hair whipped at her face as she pushed back against it. None of this was possible and she had to be dreaming. It was the only explanation.

Jump.

"Shut up!" She stumbled back another step despite the strengthening gale. The envelope flew from her hand though she still clung to the letter. Flower petals—purple, black, and red— fell out and were caught by the wind. She watched them as they were captured in an updraft before zipping down out of sight. She found herself longing to follow them. Before she realized it was happening, her feet had carried her closer to the edge. Dirt gave way beneath her toes and another gust pushed on her back.

"No!" She wasn't asking or pleading this time. It was a demand that echoed throughout the canyon. The wind ceased its efforts and Aleyna stumbled backwards. "What the fuck is going on here?"

There was no answer. She looked at the note still gripped in her hand. The message had changed. It now said 'You have the power. It's your decision to make'. It reminded her of the last thing that Grandma had said. Words she still wasn't sure she understood.

A gentle breeze stirred the grass at her feet and lifted a petal that hadn't followed the others into the canyon. Aleyna picked it up and marvelled at the texture. It looked as soft as crushed velvet and felt smoother than silk. Floral and spice drifted up from the petal, but under that was something less alluring—death and decay.

She let it go and the breeze took it. Twirling and swirling, the petal floated towards the cliff and vanished in midair. Aleyna took another step back from the edge and stared at the space where the petal had disappeared. It couldn't be possible for something to vanish like that, but there was only one way to be sure. She picked up a rock and threw it at the same spot. It disappeared as well.

"Okay, that's weird." Once again, the urge to jump, to see if she too would cease to exist in this world, tempted her. She didn't want to die, and that was the most likely outcome, but the thoughts remained—*what if she didn't fall? And where did the petal and the rock disappear to?*

She half expected to hear the voice telling her to jump again, but it was silent. If she were to believe the note in her hand, it was her decision to make. She stared at the spot, torn between reality and what she wanted to believe.

"Fuck it." Aleyna ran towards the edge and jumped.

# CHAPTER TWO

Feverish aching coursed through every fibre of her being. It was how Aleyna knew that she was alive. Somewhere overhead a storm grumbled in muted ferocity, wind rattled branches and carried to her a scent she recognized. It was the petal that she had followed to wherever she was.

Not sure what sight might greet her, she peeked out through her eyelashes and found herself staring up at a bruised and swirling sky. Lightning danced wildly and, in the center of it all, a crack of bright blue stared unblinkingly back at her.

Her hand was still crumpled around the note. Somehow, she had managed to keep a hold of it. She wondered what it might say now, and there was only one way to know. She smoothed out the page. *Find them.* It made as much sense as jumping off a cliff. She slipped the paper into a pocket and closed her eyes. She had no idea what to do or where to go from here.

"Caw!" Aleyna looked over to see something akin to a crow sitting on the leafless branch of a nearby tree. Blood red eyes and the long, hooked beak were where the resemblance ended. She pushed herself up, her hands sinking slightly into the soft ground, and looked around.

Black trees, much like the one the crow-thing was sitting on, dotted the field of wilted grass in which she lay. Nearby, a lake lapped gently at the shore, and a lamp gleamed warmly beside a dock in the dim light. Low laying fog blanketed the ground and left the rest of the landscape a mystery.

Nothing was familiar. She pushed to her feet and the ground yielded beneath her. This was not a place she could stay and contemplate how many levels of fucked up things were right now. Her eyes locked on the lamp by the lake; there had to be someone nearby to tend to it. "But where would they be?"

"Cah-caw!"

Aleyna looked back to the crow-thing. "So helpful. Thanks."

"Cah?"

She frowned and wondered if the bird was responding to her question, but that was ridiculous. Turning her back on the creature, she made her way towards the lake. She picked her way over the uneven ground of what was probably a marsh in the rainy season.

"CAW! CAW!"

Aleyna glanced to her left and wondered if the bird screaming at her was the same one. It seemed likely as it fluttered to another tree ahead of her. "What do you want?"

It cocked its head at her. "Cah."

"Great. First I throw myself off a cliff and now I'm talking to a stupid bird." Aleyna sighed and pressed a hand to her forehead. "Keep it together, girl."

There was no response from the bird this time. She walked up to the small dock, stopping near the shore. Dark water lapped at rotting wooden posts and more than half the boards were cracked or broken. It didn't look like anyone had used this spot in a long time, but the light still glowed.

Curious, she moved closer to the light when the crow landed on it, looked her in the eye and screamed at her again. Aleyna hesitated. Some birds could be aggressive, she knew that, but she didn't know if this one was. She reached for it and was rewarded with another aggressive caw.

"Fine." She turned to look around the landscape as if being a few yards away from where she'd arrived could change anything. No other lights could be seen, and she wasn't keen on the idea of being lost in this place. She didn't even know what time of day it was here, for all she knew night could be upon her soon.

"Now wha—" Aleyna slammed face first into the ground. She spat out dirt and clutched desperately at the clumps of grass to stop herself as she was dragged back towards the lake. She kicked at whatever had a grip on her ankle, but it held tight.

Icy water soaked her leg. At this rate, she'd be under within a minute. Flipping over, she tried to see what had grabbed her, but all that was visible was a large black tentacle rising from the lake. She slammed at the portion that gripped her, but it provoked no reaction from the beast.

She grasped at one of the posts of the dock as the water reached her chest. Her arms ached, and the creature steadily increased its pull on her. Her fingers were slipping. There had to be something she could do. Aleyna let go of the post and was dragged under the surface.

Eyes closed, she grabbed at the tentacle on her ankle and dug her nails in, but it made no difference. Her lungs burned for air as she yanked as hard as she could. She opened her eyes, hoping that it would help and regretted it. All she could see in the dim light was the glint of razor-sharp teeth.

Anger, fear, and desperation filled her, as she redoubled her efforts to get out of the grip of this beast. Light surged from her hands as she hauled on it and the creature let go. Kicking hard, she swam for the surface. Gasping as she broke through, Aleyna swam to shore as fast as she could and didn't collapse until she thought she was far enough away from the lake's edge to be safe.

"Cah-caw. Caw."

"Shut the fuck up." Aleyna grumbled at it as she lay on the ground, catching her breath and shivering.

"Rude."

She sat up at the sound of a man's voice and saw a figure sitting on a branch where the crow had been earlier. She looked around and then back at the man in the tree. "What?"

"I said 'rude'. You swore at me." He leapt down from the branch, landing silently on the ground.

"I swore at that stupid bird," she said.

"And you insult me as well." He was only a few feet from her now. She could see his bright red eyes despite the shadows cast by the hood on his cloak. "I was of half a mind to help you, seeing as you managed to survive your own brush with stupidity. Everyone knows not to go that close to Sounding Lake when you're in Lornemoore. Kretchen has called these shallows its home since the Shattering and protects them fiercely."

Aleyna stared at him as he talked, trying to wrap her mind around everything he was saying. "I... um... what? I'm sorry. I'm new here. I don't even know where I am."

He cocked his head in the same way the bird had. "That's not possible."

"What? Why?"

"The only way in or out is through that." He pointed at the bright spot of clear sky above. "But the storm destroys anything that tries to pass through the world's eye—in or out. That's why."

Aleyna stared at the storm overhead. Lightning flashed and thunder rolled, but there still hadn't been a drop of rain. "Where am I?"

"You really aren't from around here, are you?" He knelt beside her, pushing back his hood to reveal a shock of bright white hair. "So, how did you get here?"

"I jumped off a cliff," she admitted. "Other than that, I haven't a clue."

"Well, then, that will make you quite the novelty in these parts," he said with a grin. "Welcome to Tenebris. Also known as the Land of Shadows—what's left of it anyway."

# CHAPTER THREE

It answered only one of Aleyna's many questions. Her ankle throbbed where that creature had grabbed her, and she shook with the damp chill sinking into her bones. It was proof that this wasn't some sort of delusion or dream. This was her new reality.

"Do you have a name? I am Rappen." He cocked his head the other direction. "You look cold."

"Aleyna," she said through chattering teeth. She wrapped her arms tighter around her body. "And of course, I'm cold. This isn't exactly a tropical paradise."

"Why aren't you using your power to dry yourself?"

"My what?" Aleyna frowned, trying to understand what he meant.

"Magic, if you wish."

"I don't have any magic." As the words left her lips, she wondered if it was true. Something strange had happened when she'd fought back against that monster.

Rappen chuckled. "If you were ordinary, you'd have not survived coming here. This is not a land where one can exist without some sort of magic. Perhaps you don't know how to use it? All it takes is focus and desire."

Aleyna thought about warmth, desired to be warm, but nothing happened. She tried to remember how she felt when the tentacle had let go of her. She squeezed her eyes shut and focused on recreating the moment in her mind. She wrapped a hand around her locket, courage seemed essential for this task.

"Easy there or you'll singe yourself." Rappen chuckled. Aleyna opened her eyes with the intention to glare at what she thought was a sarcastic comment except he was right. Even the air around her was almost hot. "See? You have power."

She let go of her locket and stared at her hands. Twice now she had done the impossible. Magic didn't exist; that is what her logical mind kept telling her, but the evidence proved otherwise. "This isn't possible."

"Say, that's a shiny bauble on your neck. What is it?" Rappen leaned in close to look. "Very pretty design."

"It's one of the few things from when Grandma found me. It's broken though, won't open." Aleyna touched the locket gently, feeling the intricate carving on the metal beneath her fingers.

"Foundling? From up there?"

"If that's Earth on the other side, then I guess so?" Aleyna shrugged. She had no idea if that's what was up there, but since it was the only way in or out of this place according to him, it was probably true.

Rappen pursed his lips as he studied her. "I have no idea the name of it, but it's a place without magic. 'Earth'. What a boring name, but where else could you be from? This is interesting…"

"Interesting how?" Aleyna stood up and brushed off the bit of dirt and debris that clung to her clothes. She couldn't stay here forever, but she didn't know where to go next. She'd need all the help she could get.

"Well, the last time anything got sent out to the other world was before the Shattering happened. Those that could, escaped. Most couldn't." Rappen frowned. "Some wouldn't. It depended on what side of the divide you stood on. Complicated matter."

"Right…"

"I suppose it doesn't matter much to you, but I bet Bardrekk would love to meet you." Rappen gave a firm nod as if it were decided. "It's a bit of a trip by foot. We should probably get started unless, by chance, you have another form that can fly. It would be safer and quicker."

"Um, how would I know?"

"You should just know." Rappen sighed and motioned for her to follow him. "I guess we walk."

Aleyna stayed where she was even though she didn't want to be left alone. She needed his help, but she wasn't willing to walk blindly into danger. "Who is Bardrekk and where are we going?"

"Bardrekk is the Grand Ruler. Without him, this land wouldn't even exist. He anchored our fragment to another world, the one you came from I suppose. He resides in Shadowskeep."

"How far is it?" Aleyna asked, still hesitating to follow Rappen willingly. She could feel a knot growing in the pit of her stomach. Something wasn't right here, but she wasn't sure what other choice she had.

"A week or so maybe? I haven't been there for a long time, and when I do go, I fly." Rappen fluttered his fingers at her. "I was going to choose the shortest route, which takes us this way around Sounding Lake, but it means we'll have to pass through Deadfell Forest. Lots of nasty creatures. It is safer to go the other way, but it takes three times as long. I suppose I should leave that decision up to you. Unless you have a better suggestion?"

"Is there anywhere else to go? Someone who might help me get home?" Aleyna asked, even though she had little to return to but a boring, dead-end office job. She had no family left there. On Earth, she'd been a social outcast, but it was the only home she'd known.

"I'm sure one of the scholars in the library at Shadowskeep would have the answer to how to get you home—if it's possible," Rappen said. "And there is nowhere else really; those who do not live there are mostly outcasts, hermits, or monsters."

"And which of those are you?" Aleyna didn't miss the implied context. He'd said that he rarely went there.

Rappen chuckled and winked. "You are a clever one. I am an outcast, though it's by my own choice."

"Isn't that the same as being a hermit?" She wanted to like Rappen, if only because he seemed to want to help her, but that pit in her stomach wouldn't ease.

"Not quite. I rather like people, but not so much those that are found within the walls of the keep. Now, have you made a decision, or do you wish to keep stalling?" he asked, a playful smirk on his face.

"I don't suppose there is much of an option from the sounds of things," Aleyna admitted, ignoring the screaming at the back of her mind that this was a terrible idea. "I guess we go to Shadowskeep."

"And do you wish to take the longer and safer route or the quicker and more dangerous one?"

She thought about the monster in the lake and her newfound power. If she could learn to harness that magic, then the dangerous route wouldn't be so bad. "I'd rather not take the long way, but can you teach me how to use this power?"

Rappen gave a small bow. "Of course I can."

"Then I guess we'll take the shorter route. I don't want to be stuck here longer than I have to," Aleyna said with more conviction she felt.

# CHAPTER FOUR

"Try again," Rappen ordered.

Aleyna focused on the fire in front of her and tried to control what it was doing. Dampen it, and then release. It should have been as simple as desiring it to be so, the way Rappen had described the process. So far, all her effort had amounted to naught.

She slumped over, staring at her hands. "This is pointless. I can't make it work."

"Why not?"

"How the hell am I supposed to know the answer to that?" Aleyna snapped back. She had been working at it for several days. Every time they stopped for rest she'd try again. "I'm doing what you told me to, and you've seen the lack of results."

Rappen rubbed two fingers on his forehead, an action she had become accustomed to seeing. "It's because you are still trying to make it work with logic, not emotion. Logic has no place in this."

"I'm trying!" She slammed her fists into the ground. "Obviously, I just can't do it."

Rappen perked up and his eyes narrowed. "Of course not. You can't even follow the simplest of instructions even after begging me to help you. I don't know why I'm wasting my time. Hell, I ought to just leave you to your own fate out here."

Aleyna gritted her teeth. "You're the one who wanted to take me to this stupid place. I don't even want to be here. I want to go home!"

"Yeah? Well, I doubt they'd even want your useless ass back!"

Anger flared up inside her at that phrase. It hit too close to home. She wasn't even sure anyone back on Earth would remember her name in a year. The only person who ever cared for her was gone. No one, not even her own parents, had cared enough to stick by her side.

Aleyna screamed shrill and loud as the ache in her heart grew, and the crack in her façade that she had plastered over with platitudes split open.

"Yes! That's it." Rappen stumbled backwards as the fire shot up high into the air, twice the height that he stood. "There's the emotion we need. Well done!"

Aleyna scrambled backwards as well, heat blasting her face until it was almost unbearable. She looked down at her hands, surprised that she had managed to make the fire do anything other than be what it was.

"You can let it calm down now, we don't need every creature for miles knowing where we are."

Aleyna ignored him as she studied her hands, more specifically her fingers. Her skin had turned a brilliant cerulean, like the summer sky on a quiet afternoon. She rubbed at them, but the color seemed permanent.

"Aleyna?" Rappen's black hand took her own. "Don't be afraid. It looks as though you are Becoming."

"Becoming what?" Aleyna looked up into his blood-red eyes and wondered if he too had once appeared normal.

"That's what it used to be called when this land was whole. Not everyone had power, but most that did, well they had to go through the Becoming." Rappen let go over her hand. "Of course, none of the normal people survived the Shattering and those with magic that hadn't or couldn't Become, well... you'll understand when we get to Deadfell Forest. There hasn't been a Becoming in a long time."

"I don't understand any of this." Aleyna looked past him at the still raging pillar of fire that she had created. She was doing nothing to maintain it but somehow, her anger and pain had been responsible for creating it.

"You are the power; you don't have to work to access it when you Become." Rappen shrugged. "It's hard to explain. Even if you hadn't Become, you would have had time before you ended up like the others."

"Like the others?" She frowned. "The ones in Deadfell?"

Rappen glanced at the fire as if the conversation were a reminder that the bright beacon still stood. He reached out a hand towards it and it shrank back down to the small campfire that it had been before. "Yes, I would like to say that we will be unlikely to meet any, but they are attracted to those that have Become."

Aleyna chewed on her lip and asked the question she wasn't sure she was ready to know the answer to. "What happened to them? And what happens if we encounter them?"

Rappen placed a gentle hand on her back and guided her to where they had been sitting before. Aleyna stood as he left her to crouch on the other side of the tamed flame. He stared into its depths, not answering either of her questions. She was willing to wait him out for a bit.

They sat in silence. Aleyna was lost in her own thoughts, staring at her fingertips every now and again. As tiredness stole over her, she debated on pestering Rappen for the answers she sought. It was his distant gaze into the fire and furrowed brow that kept her from doing so. He hadn't forgotten what she'd asked, but it was obvious he wasn't ready to answer her yet.

"Ahem."

Aleyna's head jerked up. She'd almost fallen asleep without realizing it. She blinked a few times and saw Rappen staring at her over the dimming coals. "Immawake."

He smiled at her mumbled attempt at speech, but it was a paltry shadow of the grins she'd seen from him before. Whatever he was about to tell her, she didn't think it was going to be good. "Are you ready for me to tell you about those who dwell in Deadfell Forest?"

"Yes?" Aleyna hadn't meant for it to sound like a question.

Rappen nodded. "Few travel through there unless they are confident that they can protect themselves from the wraiths. While other beasts of lesser magic survive well in that area, those who have Become are in constant danger."

"Wraiths?" Aleyna frowned. Had she known about these creatures, she would have chosen the longer path, but it was too late to turn back now.

"They are what remains of those who did not Become." Rappen took a deep breath. "They are soulless creatures in search of only one thing—power. Perhaps in hopes that it could make them whole again. They are relentless in this pursuit, but they do not leave the forest—they cannot leave the forest."

"Why not?"

"The forest didn't used to exist. It grew around what used to be the town of Carcavell. It was there that people went as the dark illness took hold during the early stages of the Shattering." Rappen looked up at the never-ending storm, and his voice took on a wistful tone. "Nothing but ruins left now, and the forest that appeared around it one day. Slowly at first, a tree at a time as those that waited for a cure from the healers faded into their illness and became nothing more than a shadow of the living beings they once were."

"You sound like you were there."

Rappen snorted. "Everyone alive here today was around then, except for you. Time, in many ways, has stopped here. Have you not noticed that the center of the storm is always in daylight? We are not simply tethered to the world you come from; we are connected to a single point in time."

"Oh." Aleyna attempted to stifle her yawn with little success. "If there is no time, why am I so tired?"

"Time has stopped here, aging has stopped here, but our bodies continue as if time existed. Don't ask me how it works, ask Bardrekk when we see him. This was his doing to keep us from disappearing into the Void." Rappen stretched out on the ground. "For now, we sleep since such things are still needed. Do not worry about the wraiths, I can protect us. There is no way I would have suggested it if I didn't think we could make it through."

"What is the Void?" Aleyna asked even as her eyes grew heavier with each word.

Rappen mumbled something else she didn't quite catch before drifting deep into sleep.

# CHAPTER FIVE

The dark and barren trees of Lornemoore had nothing on the craggy, twisted monstrosities that stretched across the horizon, even extending into Sounding Lake. Large white rocks stood at intervals around it. Rappen had told her that they surrounded all of Deadfell Forest—security to keep the wraiths where they belonged. As with the rest of the land they had passed through, a perpetual low-lying mist shrouded the landscape.

"Nice place for a picnic," Aleyna quipped.

Rappen laughed and shook his head. "It's good to keep a sense of humor about you, but also be on guard. There is no light beneath those branches than can stand against the wraiths. It sometimes seems as though the trees steal the light for themselves, leaving you near defenseless."

"You said you were confident about going in there? That it would be okay?" Her early bravado dissipated at the reminder of what awaited them.

"Nothing is a hundred percent." Rappen shrugged and walked up to the giant white stone nearest them. He placed a hand on it and closed his eyes. "Mmm, yes. Nothing too close to this point right now, but we should travel a bit more inland first so that we're not near the lake."

"Why don't we want to be near the lake?" Aleyna eyed the water that lapped against a small rocky beach not far from where they stood and edged a bit further away from it. She hadn't forgotten her encounter with the tentacled beast.

"Wraiths aren't the only danger and these woods attract some of the worst of the creatures to be found." Rappen motioned for her to follow as he marched inland. "Kretchen, the one who attacked you, is semi-intelligent and not actually evil, just angry. Unless my memory deceives me, it used to be someone's pet before the Shattering."

Aleyna shuddered at the thought of that thing being a pet, but this wasn't Earth. Not even the grass beneath her feet was familiar. It would stand to reason that the pets in this place wouldn't be what she was used to either. "Is there any creature in this world that might not try to kill me?"

Rappen paused at the question. "Hmmm, I suppose the woerhk is a fairly innocent creature. I mean, it might want to kill you, but it's entirely incapable of doing so."

"So, this place is pretty much a dark and twisted version of Australia?"

"I don't get that reference." Rappen shrugged and continued up a small hill. He placed his hand on another stone that stood on its crest and closed his eyes. "No, not here."

"What are you doing?"

"Checking for signals. The lapidemia do more than mark the boundary and keep the wraiths contained. Though few have ever tried to leave, they tell you if it's safe to enter." Rappen stepped away from the stone. "Would you like to try?"

Aleyna brushed her fingers across the smooth stone, surprised by the warmth of it. She followed Rappen's example and closed her eyes, not sure what would happen. Heat shot up her arm, her vision turned red and screaming drowned out the thunder above. She stumbled backwards, the sound of tormented shrieks still echoing in her head. "What the hell?"

Rappen was at her side before she finished uttering those words, a comforting arm around her shoulders. "That shouldn't have happened. I'm sorry. Are you okay?"

"What would..." Her question went unfinished as she realized that she could still hear a faint screeching. She looked towards the forest to see tree limbs trembling as if a strong wind blew, but no breeze stirred the air. Within the shadows, small white lights flickered.

Her hand wrapped around the locket as the shrieking grew louder. She barely even noticed that the blue had inched up onto her hand. "Are those the wraiths? Do they know we're here?"

"Let's go, this way," Rappen whispered, his eyes on the trees as he guided her away from the boundary and further inland. "We can talk about it when we're far enough away."

Aleyna was more than happy to leave the sound of those things behind her. She kept darting glances at the forest, wanting to be sure that they weren't being followed. Eventually the trees they passed were still, and the screaming could no longer be heard.

Rappen had let his arm drop when they could no longer hear the wraiths. She heard no sound from him, but his lips moved as if he were muttering something to himself. His own gaze was downcast, and they passed two of the stones without him reaching out to touch either. He didn't talk about what had happened and Aleyna wasn't ready to ask.

"We can go around."

Aleyna jumped. She hadn't expected him to speak. "Around what?"

"Deadfell Forest." Rappen stopped and turned to her. "I'm not entirely sure what happened when you touched that lapidemia but I'm worried that it'll happen again when we cross through the barrier. If it does, we will never make it through—not even at the narrowest part of the forest."

"How long will that take?" Aleyna didn't look at him, her eyes were fixed on her hands and the questions she was afraid to ask.

"It's a large forest."

"That doesn't answer my question." Aleyna put her hands on her hips and glared at Rappen. He looked away from her and towards the forest that darkened the horizon and the barely discernible mountains beyond.

"I don't know," Rappen admitted. "I've never had to go around before."

"Right, you flew." Aleyna considered what it might mean to stay in this place longer. "Will I be able to go back home if I've Become before I return? Is the reason I survived this trip because I could Become but hadn't?"

She held her breath as Rappen considered her questions. "If you Become, then you are stuck here. As for the rest, I don't know. Maybe, but I don't know."

"Then we go through."

"You won't ever get back if you die here." Rappen crossed his arms and glared at her. "Would you rather die than be stuck here?"

"We're going through." She wasn't about to stand here and argue the possibilities with him. She'd made her decision and it was final. "And if you aren't willing to help me, I'll go myself."

Rappen sighed, his shoulders drooped, and he shook his head. "Fine, but we're going to head up to the narrowest portion of the forest, rest, and then attempt to pass through. It won't do for either of us to be tired if we have to fight."

"Fair enough," Aleyna agreed.

Rappen mumbled something under his breath, but Aleyna was in no mood to ask him to repeat himself.

# CHAPTER SIX

Aleyna listened to the constant thunder that had gone mostly unnoticed since her first few days here. She wished it would drown out the whistle-snore of Rappen's breathing. Sleep hadn't come easy and left her too soon. Fear and worry held a tight grip on her mind, assaulting her with images and thoughts that she couldn't ignore.

She strained for any hint of the screaming wraiths from earlier, but there was nothing else to be heard. They had traveled for hours before Rappen had called a rest. He hadn't touched a single stone since the incident.

"Erm...ah..." Rappen yawned and rolled over. "Happy waking."

"About time."

Rappen frowned. "Worried about today?"

"No, I'm worried about the fate of the stock market." Aleyna pushed up and brushed the clinging grass from her clothes. She needed a shower, and new clothes, but that wasn't likely to happen anytime soon.

"The what?" Rappen stretched as he stood up, the small fire he had created before falling asleep disappearing as if it had never been.

"Not really important." Aleyna stared towards Deadfell Forest which was little more than a dark patch in the fog from where they stood. "Let's get on with this."

No other words were exchanged until Rappen paused. Had he chosen to do so; he could have touched one of the large rocks that marked the barrier. Instead, he stared at it, a frown pulling at his face. "I don't know what will happen when we cross this point but be prepared to run and possibly fight."

"You never told me how to fight these things, I've barely managed to control the fires *you* create." Aleyna held up a hand before Rappen could respond, took a deep breath, and focused on grounding herself. This wasn't the time for panic. That would have to come later. "No, that isn't important now. We will do this and deal with what happens as it happens."

Rappen raised an eyebrow but made no comment. He took another step closer and paused. "Do not run unless we are in imminent danger. Do not speak unless necessary. Do not fear. Stay calm, stay quiet, and maybe we'll make it through."

Aleyna nodded and took a step closer as well, and Rappen raised his arm to stop her from passing. "If they start screaming before we reach the trees, then we backtrack as fast as we can."

Aleyna shoved his arm out of her way and fixed him with the angriest glare she could manage. "I'm not an idiot."

Rappen's eyes deepened in color, but he said nothing as he let his hand drop. He cocked his head to the side as he stepped across the invisible barrier. Aleyna watched him closely and when he looked to her, she did the same.

There was a slight tingling that suffused her body and she felt as though she were connected to something greater than herself. Another step and the sensation disappeared. Rappen reached for her but paused and held up a finger instead. Aleyna wanted to get moving now, but she understood his caution.

Nothing stirred and the only sound was the never-ending thunder. Rappen slowly approached the edge of the forest. It had looked menacing to Aleyna from a distance, but as the individual trees came into view, a shiver ran down her spine. Each bare, twisted limb clawed at the sky, reaching up from sickly grey trunks shot through with black streaks that created the illusion of screaming faces trapped within.

"Don't stare, don't think too long on the unnatural origins of this forest. It will only bother you more," Rappen whispered as they walked beneath the canopy.

Aleyna tried to heed his words, but the deeper into the woods they traveled, the more the trees seemed to cry for her attention, each face becoming noticeably more human, more familiar. She stopped at a tree that had a wrinkled face that looked exactly like

Grandma. Her weathered features, that sardonic grin—it was more real than a picture. She reached for it, but Rappen's hand shot out and gripped her wrist hard enough to hurt.

He tugged at her to move along, and Aleyna knew she should, but the tree called to her. She needed to touch it; the urge was even more overwhelming than the urge to jump off that cliff.

"No." Rappen's harsh whisper seemed loud within that silent canopy. It touched something in her mind. A reminder that this was not Grandma. She had died in a different world. Aleyna looked back at the tree and the likeness faded. It could have been anyone.

She gave her head a shake and nodded her understanding. Rappen released her and she stared at the passing, barren ground to avoid another incident. With the thunder silenced by the bare, entangled branches overhead, the only sound to be heard was their own footsteps echoing through the forest.

A sharp gasp made Aleyna look up. Lights danced ahead of them, blinking in and out of existence. It was a sight that was stuck in her memory from the previous day. She held her breath, but there were no tortured screams this time—simply silence.

She looked to Rappen for guidance, but he stood like a statue in front of her, his gaze fixed on those dancing lights, every muscle seemingly tight with tension. She wanted to get his attention, but she feared what would happen if she made a sound or moved more than necessary. He had said the wraiths were attracted to those with power, those that had Become, but these didn't look like what she had imagined wraiths to be.

They were sort of pretty. Almost mesmerizing. She watched them flicker in and out, swirling and twirling amongst the dreary, grey trees. Even though the thought of moving made her pulse beat wildly, she had to get closer. Her foot refused to move, and she tore her eyes from the dancing lights to see that roots had taken hold of her.

Aleyna looked over to see the same roots encircled Rappen's legs, disappearing under the tattered black cloak he wore. She tugged harder and the roots broke away. When she looked back up, the lights no longer held the same sway.

She didn't care what might happen if she acted now, they needed to get out of here. Away from the lights, and from the trees that were trying to trap them. If she wanted out of this horrid world, she needed to make it to Shadowskeep.

She slammed into Rappen as hard she could. He swayed but didn't budge. His eyes rolled to look at her, but that was all. A root reached out from under his cloak to wrap around her arm. She yanked back, but it grew tighter. This was stronger than the ones that had grabbed her foot. Her arm began to tingle, and she tried to tug again but the muscles refused to listen.

"No!" she screamed as a root reached for her other arm. She grabbed at it and that same surge that had saved her from the creature in the lake flowed through her. The root turned to ashes, crumbling in her grip. She reached for the next bit of root she could see and tried again with the same result.

She ripped frantically at the root on her other arm before turning to free Rappen while fighting off the roots that tried to restrain her. She had destroyed more than half of what had wrapped around Rappen before they retreated back into the ground. No longer supported, he collapsed into a heap.

Aleyna grabbed his arm and tried to drag him in the direction they had been heading. He was heavier than she'd expected but leaving him behind wasn't an option. Panting and cursing under her breath, she kept tugging him along.

"Stop."

Aleyna let go of him and jumped back.

"Umph." Rappen's muffled voice came from under his arm where she had dropped it. "Help."

She lifted his arm off his face and placed it beside him. "Sorry."

"Feeling is starting to come back, should be able to move my limbs soon enough." He closed his eyes and sighed. "Sorry, I hadn't even considered the few creatures that do find shelter in these woods. My only thoughts were on the wraiths."

"That wasn't the wraiths?" She looked back at where they had come from. The lights were gone now, but she had hoped the worst of the dangers were over—that perhaps they'd been silent this time, that their screaming the other night had been an anomaly.

"No, I—" Rappen cocked his head and Aleyna did the same, not knowing what she was listening for. She heard little in the silence beyond her own labored breathing and the light rattle of the tree limbs.

Whatever he heard caused his eyes to widen. Rappen struggled to move but it resulted in little more than a couple of twitching fingers. "We need to get out of here."

"I am tired. I can't drag you much further," Aleyna said, her words coming out sharper than intended. She softened her tone as she continued. "Are you sure there is something to be afraid of?"

"Do you hear that? That rattling of branches in the distance?"

"The wind?" she asked, incredulous that it was something so simple that had caused him to be so scared.

"Aleyna, there is no wind here." His voice was soft. A reminder that was far kinder than she thought she deserved considering that this was something she had already learned of this land. She wanted to curse her own idiocy as the rattling became louder, but she wasn't about to waste her breath.

Grabbing Rappen's arms, she did her best to drag him through the woods in what she hoped was the right direction. With each small step, the rattling came closer until it sounded as though the creature was on their heels, but she could see nothing when she dared to look.

Then she heard the sound she'd been dreading. A shrill, lonesome wail sent an icy shiver down her spine, and her heart stammered in her chest. All of this would mean nothing if those things got to them and, try as she might, she couldn't go any faster. She gasped as panic squeezed at her chest.

"Go. Run hard and you might make it," Rappen said.

"I can't leave you helpless like this." Aleyna let go of him even as she said it.

"You can and you will," he insisted as the wailing grew louder. "You already risked enough saving me the first time. You owe me nothing."

Aleyna stared at him, unsure of what to do, her heart pounding wildly and each beat a single command—run.

"Fuck." Aleyna moved to stand over Rappen, not sure how she was going to protect him from what was coming. She knew how to make heat which did a good job on the roots and for drying herself off, but she didn't think a wraith would be affected by something so simple.

"What are you doing? Go! Now, before it's too late!"

Aleyna ignored him as she watched the surrounding forest. Lights flickered through the branches as the wraith moved towards them. The difference between these lights and the creatures from earlier was evident at this distance. These lights didn't so much flicker as blink and they moved in pairs much like… "Eyes…"

"Too late," Rappen groaned. "I'm sorry."

# CHAPTER SEVEN

It held back, circling them. She had no idea what drove these creatures, only that they wanted power, were drawn to it, and would kill for it. She tried to look everywhere at once, wishing she could cover her ears, but she wanted her hands free to do... whatever it was she might end up doing.

Aleyna hoped instinct would guide her. No doubt, this would only serve to advance her Becoming—if she survived. Even in the dim light beneath the dead branches, she could see that the color had moved further up her arms, disappearing beneath the frayed and filthy cuffs of her jacket.

"Come and get it you motherfucker!" she screamed as loud as she could, not even sure she'd be heard and the effort making her already-stressed throat burn. She held her hands low, fingers tensed into claws as she waited for it to attack. "Come on!"

It stopped, eyes floating in the darkness in front of her, and a perfect silence descended—broken only by the ringing in her ears. Aleyna tensed as she waited for what it would do next. Branches rattled as it moved from the shadows of the overhanging branches to where she could finally see it clearly. Eyes glowed from a face that looked like the charred remains of some monster's skull that sat on a body that shifted and oozed, unable to remain completely still.

There was no evidence that this thing had once been a person. It was simply a monster, as it opened its mouth to reveal glistening rows of sharp teeth. It screamed again, the sound near deafening at this distance. Aleyna held her ground, not daring to move a muscle.

Another shrill shriek filled the forest and, somewhere in the distance, another wraith answered the cry.

Without thinking, her hand inched up to wrap around the locket. Courage flowed through her and, with it, the urge to run. Not away, but towards the wraith. Like jumping off the cliff, it was suicide to even consider doing something like that. She didn't feel as though she were any match for this creature, but still, the desire remained.

The wraith's head cocked at the movement and the lights that she assumed were eyes blinked. It charged at her and Aleyna gave into the insane impulse to meet it halfway. Letting go of the necklace, she crossed her arms in front of her on instinct, hands pointed out.

Darkness swarmed over her, the first true darkness she'd known since arriving in Tenebris. It was a darkness edged in pain, confusion, and anger. It cut through her, into her soul, and tore her mind to ribbons. She wanted to cry and scream, but there was only darkness.

"No," she cried as the emotions of the wraith pulled at her own memories. "No, no." Loneliness and isolation. Not a part of the world, but simply another parasite in the wrong place, barely hanging on for life. Aleyna tried to focus on something else, to turn from the pain as she always had.

*Grandma.* Warmth. Love. Those emotions pushed at the agony, made it recede until it was bearable. That was how it had always been. Rejected, hurt, broken, alone, but with a single look Grandma had always made it better. She wondered if what this creature wanted wasn't power, but warmth. Specifically, an emotional warmth, the ability to feel alive, vital, and connected.

Every bit of love, affection, and acceptance that she could find in herself, Aleyna tried to let pour out. A gift from her to the darkness that was this tortured, lonely creature. She tried not to dwell on if this was the wrong move, if the only result she achieved was her death then she had tried—and that was what was important.

A nearly inaudible gasp broke her focus. Aleyna opened her eyes, the darkness was gone—and the wraith with it. Instead, a woman stood before her, or the ghost of a woman. Dark red hair framed a heart-shaped face and bright blue eyes. She looked human.

"Beanna?" Rappen whispered the question, his eyes fixed on the ghost woman. "It's not possible."

The ghost approached, each step slow and deliberate as if she were trying to remember how to walk. Aleyna stood her ground, unsure of what to do or if this was some sort of trick. "Rappen? What's happening?"

"The impossible." With what little movement he had gained, Rappen dragged himself towards the ghost. He reached out to her and she mirrored the gesture, her fingers brushing against his. They held that position for a moment before she faded away completely.

Closing his eyes, Rappen sighed and collapsed back to the ground. Aleyna took the moment to listen for the sound of any other approaching wraiths, but the forest was silent. She counted to twenty before daring to say anything. "What the hell was that?"

Rappen pushed himself up to his feet, catching himself on the nearest tree to keep from toppling over. "That was—" His face pinched in pain and she could see him struggle to get the words out. "That used to be... my wife. She couldn't Become and—"

Aleyna walked over and put a hand on his shoulder. Even if much in this world still confused her, loss was universal. "I'm sorry, Rappen."

He turned sharply to face her; his red eyes boring into hers. "What did you do? That should not have been possible."

Aleyna wanted to shrink back from that intense glare, but she forced herself to stand taller instead. "I gave the darkness light and love."

"You gave it..." Rappen gave his head a shake. "You are an oddity. It should have consumed you and left behind nothing but a hollow corpse to be swallowed up by the hungry roots of this forest. Instead, you released her from what should have been an eternal torture."

Aleyna looked at her feet, not sure how to respond. "We should get going."

"Yes, we should," Rappen agreed. "I don't want to take a chance that you can defeat another wraith as easily."

He cocked his head, listening for sounds of movement. Aleyna found herself doing the same. Somewhere in the distances she heard a rustling. Rappen took a few tentative steps away from the tree, each step steadier than the next. "As fast as we can then."

Aleyna nodded and matched her pace to his.

# CHAPTER EIGHT

As they passed the lapidemia into safety, they were running full out. Wraiths wailed and the forest moved as if waving goodbye or, more likely, attempting to beckon them back into its depths. Aleyna bent over, hands on her knees, as she struggled to catch her breath. Her lungs burned with each attempt.

"We should rest, but not this close." Rappen pushed the words out between his own ragged breaths. He stumbled forward a few more steps and collapsed in a heap. "Yeah, this is far enough."

Aleyna snorted and shook her head. "Not dragging you. Come."

She didn't spare the energy to make sure he followed. All she wanted to do was sit down by a fire and eat whatever strange-ass thing that Rappen could manage to conjure. She probably would have starved to death without him.

She thought about stopping near the small copse of trees, but the nightmare of Deadfell Forest made her rethink that decision. Instead, she found a relatively flat area and decided it was good enough. Much like Rappen earlier, she let herself collapse on the ground, and wished she had energy left to feel happy about being off her feet. A thunk and groan from nearby told her that he had followed her. "Fire? Food?"

Another groan greeted her inquiries. "Give me a moment."

Knowing she couldn't eat laying down, Aleyna pushed herself into a sitting position in time to see the fire start with a woosh. It was quickly followed by the appearance of a bowl filled with a tasteless, colorless gruel that she had been assured was nutritious.

She ate her food in silence as she stared across the flame at Rappen, her mind going over everything that had happened since she'd arrived. It was surreal to find herself in this position, wanting to go back to a place that she didn't even like that much, full of pain, emptiness, and heartache.

Peeling off her jacket, she studied the color that now was spreading onto her torso. By the time they made it to Shadowskeep, the possibility of going home might be denied to her. It would become little more than a distant dream. Her gaze moved upwards to that steady circle of light that connected this place with Earth.

"Thank you." Rappen's somber tone caught her attention more than the words. "Not for saving me, although I appreciate that, but for Beanna. I never thought there was hope for her, for any of them. What you did, not even Bardrekk could do. And he was the most powerful one left when the world Shattered — which was why he was able to save this piece of the world from falling into the abyss."

"I'm happy that I was able to do something to save us." Aleyna stared into the fire as she gathered her thoughts. "Can I ask you something?"

"You saved my life, and the soul of my departed wife. You can ask me almost anything and I will answer."

"I know there are things you're not telling me, and I don't really care why. It's not like I have a lot of other options to find help around here. You're the only person I've seen since arriving. I'm not even sure why you're helping me."

"Because you're interesting, something different in a world that never changes." Rappen gave a half-smile that did little to convince her of his words.

"You didn't help simply because I was new and amusing. Was there another reason?"

Rappen didn't answer the question immediately and it was enough to confirm her own suspicions. More than once she had caught him staring at her locket when it had come out from beneath her shirt. She resisted the urge to reach for it now, not wanting to give away what little she knew.

"I figured Bardrekk might find you interesting as well. As I said, you are a novelty in these parts. That still holds true." Rappen kept his tone serious and somber. "And you are right, I have not been fully honest, but I intend you no harm. I have only omitted some truths to make it easier on you. This is a hard land, a dangerous land, and there is much you do not know about it."

Aleyna thought about his words and nodded. She hadn't forgotten that sinking feeling when she first agreed to go with him, but as they had travelled, she'd come to realize that it wasn't Rappen that gave her that feeling, but their destination. "Shadowskeep, are you lying to me about that?"

"About what?"

Aleyna cursed her own impulse to ask but it was out there now, and she couldn't take the words back. "That I might find a way home, or anything? I don't know. There's this feeling that I can't shake."

"What sort of feeling?"

"That sinking feeling you get when something isn't right, like everything is about to go terribly wrong when we get there."

Rappen looked away from her and towards the peaks that surrounded and protected the only remaining city of this land. "I wish I could assure you that nothing will go terribly wrong, but I can promise that I will do my best to make sure you are safe. I owe you that."

Aleyna wasn't sure what to make of his words. While she had her suspicions, her instinct was to trust him. He'd put his life on the line for her, had told her to save herself when the wraith first attacked. Rappen had proven his integrity in those actions. "Thank you. How much longer now? What comes next?"

"Ah, the next part is a walk in the park. There are some dangers, but they are far and few between." Rappen turned back to her smiling. "I think the worst of it is over now."

"Never say that." Aleyna smirked and winked. "That is like laying out a welcome mat for trouble."

"Ah, my mistake. I take those words back then. We'll have many dangerous obstacles that stand in our way between here and Shadowskeep." Rappen grinned as well.

"Too late, you already said it." She struggled to get the words out as she yawned.

"Ah well, we will have to just live with the consequences then." Rappen mimicked her yawn and stretched out on the ground. "Rest well."

# CHAPTER NINE

Aleyna stared up at the towering plateau on which Shadowskeep was built. Although 'pillar of rock' would have been a more accurate description. It was if someone had drawn a giant circle and pulled the land straight up into the sky. From the base of the plateau, she could barely even see the dark stone wall that marked the southern edge of the city.

These odd mountains in the center of the land had been pulled from the ground as well, according to Rappen, as a form of protection, but he hadn't told her from what. She had met a few monsters here, but nothing that made something such as this seem necessary.

She eyed the steep, narrow trail with a wary eye. It only differed from the rest of their journey through the mountains in that it featured a steep drop on one side.

"Is there no other way up?"

"Of course there is."

Aleyna sighed with relief. "Then why were you taking me this way? I've already jumped off one cliff and I am in no hurry to do it again."

"Because you can't go the other way," Rappen said as he marched up the trail. "The other way is to fly."

"Is that what most people do?" Aleyna asked, following him and staying as close to the inside of the trail as she could.

"No," he said, ignoring the rocks that his feet kicked over the edge. "Not many have a bird type form."

"Oh," she mumbled, focusing most of her attention on where her feet were landing. One wrong step, a rolled ankle from a rock, and she would be tumbling to her death. Rappen didn't seem that concerned about the dangerous drop, but he had the benefit of being able to fly.

Halfway up, a thought occurred to Aleyna. "What happens if someone is coming down?"

"Not likely." Rappen's sharp answer made her wonder what he hadn't told her about the city above them. Once again, anxiety about their destination gnawed a pit in her gut. If she weren't so focused on where her feet were going, she would have given it more thought, but not falling to her death took priority.

Her legs ached with each step and she'd lost track of how long they had been climbing. Aleyna didn't dare look up to see until she stumbled. She squeaked in fear as Rappen grabbed her arm to keep her from falling—not over the edge but into him. She looked up and saw a massive door in a stone wall blocking a wider section of the path ahead.

"Is this it?"

Rappen chuckled. "No, just the first entrance. If anyone were to even attempt to attack Shadowskeep, they would first have to navigate this narrow path and then get through both entrances."

"Who would attack?" Aleyna asked, but Rappen ignored her question as he walked up to the door. He banged on it with his fist, two solid knocks, before stepping back and looking up at the top. She followed his gaze and saw a dark green face looking back at them.

"State your name and business."

"Rappen Acrovada. We have come to visit the library."

"And who is that?"

Rappen looked at her and nodded his head for her to answer.

"Aleyna Banrey. I'm with him."

The green head nodded and disappeared again. Rappen took that moment to lean down and whisper to her. "He's double checking the lists to be sure that neither of us are known threats to the ruler."

"Makes sense." Aleyna chewed at her lip as she waited and reached for the locket. Nothing about this felt right to her, but she still had no idea what to do.

Rappen noticed the motion and pushed her hand back down. "Keep that hidden."

"W—" She didn't even get to finish the word when the doors swung open and she finally got a good look at the guard. Lighter blue specks were scattered across his face; they reminded her of freckles, and his eyes were navy. She couldn't see his hair; it was hidden by a matte black metal helmet.

"Enter." He gave a small nod to them as they passed by.

"Thank you." Aleyna smiled at him and Rappen gripped her arm. He jerked her forward while glaring at her. "What?"

He simply shook his head and continued to drag her until they were several yards away. "You don't thank the guards. You don't talk to them except to answer a question. That's it."

"Why?"

"Because that's the way it is."

Aleyna would have protested more, but she saw no point in it. This wasn't her world or her culture, she had no right to pass judgment on what she didn't understand. Perhaps if she were stuck here longer, she could try to learn more.

As the trail narrowed again, her focus turned back to her feet, but it didn't last long. Another gate blocked their path, and this time the wall extended out from there along the edge of the cliff in both directions. They were finally here. A buttery-yellow face popped up from the rampart above them. "You're expected."

Rappen stepped in front of her, his arms out as if he were trying to protect her from something when the doors swung open. More than a dozen guards ran towards them, some with weapons drawn. Aleyna started to back away as Rappen waved his arms and called out, "That's not necessary! Don't!"

Before she had time to process what was happening, one of the guards had reached her and shoved her to the ground. He clamped something around her neck. She looked over expecting to see the same happening to Rappen, but instead he was arguing with a guard. "Wha—"

A sharp pain in her cheek caused her head to spin and her ears to ring before the world went black.

# CHAPTER TEN

Cold stone pressed against Aleyna's cheek and her head pounded like she'd been on a three-day bender. Instinct screamed at her to stay still as her mind struggled through the fog of pain and exhaustion to remember how she'd ended up in this position.

Soldiers, Rappen shouting. Something wasn't right. She replayed the scene over in her head. He'd known the soldiers would be there, he'd moved in front to protect her before the door had opened.

She ran through the series of events several more times. It was clear that Rappen had betrayed her. No one here knew who she was or where she had come from except him. But that didn't tell her how they knew or, more importantly, why.

A rhythmic, loud clanging of metal on metal made her head throb even more. She didn't think it could get any worse until a voice hit her ears like sandpaper on a wound. "Get up, foreigner."

Aleyna opened her eyes only enough to let the light filter through her dark lashes. Still, the dim light stabbed into her. She closed her eyes again and wished for a handful of painkillers. More clanging made her raise her hands to her head despite the protest of the muscles needed to do so.

"I said get up!" That rough voice shoved its way into her head, and she found herself being hauled up to her feet. She tried to strike out, but it was too much of an effort. "Oh, you don't like that? Too bad. So long as that suppressor is on you, you'll just have to deal with it."

Aleyna guessed that was the thing on her neck. She reached up to touch it and her entire body filled with pins and needles. She let her hand drop and it subsided.

"Yeah, not a smart move. The Grand Ruler would like to see you before you're executed. Come along now." Aleyna didn't fight against his rough jerks and pulls. She stumbled along after him. It wasn't until she was thrown back onto the floor that she even attempted to see where she was.

Looking up, the first thing she saw was Rappen, his worn black cloak replaced with a resplendent, shimmering outfit that matched his eyes. He stood stiffly near a broad, navy man with close-cropped black hair. Though the pain of doing so made her nauseous, she met his gaze as steadily as she could.

"So, this is the remaining Banrey." He looked at her as though she were nothing more than a piece of livestock that he was about to bid on. "I must say, even when the guards reported that the color was right, I still had my doubts that someone like you would give up so readily on the royal family that you once fought so hard for."

She spared Rappen a small glance, but he looked straight ahead, not even acknowledging that he had been spoken to. The man, whom she could only assume must be Bardrekk, walked over to where she knelt. He crouched in front of her and studied her face. "Not even fully Become yet. This is almost too easy."

He reached towards her, his hand hesitating halfway to her chest where she could feel the locket hanging heavily. He made a fist instead and whirled away. "Your pardon is complete, Rappen. I never thought there would be a day I'd say those words, but here we are."

"And her?"

Bardrekk raised an eyebrow at the question. "That is no concern of yours."

"Of course. Apologies." Rappen gave a stiff bow.

"My advisor will handle the necessary documents and arrange for you to take an oath of fealty." He waved a dismissive hand at Rappen. "Now, go."

She ignored the stare that he gave her and kept her eyes locked on the man who now held her fate in his hands.

"I can't." Those two words broke her focus and she spared the energy to look at her former travelling companion. "I won't."

"I should have known. Once a traitor, always a traitor," Bardrekk growled. He raised a hand, but whatever he was about to do was interrupted as Rappen slammed a fist into the floor. A bright flash flooded the room. Aleyna thought the dim light had hurt, but this felt like doing a swan dive into the sun and surviving even though every atom of her being had been torn apart.

As the light faded, the pain and lethargy that had plagued her since she awoke melted away. Head spinning, and ears ringing, she pushed herself to her feet. She shuffled forward, sending shattered pieces of dark metal clattering across the floor.

Her eyes followed one of the pieces that came to rest against Rappen's closed fist. He lay still and she couldn't tell if he was still alive. Whatever he'd done had taken a lot of effort.

A bright white light scorched the floor near Rappen with enough force to send the piece of metal soaring across the room. Bardrekk knelt not far away, his hand raised like he was trying to grip the air. A glow formed and he threw it. This time it landed closer to his goal.

"No," Aleyna cried as she stumbled forward, not sure what she was going to do. Bardrekk turned to face her, his eyes growing wide at her approach. Already the light was forming in front of his hand as he shifted to be better able to aim the fireball—or whatever it was—at her this time.

Her feet tangled around each other and she came crashing down to the floor. A barking laughter forced its way through the ringing in her ears. She pushed herself into a kneeling position only in time to see a bright light streaking towards her. She lifted her arms and closed her eyes.

Screams replaced the ringing sound and she opened her eyes. Everything flammable in the room was on fire but her and Rappen.

Aleyna grinned even as Bardrekk extinguished the flames that clung to him. "Let him go, let me go, and I swear I won't hurt you."

"You really think I would let a Banrey go free? You deserve to pay for the part your family played in tearing this world to pieces." Bardrekk glared at her as he stood on shaky feet. "I saved this world when they abandoned it, and I will not let some foreigner take it from me. I don't care what your bloodlines are."

"I don't have a family and I don't care what my bloodlines are, all I wanted to do is go back home. Please, let us go." She stayed where she was, not wanting to waste any energy on an attempt to stand up. If he thought she was begging, so be it.

Bardrekk didn't bother with words as he shot another bright white fireball at her. She blocked it with a single arm, causing it to shatter, shards of bright white light shooting out in multiple directions. A scream came from to her right and Aleyna's eyes went wide as she turned to see Rappen, who had crawled over to lean against the wall, clutching his chest. Beneath his hand, charred fabric showed.

She ran towards him, wanting to be sure he was okay. She'd barely made it halfway when he shouted something at her. Aleyna didn't have time to register the words as she flipped around and formed the barrier again—it was getting easier to do each time and had become an almost unthinking reflex. Another fireball shattered against it.

"You mother…" She didn't bother to finish that sentence as she reacted on instinct. A warmth and energy filled her body and she focused it on a single thought. To stop Bardrekk from hurting her. Light poured out of her and took the shape of several giant serpents that swarmed her attacker and toppled him to the ground.

"Aleyna…no…don't…" She ignored Rappen's entreaties to stop as she walked over and stood above Bardrekk. He struggled under the weight of the coiled serpents and tried to shoot another white ball of flame at her, only for it to be swallowed by one of the shimmering snakes.

"Tell me you will end this. Don't make me do something I don't want to do."

Bardrekk stopped struggling. He glared at her and took his time before conceding. "Fine. You're free to leave."

"That's a wise move." She wasn't sure if she believed him, and he had no way of knowing that her threat to kill him was only a bluff. Killing in self-defense was one thing, but he was at her mercy right now. Murder was not something she wanted to be part of. "I'll allow them up when we are leaving. I don't trust you enough. Not yet."

Aleyna walked to where Rappen leaned up against the wall, a hand still over his chest where the fireball had hit him. She helped him to his feet, and he leaned on her as they walked towards the exit. Though it was unnecessarily dramatic, she used her power to slam the double doors open on their approach and released the serpents at the same time.

With a twist of her fist she was about to shut the doors behind them when she caught a glimpse of light in the corner of her eye. There was barely enough time for her to pull up a shield and she put more power into it than she'd intended.

As her eyes readjusted from the bright flash, she found herself staring at an empty room. Bardrekk was gone.

# CHAPTER ELEVEN

"I want to say that's not possible, but with you, that seems to be the norm." Rappen wheezed out the words as he studied the empty room. "But you shouldn't have done that."

"I didn't mean to." Aleyna lowered him to the ground now that the immediate danger had passed. "Did I do that?"

Rappen looked at her with a sadness that she didn't understand. "I know it wasn't intentional, but..."

"But?" she asked, wanting him to finish the sentence.

"It's nothing." He winced and moved his hand away from his chest. Large blisters had formed, and blood soaked what remained of the finery he had been wearing. "I think I may be in dire need of a healer."

"Do you want me to try?" Aleyna asked, lifting her hand as she did so.

"No," he said. "Not if you still want to go home. You can't risk it."

"It's worth the risk," she pressed, and Rappen didn't try to stop her this time as she focused on healing the wound she had caused. She bit her lip as she pulled her hand away, but only smooth, shiny flesh could be seen now. "Does it feel better?"

"Yes, but you still shouldn't have bothered," Rappen insisted as the ground trembled beneath them.

"What was that?"

"It's not important, let's get you to the library and find out how to send you home before it's too late." He stood up as a guard came charging up the hallway.

"Where is the Grand Ruler? What happened to him?" he demanded when he was close enough.

Aleyna looked to Rappen for guidance, unsure of what to say and dreading being thrown into the prison here. He stood as tall as he could and took a deep breath before speaking. "He is no more."

The guard's face went from worried to terrified at this statement. "By who? How? Someone must—"

"I know, and someone will be found to do so. Go to your commanding officer, inform them of the situation. Time is of the essence. You know what needs to be done," Rappen commanded. The guard nodded and took off at a run. "Okay, let's get you home."

Aleyna stood where she was, glaring at him as the building trembled beneath her feet again. "Why is time of the essence? What is going on?"

"It's really not as important as getting you home. That's what you came here for."

"Don't evade my questions," she said.

Rappen sighed. "Fine. Without someone with a strong enough power to maintain the connection to your world, the magic that keeps this piece of Tenebris stable will eventually disappear into the void too."

"Oh." Aleyna clutched at her locket. "There aren't many who do have the power to do so, are there?"

"No." Rappen winced at the question. "I don't have the power and I know of no others that do either."

"Except me?"

"You may not even have fully Become yet, but you are more powerful than anyone else I know. Thank your bloodlines for that." Rappen stared at the floor as he nodded in response to her question. Another shudder ran through the building and the floor of the room cracked down the middle. "We should get to the library before the connection is lost."

"You have the power. It's your decision to make," Aleyna murmured, remembering the words the note had said before she'd jumped off the cliff.

"What?"

"I'll do it," she said.

"If you do it, you'll be stuck here. You've risked enough," Rappen insisted. "Someone will be found and, if not, it's not your responsibility or concern. This isn't your home."

Aleyna stared at him as she tried to determine if he was telling her the truth and shook her head. "You don't believe that."

"Aleyna, please, don't," he pleaded with her. "Go home. Go back to where you're from and let this all become nothing more than a bad dream."

"Tell me how," she demanded. If she was going to this, then it needed to be now. She might lose her courage if she took the time to think about what it might mean.

"Over there, behind the curtain." Rappen nodded towards the other side of the room as more trembling caused dust and debris to fall from the ceiling above. Not knowing what else to do, Aleyna marched towards the curtain. She threw it open and saw a dark sphere floating between three pillars. She looked back at Rappen, unsure of what to do now, but he wouldn't even look at her.

Biting her lip, she gripped the locket with one hand and shoved the other directly into the sphere. A voice, a familiar voice, whispered in her ear. *Find them.* It was the same voice that had told her to jump off the cliff repeating the nearly forgotten words on her note.

*Find who?* she asked of it.

*Not who,* what. *Find them.*

Aleyna stumbled backwards, losing contact with the sphere. Power, stronger and unlike anything she had experienced, flowed through her. It was beyond anything she could have imagined, and it made her feel as though she could capture a star in her hands if she wanted to—though there were no stars here.

"Aleyna?" She glanced back at Rappen who stared at her from the doorway where she'd left him. She walked towards him to see a sheen of tears on his cheek. "I'm sorry. I should never have brought you here."

"Don't be sorry. It is what it is," she said, even as she wondered if she would ever see her home again.

He reached out, his fingers brushing over a strand of her once-dark hair. Glimmering silver, like a handful of precious metal, caught her eyes. "You've Become."

Aleyna nodded. "I know."

"I'm sorry," Rappen apologized again.

"Now, what?" she asked, not wanting to focus on what she'd lost.

"There isn't much to do." Rappen shrugged. "Those that live here have no choice but to accept you as the new Grand Ruler if they wish to live."

"Oh." Turning away from Rappen, she walked over to one of the narrow windows to look out on the world of which she was the unwilling ruler. Her new home, this dark and broken land.

*Find them.* Those words still echoed in her ears. She patted her pocket and pulled out the piece of paper. It looked as if it had never been in a lake, or across a land in her filthy, stained jacket. She unfolded it, wondering if the message had changed.

It had.

*Welcome home, Queen Aleyna.*

# MIST SHROUD
*Melissa Matos*

## CHAPTER ONE
*The Web*

Tinny kept her back to Losta as he slipped into the hall and shut the door behind him with a light click. Her eyes remained focused on her book and she held her breath, straining to hear his steps, though she knew it was pointless. He would tousle her hair or try to snatch her book before she realized he was beside her, and she would pretend to scold him for sneaking up on her again. It was always a good day when Losta visited. They didn't get many visitors, and there were few other dark elves in Odari, so it brightened her father's day as well.

She waited a few beats longer than usual but refused to turn around. Losta could blend into the shadows at will and had tricked her more than once, pretending he was no longer there and then jumping out from behind a plant or chair. She waited a full minute, but there was no jump or bump or sudden shout from Losta. Instead she heard the light click of a door at the other end of the hall. Shutting her book with a snap she twisted around, risking a surprise attack, but there was nothing. The hall was empty, curtained with shadow, barely lit by the blue lamps that protected her father's eyesight. The door at the far end of the hall led not to her father's rooms, but to the Alchemist's office.

She set the book aside and ran to a section of wall between two large columns. Behind a massive potted plant was the entrance to one of the between spaces that was Tinny's favorite feature of their home. Because of the odd construction there were hidden spaces and passages between most of the rooms, and Tinny had spent hours of her childhood exploring them. It was difficult to get through all of them now that she had stretched taller and filled out in places, but many were still passable. She was sure her father knew about the hidden passages, and that she spent hours in them watching him and whatever visitors he received, but he had never mentioned it.

This passage led to a corner of the Alchemist's office, an oddly shaped room attached to his private chambers in the east wing of the house. His rooms were always brightly lit, so she had to squint to see into the room. She arrived there in time to watch Losta hand over a bundle wrapped in white gauze to the Alchemist. As he held it out he bowed low, but his movements were slow and stiff as though it pained him to bend. The Alchemist took it in both hands, bowing in response and muttering something to Losta. Losta nodded in reply, and opened his mouth to speak, but no words came. Instead he nodded curtly again, turned and walked out of the room, still moving as though pushing through water.

Back in the main hall, Tinny studied Losta carefully. His steps were short and he stumbled at the end of each motion, his arms stayed close to his body, his head drooped forward. As she stared she began to notice tendrils of shining thread like the strands of a spider's web clinging to his arms and legs, tangling around his body, hindering his movement. She frowned and pushed out of her hiding place.

"Losta! Losta, wait, what's wrong?"

Losta stopped and looked up, but didn't raise his head all the way. "Hello, Tinny. Looks like you got the drop on me for once." His smile formed slowly.

"What's the matter? What do you have wrapped around you?"

He looked confused and looked down at his body. "What? What are you talking about?"

"These threads. They look like they are hurting you. Maybe I can-" She reached out and grasped the threads on his arm and tried to pull them off. They stretched and clung to him like taffy. What little she had grasped stuck to her fingers. Losta grunted in pain and pulled away, slapping at her hand.

"Stop, Tinny, that hurts. Don't pull at me."

"But it's not you, it's this." She showed him her palm.

"I don't know what you're playing at but it isn't funny."

"No, it's not funny at all. This is all over you." She thrust her hand at him again but he pushed her hand away roughly.

"There's nothing there, Tinny. Stop." He tried to turn away and hurry for the door, but his steps stayed slow and muddy. This time she grabbed a thick bundle of threads attached to his leg. He yelped and pushed her back and she stumbled into the wall. "I told you to stop." He raised his arm and stalked toward her, his face twisted and turning deep blue in his anger.

"That's enough." Tinny's father's voice echoed through the hall, and Losta froze. He looked at his arm as though surprised at its position, lowered it, and turned to face her father.

"Forgive me, Morion. I don't know what came over me. Please, I meant no harm to her." Losta clasped his hands together and looked at Tinny with glistening eyes. "I know you weren't trying to hurt me. I'm sorry."

"I'm fine Losta. I'm sorry I hurt you." She looked down at the residue on her hands. "I was only trying to help."

"I think you should go now, Losta. Your business is complete." In two long strides Morion was beside his daughter, looming over Losta. For a moment the hint of a dark flame formed around his fist. Tinny had seen her father use magic before, but never against Losta, or anyone who had been welcomed into their home. Losta shrank back and nodded, then shuffled out of the house as fast as the webs allowed.

Morion relaxed and the fire faded and Tinny remembered again how old her father was. His skin was darker than Losta's, more purple than blue, his long hair pure white. He stooped some, but was still taller than most men. The hand he held out to her was thin and spotted, but still held hers in a firm grip.

"Are you all right?"

"I'm fine papa. Really. Please don't be angry with Losta. I caused him pain. That's why he reacted that way." She could sense her father was expecting a hug. He had his other arm open to receive her. But she couldn't move any closer to him. The same threads she had seen around Losta were around him too, but thicker, grayer, older.

"That's not an excuse." Morion lowered his arm and let go of her hand. "He will not be visiting again. Though I fear that would have been the case even without this incident. He got what he wanted." Tinny was too distracted by the web around her father to be concerned about his words. How long had they been there, she wondered? How many others were wrapped in such webs? And how much stronger would her father still be without them? He was old, it was true, but not very old. Dark elves could live well into their third century if they were careful, and Morion was not yet three hundred years old. Were the threads making him old?

"You're late for your lessons." The Alchemist was standing in the doorway to the hall tapping his cane on the floor. He was as unlike her father as a man could be, a light elf, bronze skinned and dark haired. His piercing green eyes were fixed on Tinny. She sighed and headed back to her bench to get her book.

"I was finishing the reading. If you gave me more interesting books to read, I might stay awake long enough to finish my assignments the night before."

"If you paid attention during your lesson, I wouldn't have to give you so many assignments." He tapped his cane again for emphasis, and then waved her through to his office. "Come let's find out what you managed to absorb." He nodded to Morion and then shut the door to the hall.

*    *    *

Tinny recited what she remembered of the chapters he had given her to read, a complex discourse about the nature of two rare elements, one of which may have only existed in the theories of the author. The Alchemist corrected her a few times, but overall she performed well enough to warrant moving on to other things. He tried to engage her in a discussion of magical transference, a subject he knew she loved as that was something her father had perfected over his long career, but she was distracted and only answered in short phrases and nods. Finally he sighed and stopped lecturing.

"Very well, out with it."

"What were the threads wrapped around Losta?"

"Threads? Describe them to me." Her palms were still sticky, but the threads had dissolved in the hallway. She did her best to describe their appearance, how they felt, how it had hurt Losta when she pulled on them. The Alchemist listened, asking clarifying questions now and then, until he finally interjected excitedly.

"So you can finally see it! No wonder I haven't had any success getting you to see the aether before. It looks so different for you. I don't know why I expected it to look the same to you as it did for me. For my master it was auras. But you can see it! Finally! We have so much more I can teach you now!" He clapped his hands and ran to a shelf and began pulling books off and piling them on his desk.

"I'm... I mean, well, so what are these threads? Aether? I thought you said it looked like clockwork?"

"That's how it appears to me, child. But not apparently how it appears to you. You said Losta was being dragged down by these threads? I saw at once when he came that the gears of his soul were slow and rusted. You saw the same thing, only different." He dropped a tome on his desk and started flipping through the thick pages.

"So, everyone has these threads?" She stood back and looked over the Alchemist. "You don't seem to be tied up in threads."

"Hm? Oh. Well, perhaps the light is too strong in here." He snapped his fingers and the lights dimmed and changed from their normal orange glow to a golden green. "Is that better?"

She looked again, starting with his legs as they had been thickest on her father and Losta there. But his legs seemed clear. She scanned up, and finally saw the threads trailing out from his torso, but rather than clinging and sticking as the webs around Losta had, these were floating and streaming up and outward and seemed to be giving the Alchemist energy rather than restraining him.

"Well? Do you see them now?"

"I think so. But they look different on you."

"Interesting. I wonder what could have that effect on a person's soul." He changed direction in the book, flipping toward the back instead.

"They looked the same way on father as they did on Losta. Clingy and dingy. Yours are bright and floaty." The Alchemist paused and looked over his shoulder at her.

"So, they looked the same on Losta, and on your father? Exactly the same?"

Tinny shook her head. "They were much worse on father."

The Alchemist nodded. "Well, that might explain that then." His gaze shifted from the book to a plain wooden box on the shelf to his right. Tinny waited, knowing that even if she asked, he wouldn't explain anything to her. He would, however, give her a clue if she were patient. He flipped through the book some more, stopped at a page heavy with ink, and nodded again. "Did you see where the threads went?"

She looked up at the web of threads above the Alchemist, streaming in every direction. As she thought back to the web around her father, it did seem that they all lead the same way.

"I didn't. But I can find out."

Again the Alchemist nodded, and Tinny ran out of the room.

*  *  *

She slipped back into the between spaces and slid along the insides of marble caverns, clambered over a few wooden beams, and peered down at her father. He was seated at his desk scratching out a letter or contract. There were hardly any lights at all in his office, only two blue flames in lamps on his desk. In the dimness the web around her father was stark white, hanging in thick ropes from his shoulders. Rather than floating above his head like the Alchemist's his lead away in one direction. Down.

Tinny took a deep breath, slipped back down to the floor and pushed her way through an air vent and out into the west hallway. Going down the stairs at the end of the hall, she thought of finding her way to the part of the basement below Morion's office, but it wouldn't be necessary. She knew where the threads lead.

The basement was cold and so dry that it made Tinny cough. The only light was coming from under a door at the far end of a long wide hall carved from the rock foundation. Pale glimmers fell on the edges of plaques that lined the wall, each set onto a small door and carved with the name of one of Morion's ancestors. Tinny walked down the hall running her hand along the plaques, reciting each name as she passed.

The door at the end of the hall opened on its own as she reached it and Tinny squinted against the flood of golden light. Once her eyes adjusted, she stepped inside and the doors closed behind her. The room was lined with bookshelves stuffed with books and scrolls in hundreds of languages from recent and far history. The ceiling was painted blue black and dotted with all the constellations. In the center of the room was a low stone slab supporting a short sword on a silk cushion.

She stepped up to the sword and set her hands on it. She felt the familiar tingle run up her arms, and the new sensation of pushing her fingers through the web and then the world around her faded and she was standing on a hill at night with the constellations twinkling above her and the dark shapes of trees swaying in a breeze around her. A golden haired woman lay sleeping on the hilltop.

"Hello, mother." Tinny sat down beside the woman and put her hands over the woman's folded ones. Her hands were warm, and together their hands rose and fell with her breathing. "I made some progress with the Alchemist. I can see what he calls the aether. He was very happy. Normally I would be happy, too, but well, it just let me see some things that weren't so pleasant." She laid down next to her mother and looked over her carefully. She too had threads coming off of her. Hers lead in two directions, one back the way Tinny had come, and the other straight up into the sky. "I just wish I knew what any of it meant."

"You know what it means," the Alchemist said. He appeared beside them on the hilltop. "Talk it out."

"So these threads are the aether, connective energy between our hearts? Souls? And the people and things we care about. That's why my father is connected to my mother. And Losta... Losta is connected to his brother? The one that died last year?"

"Very good." He started walking in a slow circle around them on the hill. "But what's different here?"

"I could see your threads, but they aren't wrapped around you and pulling at you the way they are my father and Losta." Tinny looked up at him. "What was it that Losta brought back to you today? Has my father taken it as well?"

"Exactly! You are going to be improving by leaps and bounds now." He clasped his hands again and rushed back to her. "Come we should continue your lessons."

"What is it? That thing that Losta returned?" The Alchemist ignored her question.

"So, what do you see connected to your mother?" He stopped at her mother's feet. His gaze rose until he was staring up at the sky.

"She is tied to father," Tinny said. "But she's also tied to something up there. It's like she's being pulled in two directions. You're not going to tell me, are you?"

"I'm afraid your father wanted me to leave that to him." His gaze returned to the earth and came to rest on the sleeping woman. Though she had been asleep on this hill for most of Tinny's life she still looked healthy, her skin fair and glowing, her golden hair shining among the dark grass. No matter how much her father or doctors or mages of all kinds had tried, they had not been able to wake her.

"Tell me again about the dungeon?"

"We don't have time for stories, now, we have lessons to do. You can get into so much more advanced things now."

"Please? Just the end. Just about mother and the sword."

"I'm sure Morion has told you all about it, many times."

"Papa wasn't there really. Please, you tell it the best. Even better than Aunt Vola used to, and she's read more stories than anyone I know." Tinny pushed up onto her knees. "Please?"

The Alchemist sighed as though she were asking him to recite the entire history of Odari, but he settled down at her mother's feet and paused to gather his thoughts.

*Morion and Elen fell in love the first time they met, which was awkward considering Elen was the prison guard where Morion was being held captive. Your father being what he was, the best spell thief Odari had ever known, was being kept in a magical prison, not surrounded by iron bars, but by a single painted line on the floor. Crossing that line would doom Morion to a terrible curse.*

*Elen sought for a way to free Morion, which is how she discovered the sword. She hesitated to offer it to him, since it was not a complete solution. The sword too was a curse, and would trap the first person to touch it inside. But it was movable, and Morion agreed that once inside Elen could find someone to free him from the sword far away from the prison.*

*So Elen helped Morion escape. She slid the sword over the line, Morion touched it and was trapped within, and Elen fled with the sword. She said they could sense each other when she held it, that they had a strong connection, almost like a shared dream. At twilight and at dawn Elen was able to enter the sword and spend time with Morion, but it was only for a few hours at a time, and for a while it was enough. But then you came along. Elen went in search of the maker of the sword to find a way to free*

*Morion. That's how I met your parents. The Alchemist before me had made the sword, and Elen came to me to undo it.*

*Determined to find a way to break the curse, Elen ventured into a deep dungeon. I went with her, as did your Aunt Vola, Ace, Garnet and Vograck. We were nearly to the heart of the dungeon, when Elen came up against a powerful sorceress. One blow left her reawith, but before she could die, Morion drew on every last reserve of magic he held and switched places with her, preserving her body inside the sword and emerging in time to stab the sorcererss through the heart. She's been in the sword ever since, unchanging and undying.*

"Thank you, Uncle Lomion." Tinny took hold of her mother's hand again and squeezed it. She hadn't called the Alchemist by name since she had become his student. He was not a warm person, and was a very strict teacher, but now and then he would talk about the old days and was the Uncle Lomion she remembered.

"Right, of course. Let's get back to my office now. You have so much more to learn."

# CHAPTER TWO
## *The Shroud*

Tinny waited and watched, spending more time in the between places in the walls than she had in years. The Alchemist did not leave her much time to slip away as he drilled her on what she could see and deduct about the threads. Eventually he taught her to manipulate them without harming the people they were connected to. It was delicate work, and Tinny took her studies very seriously. But through all of it she kept one eye on the box in the Alchemist's office, and the other on her father.

Less than a week later the box on the shelf was open and empty. She knew the Alchemist left it open on purpose as a signal to her, probably more for her father's sake than for her own. Running down the stairs at top speed she reached her father while he was still trying to choose a book from the shelves in the sword room. He had the wrapped package under his arm.

"I would rather you not come in with me this time, little one," Morion said when she came into the room.

"I have a question, papa." Tinny took up a stance between her father and the pedestal.

"And you won't let me visit your mother if I don't answer?" Morion turned and smiled down at his daughter. "What's your question?"

"What is that?" She nodded to the package under his arm.

"Ah. So that's what Lomion was going on about." Morion came to stand beside Tinny and set an old book down on the podium. "This is the Mist Shroud." With one quick shake he flicked the package open. Rather than something wrapped in gauze it turned out to be a large square of gauzy material that had been wrapped in a bundle. It floated in the air where Morion and shaken it, undulating softly as though a breeze were wafting through the room. Tinny felt the temperature drop.

"What does it do?" She inched away from it, her voice low and feathery.

"You know the between places you like to hide in the walls?" Tinny nodded. "There are places between planes as well, between here and the place where our souls go when we die. When a person is wrapped in it, they can die for a short time. Their soul travels into the between realms, but is able to return to their body so long as it is still wrapped up."

"And you've been using it to talk to mother?" Tinny was wounded. It stabbed to think there was a way to talk to her again but that he had kept it from her.

"I've been trying to find her." Morion ran his hand over the shroud. I billowed under his touch but didn't sink. "Her soul is trapped in between here and the next place. I'm trying to bring her back."

"We can't just wrap her in it? It won't help bring her back to her body?"

"I tried that. We had wrapped her in it for weeks. Nothing changed."

"But papa," Tinny took hold of his hand. "Do you know what it's doing to you?"

Morion frowned and knelt down so he was looking into her face. His eyes were cloudy with concern. "What do you mean?"

"It's like what happened to Losta. It ties you to that place and wraps you up so that you can hardly move here. So that you don't want to move here. It's going to drag you away." Tinny took a long shaky breath and pressed her eyes shut until the threat of tears passed. "I don't want you to go away, too."

"Oh sweetheart." He gathered her in his arms. "I'm not going to leave you. But your mother did so much to save me. I have to do what I can to save her."

"But what if it doesn't have to be you?" She pulled away to look into his face, her maroon brown hands stark against his blue cheeks. "You can't see the threads that connect her to here. But I can. I could follow them to her. I know I could."

"I couldn't let you go in there. You have no idea what it's like. I couldn't even tell you. It looks so different for each person." He pulled her hands away from his face. "No, Tinny. You can't."

"I can, papa. I can and I will. The only way you can be sure that I don't go looking for her is to get rid of the shroud. And I know you won't do that." She pushed her chin up and set her jaw. Something fractured in Morion's gaze and he looked away.

"You're as stubborn as she is," he muttered. He pulled himself up, his knees creaking with the effort, and grabbed hold of the shroud. It collapsed into a regular drape of fabric in his hand. "I will allow it once. Only once. And we are going to need Lomion's help. I can assist you while you are in between, but it's easier when he's around."

*       *       *

When they presented their plan to the Alchemist he lowered his eyes and nodded as though he had expected this exact idea for some time. He reached over to a shelf in his offices and pulled down a battered carpet bag that clinked when he set it down. Opening it, he glanced inside quickly, and then looked to Morion.

"Do you have something you can offer?" The Alchemist asked.

Morion nodded, squinting against the bright light. "I have a few things. Stay with her while I gather them?" The Alchemist nodded and Morion slipped away.

"While you are in between," the Alchemist said, reaching into his bag. "We will be around you at all times. We will have precious items with us that we can sacrifice as necessary to assist you. But we will not really be with you." He pulled something from his back that looked like a wrench made of clear crystal. "I will also do my best to be sure that the threads tied to you stay strong, but that you do not get caught up as your father has."

"He wouldn't let you help him?"

"He did at first. Once we returned from the dungeon we all remained with him for some time, taking turns assisting as he went in search of Elen." Lomian sighed. "Then he began stealing again, even from us. It became very costly as each lost more and more of our own magic to help him through that place. They tried to look the other way, after all, it was to help Elen. Over time each of them moved on to other things. They still come to visit, now and then, but it is not the same. Now he goes whenever he wishes, and doesn't ask me for help anymore."

Morion reappeared in the Alchemist's office with a different bundle in his arms. Tinny had assumed he had gone to his own office, or his rooms, but he had gone to hers. The bundle was wrapped in her old baby blanket. He set the bundle down on the desk, and she could see a doll, a hair bow and other things.

"Would you like to go now, or-"

"Yes, let's go now." Tinny set her hands on the Alchemist's desk. "You've tried long enough, papa. You did your best, but I want to help, too." Her father wasn't looking at her, but Lomion smiled down at her and nodded.

"Let's go now, then." He patted Morion's shoulder as he passed, and together they travelled down the stairs to the catacombs. The Alchemist had brought a light for himself, but he stayed behind Morion and Tinny. The doors parted for them, and they were again in the golden chamber with her mother's sword.

They entered the sword space. Morion sat down by Elen's head, and put his hands on her forehead, closing his eyes. The Alchemist spread the shroud out and it floated to the ground beside Elen, hovering just above the grass.

"Lie down," he said to Tinny. She swallowed hard, but did as she was told. As soon as she did, the shroud wrapped itself around her. It was not tight, but soft, like being wrapped in a cloud, but it was cold and wet. She began to shiver.

"Take slow, deep breaths. Try to relax and let it do its work." Lomion sat down at Elen's feet, and kept speaking in soft, low tones. "Just rest, like going to sleep. Do not be afraid of the darkness. That is only the beginning."

Tinny tried to shut the cold out of her mind, focusing on the numbness that spread over her. She pushed air in and out of her lungs and counted, in one two three, out one two three, until the numbness reached her mind. The golden glow outside her eyelids flared to red, phantom shapes lingering, until it all faded to a deep black.

Then her breath ceased. She tried to bring air into her lungs but it would not work. Her mind screamed for her body to shake loose of the bonds, to break through the cold and live, but nothing responded. She could barely hear Lomion speaking, trying to calm her down, but everything within her kicked and squirmed against the darkness that dragged her down.

# CHAPTER THREE
## *In Between*

She opened her eyes to a land covered in dark roiling fog. The tips of spiky trees poked through the mist. Now and then the earth trembled as thunder rolled across the sky. There was no lightning. Her eyes scanned around for any sign of the web. In the ground at her feet there was a stirring in the earth as though something were burrowing through the dirt. She crouched down to look closer.

The ground at her feet erupted in a fountain of gravel and dust, throwing Tinny back and sending her rolling along the ground. A massive worm shot up from the ground and screeched at the sky though a sharp glistening beak. While it pulled its soft body from the ground it began floundering around blindly.

Tinny scrambled to her feet, sliding on the rubble the worm had disturbed and ending up at the bottom of a hill. The worm pulled itself free of the earth and started undulating down the hill after, each slap of its body against the ground shaking it and splitting the earth even farther. Tinny finally found her footing and ran, jumping fissures in the ground and hopping to the side each time the worm struck out at her.

She managed to get far enough ahead of it to run on even ground and took off at her top speed. The worm screeched again and burrowed back into the ground so it could move faster. The rumbling tunnelled toward her. Just as it erupted again, she leapt for the edge of the trees and grasped for a branch, pulling herself into the spiny evergreen.

The worm screamed in fury and smashed against the tree, impaling itself on the pointy branches. Tinny swung around to the far side of the tree and tried to shelter herself in the thick needles but she was still spattered with hot, greasy globs that flew from the worm's wounds. The tree shuddered under the attack, branches ripped off caught in the folds of the worm's thick skin until it tore itself apart. It collapsed into a shredded heap of gore at the base of the tree and dissolved into a dark puddle. Small bubbles surfaced and released a smell like tar and blood mixed together.

Tinny waited until the bubbling stopped, then inched back down the tree trunk. Before letting go of the lowest branch she pushed at the puddle with her toe, sending slow ripples across the surface. It was cold, and clung to the tip of her shoe. Hoping to miss wading through it all, she swung herself as far from the trunk as she could, coming down towards the edge of the puddle and sinking much farther than should have been possible.

She ended up chin deep in freezing cold slime that immediately began pulling her even further downward. She had to tip her head back to keep her mouth and nose out of the stuff. Slowly, as her father had taught her, she inched her way to the edge of the puddle but it felt like the slime was resisting her every move. The shore looked farther and farther away with each step. The tips of her fingers were numb, and her chest cramped with each breath.

She stopped moving, letting the thickness of the murk keep her upright. Taking another step would just prolong her pain. Staying still allowed the cold to numb the pain of breathing and quiet the panic in her mind. It was much easier to rest and let the chill drag her mind into sleep. As her eyes closed she noticed a waving figure on the shore, and wondered if another worm was coming after her. But then it shouted her name.

Her eyes flew open and she saw the Alchemist standing on the edge of the pool, waving his arms wildly and shouting at her. She tilted her head, lifting one ear out of the oily murk, and her opposite cheek cringed when it touched the icy chill.

"Just one step," he shouted. "Take one step up and I can get you out. Hurry, Tinny, take a step." In addition to flailing he was imitating taking a step up, pretending there was a stairway beside him.

Tinny's legs stirred a little against the mud at the bottom sending shooting pains through her muscles. She groaned and furrowed her brow, staring at the Alchemist through narrowed eyes.

"It hurts," she tried to tell him, but her mouth wouldn't form the words, and it came out as another groan.

"Just one step, Tinny. Or are you getting lazy on me?"

She huffed, sending a spray of liquid towards him. He was always accusing her of being lazy and avoiding classes, even though most of the best breakthroughs had come from her out of class activities. She grit her teeth and took a step forward.

Beneath her feet a moving set of stairs rose up and pushed her out of the murk and toward the shore. Not only was the Alchemist there to catch her as she tumbled off the stairway, but her father was there as well, wrapping her in her old blanket and rubbing her arms and legs to get her blood flowing again. They looked different here. The Alchemist looked like he was made out of metal and gears, a complex and delicate mechanical person with glass eyes and rubber coated hands. Her father was scaled and muscled, with a long snout and wings, but otherwise still shaped like a man. Despite their appearance, she knew exactly who they were.

"Do you think you can walk now?" The Alchemist was kneeling on the edge of the pool. Tinny was wrapped in the blanket and in her father's arms, and he wasn't letting her go.

"Give her a moment," Morion growled, and held her tighter. His warmth crept through her limbs and pushed away the aches.

"I'm all right now." She sat up and hugged her father. "Thank you. Thank you both. I'm all right now." Morion let her go and she stood, stretching her stiff limbs. "I wasn't expecting it to be this dangerous as soon as I appeared. You didn't mention that there would be creatures here."

"It's different for each person who enters," the Alchemist said.

"I didn't think you would have that much anger in you," Morion said. His voice was heavy. "Perhaps you should come back."

"No." Tinny pulled away from her father and looked out over the hills where the worm had sprung up. It was empty now, there were no more worms or tremors, only the mist and the trees. The warmth of her old blanket had calmed her. She hadn't thought she was angry when she laid down in the shroud, more afraid of the cold and the stillness, but as the care of her father washed over her, she felt it leave. She had been angry, at him and at the Alchemist, for keeping all of this from her.

"Are you sure? There may be worse things in here than that." The Alchemist's gears whirred faster and he set his hand on her shoulder.

"No, I'm going further in. I'm not coming out until you have no way to help anymore." She looked up at her father. "Not until there's nothing left, all right?"

Morion nodded and they both faded into the mist.

*       *       *

Tinny followed the threads of the web that stretched between her mother's body and her soul through a maze of sharp trees, over miles of gray rolling hills, and pushed a raft through a mirror-still lake of black water. On the far side of the lake she found a tall mansion crowned with crooked towers. She had never liked her mother's family estate, but this was even more warped and broken looking than it had ever been in life. Tinny ran the boat onto the gravel shore and trudged up to the gates.

The door gaped open onto a dark hallway echoing with squeaking laughter. She followed the sound up a winding staircase and down a hallway that twisted and turned far beyond the bounds of the building. It led to her mother's room. The doors were shut, and her grandmother and aunts were at the door, laughing and taunting.

"Come on out Elen, show us again what a brave soldier you are." Her aunts looked like cats, their claws out and scratching on the door. "Tell us again about your last battle."

"Yes, and then all about how well you guarded the prison when you came home," her grandmother added. "And the hound dog of a man you saved from his cell." They hadn't noticed Tinny arrive. She looked around the hall and spotted a dainty wooden chair. One hard kick splintered the chair. She picked up one of the legs, now sharp and jagged at one end and pointed it at her mother's family.

"Get away from the door or I'll run you all through," she growled, doing her best impression of her father's voice.

148

"Oh look, it's her precious little girl." One of the cat-aunts crouched down and dug her claws into the carpet. "The one who's supposed to see beyond the fabric of the world. What can you see now, little girl?" Her aunt pounced at her, and Tinny slashed at her nose, jumping backward to avoid her claws. The cat covered her nose with her paws, dripping blood on the carpet.

"More than you can," Tinny answered. "I can see how beautiful and strong my mother is. And how petty and ugly you are. Get away from the door." All three turned on her. Her grandmother didn't look catlike. She was still tall and regal and picture perfect, but her eyes glowed green and her nails were like blades on her hands. They lunged at her.

The door to her mother's room burst open and golden light flooded the hall. "Don't you touch my girl." Elen's voice sounded like a trumpet. Grandmother and aunts cringed away from the light and scrambled along the edges of the hallway, still slinking toward Tinny. Morion had stolen magic from dragons and could breathe fire and fly. But Tinny's mother spoke to the stars, and had commanded a much more terrifying power.

Brilliant rays of light flashed out from Elen searing through the darkness and turning the cats and her grandmother to ashes. Once they were gone, the light faded, and Elen slumped to her knees in the doorway. Tinny ran to her mother and tried to help her up, but Elen shook her head and took a shaky breath.

"Not yet. Let me rest a moment." She looped her arm around Tinny's shoulders and kissed the top of her head. "What are you doing here, little girl? This is no place for you."

Tinny couldn't answer at first. She buried her face against her mother's shoulder and breathed in the warm gingery scent of her. It took all she had to keep from falling apart in tears.

"I'm here to bring you back, mother." Tinny's words were muffled and Elen asked her to repeat herself. Tinny said it into her ear.

"Oh darling. I will try."

Tinny's brow scrunched and she pulled back to look at her mother's tired face. Then she looked over the rest of her. She too was covered in webs, thick heavy strands clung to her legs and arms and wrapped around her waist. Most of them trailed back the way Tinny had come, but not all of them.

Elen stood up and leaned against the doorframe. The hallway had changed, one end leading straight back toward Elen and Tinny's bodies, the other bending upward to an opening that showed a clear patch of starry night sky. As Elen moved out into the hallway, Tinny could see a long bright strand leading through the hall and up into that sky. She tried to make her way down the hall with Tinny, but the thread to the sky was strong and didn't stretch the way the other threads did. Elen struggled for a few steps and nearly fell again.

"Sorry sweetie." Elen grabbed at the wall but there was nothing to hold onto. The hallway stretched away in front of them, and shortened behind them, pulling them closer to the opening in the ceiling.

"I can get help. I can call for help, now that I know where you are." Tinny stepped away from her mother and headed for the long dark hall, but something tugged at her. She spun around and saw for the first time her own threads splitting out in many directions, all light and glowing. One thread connected her to Elen, and was the one that pulled at her now. She looked up into her mother's eyes and held back a sob.

"Elen!" Morion's voice cracked like thunder. He flew down the hall, his dragon wings brushing against the walls, pushed past Tinny and grabbed hold of Elen.

"Hello love," Elen said. She looked like a bright flame glowing through membranes of his wings.

"Tinny found you. I didn't want her coming in here, but she's as stubborn as you are." Morion laughed and turned to pull Tinny into the hug as well. "And now we are all together again. Let's get you back."

Tinny sobbed again, out loud this time, and shook her head, pushing against her father's strong embrace.

"It won't work, papa." Tinny's voice was swollen. "It won't work."

"What do you mean? We found her. We can just bring her back."

"No, papa. She needs to go that way." Tinny pointed toward the sky.

"No." Morion moved around Elen, between her and the opening. Tinny looked at the threads again. The thick thread she had followed was no longer leading down the hall. It was lying slack beside her father. As she watched it started to shrink, wrapping tighter around them all. Morion followed Tinny's gaze, and noticed what was happening. He began clawing at the heavy threads pulling Elen away. Elen cried out and bent over. Morion was at her side immediately. "I'm so sorry. I didn't know it would hurt you."

Tinny took a few steps away from them, but the connection to her father was shrinking as well, and she couldn't get more than a few steps away from them. Elen pushed up, leaning heavily on Morion, but her eyes were focused on Tinny. She tried to speak, but couldn't force out the words. Instead, she nodded at Tinny.

Tinny shut her eyes, counted to three, and wrenched the thread free that connected her to her mother. She felt a pain deep in her gut that stole her breath and wrenched tears from her eyes. Elen cried out again and tried to keep a hold on Morion, but the web behind her was too strong and yanked them both down the hall until they were at the edge of the opening in a pool of starlight. Morion beat his wings, stirring up a storm of ash and dust, but couldn't move them back.

"Elen, come on." He took firm hold of her wrist and began clawing his way back down the hall. Elen screamed as the rope behind her refused to give, even as the web connecting her to Morion pulled her forward. "Elen?" Morion stopped and slid back to the place under stars, clinging to her.

"I can't," Elen said, her voice raspy. "I'm sorry." The webs began to close in, pulling Morion closer to her.

"Papa, get away from her." Tinny ran to them and started pulling at the webs, but Morion wasn't listening. "Papa, please, it will pull you both away." Each time she snapped a thread she could see her father wince, but his eyes remained on Elen.

"She's right," Elen said. She set her hands on his cheeks. "Are you going to make our little girl go home alone?"

A low growl began in Morion's chest, and he doubled his efforts to pull her away. Elen cried out again but he ignored her. The webs wove tighter.

"Papa, I can't do this by myself." Tinny scratched at their webs wildly but nothing worked. It was too old, too thick, and growing thicker by the moment. One last croaking roar left her father's throat. He gripped the rope in his heavy claws.

"Say goodbye, Tinny," Morion said, his legs shaking from the strain.

Tinny smiled through her tears at her mother's glowing face. "Goodbye."

"Goodbye baby," Elen whispered. She leaned forward and kissed Morion.

With one final wrench Morion tore through the webs. Elen was yanked back and up into the night sky, disappearing into the glistening darkness. The remains of the webs around her father began to wither, and blew away like dust. They sat slumped in the hallway for a few moments, Tinny sniffling, and Morion crying silent tears. Tinny stood up and started back, and Morion followed, but it was like dragging a reluctant dog back into the house. The bond between them stretched thin in places and Tinny would have to wait alone in the swirling fog until Morion caught up.

The longest wait was on the hill where she had entered. It felt like hours before Morion arrived, his steps slogging as though he were moving through the murky remains of the worm that had chased Tinny earlier. She faced him, hands on her hips, as he reached the top of the hill and stood staring at the gray green grass.

"Do you want to just stay here?" Tinny's voice bit through the fog and Morion flinched away from her. "Or are you mad that I finally invaded this place?"

Morion's eyes darkened, and he looked up at her then. "What do you mean?"

"I mean, you kept me away for so long. Did you want to make this another place for just you and mother? And I ruined it for you? Why didn't you tell me any of this?"

The ground shook as she stomped her foot on the hill. A low rumble responded from deep within the earth.

"Don't Tinny. That's not fair."

"Fair? None of this was fair." Thunder rumbled over them. "But I could have helped you. We could have borne this together. And instead you just let yourself get pulled away." She was trembling and hot tears spilled from her eyes. Beyond Morion she could see the furrows of dirt traveling toward the hill. "So do you want to stay here?"

"No. We need to leave. Now." Morion had noticed the rumbling and moved to take his daughter's arm. She pulled away.

"You first," she spat at him. Morion nodded, and then dissolved into the darkness. Tinny watched the worms plow towards her and left a moment before they reached the hill.

*       *       *

She awoke with a gasp on the night hillside beside her mother. Morion was leaning over her, and sighed when she looked at him. The shroud was still wrapped around her, cold and damp, but where it touched her skin it steamed as though she were burning hot.

"Get this off me," she croaked, still gasping for air. Morion started to unwrap her, but as soon as she was able to budge she lashed out, tearing through the fabric in places. Morion blinked and stopped, but then the cloud passed from his face, and he began tearing through it too. The pieces of shroud dissolved into mist and floated away.

They were left breathless and sweating on the hill. Lomion had moved away down the hill, keeping a curious eye on them. They turned to look at Elen. Her breath was gone, the light of her skin and hair faded and pale. The skin on her face looked taught. Tinny reached out to touch her, but her hands were cold.

Morion stared down at his empty hands. Tinny could hear the growl beginning in his chest again, but before the magic could come roaring through him, she inched over and pushed her hand into his. The growl died, and he pulled Tinny into his arms. She wasn't sure how long they sat there, crying onto each other's shoulders, but they were both stiff when they went to stand. Lomion had left.

Morion pulled them out of the sword. The room was dark now, lit only by a dim blue light that the Alchemist started when he left. They exited the chamber, and Morion shoved the door closed. They didn't speak as they ascended the stairs, but Tinny could see that his steps were easy and long, and he no longer walked stooped over like an old man.

# CURSE OF THE DARK LAKE
*Michael D. Nadeau*

## CHAPTER ONE
*What Lies Beneath*

The wind blew in off the lake, taking the boy's hat and carrying it along the road against his will. His little legs pumping, he chased it as it flitted away as frustrated cries of obscenities spewed from his young mouth. Timmy might have only been eleven summers old, but his father was a fisherman and he had learned some inventive phrases. He stumbled, his fingers almost clutching the hat as he tumbled over the gravel road. His breeches ripped on the sharp rocks, and his shirt filthy from the dirt, Timmy sat up and watched his hat fly around in a lazy circle on the road ahead. The wind whipped his shaggy black hair in his eyes as he stood, determined to retrieve his favorite hat; the one his dad bought for him. As

Timmy walked towards it, the wind picked it up with a gust and tossed into the water.

"At least now you won't fly away from me," Timmy said as he got to his feet and rushed towards the edge of the lake. Timmy hesitated on the bank, staring at the aptly named Dark Lake with apprehension. He had been told to never go into the water alone because of the panic that could set in. *For Sithar's sake, I'm eleven, not five,* he thought, invoking the death god's name. Timmy stepped into the water, inching his foot forward with little prods to make sure he had ground underneath each step. The dark water had an odd property of being impenetrable to vision. It was pitch black, so nothing could be seen once submerged. If you were sitting in the water, you could look down and not see any part of yourself under the water. The legend around the nation of Llal'rin said that if you went under all the way, you actually disappeared forever. *Horse's breath. That's only a story to keep lil ones from going into the water without their parents watching them.*

Timmy had gone out far enough now to almost reach the hat; the water up near his waist. The wind was pushing the hat like a ship with full sails, carrying it out to open water and away from his reach. It was now or never. Shuffling a step at a time because he couldn't see the drop off, he reached out once last time, stretching out as far as he could without stepping further. His heart hammering in his chest. Timmy had one finger on the rim of the hat when something touched his leg. Screaming in shock and fear, he stumbled forward, one foot meeting nothing as it plummeted down unsupported. Timmy flailed with his arms, desperately trying to keep his head above water. He kicked his legs as hard as he could to tread water as he sputtered, spit, and sunk slowly. Agonizing seconds later he stopped sinking and leveled out, yet his panic didn't abate.

His breath coming quicker, he was starting to become lightheaded as he looked around for the shore. He was at least thirty feet from the weed covered bank. *It was just a fish, it was just a fish, it was just a...* Something hard wrapped around his leg and tugged. It didn't pull him under, only tested its grip, yet Timmy couldn't know that; all he knew was fear. "Help me!" he screamed, though no one was near enough to hear him. "It's got my foot!" He was on the long stretch before the town of Alsir to the north and trade wagons weren't out this late; there was no one to hear him. He was pushing it being out this late himself, but he thought he could make it to town before the sun set.

The next tug on his leg dragged him fully under, his eyes stinging as he submerged, and water flooded his mouth as he kicked with his other leg uselessly. Panic had settled in, making his attacks ineffectual at best. He looked down and let out a horrific scream, water backfilling his throat while bubbles escaped towards the surface... a surface he would never see again. He could see everything, now that he was under the black surface of the water, and he sunk with the horrible sight of what gripped him burned into his eyes. The water filling his small lungs, he twitched for a minute, struggling to get air. The light left his eyes as he went to dwell with Sithar of the Ravens.

# CHAPTER TWO
## *The Gathering*

The High Lord of the Llal'rin nation paced before his throne and cursed the day he married that spiteful wench. Garar Valstein was a dazzling fighter in his youth, yet now in his sixtieth winter he only drew his sword in ceremonial gestures. He sighed as he took his seat on the throne and waved for his steward.

"Yes milord?" the man said, coming over looking quite bored.

"Falas, are you *sure* you summoned them?" Garar asked for the twelfth time.

"Quite, sir."

"Where could they be?" Garar asked, not really looking for an answer. He had summoned the infamous Company of the Black Sword to his chambers five hours ago, and it was only a short ride through the city of Lortil to get to the castle.

A commotion in the outer hall made them both look up with renewed enthusiasm, eager to end the awkward silence between them. The four adventurers walked in, their demeanor radiating confidence and bravado. They were the best in the north and they knew it. Their leader, Kasha Anar, stepped to the fore and bowed slightly.

"Great High Lord, we have been summoned to your throne. What do you need done by the Company of the Black Sword?" she asked, her violet eyes never leaving the high lord. She was a dusky skinned warrior in tight, dark leathers with grey hair and dual Sakar—short unbreakable sticks made from the rare Aril tree. Kasha was an anomaly among her kind, a Hal'rhan. The Rhan were elves and had two sides, light—Lin'rhan, and dark—Dal'rhan. A Hal'rhan was a half breed of a human and one of the Rhan, and was often shamed because of their heritage. This warrior, however, had made a name for herself as a competent fighter as well as the group's leader and healer.

"Yes I did Lady Anar. There is a problem around the Dark Lake, and I need your company to investigate."

"Please, lord. Kasha is fine; I don't need titles to get the job done." Kasha stood proud as her companions behind her Bickered among themselves.

"What is all this?" a female voice interjected, walking in behind the company of adventurers. "I thought you were going to handle the Dark Lake problem, Garar?" The woman was short and stout, dressed in a ridiculous flowered dress.

"The High Lady Faralda Valstein," Falas announced, smiling like a man who had his revenge. He walked out of the throne room after that, chuckling softly.

"I said I was handling it, and I am!" the high lord roared, standing and shouting at his wife. She stormed right up o him and jammed her finger in his chest as he put his hand on the hilt of his sword.

"Might I intercede here Lord and Lady?" Kasha asked, not quite getting their attention.

"Right, that's it," an onyx skinned woman said from the ranks of the companions. She was a Dal'rhan wizard, her long robes cut up the side to show more skin and her deep, black eyes promising nothing but death. She had long white hair the color of bleached bone and her smile was distant, never quite touching her eyes. She waved her hands and brought her finger to her lips. "Alsalam," she whispered, the word or power vibrating in the air. "Shut up!" she said as her voice echoed throughout the court, reverberating off the walls as the magic enhanced its volume. Raervyn knew some of the most powerful words of power, and always let people know it.

"Thank you, Raervyn." Kasha stepped up to the stunned couple and smiled apologetically. "If you just give us the details and payment, we will be out of your way."

Garar shook his head and sat back down, ignoring his wife as she sulked off to the side, mumbling to herself. "People have gone missing all around the lake, from Asir to Faer'dran. Young and old alike, there seems to be no pattern and my court sorcerer is stumped."

"Big surprise there," an alabaster skinned elf said in the back of the company. He had long white hair, azure eyes, and was dressed in white silk. He was a Lin'rhan wizard who carried the namesake of the company; a black sword with a blade as dark as night.

"Illistyn, enough," Kasha scolded.

Garar continued without questioning the wizard's words. He wasn't entirely sure he wanted to know anyway. "I will pay you five hundred gold shards if you can investigate the problem and stop it."

"High Lord Valstein, you have yourself a deal." Raervyn said, accepting for the group. She walked up and shook his hand, ignoring the scowl Kasha gave her. "We'll be in your finest Inn for the night and leave on the morrow at first light."

"Or maybe highsun, at the very latest," Illistyn corrected, bowing low to the high lord as they walked away.

Once they had exited the throne room, Faralda walked over to her husband and laid her hand on his arm. "Do you think they will stop it?"

"I don't know. Let's see if they can figure out what it is first." High lord Valstein slumped back in his throne and rang the bell for Falas once more. He was going to need drinks for this night, he could feel it.

*　　*　　*

They left the castle already making plans on how to start this investigative journey. Kasha walked next to the biggest member of the company, looking up at him as they went. "So, Albriar, what do you think about the high lord and his quest?"

"It'll be fine," the big warrior said, not even cracking a smile. Albriar was human—the only one in the group—and a formidable fighter. He typically fought with methodical silence, never talking once blows were exchanged, and the polar opposite of the rest of the company. The group had taken to calling him The Silent One, though he never really answered to it. Even out of combat, the big man rarely spoke unless it was important.

"Everyone keep your ears out for rumors tonight in the inn. You would be surprised at what the commoners know that the lords don't," Illistyn said, looking at the fine women as they walked down to the lower city from the castle.

"Must you stare at every female that walks by?" Raervyn asked, hitting him in the shoulder.

"Will you sleep with me?" he asked.

"Most certainly not."

"Then, yes, I do."

# CHAPTER THREE
## *The Tale*

Illistyn Irial cheered when they arrived at the Ebonmire Inn, ignoring the looks his companions gave him. He wasn't like most stuffy Lin'rhan who thought they were better than every other being, he enjoyed the finer things in life; women, wine, and adventure. He had studied magic at the Spire of Ash in Rho'san, and at over one hundred and thirty summers of age, he was an accomplished wizard. The fact that he also fought with a blade was off-putting to most other wizards, but he had been trained since birth by his father to wield the family sword. The blade, Ashryn, was his most prized possession. Along with his magic, there weren't many who could match him in battle.

He looked around the empty streets of Lortil and had to laugh at the humans scurrying to and fro as they packed up their wares.

The companions had arrived shortly after getting to the lower city as the pale sun was finally giving up and setting below the dark clouds. The people were getting their last-minute affairs in order; markets closing and shops lowering gates. No one went out at night unless they absolutely had to, even inside of a city. Taverns and inns were the only exceptions, their patrons too drunk to worry about what could lurk in the dark. The Ebonmire was in full swing when they walked in, with a bard on stage singing a song as the crowd ignored him. It was a fine establishment with almost twenty tables, a stage, and seven rooms. Their stables were some of the best in the north, and were cheaper than most big city stables.

"They better have Dal'rhan ale," Raervyn said, pulling a chair out and sitting. She had picked the far table in the corner and everyone settled down with her.

"We're in Llal'rin, Raer, they won't have it and you know better." Illistyn smiled as he flagged down the serving girl with a flick of his wrist. "This is a Lin'rhan and human nation, and they hate importing from your homeland."

"Speaking of that, why did you bring that filth in here, Lin'rhan?" the bard asked as he walked over to their table. He was tall and fair of hair, handsome except for the scowl he wore and the open contempt in his eyes.

Kasha was quick to take the lead before things got rough. "Why don't you have another drink and forget about us friend," she said, tossing a half shard to the man. Her hand went out to make a fist in front of Raervyn; a subtle sign to hold until Kasha gave the open hand signal that meant she could act. This problem wasn't new to the companions.

"Now I'm expected to take shards from a half breed?" the bard asked, throwing them back. "No thanks, bridge-trash. I'd rather let Dal'rhan back into the world so they can break it again."

Raervyn caught the shard in mid-air like it was nothing, smiled, and set it down in front of her. "And what do you know human *gos*?" she asked, using the term for filth in her language.

"Jobe..." the bard's friend said quietly as he followed behind.

"Not now, Kendrick." He ignored his friend and stepped up, actually leaning on their table. "I know that your people messed with a powerful artifact against the gods' warnings and caused a wave of darkness to wash over the land, infusing the very earth with dark energy and wilting most life." His chin up in defiance, he turned to the room and went on, spinning his words like the performer he was. "The Rhan used their magic to preserve their own forests, yet could do nothing for the animals within. No care was given for the rest of us though, so humanity gathered in their cities and held out against the darkness with only their prayers to the gods." He had enraptured most of the room now, the people nodding agreement to the ancient story that even their grandfathers, fathers couldn't recall. "The gods grew tired of what their creation had become and soon, without warning, the three gods of order and goodness abandoned this world. Darkness ruled the land and the creatures that were twisted by the darkness ruled the night." He spit on the companions table at this and glared at them. "Even when the sun rises in the sky, it is more of a pale light then truly bright now, thanks to the Dal'rhan."

"Jobe!" Kendrick called out again to his friend, his urgent cry going unheard yet again.

"You forgot a couple of points, dear bard," Illistyn said, leaping up on top of the table they sat at, his light frame barely a strain on the wooden platform. He flicked his white hair out of his eyes and scanned the room, making sure he had their attention before starting. "This dark wave also had an unforeseen consequence for the ones responsible for breaking the artifact, called the Orb of Madra, by the way. The two clans of Rhan that worked to break the orb were also infected by this darkness, turning their skin coal black and changing their eyes to violet or even black in some cases. Our race fractured into the Lin'rhan and Dal'rhan—meaning light and dark elves for those of you uneducated in such matters—turning upon their own and banishing them to the far northern forests. You *humans* were too busy surviving on your own, so that left the Lin'rhan to clean up everything by themselves. The Dal'rhan were pushed back past the Linial River, but they dug in there. Admitting defeat, The Lin'rhan let them have the area you call Valan'tir and then helped you all rebuild." Illistyn turned with a grand gesture, twirling his long shirt as he did. "Yet in the years to come, the Dal'rhan learned to repent, even opening their borders to aspiring wizards who wanted to learn at the Spire of Ice. Lament them not, fair bard, for they have shown more tenacity in this life than you have to be sure." He bowed to the rapt crowd, their angry muttering ceased; stares directed to the bard now.

"Jobe," Kendrick whispered insistently in the hanging silence.

Jobe turned to his friend, ignoring the glares of the patrons. "What, Kendrick? Can't you see that I'm busy?"

Kendrick smiled sheepishly and pointed to the companions. "A Dal, a Lin, and Hal, with a human... Does that sound familiar to you?"

Illistyn unsheathed his sword and flourished it as he hopped down off the table, the black blade shimmering in the pale glow of the torches. It almost seemed like it was devouring the light around them, such was its luster. The Lin'rhan wizard saw the man's face fall and knew that they had been recognized. Sometimes that was a good thing, other times it went south very quickly. "Were you ready to leave now Jobe?" he asked, looking to Kasha. Her hand was still in a fist, so they couldn't act out yet.

"I... I'm..." Jobe turned and fled, pushing over people to get to the door.

"Are you truly the Company of the Black Sword?" an older man asked from the other side of their table as the room laughed at the fleeing bard.

Kasha lowered her hand, keeping a steady eye on Raervyn until the Dal'rhan nodded that she was alright. "Yes we are, good sir," she said, turning to face him. "What makes you ask?"

"Are you here because of the disappearances then? Around the lake?"

"The lake you say?" Illistyn asked, knowing that this could be what they needed. "Who has gone missing?"

"Whom," Raervyn corrected.

Illistyn shot her a look as Albriar laughed, breaking his usual silence. "Anyway, do go on good sir."

"Well it's not just someone; it's a lot of people. Word is that over thirty people have gone missing around the Dark Lake and the High Lord can't stop it." The old man shifted his chair over to better talk with them quietly.

"Well the High Lord has asked us to investigate, so consider it solved," Raervyn said, her cocky bravado shining through again.

"Easy there Raervyn," Kasha said, sliding the man the half shard left on the table. "This is for any more information you might have, or pointing us in the direction of someone that knows more."

"Well, I do know that most people have gone missing up near Alsir, yet no one has heard anything from Faer'dran, across the lake, in a tenday." He stopped as the serving girl came by with a round of drinks and a platter of mutton for Albriar.

"Compliments of the owner," she said, smiling at Illistyn before bending over to pick something up off the floor and walking, ever so slowly, away.

"It never ends for you does it?" Raervyn asked, hitting the Lin'rhan wizard on the shoulder. "Just keep your sword in its sheath, will you? We don't want another episode like the chase in Bridgewater."

"How was I to know it was the Lord's daughter?" he asked as he stood and bowed to the table. "I should be ready around first light, Kasha, whichever destination you settle on." Illistyn sheathed Ashryn and followed the serving girl across the room, leaving the others to talk, eat, and relax until they set off in the morning.

# CHAPTER FOUR
## *Across the lake*

Kasha Anar sighed as they waited at the docks for Illistyn. She was the leader of the company and was still amazed that they all listened to her. She was Hal'rhan, a half breed, and usually she was treated like the dirt on the bottom of most shoes because of her birthright. Her father was a human pirate and her mother was a Dal'rhan ship wizard. Her mother had been caught, tortured, and raped by the man and left for dead in their ship's hold. She had escaped, killing them all and fleeing home, yet she had been left with a burden in her belly. Months later, Kasha was born. Her life had been hard, growing up in Valan'tir a bastard, and only training with magic and weapons had gotten her through those years. She found refuge in a temple of Sithar of the Ravens; god of death, magic, and nature. She was raised to heal when others were hurt, and to kill those who hurt others. She could cast healing spells with water, and even scrying spells, but it was her martial prowess that made her truly stand out.

In fact, she was about to pull her Sakar and hunt down Illistyn for making them wait when he finally appeared on the rise, skipping down the road. His clothes were a mess and his hair looked like it had survived a windstorm, yet he was here.

"Oh Sithar of the Ravens, we're going to have to endure the stories of conquest from him all day," Raervyn said, invoking her god and rolling her eyes. She stormed off to the ship docked behind them, the *Dusk Runner*, without waiting for everyone else; even Albriar chuckled at that.

"Thank you for showing up dear wizard," Kasha said, bowing to him then turning on her heel and striding away towards the boat. Some days she would love to turn over the leadership to one of them, just to see how they handle things like this, yet she enjoyed the challenge to be honest.

"Hey, in my defense I did say highsun at the latest, in the high lord's court." Illistyn quickened his pace as they boarded the small ship bound for the other side of the lake, straightening his clothes as Raervyn ignored his presence.

Kasha sighed and looked out across the black surface of the lake, recalling the urban myths of submerging oneself under its inky waters. *Rubbish all of it, it is just water, black to be sure, but water all the same,* she thought as she headed towards the captain of the ship. "Good sir, have you had any trouble on the waters lately?" she asked, leaning on the rail as he looked at her askance.

"Trouble? Oh you mean like the people gone missing?" Captain Lar asked, spitting over the side. "Nope, not on any of my trips so far. No trouble except the wizards up north."

"You mean the Spire of Steam?" Raervyn asked as he walked up to them. "I heard those wizards and sorcerers are a bit off their slates."

"This coming from you?" Kasha asked. She couldn't resist the shot since Raervyn was always acting like she was special. Kasha knew it was only an act meant to throw off her enemies and have everyone think she was a loose cannon, yet the woman was as dangerous as they came. Raervyn was close to attaining the rank of Archmage and that was truly impressive.

The captain laughed at them as the sails filled with wind, the ship breaking the dark water and sending onyx waves rippling away from them. "Yeah, we stay clear of the northern shores unless we're well paid. Speaking of payment..." He let the words hang in the air as he turned his gaze away.

Kasha laughed and walked across the quarterdeck, pulling out a small pouch of gold shards. "Here is the agreed amount for passage, Captain." She slapped him on the back and pointed to Illistyn as the Lin'rhan wizard sauntered up to one of the female deckhands down below on the main deck. "However, our wizard may be servicing some of your crew for free."

"Captain, movement to starboard!" the crewman in the crow's nest called out.

Everyone rushed to the railing and scanned the water; they all saw the same thing. Something in the water was making a line right towards them. "Captain, is there anything in the lake that would do that?" Kasha asked, knowing the answer would probably upset her.

"Aye, that's a Kione for sure, but they don't travel alone." The captain pulled the wheel of the ship, sending it to port as the men and women of the *Dusk Runner* grabbed up arms.

"Don't worry captain; the company of the Black Sword is here," Illistyn called, shoving the woman he was flirting with behind him as he drew Ashryn and shouted a word of power to make his strikes faster. He often used wind magic to compliment his fighting style, much to the disappointment of Raervyn. She always teased him about not being a wizard since he fought with a blade.

Kasha saw the ripples vanish as the thing sank down, then a vibration came up through the ship as whatever it was struck the hull below the waterline. She drew her own weapons, the Sakar rods she used, and faced the port side of the quarterdeck, assuming that the first one was more than likely a distraction and that they would try and take the helm first; it was what she would've done. Sure enough, two pairs of scaly hands clawed their way over the rails in eerie silence, fluidly vaulting over onto the quarterdeck searching for targets. They were hideous to behold and Kasha had to admit that they gave her pause. She had faced some terrible creatures as leader of this company, yet these things looked by far the worst yet.

They stood like a human would, yet the comparison fled there. Their scaly hide was a putrid mix of light green and black, swirling together like an artist's fallen palette, and their wide head held large eyeless holes filled with milky orbs which pulsed like a heartbeat. The back of the Kione was covered in a row of long spines that quivered as if sensing prey. Their webbed feet had long spines in the back of the heel that dragged across the deck as they moved, and their long arms ended in vicious claws with black liquid dripping from them. Whenever the liquid hit the wooden deck it hissed, smoking as it started to erode the surface. Kasha knew instinctively not to let those claws touch her skin. The smell was by far the worst though, a nauseating aura of death and rotting vegetation that would cripple lesser men as they neared, such was the power of it even from this distance.

She leapt at the first one near her, knowing that there was no way to avoid combat at this point. *Better to strike with surety then react to aggression,* she thought, remembering her lessons and the painful bruises that came with them. Coming in with balanced steps she swung low, hitting where the joints connected in the legs, hoping to at least knock the things down, or immobilize it. Her Sakar hit once, twice, three times in rapid succession and the Kione screamed a terrible howl of pain and anguish as it fell, its leg a ruined mess of bone and sinew. It swung its vicious claws at her as it fell, but Kasha ducked under and went to the next in line. "Captain, finish that one off while I tend to this nuisance," she called out, her words sounding braver than she was feeling and spun to the next one, connecting with a double strike to its head. She kicked it backwards into Albriar's sword as he came up the stairs to help and took a breath. The big man lifted the almost seven-foot-tall creature impaled on his sword and flung it off the ship in silence.

The quarterdeck cleared, Kasha looked out at how the rest of the ship was faring and had to smile. Her companions were doing well, though it did seem that Illistyn had been wounded. He was standing around three bodies, chest heaving with exertion as he cast again, sending the last opponent back over the rails with a gust of wind. His sword, Ashryn, was dripping dark blood. Black holes were all around his feet on the wooden deck and his shirt was burned away down his bloody arm. The female crewman behind him had done well too. Her sword was broken, yet the thing was dead, twitching at her feet.

Raervyn, by comparison, hadn't been touched. As usual, the body count around her included allies as well as foes, yet she stood victorious in all her splendor. The bodies of the Kione had been burned, broken, and torn apart—pieces strewn across the deck as her spells of wind and fire ripped through their ranks. Two crewmen lay at her feet as well, but the rest of the ship cheered as the day was won. The celebration stopped, however, as screaming from the water drew their attention. Kasha ran to the rail and looked down, the couple of Kione that were thrown off the ship thrashing in the water. They were dragged down, screaming in fear, disappearing under the pitch-black water. Because of the lake's unique property, nothing could be seen once it was submerged.

"What could make something like that scream captain?" The woman behind Illistyn asked, as she fawned over her Lin'rhan protector.

"Nothing living that I've ever seen Serra." The captain was as shocked as the rest of them and it showed on all their faces.

"Well that can't be good," Raervyn said, coming up to the quarterdeck, wiping her hands on her robe. "So are we there yet?"

# CHAPTER FIVE
## Faer'dran

Raervyn Halloran smiled as the *Dusk Runner* pulled into the docks late the next evening, no welcoming committee present to meet them. She liked it better that way as most people were uncomfortable around her because of her heritage. Being one of the rare Dal'rhan seen outside of Valan'tir meant that she was the target of prejudice and hate, and she really couldn't blame them. Her race had broken the world and forced the gods of light to vanish. The entire land was soaked in darkness and shadow and it was linked to her blood. She had worked hard to climb out of that shadow, but when your very skin reminds everyone of the pain they've suffered, even more than five centuries ago, it still tends to sting

"Typical," Captain Lar said as his crew tied the ship up and lowered the boarding ramp. "Once night falls no one comes out down here."

"Can you blame them?" Raervyn asked, seeing the captain flinch as she walked by. She stopped and turned a cold gaze on him, raising one eyebrow. "I told you captain; those men were killed by the Kione, not me."

"I know, I saw the marks, but it's your reputation that scares me missus," he admitted, taking off his hat and bowing his head as an apology.

Illistyn walked by, arm in arm with Serra, smiling at them both. "Don't mind Raervyn, Captain, she's always like that." The Lin'rhan wizard dodged as Raervyn swung at him, laughing as he walked into the deserted town.

"Thank you for letting us sail with you Captain Lar, if you're still here when we're done, may we hitch a ride back?" Kasha asked, putting her arm around Raervyn to calm her down.

"Certainly, you all will always be welcome aboard the *Dusk Runner*."

Raervyn and the rest of her companions walked into the town of Faer'dran and couldn't help but feel like they were in a ghost town. The packed earthen streets were empty, as were the abandoned merchant stalls. The sickly pale moonlight illuminated some of the windows of the houses, yet no lights came from within.

"It's too early for them all to be asleep," Albriar said, making the entire company turn towards him and draw their weapons. He spoke so rarely that when he did, they all knew that something was wrong. He slowly drew his own great sword, one that most men could barely lift, never mind swing with precision and accuracy.

Raervyn slid to the back of the group and scanned the shadows, her eyes more accustomed to the dim light of the torches burning down the main street. Nothing moved, not even an animal scurried in the shadows. *I expected chaos and screaming at the least.* As if reading her thoughts, a cry caught her attention as the group spun towards the sound; a woman in distress, yet the timing was too perfect. "Wait Kasha, don't." Raervyn tried to warn her, but the warrior was already off into the gloom, Sakar out and ready.

"What is it, Raer?" Illistyn asked, dropping back as Albriar followed Kasha's lead.

"I'm not sure; the timing of that cry was too perfect. Right when I was thinking of it," she said, her hands moving through the patterns of a spell. "Reven!" she called out, saying the word of power to reveal hidden objects. Four, then five, and finally seven creatures became visible down the path Kasha and Albriar took, their magic washed away by Raervyn's spell. They were surrounded by Gnomes.

Gnomes were small creatures, grey skinned and wicked. Standing at only three feet tall and wire thin, they had sharp teeth, very little hair, and wicked claws that they used to rend flesh from bone. They could spit a semi corrosive spray that would melt flesh as well, but tended to use this only in desperation; they liked their meat fresh. These creatures loved to steal people and feast on them for days, prolonging the death as much as they could, savoring it. They would eat the extremities first, spraying the wounds with their corrosive spit to close them. It was said that gnomes would eat an entire village to keep fed through a winter.

Illistyn drew Ashryn and moved through the spell for a potent gust of wind with his other hand. "Toren!" he cried, thrusting his hand out and blowing the closest two away from Albriar. He waded in then, stalking one that was eyeing Raervyn. "Help Kasha," he said, spinning his blade in a defensive pattern. "I'll keep them off of you."

Raervyn scowled at his heroics, secretly admiring his ability to cast with only one hand. She had always found him attractive, yet could never tell him. The possibility of rejection would be too great from such a close friend. No one wanted to be with a Dal'rhan. Raervyn looked at Kasha and saw the warrior spinning her twin Sakar, bashing any hand that snuck in through her defense; yet that's all it was, defense. She was surrounded by three of the murderous little creatures and they were keeping her quite busy. Raervyn wove a spell with her fingers, then chopped straight down with her other hand. "Burnan!" A line of fire raced out towards the three gnomes, catching the toe in her sight and engulfing them in flames. Screams went up that echoed across the lake, sending the flaming creatures running for the water. The joke was on them though, that fire wouldn't go out for anything except magic.

"Thanks, Raer," Kasha called, hammering the remaining one to the ground with quick strikes.

The Dal'rhan wizard looked towards Illistyn and Albriar to see that the two had made short work of the rest, nary a scratch on any of them. *Gods but he is infuriating,* she thought, trying not to think of what she would do to him given half the chance. It was why she got so mad when he caroused with anything with a heartbeat. *Oh to be normal.*

"Quick thinking Raervyn," Illistyn said, walking over with the big warrior behind him. "That could've turned out far worse had they struck first."

"Well it's not over yet. We still have to find the rest of the town and see how many are left." Raervyn turned away so that no one could see her blush.

"Did you come to save us?" a small voice asked from one of the darkened windows.

"Yes, how many were taken and where did they go?" Kasha asked, smiling at the little girl that came out to talk with them.

"They took most of the men down that lane," she said as her mother came out as well.

"Thank you. We'll be back soon, just hold tight and get ready to treat the injured." Kasha turned and motioned for the company to follow.

They walked down the dark path Kasha had started on; Raervyn's eyes now looking for tell tale signs of ambush. Nothing else bothered them down the lane and soon it opened up into a small clearing with a cave.

"Old storage cave, perhaps?" Kasha surmised, peering around for tracks.

Illistyn picked up a discarded sign and held it up like a bard on stage. "Ye old dry goods," he said, waving his hand over the sign stating the very same thing. "Think we found our lair."

The company of the Black Sword went down into the storage cave and found the men of Faer'dran. The cave reeked of death and disease, with small piles of unrecognizable meat here and there, blood smeared over everything. Hands, feet, even some ears and noses were missing, their skin melted over the wounds to keep them from bleeding out. Of the hundred or so men taken, only twelve had died of their injuries, yet over half of them would never work again due to missing extremities. They had saved the town, yet clearly this didn't have anything to do with the lake, or the other disappearances.

# CHAPTER SIX
## *The Way to Alsir*

Albriar Vandersan watched as the group debated whether to take the ship back across the Dark Lake, or to ride around. It would be longer to ride, but they could hit two other towns on the way and see if they could pick up any other word of the mystery. Albriar was stoic and calm, with short brown hair and deep hazel eyes. He wore custom plate armor and fought with his father's sword, a great steel blade that would topple most men who tried to swing it. His father had trained him when he came of age, and always taught him that distractions in battle meant death. As such he never quipped or talked once fighting started, instead focusing on his opponent with a critical eye and tactical grace.

Kasha sighed, taking a stick and drawing in the dirt near the docks. "It would take five days of riding, with stops at Omnar and Olvar, to make it back to Lortil, yet only two days by ship." She paced after drawing and looked to each of the companions. "I'm for sailing back and riding to Alsir with haste. What do you all think?"

"I think we should ride around, just to make sure the problem doesn't stem from those towns," Illistyn said, his hands on his hips as he looked at the drawing.

"I say we sail as well," Raervyn said, sitting down on a crate and looking at her hands as if bored. "We have to get up there quick if they have a problem with disappearances."

"Albriar, it's up to you," Kasha said, turning towards him.

"Sail," he answered, keeping his answer short. It would avail nothing to elaborate to them as they wouldn't understand his decision. They all knew he wasn't fond of sailing and he could see the disappointment in Illistyn's eyes. They couldn't possibly know that Alsir was his home town. He had to get there quickly and find out if his family was alright. He was fine with coming here first, as he thought the wizard spire's proximity had something to do with this mystery, but now...

"There we have it, we'll sail with captain Lar when he departs back to Lortil, then grab horses north up the coast." Kasha walked away to go find Lar, leaving the other two to stare at Albriar.

"Well?" Illistyn asked, obviously stumped.

"Don't worry about it Lyss," Raervyn said, using her nickname for Illistyn that he hated. "You lost, get over it." She walked away as well, following Kasha and swinging her hips to make Illistyn stare.

Albriar shrugged, leaving Illistyn alone with his thoughts, and walked after her. He would never understand why those two hadn't gotten together yet. It was obvious to him that they both cared for each other, but they were stubborn to the core. *Rhan*, he thought to himself as he walked, *and they think they're so superior.*

*     *     *

The trip back to Lortil was uneventful, though Albriar swore he saw a hand poke up through the water on the morning of day two. The others laughed at him and patted him on the shoulder, until they saw more as they neared Lortil. Raervyn tried some magic, but nothing happened that he could see. The rest of the trip was made in silence, the rest of the crew of the *Dusk Runner* making the sign of Sithar of the Ravens whenever they neared the railings. It's funny how everyone pays death homage when his touch is near. Albriar didn't revere the god of death and nature, instead putting his faith in Lareth of the Blade, god of violence and war.

They paid for horses and headed up the jagged coast the next morning, the rising sun slowly burning off the fog as they rode. The lake looked eerie as they went, the rolling fog dancing across the pitch-black water. They couldn't make it to Alsir in one day, and so had to make camp off the road. This was the main reason for heavily guarded merchant caravans, as things came out after the pale sun set that most people never wanted to see. With just four of them they slept in shifts, with Illistyn and Raervyn keeping a bright light shining throughout the night. It was the one word of power that Illistyn knew for fire magic.

On Albriar's shift, with Raervyn, he could hear voices outside of the circle of light. They were taunting him and calling for him, sometimes in voices he recognized, oftentimes not. A couple of times a black hand, faded and gnarled, would try and reach through, but pull back once the light started burning it. These were the times he put his faith in his companions, and especially the Dal'rhan wizard that he had come to rely on. It was too bad she didn't realize she was that cherished. He might be quiet and often considered slow to the others, yet he saw things most people didn't.

Other than that, the only weird thing was the sound of children laughing. This happened during both shifts and sounded far away, yet persisted until dawn. Tired and weary, the company of the Black Sword continued on towards Alsir and in the late afternoon, arriving to closed gates.

"Who goes there?" a guard asked as they rode up and dismounted, stowing their riding cloaks and gear.

Kasha stepped forward; business as usual. It was one of the things they all agreed on, and why she was the leader. No one else wanted to deal with people. "We are sent from Lortil, hired by High Lord Garar Valstein to assess the disappearances around the Dark Lake."

"No problem here, thank you for your concern," the voice said.

"Did he just say thank you for your concern?" Illistyn asked, half drawing Ashryn.

Albriar put his hand on his friend's arm and shook his head. "Open the gate for the Company of the Black Sword," Albriar said, his deep voice echoing across the fields. It was the most he had said for a month.

"Albriar? Is that you?" the voice asked, a head now peaking over the wooden palisade. It was a man, maybe thirty summers and covered in freckles. "My gods it *is* you!" The head vanished and footsteps were heard across wooden decks. "Haren, open the gate it's Albriar!"

The gate opened slowly, enough time for his companions to openly stare at him and shake their heads. "What?" Albriar asked.

"You're from Alsir?" Kasha led her horse towards the opening gate shaking her head. "We've been traveling together for five years and this was your big secret?"

"Yeah, I figured he was raised by the dwarves in Oran," Illistyn said, laughing as he too walked into the small town.

Raervyn just patted him on the shoulder, like she was showing him pity, and followed, leaving the big man to stare at his feet. He never wanted to come back here after the death of his father. Some things were just too hard to face. *If you never lift the sword, then you'll never win the fight*, he said, repeating his father's mantra he learned during his training. It had saved him from many battles, when indecision had frozen his fellow soldiers and companions in the past.

He walked in after a couple of deep breaths and held his head high. He would meet this like any other challenge; with determination and courage.

# CHAPTER SEVEN
## *Laughter at Night*

Illistyn walked down the main street with a wary eye. He had a bad feeling about this little town when they arrived to closed gates in the middle of the morning. Even though people were afraid of the night and the darkness within it, they always threw open the gates as the sun came up; it was like a ritual. For this town to keep its gate closed all day caused his spine to tingle, and when that happened there was always trouble.

He was also trying to work through the startling revelation of Albriar growing up here. Not that there was anything wrong with that, but the big man just didn't act like the frontier fisherman type.

"You're being way to quiet Illistyn," Raervyn said, coming up behind him as he walked along, leading his horse. "What's wrong?"

"It's probably nothing... just a bad feeling, that's all."

"No sarcasm or witty remark?" Raervyn acted like she had been shot with an arrow, clutching her chest and staggering backwards. "Kasha, it's not Illistyn... It looks like him, but it cannot be!"

"Enough you two. Let's get to the tavern and stable the horses, then you can fool around all you want."

They found the stable and paid the man for the care of the horses, gathering in the tavern aptly named the Fishnet. Albriar got a table for them in the corner and signaled the serving girl.

"So you grew up here?" Raervyn asked after an uncomfortable silence stretched on between them all.

Albriar sighed, sliding his chair back and relaxing. "Yes, I did. My father was the Master-at-arms for the Lord here, and I trained under him for years. I left after my father died and never looked back."

"How did he pass?" Raervyn asked as the rest of the group gave her the look. "What? Like you all don't want to know?"

"It's fine. My father died from Root Fever. The local priest of Sithar of the Ravens tried to save him, but the rot had set in too quick for any sort of healing," Albriar said, drumming his fingers upon the oaken table. He looked down at his hands as he spoke, wringing them as if trying to work through something. "They think he caught it from a bad batch of stew. The town lost seven people that week."

The serving girl came over and Illistyn smiled up at her, then faltered. This was no young wench he was looking at, but a woman in her fiftieth winter at least. Once she took their order and left, he leaned over to Albriar. "Why are there no young ladies in this Inn?"

Albriar shrugged, back to his quiet old self.

Kasha must've overheard them, because she leaned in as well. "Come to think of it, I haven't seen any children since coming in the gate, and we usually attract them like flies to a picnic."

Illistyn's hair was standing up on his neck now. Something was horribly wrong here, yet all seemed fine to his eyes. *What are they hiding?* He got up and sauntered to the bar, leaning on it casually and met the gaze of the serving girl with his azure eyes. "Excuse me miss, could you do me a favor?"

"What do you need Lin'rhan?" she asked, leaning in and looking him over. She was almost licking her lips as she did.

"Could you find me a small child to act as a runner for an important message?" he asked nonchalantly. "I like to spend my coin on them so they feel good earning some money for the house too."

The woman blanched, then backed away. She had the look of someone that had been caught with her hand in the proverbial cookie jar. "I... I'll see what I can do. Very busy though, very busy." With that she disappeared out back.

Illistyn walked back to the table, his mind racing furiously over the possibilities, yet could think of none. He liked to be one step ahead, that way when everything went south, he was prepared, yet this confounded him. He sat and drank with the rest of the company, listening to the gossip around the Tavern. As night fell outside bells rang and people finished up their meals and drinks.

"Why is everyone leaving?" Raervyn asked, looking at them all saying good night at dusk.

"We don't take chances here, Dal'rhan. When that sun goes down, we shelter behind closed doors until the pale sun rises." This from an older man at the other side of the room as he stood up, ready to go. At the door to go outside he turned once more and fixed them all with a critical eye. "If I was you, I would get a room and stay in there for the night."

"What a lovely town you grew up in Albriar," Kasha said, laughing in her mug as she drank. She got up and walked to the bar to purchase two rooms for the night, paying extra for adjoining rooms. They took their drink with them, even ordering food to be brought up later.

It was in these rooms, hours later, that the sound of children giggling could be heard. The company was all in one room for now, going over what in the hells could be wrong with Alsir, when the children were heard. Illistyn looked out the window and saw small figures rushing around the streets, scurrying from house to house. "Guys, there are children out there. Maybe they know what's going on," he said as the group all nodded in quiet agreement.

"Levian," Raervyn said, using the word of power for air as she wove her hands in the gestures of a spell.

Illistyn felt the tendrils of wind wrap around him as he climbed out the window and gently floated to the ground. He waited for the others to join him and they padded softly after the children as the pale moon broke through the clouds. The children were all headed to the outskirts of the town, funneling through the streets and alleyways to a large fenced in plot of grass filled with upturned boats. At the head of each boat was a headstone, each stone carrying a single name with no dates. There had to be almost fifty boats.

"What the hells is this?" Raervyn asked, her eyes going wide.

"It seems like a graveyard," Kasha said, inspecting the boats.

Illistyn looked around and saw a path to the back walls and a door, wide enough for a wagon to pass through. By the looks of it the door seemed to lead towards the lake, yet there was no other traffic from the town to be seen coming this way. *Strange indeed,* he thought as a child laughed right near his ear, making him jump. The ghost children swarmed them, giggling and tugging on their clothes. At first playful, the tugs became aggressive and the laughter turned into growls. The companions struggled to break free of the angry spirits and both Illistyn and Raervyn hurled spells of light to turn the children away.

"Back to the tavern!" Kasha said, turning and running for the building.

Illistyn ran after them all, covering them with his light spell. He knew that they could do nothing else until dawn, yet the entire thing baffled him. *Why are the children haunting just the town and how has the town's priest not fixed this?*

# CHAPTER EIGHT
## *More Questions*

Raervyn sat cross-legged as Albriar and Kasha slept. As one of the Rhan, she didn't need to sleep. She simply would close her eyes and peacefully reflect on her life. Both sects of Rhan called this *the haze,* and it connected them all in a sort of dream place, though the Lin and Dal never crossed paths there. In this state she was fully aware of her surroundings, and when the others stirred, she was ready.

"Anyone else have strange dreams of little kids ripping your face off?" Kasha asked, rubbing her eyes and stretching.

"No, yet the events of last night did trouble my Haze," Illistyn admitted, smiling at Raervyn. "How was yours?"

Raervyn looked away, unable to admit that she tried to find his mind in the dream state again. It was something she had tried since the image of him drove her to distraction, yet his mind eluded hers. They had always been told that Lin'rhan and Dal'rhan couldn't haze together, yet she couldn't believe that. "It was fine, though those kids did creep me out."

"Well we're going to get answers today." Kasha strapped her armor on and sheathed her Sakar, heading for the door.

The others followed their leader, with Raervyn taking up the rear this time, watching everyone they passed for signs of betrayal; it was who she was. Of the four of them, Albriar seemed the most upset, as if the dead had troubled him more than usual. The people quieted as they passed, all talk ceasing in their wake with mumbled conversations picking up once they went by. Raervyn had seen this before, usually revolving around her heritage, yet this time they all were getting the look. The lord was coming down the street towards them, mounted with his guard beside him, weapons drawn. Raervyn loosened her shirt a bit and undid one of the ties, exposing her breasts a bit more, the crisp morning air making her shiver. It usually helped when they were approached by town guards, often distracting them long enough for her to get a spell off.

"Who leads this company?" the lord demanded, his tone smug and off putting. He thought he was better than them and flaunted it. Little did he know who he was toying with.

Albriar stepped forward, his large arm barring Kasha for once. "Lord Parin of Alsir, I presume?"

"Albriar? Is that truly you?" Lord Parin asked, looking to his guards. "I had heard you were in town, but surely you can't be in the company with these scoundrels."

"Have a care what you say about my companions, *lord*, we are chartered and tasked by the high lord himself." The threat hung in the air so thick that people backed away and went indoors. "Yet I am not the leader of this company. I only spoke out of turn to assure you we mean no harm here in Alsir." Albriar bowed to Kasha and waved her forward.

"That has to be the most I've heard you speak in public ever. Thank you," Kasha said quietly as she walked forward. "I am Kasha Anar of the Company of the Black Sword, and I request to talk privately.

"As long as it is a peaceful talk then you have my residence. Follow me and we shall break your fast with fine breads and talk awhile." He turned his horse without waiting for her answer and rode off towards the keep, his guards eyeing them with sneers and hands on weapons.

"Again, Albriar, I must say what a delight your little town is," Illistyn said, walking forward.

*       *       *

A short while later Raervyn was comfy in a plush chair, bread in one hand and a glass of wine in the other; Dal'rhan spiced wine to boot. She was sitting sideways, legs over the arm of the chair and chewing loudly. She couldn't believe that the lord lived like this among fishermen who barely had anything, yet such was the fate of the people under the rule of tyrants. The only one of the companions that seemed irritated by it was Albriar.

Illistyn sipped his own wine and cleared his throat. "So tell us Lord Parin, what is the story behind the graveyard at the end of town?"

The lord shifted in his own chair, a tell-tale nervous habit that he had been doing for the last twenty minutes as he stalled their questions. "We'll come to that in a minute. First, tell me what brings you to Alsir under the High Lord's decree?" He fumbled with the paper in his hands, the official notice from High Lord Valstein

Raervyn could've compelled him with magic, yet he would remember that and the law would come down on them like the wrath of the gods. To enspell a lord was treason in Llal'rin, and most other nations. "We came here to figure out what was causing people to disappear around the Dark Lake," Raervyn said, swallowing her bite of wine-soaked bread. "Come to think of it, most of those missing people were children, right Kasha?"

Never one for subtlety, Albriar could not keep quiet. He lurched to his feet, his face red with contained anger. "What have you done, Parin? Why are those poor children haunting the town?!" His voice brought the guard pouring into the room, yet Parin's raised hand forestalled them. One man, presumably the master-at-arms, stood sneering openly at Albriar.

"Easy Albriar, I have done nothing," he said, standing slowly and setting his drink down on the small table full of wine and bread. "I don't know what you speak of, but I fear this has something to do with your father? Maybe grief is still muddling your mind?"

Albriar surged forward, his hands balled into fists, yet stopped just inches from lord Parin's face, his breath steaming from the crisp air coming in from the open windows. "That graveyard is full of child-like spirits and you know about it." He stood there, silently daring the lord to order his guards to apprehend him.

The lord sighed, trembling visibly, yet his trained voice was steady. "Albriar, I will forgive this affront because you grew up in my house. Your father was the best Master-at-arms I've ever known and..." He looked at the man behind them and nodded his head slightly and the man backed away towards the door. Jaeren now holds that spot. "You trained with him am I right?" The lord stopped as Albriar seemed to stand taller, the presence in the room undeniably shifting towards violence.

"Albriar..." Kasha started to say, but stopped when the man turned towards her, his eyes closed.

"I know. I'll be outside." He walked out, yet stopped at the door as Jaeran stood in his way.

"Well well well. If it isn't little Albriar Vandersan." Jaeran might have said more, but he was pushed out and into the wall opposite the door with such force that he slid down to the floor in a heap, his mouth open and struggling for air.

Raervyn laughed openly, getting up and handing the wine to the lord who had no choice to take it or have it drop to the braided rug below as she walked away. "That would be our cue then. Thanks for the information or lack thereof Lord."

Kasha laughed as well, bowing mockingly and heading out behind Raervyn, grabbing Illistyn as she went. "We'll be in touch!"

# CHAPTER NINE
## *Fate of the Children*

Kasha walked down the packed earthen road of Alsir and tried to figure out what the lord's plan was. It wasn't extortion, or any other money scheme, yet something definitely felt off about the whole thing. "Do you guys think the town knows?"

Raervyn stopped and turned, a horrible look on her onyx face. "Oh my gods, how could they not know and do nothing about it?"

"I say we go and ask," Illistyn said, almost skipping down the street now. "This ought to be fun." He went right to the Fishnet tavern and threw open the doors, silencing the murmurs of the people, mainly traveling merchants, gathering for their morning meal.

"Illistyn, what are you doing?" Kasha asked as she came in right behind him. "Most of these people don't even live here."

"I happen to know of a lovely woman that knows a little something," he replied, walking towards the bar.

Kasha saw the serving girl from the other night and it all clicked. Her companion had been a little distracted and that only happened when he was turned down, or was confronted by a mystery. She had assumed it was the former, but now she wasn't so sure. The woman was at least in her fiftieth winter. Not unattractive, yet definitely not Illistyn's type.

Illistyn leaned on the bar, cradling his face in his hands like a bard, and waited for her to come over to him. "There you are missing. Say, you wouldn't happen to know about all the little ghost children, would you?"

"You folks need to leave." The gruff voice came from behind them all, the rising sun blocked out by the man's bulk in the doorway.

"And who would you be?" Raervyn asked, turning around with a swish of her long bone white hair.

"His name is Gronar," Albriar said, walking over to the man. "And he thinks he is the town's best fighter." Albriar smiled coldly at the man, cracking his knuckles.

"You all have been asking too many questions about this town and we don't appreciate it."

Kasha knew the tone in his voice; it was determination. This man wasn't just a bully, at least in this instance, but a force determined to stop them from finding something out. "Let's go, guys. This place just got a little too crowded for me," she said as she made a fist and cupped it in her other hand, the sign for retreat and regroup. She had come up with these signs as they adventured to communicate to each other without speaking. It came in handy with the places they have visited and the situations they found themselves in... like this one.

As they left, she pointed to the graveyard. "Let's go see the lake," she whispered to her companions. They marched towards the boat graveyard as the folk of Alsir came out of their homes and went about the day, ignoring their stares and whispered conversations. When they got to the wall, she pointed to the wall and back at Raervyn and let Dal'rhan do her thing.

"Forsar!" Raervyn said, invoking the word of air to smash the door to the lake open as she wove her hands. The path continued down a sandy cliff towards the beach, vacant and empty.

Kasha walked up to the edge of the lake and took a deep breath. Something happened here and she needed to see it. She wasn't as powerful as Raervyn and her air and fire spells, nor was she as inventive as Illistyn with his air and water magic. No, the one and only thing she could do was water, yet she was the best at it in the company. Kasha used it to heal and occasionally to dig into the ether, a special category of magic related to the flow of the world. She called upon that now, using the word of power for seeing whatever the water had seen. "Signalt!" she cried, as her hands went through the complex movements of the spell.

"Kasha, wait. That spell..." Raervyn stepped forward but Illistyn held her arm.

"No Raer, let her do this." Illistyn's voice was devoid of sarcasm for once, instead holding a tone of awe and even sadness. They both knew this spell could turn deadly to the caster.

Kasha stood there at the edge of the jet-black water lapping at her boots and opened her eyes. The edges of her vision were blurred but the scene immediately around her was crisp and clear. Lining the beach were all the boats, their paint new and shiny. Children sat in the boats, all dressed in their best clothes. Behind them on the sand was a Lin'rhan, his white hair hanging all the way down his back. *An archmage for sure*, Kasha thought as she watched his hands move in the intricate gestures of a spell.

"Timia'vren!" he shouted, using a word Kasha was unfamiliar with. The boats were pushed out onto the lake and they kept going, drawn on by some invisible force. The adults on the beach were celebrating something, maybe a springtime ritual, and were all cheering for their children to bring them luck.

Kasha walked on top of the water and followed the boats, intrigued by the scene unfolding around her. They went out at least five hundred yards before the archmage's spell ceased dragging the boats, the smaller children whimpering in fear at the waves licking at the boats edges. Kasha turned back to look at the adults, yet could not see anyone on the beach. She could hear the children exclaiming as well that they couldn't see their mothers and fathers, and panic soon resulted in the older children trying to swim back. The two oldest disappeared from view, and then the younger children started to openly cry.

Time flowed around her as her spell sped up, showing the children growing more desperate as the days dragged on. One day, two, and more children tried to swim home, their voices raw from screaming for help. Kasha watched in tears as the children around her slowly starved to death, unable to swim or even attempt because of their fear. As the last child died in the boats, the adults came into view on the sands, shouting and crying for the kids. There were men all around her exclaiming in shock as the boats appeared before them. As she walked back to the beach, she heard them accuse the archmage of casting the spell wrong, realizing that he was only supposed to move the kids forward in time a couple of hours to speed up the ritual...

"Oh Sithar of the Ravens, no. How could you do that to the children?" she wept, falling onto her knees and sobbing as her spell wore off.

"Easy Kasha, we're here," Illistyn said, as he helped her to her feet.

"I've never seen her break down like that," Raervyn said, unease in her usually steady voice.

"It was the parents," Kasha began. "They had an archmage use a time spell on the children out on the lake. Some sort of ritual."

"The ritual of the season," Albriar said, nodding in revelation. "I know of it. It's supposed to be a daylong thing that brings them luck in the fishing season."

"Well the archmage screwed it up and stranded them in time for months instead. Most of the children drowned, while the rest starved to death on the boats, unable to get back to shore." Her tears were still flowing down her cheek, but she stood straight and set her jaw. She knew what she had to do. Striding back into the graveyard, Kasha drew her Sakar and smiled. It was time to set these kids free.

# CHAPTER TEN
## *Free at Last*

Albriar Vandersan hadn't seen Kasha this angry in many years, and he had *never* seen the fierce woman break down like that over anything. He watched her stride towards the boat graveyard and braced himself for whatever may come. This was his hometown, but he recognized little from the people today. Something had changed them, and if what Kasha had seen was true, it would explain everything he had witnessed from the people he remembered from his youth.

"Albriar, Illistyn, guard the entrance to the graveyard. Raervyn, help them all you can," Kasha said, kneeling before the first boat. The thing was upside down and the paint was flaking off, yet she touched it reverently. "I'm going to need all the time you can give me." The leader of the Black Sword bowed her head and rested it against the old warped wood. "The townsfolk are going to try and stop me from doing this, I know that now, and you can't let them."

Albriar shifted nervously, sheathing his weapon. "I'll do my best Kasha, yet I won't kill the people I grew up around."

Kasha turned towards him; her eyes red from crying. "I know Albriar, but they are locked in grief over the deaths of their children and these spirits need to be released. You saw what they are turning into."

"It's alright Albriar," Illistyn said, sheathing Ashryn and picking up a piece of driftwood. "I'll be right beside you."

The big warrior laid his hand on the Lin'rhan's shoulder and smiled. He had been with these people for many years and they always supported each other, yet this somehow felt different. They may die here, and his friend was putting away the one thing that would give him an edge against the mob surely coming. "Thank you Illistyn." He found a large piece of driftwood as well and stood shoulder to shoulder with his companion, waiting for the people.

Sure enough, within two minutes of Kasha pouring water over the boats and sending their spirits to Sithar of the Raven's embrace, the townsfolk came down the street. They weren't walking or even striding towards them, they were rushing the graveyard in a panic, wielding pitchforks, clubs, and even knives in some cases. Master-at-arms Jaeran was in the fore of the group, his cohort of guards behind him and they had actual weapons out and murder in their eyes.

"I've got them Albriar," Raervyn said coming up behind the two. "You don't mind if they get hurt right?"

"Hurt? No. Just not permanently alright?" he said, shifting his feet for the onslaught.

"Loftiven!" Raervyn called out, using the word of power for one of the most powerful air spells she knew. Her hands swept aside and the wind picked up the men in the front, throwing them aside like broken branches in a storm. Their weapons clattered uselessly to the ground, the wind sweeping them away at her direction so that the townsfolk couldn't use them.

Albriar met the first wave of townsfolk with careful strokes, taking the hits on his armor where he knew he could, and trying to take them out as painlessly as he could. Clubs and rakes were getting through his defenses as the people went down, and soon he was down on one knee, his leg shattered within his armor from a large fisherman with a steel gaff. He took a hit on his shoulder as he pushed three women away, taking one out in the leg and throwing the other with his free hand. Raervyn was trying to deflect the people swarming around them, funneling them with both air and flame to the center where the two warriors were holding.

Illistyn wove his free hand through the gestures of a spell, shouting the word of power for water and air, forming an ice shield. His strokes with his makeshift weapon turned aside picks and oars as the people came at them, and at one point stepped in front of Albriar so that the big warrior could try and regain his footing.

"How close are you Kasha?" Raervyn asked, her constant use of magic draining her vitality quicker the more she used it. Magic was great, but the caster needed to rest between spells or they tired quickly. It was a testament to her power that she was still casting as well as she was.

"Almost there!" Kasha called out; her arms wreathed in water as the spirits gathered around her despite the pale sun overhead. They seemed to be talking to her, their mouths moving quickly, like they were begging.

"No!" a chorus of shouts came from the remaining people and they rushed the warriors again.

Albriar stood on his good leg, swinging his driftwood to keep them at bay. There were too many and if he tried to actually hit them, he may kill them at this point. Hit after hit broke through his defenses, trails of blood trickling down into his eyes. He knew it was almost over, yet he was faltering. "Hold the gate Illistyn," he said, as a farewell to his friend. He backed up, leaving the gap to his friend for a second.

Illistyn brought his shield to bear on his left and spun like a devil among the invaders, kicking and pushing them back. His clothes were torn and blood ran freely down his arms as well. "I've got it, take a breath," he called back, the confidence he usually had in his voice faltering.

Albriar ran back and lifted a boat. He took it and held it in front of him, taking a breath through bruised ribs and gathered his courage.

"Albriar, no..." Raervyn said, yet she could do no more, exhaustion bringing her to her knees.

Albriar smiled at her and shook his head. The fight had lasted awhile, and they were reaching the limits of their endurance. If they had their weapons it would've been a quick fight, but he had asked them for this. Now it was up to him to save them. He rushed the gate holding the boat and called out for Illistyn to move. The Lin'rhan stepped aside, trusting in his friend, and the boat slammed into the crowd, knocking them back and to the ground in a heap. He felt the clubs and fists of the people he grew up around, pummeling him in their anger and grief. His vision dimmed as he curled up into a ball, taking the hits without striking back. In the back of his mind he heard Kasha call out that it was done, and the pressure of bodies lifted. Albriar moved to stand, but his legs wouldn't work.

\*     \*     \*

Kasha was reeling. She had sent the children to Sithar of the Raven's embrace, but it was what they had told her that really floored her; the children had been roaming the lake looking for playmates. Whenever they found someone, they would drag them down until they stopped fighting then wait for them to turn into spirits as well. They hadn't had much luck, yet they kept trying. They had begged her not to send them away, pleaded to her to let them stay with their families... and that made it even worse for her to finish the spell and send them away.

She finished the spell as the crowd around Albriar dissipated. "Need some help old man?" Kasha said, walking over and lifting him up. She had to keep her emotions in check; it was bad enough that everyone saw her break down earlier.

Albriar stood slowly, favoring one leg. "Thanks. I take it it's all done. They're at rest now?"

Kasha wove a quick spell and uttered the word of power for healing, mending his leg. "Yes, now let's go see your old friend the lord... there are some things he has to answer for, and as a follower of Sithar of the Ravens, I *will* enforce them."

"What about them?" he asked, seeming quite talkative after the fight.

Kasha looked back at Illistyn and Raervyn, sitting on the ground and just holding each other. It was touch and go there for a bit, and Raervyn was exhausted. "Let's leave them to themselves for a bit. Who knows, maybe they'll get over themselves and tell each other how they feel," she said as she looked around at the people. The injured were being tended to and the others were sobbing quietly. They would all have to grieve now, but they would be better for it in the long run.

# EPILOGUE
## *Moving On*

The High Lord of the Llal'rin nation sat on his throne and drummed his fingers on the arm. His wife was asleep, thank the Three, and he was awaiting his guests with their report. Word had come in from the north that the Company of the Black Sword had caused some havoc in Alsir, but had shown his decree as proof that they were sanctioned. He couldn't wait to hear what had happened.

"Kasha Anar and the Company of the Black Sword milord," Falas announced with flair, stepping out of the way as the four came in.

"Welcome adventurers!" High Lord Valstein said, holding his cup up as a toast. He had been drinking since early this morning and with his wife asleep, there was no one to gainsay him. He was about to make some grand speech, but the attractive Dal'rhan wizard rolled a sack across the floor at him, the cinched cloth opening, spilling a trail of blood across the marble floor. "What is the meaning of this?" He looked at his royal guards, who didn't seem to notice the scene. They wouldn't act unless he was actually approached with weapons, or he called out for them.

Kasha stepped forward, not even bothering to bow. She grabbed the bottom of the cloth sack and lifted it, letting the head of the lord of Alsir roll out and thud on the floor. "I give you the cause of the problem, high lord," she said, kicking it towards him violently. The head slammed against the throne and bounced away, the lifeless eyes open and staring.

"What? How?" Garar Valstein was lost, confused, and a little worried.

The Lin'rhan walked up, drawing his black sword, the symbol of the infamous company and looked at the guards as they too drew their weapons, yet remained where they were. "You see, milord, this man had hired an archmage to use magic on the spring ritual last year and accidently killed all of the children in the town. That would be bad enough, yet it gets worse."

Kasha cleared her throat, then crossed her arms, menace dancing in her eyes. "He refused to lay the children to rest, instead letting the spirits of the children roam the town openly, degrading into evil abominations," the leader of the company said, her face hard as she told the story. "As I sent them to Sithar of the Ravens, they told me what they had done. They travelled the lake, taking other people in their constant loneliness and searching for playmates."

"But you killed the lord?" Garar asked, horror creeping into his guts. He knew that she must be a devout worshiper of Sithar of the Ravens, but he needed her to say it.

"Yes. In accordance with the tenants of Sithar of the Raven's faith, the one who deliberately keeps the dead from him shall be killed and sent to him for judgment." Kasha bowed then, and turned away, walking out without a second glance.

Soon, only the big man was left, the massive sword in his hand bouncing off his broad shoulders. He walked forward slowly, not saying a thing. He stopped at the foot of the throne and held out his hand, eyeing the guards as well; the look in his eyes promising violence if not sated.

"Of course! Falas be a good man and pay the reward." Garar watched his steward pay the man and held his breath until he was gone. Then he took a long swig of his drink and left. He needed to sleep and forget this day already. *That's what I get for hiring the Company of the Black sword.*

# THE JAWS OF THE DEEP
## *Elizabeth Carlyon*

The sound of clicks and scrapes echoed in the deep; metal tools and axes chipping away into oblivion. Cold and damp was the air, forcing the miners into sporadic coughing fits, their lungs worn raw from rock dust. The darkness was everywhere, the only light source being dim lanterns that hung every twenty or so metres along the tunnel's length. It was not enough to see full detail, but provided satisfactory illumination for an eye used to spending the daylight hours underground to make out the shapes in the rocks. There must have been fifty men in this tunnel alone, and it was one of dozens that spiraled in an intricate network underground. If a man, or sometimes even woman, could make do with cramped living conditions, never seeing the sun for most of the year, and living off the sparsest rations, they would have a job for life. The money was decent, but it was not a path chosen lightly. Those who had worked in the mines long enough were said to develop the vision of a bat, able to navigate purely by the traces of daylight that filtered from the surface, normally unseen to the average eye. Those who had actually put in the time usually retorted that bats are blind and fifty years of eye strain and a bad headache is nothing to be proud of.

Falling prey to the dull ache of fatigue, one of the workers leaned back against the rocks. Sheens of sweat littered his leather-beaten skin, tangling in the bristles of his broad chin. His frame was thick and muscular, as was that of all the hardy miners. His work clothes were torn and dust-covered, but not much more could be expected when one set of dungarees and two shirts were to last you the year. Small scars littered his forearms, many clearly from small nicks and scrapes whilst working. There was one however, on his left arm, that was a little larger, and more jagged than the rest. Lot didn't like to think about that particular scar too much.

Lot sighed deeply as he opened his soot-ridden eyes. A man could not rest for too long down here lest the chill begin to seep into your bones. The cold makes you sleepy and sluggish. You don't work as fast and don't earn as much pay.

Muscles groaning in protest, Lot raised his chisel to the sickly-yellowed rock face once more. He supposed his job could have been worse. Those poor souls who were forced to squeeze along narrow gullies and minuscule holes to access the ore were far worse off than he. Every day, Lot counted his blessings that his shoulders bulked out too far to fit in the smaller gaps. No, his present location would do, chipping away at his own precious patch of Green. Even now Lot wasn't sure what was so special about it, but he mined it as he was told. Of course, Green was not its official name, that was something big and impressive like *key-fanan* or something, but to he, the frozen bubbles were simply green. It made sense to call them what they were.

Slowly, the man chipped away another fragment. As he turned to cast it into the pail, something on its mottled surface caught the light. Holding the piece closer to the flame, Lot hunched over to examine it further. There, on the surface of the ore, he caught a glimmer of something different. Something he had not seen before. Streaked across the dark, solid green was a sheen of black; slick, like treacle. Pressing his fingertips to the substance, he felt a chill of dampness that left cold, darkened circles on the pads. An odd smell permeated the air also, sweet, like blackberries. Raising his hand to his nostrils, Lot ascertained that it was the substance. It reminded him of his childhood, and the tarts his mother would make from the berries he and his brother collected from the forest in the summer.

'Ow curious, thought Lot, turning back toward the passage wall. Sure enough, more of the sticky substance glistened upon the Green, trickling down onto the source rock beneath. It seemed to run in rivulets down the rock face, yet as far as Lot could tell there was no source; no holes or fissures could he find. It was if the rock itself was weeping blackened tears.

'Ow very curious indeed, he thought again. This was far beyond his knowledge.

'Oi!' came a call from a worker further up the passage, 'You done wastin' time yet? I ain't sufferin' the wrath of Gotterly coz' of the likes of you!'

Gotterly was the name of the warden. A pleasant chap... as long as you didn't have to speak to him more than once a week. He wasn't a fan of workers taking breaks. Why, there'd been rumours that he'd caught Little Tarry fallen asleep amidst a pile of rubble the other week. No one had heard from Little Tarry since.

'You seen this stuff Jeddy?' Lot replied to the darkened shape of his coworker, 'All black and gooey-like. It's comin' out of the wall!'

"Yer," grunted Jeddy in return. "Found some o' that stuff a couple days back, jus' dig round it. Don't seem to be anything monstrous."

"You sure? I was brought up on Wissnane an' over there they always listenin' to signs of nature. Never know when a storm is gonna whip up and steal your slippers." Lot eyed the substance again. It was strange. He didn't know what to make of it.

'More sure that it ain't worth gettin' docked pay for, which you're gonna get in a minute if you keep standin' there like a turp.'

Lot scratched his chin thoughtfully. If Jeddy had ignored it, things would probably be okay, but still...

"Ah think ahm gonna question ole warden 'bout it anyhow," he decided affirmatively. Procedure was procedure after all, and protocol said that they needed to report any unusual happenings to the warden immediately. As far as Lot was concerned, this was a mighty unusual happening indeed. Besides, he hadn't been in Gotterly's bad books *too* much lately...

"Suit yourself," shrugged Jeddy, then slipped back into the steady silence of hammering at the rock face.

Decision made, Lot laid down his tools, then began to make his way up the winding passage toward the main cavern. His fellow miners eyed him with a judging curiosity as he passed, but Lot did not dally to tell them his purpose. His mind was made up now.

Eventually the passage came to an end, widening out into a larger cavern where Green was sorted into barrels to be hoisted to the surface. The sound of the cavern reached Lot's ears long before he could see it, and the sight was as impressive as the noise. Natural light filtered down through a small opening many feet above his head. Heavy ropes snaked down through that hole, made for carrying materials quickly and efficiently out to the surface. Thankfully the humans took a slightly easier route, albeit longer. The walls of the cavern were banded with different shades of rock. Holes dotted the different layers, entrances to tunnels that had long since been stripped bare and abandoned. A visual history of man's exploitation of the area. Long had it been since the miners had hammered away at the top, and it would be longer still until they stood on the true bedrock beneath. Layers of Green still lay dormant beneath their feet.

Lot cast his gaze around the men hauling buckets of green to and fro into the barrels. The warden should be somewhere in the middle, barking commands to speed up the slow-goers. No sooner had he begun his search when he spotted the man, clad in his traditional oversized suit, studded with large rusted bronze buttons along the opening of the blazer. Once upon a time, the suit had probably been a prized purchase, but years of surrounding himself with grime and dust had worn it rugged, with patches and fraying fabric along the seams. Even so, it was still better than anything Lot had ever owned.

Lot walked up to greet the warden, suddenly unsure if he had made the right decision. The warden was a short man, but his bite could be brutal, and no one could say he hadn't earned his right to it.

'Mr Gotterly, sir...' Lot said hesitantly. The short man spun instantly, and fixed him with beady narrow eyes. He glanced at the dirty red tie around Lot's neck that marked him as a worker of the seventh tunnel, then fixed him hard in the eyes.

"Whaddya think yer doin' 'ere? Ge' back down yer 'ole afore ah come 'n make yer!"

"Beggin' yuh p-pardon sir," Lot stammered, adding in a slight bow, "But some intrestin' stuff's just come to me attention down below." Lot held out the blackened Green for the warden to examine, "You always been a-sayin' 'at we should report t' you if we spot 'nythin' perculiar."

Violently, the warden snatched the Green from his hand and scowled closely. He turned the rock over, held it up to his eyes, then turned it over again, before throwing it into a nearby pail.

"This stuff's been poppin' up all over the place pas' few days. Noh'in teh concern yerself with. Jus' dig round it," grunted the warden, before turning to storm toward a pair of young boys attempting to get a pulley rope attached to a newly filled barrel... and failing. Gotterly's angry barks took their place once more, blending with the sea of work tools and heaving.

Huh, Lot thought to himself as he turned to trudge back to his work spot. He really had thought he was doing a right thing, bringing the Green to Gotterly's attention but... If neither Jeddy nor the warden were worried about the black substance, then it really must be nothing at all.

Even as the words passed through his mind, a rumble emanated from deep with the tunnel ahead. Lot paused, then stared. A second rumble, followed by the startled shouts of workers. All sounds of work within the cavern stilled.

"Cave in!" came an urgent cry from over his shoulder, echoed by the frantic screams of workers within the tunnel. Clouds of dust billowed out of the entrance way, followed by several loud booms. People nearby dropped their tools, then began to flee. Workers raced out of the tunnel.

"All right! Calm yerselves'! The danger's in th' seven, not 'ere!" howled Gottery over the din, but his words did not seem too successful. Cave-ins were like the boogieman to a miner, and struck the same amount of terror. The warden was right though, Lot ascertained. Despite the chaos and shudders sweeping through the cavern, the ceiling above them seemed to be secure. Beams and bolts built and reinforced over the decades saw to that. No, the danger was only to those poor souls trapped at the bottom of tunnel number seven.

*Jeddy!* Lot thought with a start. He had left him alone down there. It was a miner's unspoken responsibility to take care of your neighbor. Ain't nobody else gonna look out for you. What if he was stuck? Lot had to get to him.

Lot plunged forward toward the tunnel entrance as the last of the workers filed out. Jeddy's face was not among them. He kept going, down into the tunnel depth.

Visibility in the tunnel was zero. Whatever light the lanterns had given was blocked out by a thick haze, if any of them were even still lit and not lying broken on the floor. The air also felt hot and heavy, as if he was walking into a dense soup. With every breath, the air slid down his throat, smothering and tightening around his lungs until it was difficult to breathe. Lot clutched at his chest as he felt pain constrict around his ribcage. He wheezed heavily, then coughed. It felt like agony, but he had to keep going.

Closing his eyes to protect them from the dust, he slowly moved forward, arms feeling forward for the rock walls ahead of him.Every step felt like ten.

Gradually, a light began to form behind Lot's eyelids. There must be a lantern still lit somewhere, he assumed. With the light, the air became hotter and thicker, more like syrup than soup. It choked him, forcing his limbs to a halt. He couldn't go on... but he had to. He had to save Jeddy.

Lot's eyes flickered open briefly, then was taken by surprise. The light was not from a lantern, for it was sickly pale green in colour and much too bright to be the product of a single measly flame. His ears also began to pick up a slow rhythmic sound. A pulse, steady and constant, growing louder, almost like... footsteps.

Lot gagged once more, though this time from fear. Nothing human could make a footstep that sounded like that. It was too large... too weighty...

Adrenaline burst through his system, Lot managed to spark some last dregs of strength to life. Enough to turn and flee from the cave and whatever beast might be coming up from it's depths. Jeddy would have to fend for himself.

Lot burst back out into the main cavern, then collapsed onto all fours, dry heaving as semi-breathable air flooded back into his lungs. His vision swam before his eyes, but was slowly reforming.

When he could manage, Lot turned to look at the tunnel entrance. He almost wished he hadn't. The light was burning now, as if the fires of the very sun had been captured underground. It hurt Lot's eyes. He scrambled backwards, almost knocking into the feet of a young worker boy who too, was enraptured by the strange light pouring out of the tunnel. In fact, everyone in the cavern who remained was deathly still and silent. Even Gotterly, who was normally not phased by anything, had been rendered into a statue-like stance. Whatever was happening, they were all in this together.

All of a sudden, the light disappeared as an emerald leg stepped from the shadows; a sturdy, slender figure. Bands of moss, emerald and ivy swirled across its skin in a hypnotic storm, spiraling upwards and upwards to meet a mane of swishing vines. It was a woman, but not. Her face held no nose, no eyebrows, no cheekbones, only smooth contours, broken only by a slit-like mouth and two deep, onyx eyes. It seemed as if she had been carved from the rock to ultimate perfection. With the sight of her, Lot almost forgot his terror. She was a living embodiment of Green. For the first time, he was casting his eyes upon a specimen that deserved not the lowly, practical name.

"Kiavernan," he greeted humbly, swiftly dropping into a low bow. He thought he was beginning to understand who she might be, and why she was here. There were tales from Wissnane that told of gods, once clouds of energy, who had grown tired of an immortal life of roaming. Having seen everything there was to see, they settled down an unclaimed part of the world, as forests, lakes, or...

rock. Suddenly Lot began to wonder where exactly the Green that they mined came from. The thought made him feel sick.

"Rise, foolish mortal," snapped the figure. Immediately Lot rose to his feet, feeling rather bashful. If this was a god, how was one supposed to act? He was just a simple man, with a simple life, he wanted nothing to do with gods or mystics.

"Ahm sorry, ma'am," he mumbled.

"Whaddya want?!" a frantic miner cried from somewhere. Lot did not turn to see who had dared to be so forthright in the presence of such a being. Fiercely the stone-woman's gaze locked to one side, burning into the insolent miner's soul.

"Puny mortals," she spat, "You have no idea what you have awoken from below. We had a bargain. You would dig no further than the silver bed, and you would heed any signs to stop. You have not listened. For your insolence you dig toward your doom."

"And wha' signs would these be?" grumbled the warden as he pushed his way in front of Lot. "Yer all very intimidatin' an' all, but wha'ssa bunch a' rocks gonna do to us?" The ground seemed to groan as the stone-woman slid her eyes toward the warden. In her presence he seemed less like a tyrant, and more like a crumpled old man that would disintegrate with one flick. It made Lot shiver to think that he must seem the same.

"Things live in these 'rocks', Mister Gotterly," she hissed, but her breath was that of wind whistling through fractures in the walls. "Things older and more powerful than picks, spades and a cruel tongue. They've torn the world apart once before and they are just waiting for the opportunity to do it again. Do you wish to cause an apocalypse, Mister Gotterly? I order you to leave, withdraw your tools and flee, before it is too late."

The warden bit his tongue, watching resentfully as the stone-woman stepped backward and melted into the rock. Her words rang emptily throughout the cavern, even long after the sound of them had ceased. The men stood alone, cold and shivering. Not a soul dared to say a word. Instead, their eyes stared balefully at the rocks which, to their minds, whispered and cackled like conspiring demons. All trembled to meet their gnashing teeth.

A figure stumbled forth from the darkened tunnel, grasping clumsily against the wall for support. Trails of blood streaked from his hands, forming a thick soup with the dirt and grime of his skin. His clothes were torn and tattered.

"Jeddy!" Lot cried once more, rushing forward to give his fellow minor support. "Thank Dae you're alive!"

The cavern seemed to tremble at Lot's use of the word 'Dae', but he ignored it. His friend was more important.

With a tremendous sigh of relief, Jeddy pushed his weight onto Lot's shoulder. Close up, Lot could just about make out the signs of an angry black bruise brewing above his left eye.

"Thank *Dae* indeed," grumbled Jeddy, a hint of spite in his tone. Later on that day he would tell Lot of how he raced to escape the falling boulders, only to be slammed viciously to one side by a strange, green woman, but for now he simply rested.

"Alrigh'!" barked the warden suddenly, clapping his hands. "Tha's enough dallyin'! Ge' back teh werk yer pathetic slackers!"

Many miners jostled at the command, jumping over one another to reach their weapons of shovels and picks. Yet their minds were confused. Some, upon collecting their tools paused, staring uncertainly at the ore veins. Others simply cast their eyes to the ground. The warden's face crumpled in bitter irritation.

"Well?" he snarled, voice echoing in the empty space, "Whaddya waitin' for?"

Lot bridled at the hidden imperative.

"You 'erd what the lady said," he reminded the warden bravely. What remaining eyes that were still staring turned away.

Jeddy tensed at his side. The warden snarled like an animal as he spun to face Lot, shoulders bunched in warning.

"Am not goin' teh let some stoopid bit a' rock destroy me career. If she comes at us again, I'll smelt the bitch." The tendons in the warden's neck strained bright red. It wouldn't be long before things erupted. Lot held his ground. Mr Gotterly had been scary earlier, but the green woman was scarier on all accounts.

"Nay disrespect sir, but ah grew up on Wissnane. There's some mighty strange things goin' on that island, ah tell you, but we learnt to always listen to the warnin's from Dae-creatures. Dae-creatures know far better than man what goes on in t' world."

"Dae-creatures," the warden spat, "I don' give a flyin' monkey's about where you grew up. This is our world and am not lettin' some freaky beings tell me wha' to do.

'Now, yeh're gonna take Jedresh 'ere back up above so someone can tend to 'im. Then yeh're gonna get yehr backside back down 'ere and carry on minin', you 'ear me Lothien?"

Lot nodded somberly, but was firmly unfazed by the warden's threats.

"Loud n' clear boss," he assured the warden. "Ah'll take Jeddy up top right n' proper, but ah won't be a'comin' back down. Ah know when t' heed a warnin'."

The warden's greedy mouth gawped like a goldfish as he processed Lot's words. Never had he heard such insolence spewing from an inferior's mouth. The fury of it turned his beady face ten shades darker until it bore more similarities to a char-grilled beetroot than human skin.

Taking no notice of the little man's wrath, Lot began to waltz toward the exit... or at least he would have had his partner not been such a deadweight. Instead, Lot's pace was reduced to a confident shuffle. Jeddy was in a shocked state of stupor, his legs only moving by instinct. He was positive that one of these days Lot's impetuousness would be the end of him.

*     *     *

For three whole days, Lot remained above ground. He was supposed to be preparing for the trek back across the island to the northern farming towns. Since he refused to dig any further in Kiamore, ole Gotterly had revoked his rights as a miner, leaving him with neither a job nor lodging in the miners' village. Lot was only barely bothered. Sure, he had just lost his livelihood, but he was certain there would be a little cottage in the north with a flock of sheep waiting for him. Who knows, maybe someday he would even get back to Wissnane. Folk were certainly kinder there. Darn him for deciding to leave and see the world in the first place!

Truth be told, he had wanted to start his trek the very day he left the mine, but it had been late and he had needed time to pack. There was also Jeddy. What the doctor had thought was a broken rib in the beginning had turned into something much graver. A black rash, tracing the pattern of his veins, had broken out on his right hand, spreading slowly upward toward his shoulder. It grew worse every day, and no one knew the cause of it. The doctor had tried herbal compresses, bleeding and some odd tablets that Lot could not pronounce the name of, but nothing helped. It seemed the disease was beyond any of the resources kept on Nithos, perhaps even in the whole of Nicheitah. Lot didn't know what was going to become of Jeddy, but he felt it was only right he be there to say goodbye, if it was to be so. Jeddy had worked by his side for four of the five years that Lot had been in the mines. He owed him that much.

Lot decided to make use of himself to the nurses, whilst he was still there. He fetched water from the well and served food to the patients that were conscious. He even added his own touch of freshly picked wild mushrooms to the otherwise tasteless standard-issue broth, much to the delight of the nurses. They asked him where he had found them, but admitted straight out that they would never have the time to hike out to the mountain grove themselves. When he was not needed, he sat by Jeddy's side, keeping an eye open to the world outside.

No one had heeded the warnings of Kiavernan. The following day, Lot watched as a group of men ran screaming out of the mine. Their clothes were dripping with sweat and vicious boils had bubbled like angry mites across their skin. The nurses tried to ease their pain, but the men writhed deep into the night, shrieking that there was fire in their brains, begging for it to be put out. One man, Elyan, was one of the few who seemed to keep his wits about him. Lot had spoken to him to ask what had happened. He told him that they had been digging in the far reaches of the third tunnel when the very air had turned against them. Hot as a furnace it had grown, Elyan said, and scalded their skin. The few who made it out were not the only ones that had been affected. Elyan had watched his neighbour stumble down a low slope, only to find himself unable to stand again as his skin melted and fused to the rock. The wailing cries of dying men in agony would haunt him for the rest of time.

At the crack of dawn, one of the overseers marched into the sickbay. He relayed a report from Gotterly that the temperatures had returned to normal in the tunnel. Those that were able to stand and make use of their arms were expected back to work come morning rounds. The nurses protested, saying that the men needed more time to recover, that sending them down too early would only guarantee their return to the sick ward in an even worse condition, but their pleas fell on deaf ears. It was all they could do to provide the men with extra bandages for their sores, then send them on their way.

That night, as Lot slumbered by Jeddy's bedside, he was awoken by the light clanging of something metallic. It creaked and clunked, almost like the sound his pail used to make as he carried it back and forth through the mines. Lot blinked his eyes open, then straightened a little on his stool. It was not completely dark inside the sick ward for, although there was no moonlight and precious few windows, one of the nurses had left a lantern burning close to the doorway. Lot let his eyes adjust to the dim orange light, then looked groggily about the room.    He    reached    his    hand instinctively to the back of his neck, for it hurt something fierce after sleeping in an unusual position, then froze. Not five feet away from him, at the foot of what had been Elyan's bed, stood a tall, pale figure, it's clothing ragged and torn, as if it had been shredded by the talons of some dreadful beast. The figure swayed a little, back and forth and, as it did, it caused something in his hand to sway. A miner's bucket, just as Lot had thought he heard.

Lot cleared his throat.

"'Scuz' me?" he asked, "If you be lookin' fer nurses, ahm, you can wait by t' office."

The figure did not move. In fact, it did not show any signs that it had even knew it had been spoken to. It just stood there. The metal bucket creaked.

Unsettled, Lot dragged himself to his feet. He wondered what more had happened down in the mine during the day. Was this another victim of tunnel three? Whoever it was, they were probably in a state of shock and surely were in need of help.

It wasn't until Lot was almost next to the figure, when he was close enough to reach out and touch, that he noticed that the air was thick with the sickly-sweet smell of blackberries.

A bead of cold sweat rolled down Lot's spine. He peered closely at the tears in the man's clothing, for he was determined to not think of the figure as anything but a man now, then shivered at what he saw. It appeared that this man, just like the workers of tunnel three, had suffered extreme burns, but instead of red scars, his skin boiled with a black, weeping substance that shimmered when it caught the light. Most of his hair had been scorched right off his head and, here too, he was covered in oozing pustules of the vile fluid. Lot was certain that this was the same substance he had found on the Green down in the mines. He remembered Kiavernan's warning. What if this was the great evil she had been talking about? Maybe it had already broken through and had taken the form of one of the worker's? He had to know more.

Moving with cautious footsteps, for he was now afraid of what would happen should he wake this creature from its stupor, Lot tried to get into a better position to take a look at the thing's face. Despite intensive scarring and rivulets of Black that ran down his face, it was still possible to make out the identifiable features of an individual. Lot himself perhaps stood a greater chance of recognising the man more than anyone, for he had seen him after his most recent scarring and spotted familiarity immediately in the forced downward twisting of the left side of his mouth. However, the last time Lot had seen him, Elyan had been still full of life, and character, despite his suffering. This man's eyes were cold, glazed and white, as if Lot were staring at a risen corpse.

Lot staggered back in shock.

The Elyan-creature cast its stone-white glare upon him. The crumpled skin of its lips cracked as it attempted to form words. Black puss s seeped out.

"Gotterly must be stopped, or this sickness will spread." The voice that came out was harsh and raspy, as if even the vocal cords had been scorched and shriveled. The sound grated like nails against slate.

"I dun know how t' do tha'!" cried Lot, but the creature did not care. Message delivered, it's skin began to bubble ferociously. Flesh peeled away from sinew, revealing nothing but the black liquid that writhed and reeled inside its human host. The fluid twisted and overflowed, consuming all that remained of Elyan, until there was nothing left but a pile of sticky, sodden rags, and a large viscous pool of shimmering black.

Lot jumped up onto the nearest bed which, thankfully, was empty. The pool was spreading, and he did not want to know what would happen should the black substance touch him. It had not harmed him down in the mine, but that had only been a small amount and had not looked so... alive. The fluid gurgled and bubbled away on the floor of the ward.

As the hours passed, the substance gradually began to seep away, disappearing into the cement. By the time the nurse returned to do her routine check on the patients, there was nothing left beside rags, and a rather worked up Lot who had not yet dared to clamber down from his perch of safety.

The morning brought more reports of possessed men, or 'ghouls' as the workers were calling them, for the horrible affliction seemed to only occur to men who seemed certain to die. The workers said that terrible spirits were possessing the bodies of fallen men, and forcing them to walk once more. In some cases the ghouls went wild and attacked the workers, causing a disruption to the work in the tunnels. Others said the ghouls simply stood there, staring into the depths of the mine, babbling in an incoherent tongue.

Lot was terrified, but a course of action did not strike him until mid-afternoon. The sick ward was full again, with injuries ranging from burns, to broken bones and pick-axe wounds. But there was one bed that had suddenly become vacant.

Jeddy had passed away.

Lot did not see when it happened, he had been out collecting wildflowers to help sweeten the stench of the sick men. He had not expected it to happen quite so quickly, and neither had the nurses. When he returned, they informed him that he had suddenly burst into a fit of convulsions, and no form of sedative they knew had been able to help. When the tremors finally subsided, and Jeddy lay still once more, his heart had stopped beating.

Lot stared at the motionless corpse of his colleague, his friend. The black rash had spread across his entire face and chest, which lay exposed now after the nurses last minute efforts to save him. He supposed that he should feel sorrow. This man had worked alongside him for years. They had shared light and food and water. He was almost like a brother. But Lot did not feel sorrow. Actually, he felt relieved. Jeddy had been the last thing tying him to this place. Now that he was gone, Lot could go too. A niggling thought at the back of his head also warned him to leave as fast as he could before Jeddy decided to come back.

Free from his burden, Lot marched back to his barracks, picked up his small sack, collected some provisions from the canteen, then made his way toward the edge of the mining village. Lot had two routes he could take. One was a long route, winding around the eastern shoreline until he reached the port of Nithwae. From there he could either try to take a boat to Krokith, or continue his hike northward to Kiawae, where he would stand a better chance of finding a boat headed directly to Wissnane. He had now decided that it would be good to see if it was possible to get home first, before settling anywhere too close to the mine. His other option would take him up through the mountains. The path was reputedly well-marked, but the weather was cold, the trails were narrow, and rain could make for slippery footing. If all went well, he could maybe save two or three days and head straight for Kiawae... but a delay could cost him a week of slow trudging in treacherous conditions.

As Lot left the last of the houses behind him, he fixed his eye on the distant rocky shoreline. Through the clouds he thought he could see traces of a faint sun attempting to peek through, as if illuminating the way. Aside from leaving the mines behind him, Lot was in no real hurry. Taking a leisurely pace along the coast would be affordable, and perhaps even enjoyable.

Decision made, Lot began to climb the path that would take him up above the far reaches of the mine, then descend toward the sea. It felt so good to get away. He supposed he should be a little worried about how he was going to provide for himself in the future, but he wasn't. His mind was already back in Wissnane, remembering the lush green forests that spanned for miles, rich with all kinds of wildlife. Beside the odd copse of trees, the land here was dry and bare. Occasionally, one could catch a glimpse of an eagle, soaring around the mountain tops above the mine, but other than that the place felt lifeless. Even the very name of the area 'Nithos', meant 'barren' in the language of the Dae.

Thinking about nature made Lot remember that it was already early spring. If he was lucky, maybe he would even be able to make it back to Wissnane in time for the festival of the Sun. The thought brought warmth to his heart. It was one of the biggest festivals in the country. Children would make flutes out of willow branches, loved ones would sing songs together and there would be dancing and ceremonies around the running streams. Lot thought of his mother and wondered how she would feel to see him again. She had approved of his decision to travel south, to try to make a life on the mainland, but he knew she must miss him dearly. She used to send him parcels of dried fruits and treats once a month and, in return, he posted her drawings once a month, to keep in touch and let her know he was fine. If he'd known how to write he would have sent words instead, but the images felt like a good substitute. That was until his paper ran out. He'd tried to order new, but for some reason it never arrived. With that his communications slowed to a halt. The parcels of treats continued to arrive for several months but, after a while, they too stopped coming. He wondered if his mother thought something had happened to him. It would be good to be able to let her know in person that he never stopped caring.

A slight tremor rumbled up from the earth below. Lot paused mid-footstep, then looked at the ground. The small pieces of dirt and stone scattered along the path were dancing in a light, jittery, jig. Lot placed his foot fully down. He glanced backward toward the village.

At first, all sounded normal, just the occasional communicative shout, or the heave of machinery; then the tremors grew stronger; then screams began.

Soon, Lot could not focus on the miners anymore, for his own situation was growing gravely perilous. The ground was shuddering so violently that it was impossible to move in s straight line and very difficult to keep himself from tumbling down. It was as if the earth itself was having a seizure which, in a way, it was. Lot carried on forward as best as he could. The only thing he could do was try to get as far away from the mine as possible, only then could he be safe.

A rock shifted underneath Lot's foot, sending him crashing to the ground at an awkward angle. The rough surface grated his shoulder upon impact. Lot cried out in pain, as he tried to right himself. Fortunately, it seemed it was just a scratch, for he was still in control of all his limbs, but that didn't stop it from smarting something fierce.

The sounds of panic continued in the distance.

A large crack sounded from somewhere above Lot's head.

Lot looked up. A carriage-load of debris had become dislodged on the mountain side and was now tumbling at break-neck speed toward him.

No time to stand, Lot flung himself into a frantic sideways roll in the hopes he would avoid the worst of the impact. A small stone scuffed his upper thigh, adding to the scrapes, but other than that, he was unharmed.

Lot peeked up from between his hands. The landslide had finished, but there would undoubtedly be more. He wondered if there was a safer place for him to hide. Should he try to outrun the quake and get further around the shore? Should he head back to town? One glance back in that direction told him that several of the buildings seemed to be suffering from various degrees of collapse. None of the structures were built to withstand an earthquake of this magnitude.

As Lot was mulling his choices over in his head, he spotted something that made his blood run cold. A crack was forming in the ground, directly underneath where he was now lying. It was small, barely visible underneath the dust of the dry road, but it was undeniably present. It was also getting wider.

Stumbling frantically to his feet, Lot broke into a staggered sprint up the path. It was not easy, for the tremors confused his sense of balance and caused him to misplace his footing, but he managed to stay, for the most part, upright. However, when he glanced behind him, he saw that the crack had widened to the width of a small branch, and it was heading right towards him.

Lot put on a burst of speed. He could hear the ground tearing apart now and it sounded like all the demons of the underworld were waking up. Pain and fatigue seared through his limbs as the path took an upward turn, but he would not let that slow him. Adrenaline fueled him to push on.

Suddenly, he felt the rock beneath his right foot shift so that it was several centimetres lower than the left. In a blind panic, he veered off from the path, not daring to look at what was following him. Maybe the crack was to catch people trying to escape by the obvious route out of the village. In that case the path was doomed.

The ground to the side was more treacherous, formed from uneven outcrops of granite and boulders that sloped down towards the sea. It was a frantic scramble for Lot to keep up a faster pace and he was not sure what would happen if he reached the cliffs only to find the crack was still chasing him. He would throw himself into the water if he had to. Anything to save himself from falling back down into the darkness that he had already sacrificed so much of his life to.

Lot glanced over his shoulder. His heart sank with the bitter tang of desperation as he saw his fears confirmed true. The crack *had* changed direction and it traced a perfect line from the path, across all of the boulders he had scrambled across. It was following him, charging forward with full speed. It was as if the very jaws of the deep were widening, preparing to swallow him whole.

Lot gulped. The cliffs were coming up fast and, now he was close, they felt a Lot higher than he had imagined. The roar of the sea crashing against the jagged rocks below made an impressive sound. The hiss of the foam joined the rumble of the quake in a natural symphony of horror. Twenty paces and he would reach the edge. Fifteen. Ten... nine... eight... Lot felt his legs begin to slow. Seven... six... he had learned how to swim as a boy, but he had not practiced in years, what if his body simply sank like lead to the bottom of the ocean? Or what if he diced himself against the rocks? Five... four... three...

His feet came to a halt less than two steps from the edge. He could not do it. He could not voluntarily throw himself forward. Closing his eyes, he spread his arms out wide and waited for the crack to catch up behind him.

The ground grew silent. Wind whipped through Lot's clothes. Sea spray from the waves below splashed his face. His heart pounded in his chest and... nothing happened. No tremor shook him over the edge. The rocks beneath his feet stayed firm and undivided. The earth was still.

Several moments passed as Lot breathed in the moment, not quite sure to make of it all. He should, by several means, be dead, but he was not. Why?

Opening his eyes, Lot appreciated once more the feeling of the weak sun on his face. The light through the clouds was mottled and, almost mystical. He imagined that the eyes of a thousand gods were staring down at them, watching events unfold. Perhaps one of them had saved his life.

Slowly, Lot turned around, then all of his thoughts of salvation vanished. The crack had stopped spreading... at a grand distance of less than two feet away from Lot's own. In fact, if he looked closely, he thought he could make out a small hairline fracture running from the edge of the opening, and finishing directly underneath him. The chasm it had opened before him was huge; an open, black wound in the landscape. Come down, it said, come back into the dark. Limbs shaking, Lot gingerly began to tiptoe around the edge of the crevice, hoping to make it to safer ground, when up from the depths rose a sound that stopped him in his tracks.

*Dear miner...*

The voice was soft, deep and laced with strong will. It did not belong to any human that he knew, however he had heard it once before. It was the voice of the Green Lady. She was talking to him.

Once again, Lot stared at the crevice in horror. Had the Daewoman been the cause of this? And had she really been hunting *him*? He wanted nothing to do with this. It was not his fault that Gotterly had gone too far. Could the Green Lady not allow even a single soul to escape?

"'Ah stopped when you told us to!" he shouted down into the darkness. His voice echoed from the rock face. "Please lemme go!"

No one answered.

Well, he thought to himself, supposing that was that. After long years of toil, he'd finally cracked the bucket. Perhaps this whole damn charade had been in his head from the beginning? Maybe there had been no green woman, or strange disease, or ghoul, just one barmy old badger who was better being cast off to live as a hermit than relied on as a worker. It would certainly explain other people's irritation.

Even as he thought this, his eyes picked out something peculiar within the crack. There was a staircase. Not a regular staircase, as one might find in a manor house or castle, but a sloping, fragmented array of outcrops and boulders that zigzagged from side to side until it vanished into the darkness. It certainly didn't look like the sheer divide that he would have expected a quake to result in, and he was unsure as to the meaning.

*Come...* beckoned the voice from somewhere down below, eradicating any doubts in his mind that he had misheard it the first time.

Lot bridled. "Ah, no, a bit of earth shakin' an' spooky voices, ain't persuadin' me t' go down there! Ahm leavin', now!"

In response to his words, a soft green light began to glow in the depths. Lot's heart sunk. He wanted to believe that he was crazy, but deep in his heart he knew that his senses were telling the truth. If he didn't go down, then she, it, was going to come up here. It was she who had caused the rupture in the ground and maybe even her who had sent the ghoul to him. The green lady would follow him wherever he went, for the rest of his life, until he answered her call. People here might not respect the creatures of the Dae, but Lot's upbringing had taught him better. It was figures like the Green Lady that had helped to shape the world as it was today. They had fought wars before mankind ever evolved on this plane, all to shape the way for some future that only that knew the end of. They played a hand in creating the trees, the flowers, the animals, the streams... and they could tear it all down again, should they desire. For some reason, he, Lothien of Wissnane, had caught the attention of one of these beings. He was duty bound to find out why. Heart leaping into his mouth with every thud, Lot began to descend.

The climb itself was relatively simple. The rocks were the perfect size to step between and, if he came across any trouble or larger gaps, something would miraculously shift to make up the space. The glow faded when he was part way down, but he did not need it. He was used to working in extreme conditions and the light that filtered down from the sky above was more than enough. What made it difficult however, was the unnatural heat that swarmed up from the base of the crevice. It made the rocks toward the surface warm to the touch, which, pleasant at first, caused increasing discomfort the further down he went. He needed his hands to help steady him, but if he lingered too long in any one place, he felt the heat from the earth would char even his thickened flesh.

Eventually, he reached the canyon floor. The very air here seemed to shimmer, the same as at the height of summer in the southern isles, but this time there was no sun to warm the air. Ahead of him lay the arch of a low tunnel, trailing away underground. It looked like one of the older mining tunnels that had reached the limits of the ore, then been abandoned. A faint hue of pale, effervescent light filtered up from its depths.

Lot braced himself. Every fiber of his being wanted to turn back, to climb up to safety and run far away, but he knew that he could not. He had to find out what the green lady wanted from him. He entered the tunnel.

Within the tunnel, the conditions felt even more unbearable. The further Lot progressed, the deader his footsteps became. It was as if the very air was guzzling up the sound. It would be rather greedy if that were the case, for already the air seemed to hang with a bloated thickness that made his head ring. Beads of sweat began to pool on his brow and trickle along his spine. His breath came slow and jagged. How very tempting it was just to lean back against the rocks and sleep, yet the rocks themselves bore no comfort. Through the soles of Lot's shoes, he could feel their unnatural warmth, pervading the leather. Ole Gotterly was barmy to try and work in this.

Gradually, the tunnel began to widen, and, with a shock, Lot realized he was in the main cavern of the mine. There were no people around, but abandoned pails and barrels of ore lay scattered about, upheaved and broken during the quake. Piles of boulders lay in haphazard disarrays around the working tunnels. Stalactites that had once stood proud on the ceiling now lay in smithereens on the floor. The pulley system that had once transported goods to the surface, lay in a sad pile in the centre of the cavern, shaken free from their restraints that had held for decades. It seemed the tremors had attacked the mine in full force.

The sight that chilled Lot the most however, was not the fallen stones and work tools for, they could always be moved and recovered, but the sight of a large crack about three centimeters wide that cut a jagged divide from the roof of the cavern, down the walls, and across the center of the floor. Whilst the divide that had followed Lot had terrified him, there was something about this crack that just felt *wrong*. It seemed to him as if some dark, malevolent presence was trying to force its way up from deep underground. It made him shudder to think what that was.

"Do you see the true risk of human greed?"

Lot flicked his gaze from the crack to the far side of the cavern. He had not noticed the Green Lady's presence until now. Without her supernatural shine, the Lady's skin blended almost perfectly with the rock face. He eyed her carefully, then noticed that from her dark eyes ran faint black trails. The darkened streaks seemed to glisten. Were these tears?

"Beggin' yer pardon miss, but ah think yer takin' things too far," Lot began, a mumble at first but, when she did not cut him off, he grew bolder, "Most of the chaps who work 'ere are desperate. Money gives 'eir families food, some'ere to lay 'eir 'eads. It's Gottertly who should suffer, not 'em... mah Lady."

"These rocks are my home. I understand the needs of humans and welcomed them with open arms. Had I known the damage you would wreak... I would not have bothered." Resentment rang from her words like a bell.

Humbly, Lot bowed his head. "You did ne' want this to 'appen," he stated grimly, "Ah understand your problem 'n' all, but Gotterly won't stop. Maybe it's best t' just pack up 'n move."

The Lady fixed him with a fierce stare. "I am not mortal," she spat, "I have lived in these rocks since they first formed. It is not within my ability to relocate, for I am bound to the place as surely as the mountain is bound to the land. When I agreed to let you mine, I offered you part of my soul. You violated it."

Sorrow struck Lot's heart. He should have said more to Gotterly. "Ahm truly sorry," he apologized, "We did ne' know. Gotterly never told us naught. Ah would've done more if ahd known. Why did ne' you stop us?"

The Green Lady whipped her head back with a ferocious snarl, but her gaze caught on something in Lot's face. Sincerity. This man was different from the others. Defeatedly, she allowed her anger to drop.

"I wish now that I had," she sighed, her voice hollow, "But I haven't the strength anymore. The mines run too deep. I fear for us all when the beasts beneath gain free reign."

"Ma'am, beggin' yer pardon but, why did you bring me 'ere? Ahm certain a fine Lady such as yerself could find more important folks 'a be speakin' to," queried Lot. For someone so depleted of strength, it seemed she had gone to considerable effort to track him down. He doubted she just wanted someone to chitchat the way into armageddon with.

Kiavernan eyed him up and down with an assessing gaze. Her emotion Lot could not quite place. There was sorrow, of that much he was sure, but it was mixed with something else that was more conflicted, as if she was still debating the reasoning herself.

"I grew up with the Derandera mi'lady, 'ah know 'at you Dae creatures don't do nothin' withou' purpose. I ain't afraid. Tell me." Lot was afraid. He was very afraid, but it felt like the right thing to say. Kiavernan could probably see straight through him. She pursed her lips.

"These mines need not to be emptied, but to be destroyed. The destruction needs to be big enough to ensure that no one, ever again will try to mine here. At the same time, the collapse will seal away the things that lurk below."

Lot thought about the words. He could not disagree with her, for he was not a mystical being and knew nothing about their behavior. He did however know Gotterly and men like him. Maybe after these events the mine would close for a week, maybe even a month, but eventually a new wave of workers would be sent down. The old wounds would be opened, the curses would start afresh and whatever waited in the depths would be awoken and released. That could not be allowed to happen. A heavy realization began to settle in Lot's heart as he began to suspect what it was the Lady wanted from him.

"You said yer powers ar' depleted ma'am?" Lot questioned carefully, not really desiring to hear where this conversation would lead.

"That is correct," she affirmed.

"So, you don't 'ave the strength t' shut down the mine?" The Green Lady's gaze told him that the statement was true. Lot breathed deeply, forcing himself to continue, "Ah 'eard once that a man's soul is concentra'ed power. 'At is what gives 'im breath, 'n' thought."

"More or less," she said, her eyes now fixed intently on his. He knew his fears were true.

"Then bloody go on 'n take it," Lot said, flinging his pack to the floor. The realization that he probably was not making it out of these caves alive had brought his attention back to the fact that he still had it about his shoulders, and it felt impossibly heavy. "'At's what ye' want, isn' it?"

Kiavernan nodded with one long, slow bow of her head.

"Yes," she answered.

With that, Kiavernan closed the gap between them with footsteps so smooth and gracious that Lot could distinguish one stride from the next. The closer she came, the more overwhelmed by awe he felt. She was immense, at least three feet taller than he, and beautiful in a way that made him think of, well, statues. She was also terrifying.

Carefully, she placed a hand against Lot's cheek. The stone was cooling to Lot's skin, and it felt strong. He was certain that with just a slight flick of her wrist, the Lady would be able to crush his skull to smithereens. He hoped that wouldn't be how this would end.

Suddenly, the Lady's stone lips were pressed against his. An icy chill spread through his body. He tried to recoil but found himself locked in place, completely unable to move even if he wanted to. A cold nausea pelted through his stomach. It was as if something cool and slick was being wrenched upward from his gut. His throat gagged reflexively to pull it back down, but naught could be done. Slowly, Lot's skin began to shrivel, his reddened skin clinging madly to the bone. Sweat turned to leather as his form set. Eyeballs tore from their sockets, fingernails seemed to grow, hair shriveled black and dry. The muscles in Lot's torso bucked in agony as the spectral chord was pulled from his mouth. Only the Green Lady's stern grasp held him in place.

With an agonizing heave, Lot was wrenched back to reality. He collapsed to the floor, blood pumping ferociously in his veins. Frantically, he touched his face, his arms, his legs. His skin was whole and unharmed. He looked up at the Lady, the memories of pain still searing his flesh. As he watched her patient gaze, he understood. She was giving him a final choice, showing him what his destiny would be if he offered his help. He was not sure if he would have been better off not knowing.

"A fella's got t' go sometime," he joked, but his voice was hoarse. As far as he saw it, he had no family reliant on him, no children, and no long-term debts. He was the best man for the job. He found it bitterly ironic the same factors that had made him able to escape the mine would also bind him to it.

"There is no changing your mind once the process begins," she informed him.

Steeling his emotions, Lot dragged himself to his feet.

"Ahm aware 'f that milady."

Kiavernan placed her hand back against Lot's cheek. A bolt of panic rose in his chest, but he fought it back.

"What is your name, brave miner?" the Lady asked in admiration.

"Lot ma'am," he answered immediately, "Short for Lothien, born in Rekkentara on Wissnane."

A glimmer of a smile danced about the Lady's lips, "You are a valiant man, Sir Lothien of Wissnane. It is an act that will not quickly be forgotten," she vowed. Her words sent a thrill to Lot's trembling heart.

"Valiant," he mused, "'Sir', ain't nobody ever called me tha' afore."

The Green Lady smiled as she took one final look at Lot's face, then pressed her lips to his once more.

\*        \*        \*

The chaos above ground was immense. The ground shook and crumbled in a way that made the previous quake feel like nothing but a stomach grumble. Men scattered in all directions. Some tried to hide. Others ran. For those on the outskirts of the village, some hope lay in running for the coastal paths. They would need to avoid landslides and keep a wide berth of the crumbling cliffs, but maybe they would be able to race to safety. Those that were closer to the mine entrance had no chance of escape.

The collapse started above the central cavern, then spread quickly outwards. It appeared that the land was cannibalising itself. Heavy rockfalls shook free from the nearby mountain, debris filling up the crater at the same time as it was created.

Gotterly ran back and forth amidst the chaos, gathering what traces of polished green he could find from the remains of the crumbling storehouses.

"Get back 'ere!" he shrieked at some of the workers, fleeing for their lives.

He would not be defeated, not now. There was too much pressure. They had to reach their quota set by the Weskain Merchant House lest their trade permit be revoked. It was just an earthquake, like all the others. The land would quiet and they would be back in business come nightfall.

"Anyone who abandon's 'is post loses three weeks' pay!" he yelled, picking up another piece of green. That would teach them.

The remains of a stone wall gave way, crumbling in Gotterly's direction. He looked up, then twisted violently out of the way. His arm hit heavily against an old metal casket. The bone cracked and he fell to the floor, causing him to drop the green he was carrying. Pain seared up and down his arm. He tried to move it, but it screamed in agony. The bone was protruding from the flesh.

"Help!" he yelled, looking up, but there was no one around. Everyone had fled.

The earth shook.

Gotterly sobbed, then attempted to prop himself up. When he saw what lay in front of him, he wished he had not.

The village was being destroyed. The crater was expanding outwards and outwards. Rock, dirt and tools roiled together like waves on the sea, moving closer and closer to the warehouse where Gotterly was sitting.

He did not move. He could not. His entire livelihood was collapsing upon itself. Even if he stood a chance of getting away, there was nothing left for him. In the end, there would be nothing left but a crater where the mine had once been, filled with rubble and debris that would take decades of digging to clear. Such an expenditure of resources and time would prove too costly. The mine would close and Gotterly would lose everything. Better to end it here, than as a society cast out with no status. He waited to embrace his fate with open arms. The jaws of the deep had won.

# TREE CRYPT

*Sam Claussen*

Prince Felix Okar stared into Tree-Crypt and within saw a version of himself he both despised and longed to be. Felix was fifteen and uncomfortable in his current state. He could not grow a beard. His voice was too high and his body too skinny. He was not prepared to rule, yet still the War-King, his father, lay bitter in his death bed. The man in the Forest, though, the image of Felix's future self that stood stoically beneath the low-hanging branches, was tall and muscular, with a big red beard and smiling eyes. Men would follow him. Felix would follow him.

"Stay away from the Forest, Flea," Queen Mother said. She sat amongst flowers and placed the prettiest behind her ear. She had just come to the age where her looks suggested a beautiful youth. Two royal guards stood nearby, staring uneasily at the Forest.

"I see a man in there, and that man is me," Felix said.

"Speak up, Flea," Queen Mother said. "You must speak clear and without question if you mean to rule."

"That man in the forest." Felix placed an insecure hand on the hilt of his freshly finished sword. An Okarish emerald was placed in the pommel of the blade, as worn by all royalty, and the same blade hung at this mysterious man's belt. He grinned faintly from the shadows at Felix. "He is me, one day."

"That's not possible." Queen Mother stood, dusted off her flowing dress, a white daisy tucked behind one ear. She came and stood next to Felix, placed a domineering hand on his bony shoulder. "For no son of mine will ever venture into the Forest. Those that do are lost to the darkness. You know this, Flea."

"I know that is what I've been told," Felix said. He stood straight. "I will go where I wish."

"And be buried there." Queen Mother flushed, and then sighed. "We've already lost three sons. Must we lose another? Must you throw your life away, when your brothers and countrymen laid down their lives to defend it? You're too old for these childish daydreams, Flea. Come, the day grows old and I suspect this afternoon will be blistering. Let's retire indoors."

Felix turned and walked quickly away toward the squatted stone castle.

"Speak to your father!" Queen Mother called after him.

*      *      *

Felix sat next to his dying father. He was the King of Okaral and Emperor of the Known Lands. The former title of King he'd inherited from his father, but the War-King had earned the latter title of Emperor himself. He conquered all lands to the south of Okaral to the Baron River, swept east to the Dunes, and had even chipped away at the blessed lands of Inohmipa in the far west; an empire that had stood for two-thousand years. Now on his death bed, the War-King knew peace for the first time in 40 years. He did not find it agreeable, falling ill so soon after peace was made with the Dunish. A man needs purpose.

The only land left unscathed from the wars was Tree-Crypt, which bordered Okaral to the north. It went by many names, whispered in taverns and inns across the Known Lands: Greywood, Ill Timber, or commonly the Forest. Tree-Crypt held nothing for man except death in an unknown land, and a burial amongst the trees where no family would bless you. The War-King had had nowhere to go save south in search of reward.

The King's room was piled with treasures from far-away fiefdoms. Well-wishers whose only true wish was for the War-King's quick death so they could retake the lands of their forefathers and rule as kings once more. Felix was studying a gilded sword when his father woke.

"Benji?" his father asked hopefully, his eyes still closed. "Is that my Benji?"

"No, father. It is Felix. Benji is dead." Felix had been so young at the time. He remembered his father riding back from the south in black silks, and how at the sight Queen Mother had burst into tears. As with all royal deaths, the funeral date was marked and remembered each year, but Benji's was as much a holiday as Blood Moon Day. He had been loved by the people, his exploits in the Dunes still talked about in taverns, celebrated with drunken cheers.

"Buried in the Dunes." The War-King shook his head, opening his bloodshot and wrinkled eyes. He looked at Felix, or at least in his direction. "No place for an Okaral Prince to rest. A great disrespect, that his body was not recovered."

"Yes."

"We should have words with them," The War-King muttered. Drool spilled from the side of his mouth. "Words or blood."

"We are at peace, father."

"Peace dies with the King. Soon they will be at our door." The War-King became conscious of himself for a moment, wiping the spittle from his chin. "You will bury my kingdom with me." The War-King gestured to his portrait on the wall, of him riding a white steed, sword drawn, riding south to victory as a younger man. "What will your portrait be? Either clinging to your mother's dress or buried in an early grave."

"I hope to prove you wrong, father."

"Hope." The War-King coughed, blood bubbling at his lips. He snorted and spat at Felix's feet. "Hope will dig you an early grave. You need to sharpen yourself, Felix. You have been pampered and ruined by your mother. War would do you good."

"It did not do my brothers any good."

Straining pathetically, the War-King reached over and slapped Felix across the face. Not very hard, but the meaning behind the strike left its mark even though the hand had not. "Your brothers died with honor. You live with none and die with none. Leave me," he said.

Felix laid the golden sword across his father's lap. He stood and walked to the door before looking over his shoulder. "I saw myself in the Forest today. Perhaps it was an omen," he said.

The War-King's skeletal hand tightened around the grip of the gilded sword. "At the very least, you are my only heir. You will not go frolicking in Tree-Crypt. You will learn to rule, or at least, learn enough to bed some poor wench. Perhaps your future son will have a better mind for the throne."

"You would be proud of me." Felix looked past his father's grand bed of red silks and out the open window onto Tree-Crypt. Black as midnight under the canopy that drooped low over the grey bark dripping with red sap. "If I brought you the North."

"You would bring ruin upon our name and nothing more." The War-King closed his eyes. "I wish you war, to strengthen you. And if you refuse to be honed, then I wish you honor in death." The War-King closed his eyes, hand still firmly gripping the gilded sword.

*　　*　　*

Felix stood a safe distance from Tree-Crypt. His palm perspired on the grip of his sword. He wore traveling clothes, his hood up and his cape drawn close to hide his frame. It was night, and those of import were busy within the castle walls. Guards patrolled the edge of the Forest, but Felix knew their schedule. He had a while longer before he'd be discovered.

The night was crisp and silent. No beast called Tree-Crypt home. The air smelled of wet leaves and crackling meat, of roasted apples and warm pies and laughter over dark ales, huddled close to fires and away from windows that poorly kept the bitter breeze out. It was a brisk evening that reminded him of many comforting nights beneath feathered blankets, sleepily half-reading a book of adventure and unrealistic survival. These memories, once comforting, now only reminded Felix bitterly of his spoiled, undermining upbringing.

The Forest waited impatiently, sap audibly dripping into thick red puddles that surrounded the base of the grey trees. None who ventured into its depths, it was said, ever return. It was an unnatural place, abandoned by man generations ago. The spirits of dishonorable men are said to walk beneath the black, blanketing shroud of Tree-Crypt. Felix felt as if a thousand eyes were watching him. He looked up and could not say where the dark needles of the trees ended, and the starless night began.

Suddenly Felix saw his future self again, standing deep in the Forest, the only visible thing within the endless black. He smiled at

Felix, a gloved finger playing with the emerald in the pommel of his blade. Felix took a step toward the Forest edge, mesmerized by the man he could be if only —

"That's far enough, Prince," a gruff voice came from behind him.

Felix jumped, lost his footing and almost fell to the ground. He composed himself, standing royally before turning to find Captain Gall, a veteran of a dozen named battles and countless skirmishes. He had served next to Benjimar, Felix's eldest brother, in the Dunes, and after Benji had passed had served under Prince Arkin in the South and Prince Wym in the East. He had been at the burial of all, something Felix could not say. He stood tall in his weathered armor, scars littering his face and exposed hands.

"Gallows," Felix said, relieved. "I didn't hear your approach."

"Forgive me, my Prince, but what are you doing so close to the Forest at night, with no guard at your side?" Gallows eyed Felix's garb, hiding a crooked grin. "If you plan to sneak away, perhaps you should hide that sword of yours. Okarish emeralds rarely grace the steel of peasantry."

Felix quickly covered the hilt of his sword with his brown cape. "I saw my future in the Forest," he said, looking at the bleak dark with dreamy eyes. "I saw the man I could become."

"I should hope not," Gallows said, walking up behind him and placing his callused hand on his shoulder. "Tree-Crypt is the final destination for those who die without honor. Not to mention any number of monsters and ghouls."

"You really believe in those old wives' tales?" Felix looked up at the gruff man.

Gallows considered the Forest for a moment, his eyes taking on the black of its shadows. "I've seen children play along its edge. I've never seen anyone go into the blind night of it, though. But if you held that fancy sword to my neck, and I had my back up against

Greywood? Well. I suppose I'd turn and flee into it. Make of that what you will, but do so safely behind doors, if you don't mind."

Felix, a pampered prince his whole life, found it easy to ignore the advice of underlings, even if not on purpose. He was transfixed by the Forest, was drawn to it as his father had been drawn South to war. It was his purpose, and if a boy turned from his purpose, does he ever truly become a man?

Gallows hand tightened on Felix's shoulder. "C'mon, Flea. Tonight is not the night to prove yourself."

"When, then?" Felix turned from the Forest. "When do I stand? When will my father look at me as he did my brothers?"

"You will be king one day."

"No man can rule an empire if he cannot rule himself." Felix looked at the Forest once more. "Or his fears."

"I cannot allow you—"

"Yes, I know. I will retire."

Felix walked across the yard to the castle, looking up at the candlelight flickering in his father's room. A gust of wind rushed across the yard, originating from Tree-Crypt, chilling Felix to the bone before rushing through his father's window and extinguishing the candle within. Black smoke curled out and rose into the brisk night.

*　　*　　*

The War-King died in the night. Black mourning flags rose with the sun, marking a Day of Silence across the empire—which was only observed within earshot of the royal guards. The following morning the War-King was placed on the deck of a sailboat with black sails.

Felix stood on the dock in front of his people. He would be crowned King once his father set sail. It was a warm autumn morning, the sun melting the ice that had crisped the dead leaves that piled up against the reeds of the river. The water flowed briskly south. Everyone waited for the Prince.

"It is time, my Prince," the Reed-Priest said. His only purpose was to oversee the funeral proceedings of royalty. He was an old man, and almost seemed excited at the opportunity. The bodies of the other princes had been left in their respective war theatres, so the Reed-Priest hadn't had an audience since the days of King Metra, the War-King's much mocked father. His speech had been labored over for years and felt as dusty and drawn as a withered tome, making most the mourners irritably tired.

The Reed-Priest finally cleared his throat, ending his speech to a relieved sigh from all those present. A breeze had picked up, and the boat tugged at the ropes that anchored it to the pier. The Reed-Priest turned up his green hood against the cold. "If you don't mind, my Prince," he said, "It is time for you to speak the Words of Passing."

"I've not prepared anything," Felix said under his breath.

The Reed-Priest nodded with a smug smirk. "Of course, my Prince. It is hard in such times to express how you feel. If I might be so bold, I've taken the liberty to write a piece in our War-King's honor."

The Reed-Priest took from his robes a parchment. Felix took it without question or review. He walked down the dock and boarded the boat unsteadily. He looked down at his father, two Black-Holy Flowers placed over his eyes. The Reed-Priest had somehow gotten the War-King to smile in his rigid death. It looked unnatural and almost painful on his face, all the wrinkles he'd earned from his endless frowning trying their best to rid themselves of the dopy expression.

Felix unrolled the parchment, squinted at the scribbles, and read aloud:

*And so, we say goodbye*
*To our King and father.*
*Here his body lies,*
*Though his spirit wanders.*
*He is with the Gods,*
*And we mourn in his wake.*
*His body amongst the river rods,*
*His teachings we will take*
*To build a better land*
*For all that praised his reign —*
*From the Dunish sands*
*To every conquered plane.*

The mourners muttered their agreement. Felix nodded and ignored how tone-deaf the poem had been. The Reed-Priest soaked in the praise of his work. Queen Mother, her nose red, black tears running down her cheeks, looked absolutely without direction. Felix stumbled forward and grabbed the tied ropes that hoisted the sails. It took him an embarrassingly long time to unfurl them, having never stepped foot on a boat, but eventually the sails fell and immediately tugged the boat down the river until the ropes snapped tight and stopped the advance, causing Felix to fall backward over the War-King's body.

There was an astonished hush that fell over the crowd, along with some light snickering among the youngest present. Felix stood quickly and jumped onto the pier. He walked blushing through the crowd and up to his castle, where the next festivities would take place. The Reed-Priest said his final words, thrown off by the Prince's sudden departure, and cut the ropes that held the sailboat to the dock. The river immediately took it and off the War-King went, down the King's Way River that flowed south past the eastern Dunes, and then onto the Border River where the Western Sea Lords brood, and then past the Blessed Lands of Inohmipa in the West. The whole of the Empire would gather along the banks to see the War-King's final march south.

Every conquered man would know that the War-King is dead.

Felix was crowned King. A banquet was held where many riches were bestowed upon him. Roaring fires lit the tall stone hall. Bubbly women and intoxicated men danced and drank endless wine and ate roasted pork and an endless assortment of meats, breads, and desserts. Their voices echoed in a deafening muddle of drunken nonsense and hurrahs. And all the while Felix sat at the head table, surrounded by strangers who cautiously called him King. Gallows stood stoically in the back with a reassuring yet expectant gaze in Felix's direction.

"What about a Dunish girl?" Queen-Mother asked him. She had never treated him as a man until she'd lost the one she'd relied on. Now with the War-King gone, Felix had hardly been able to rid his presence of her for more than a few moments. "They are pretty in a foreign way. I've heard the Governor's daughters are quite fetching." Queen Mother's hand shook as she took a drink from her goblet. "Your father had said so himself."

"Aren't we moving a tad quickly?" Felix muttered, rearranging the crown on his head. "They haven't even fitted this damned thing for my head yet already you plan my wedding."

"The death of a king is an omen for chaotic times, Flea—my King. *Especially* the death of the War-King. He held the country together."

"By force." Felix held out his goblet which was immediately filled by one of his many servants. He downed the cup and held it out for more.

"How else?" Queen Mother placed a hand on his arm, lowering his goblet. "We need to forge alliances quickly. If we take a Dune girl as your bride, they will lend their armies to our cause. Make no mistake, the territories will rebel. We must make friends. The Dunish are fierce and savage warriors."

"Is this my first war council?" Felix stood shakily to his feet. "I wish to retire."

"There are still gifts to present." Queen Mother smiled at the crowd of people.

"They're all yours, mother." Felix walked out of the banquet hall and up the steps to his father's room, *his* room.

He shed his black mourning robe, sewn of the finest silk, and took the golden crown from his head. The heavy green emerald embedded in the band had caused the misshapen crown to slide down his forehead all day. He tossed it on the bed and walked over to his window that looked out onto Tree-Crypt.

He thought he saw his older and successful self again within Tree-Crypt, the *real* King. *And what type of king?* Felix thought. *Another War-King? Or, perhaps...* He saw him clearly now, at the edge of the Forest. The bearded, confident man grinned up at Felix. *The Forest-King.*

*        *        *

"You requested me, my King?" Gallows said, handing his weaponry to the guards outside the King's private chambers.

"He can keep his weapons," Felix said, feeling ridiculous as he sat behind his father's large marble desk.

"It is against custom, my King, to allow an armed man within your presence," the guard said.

"He is Captain of the King's Men!"

"It's alright, my King," Gallows said, taking his sword belt off.

"No." Felix stood. "It isn't. I said to keep them."

The two guards looked at each other, and Gallows smiled grimly. He took his dagger and sword back, nodding to the men. "You heard your King. That will be all," he said in a friendly way, a management technique that Felix had yet to learn.

The two guards bowed and exited, closing the tall wooden door behind them. The room was alive with the flicker of the great fire that smoldered at all times in the charred fireplace. It was hot and humid, and Felix sweated profusely. His clothing reeked of smoke, as did the curtains, the bedding, the whole room. It made him sick. Felix sighed once the guards had left, slumping in his chair.

"The crown suits you," Gallows said, approaching the desk.

"Don't mock me." Felix rubbed his forehead where the crown had scraped him all day long. "I've not done any legislating or warring, yet already I grow weary of this charade. Would you care for some wine?"

"Allow me." Gallows poured two glasses of wine, admired the glassware before selecting what he thought was the best of the pair and slid it across the littered desk to Felix. Gallows sat back, allowing the silence to brew for a moment before saying, "It is your first day. You can hardly expect to hang your portrait yet. Give it time."

Felix drank deep from his glass. His head was swimming from the amount he'd drank that night already, anything to quiet the contradicting voices in his head. "I haven't time. You know this. Every man who sees the War-King's lifeless body bobbing down the King's Way will arm themselves and revolt. Tell me, Gallows, you were there. Were the territories happy to be conquered?"

"They were happy for the war to be over." Gallows chair creaked beneath his weight. A little belly had developed since his return from the south, but he was mostly calcified muscle. "The small folk, anyway. The rulers are never happy, of course, but the small folk never want war."

"Who cares what the peasants think if they make no difference in what is done?" Felix threw his glass into the chimney. It shattered against the blackened back, leaving a purple stain that dribbled down the wall. It sizzled and burned and charred, smelling foul. "Apologies."

Gallows nodded, not easily offended or taken aback; he had served three princes and knew how royalty was short to anger and quick to questionable decisions. "If I may, my Lord. They matter most. Your kingdom has stood for generations, but others are not so lucky. There are rebellions every day, some smaller and others much larger, who have had quite enough of fighting our wars while we rape their women and ravage their crop. When you treat peasants like kindling for war, you can't be surprised if they burn the whole kingdom down."

Felix rubbed his bald chin inquisitively. He had hardly heard a word Gallows had said. He was not cut out to be a king, yet here he sat, like a jester courageously wearing the crown for laughs. He had not earned it, like his father had. War would come, that much he knew; and if the kingdom was to stay intact, he must become a king.

"I'm going into Tree-Crypt," he said.

Gallows flinched, as if someone had snuck into the room and stabbed him in the back. After a moment he nodded. "You take your omen seriously, then."

"I do."

"Your guards will not allow it."

"I plan to leave in the night."

"You will be found out."

"Not if I have your help."

"Ask, then, my King." Gallows shook his head and then drained his glass before quickly pouring another. He took another drink before looking Felix in the eyes. He sniffed. "I've mourned three princes and a king in my life. I've seen them all buried. I do not plan to lose another."

Felix grinned. "Well," he said, standing. "That is good to know."

"Know this as well," Gallows said, standing. "I think this the wrong path to earn your portrait. The kingdom needs a leader now more than ever."

"Yes." Felix walked over to the window, looking out at the Forest. "Let us go find him."

*      *      *

It was well past midnight when Gallows hissed up at Felix's window. Felix got out of bed—a bed he hadn't been able to sleep in—and looked out the window at his frantic captain. Gallows was glancing all around, pale in his face, nervous to be caught whispering at the King's window. Felix nodded down at him and then quickly threw his traveling cloak over his bony shoulders, laced his sword belt through his pants. The emerald embedded in the hilt glittered majestically in the dying embers of the fire.

Felix looked up at his father's first portrait, of his successful march south. The War-King's black eyes were alive in the warm flame that sputtered within the chimney. Many more portraits were hung, singing of his father's exploits and campaigns, but a King's Portrait was always his first, and it was to capture how he had earned his title. It shaped his entire rule.

There was a place made on the stone wall for Felix's portrait. A square that was lighter than the charcoal grey of the stained stone walls. The least worthy of the War-King's portraits had been taken down to make room. Felix put his pack over his shoulder and went over to the window, threw down a rope periodically knotted for easy climbing. Gallows had done that for him earlier.

"I won't have the King falling three-stories to his death, screaming all the way, with me to greet the guards," he had muttered as he'd tied the rope securely to the bed frame.

Felix stepped over and out the window and sat saddled on the sill, Tree-Crypt looming tall and malicious over the castle like a huge, inky wave rolling toward land. He cautiously lowered himself onto the rope, felt its coarseness burn into his uncalloused hands. At first his tender grip failed him, and he slid before his thighs could grip tightly the hemp. He hissed as it cut into the skin beneath his leather legwear, the smell of its burning pleasant to his nose, sweet and earned. He took his time to make it the rest of the way, eyes closed until he felt Gallows pat him on the back. Felix dropped to the ground, sighing.

"Well." Felix brushed his garb off and looked at his red, soon-to blister hands. "That went faster than I expected."

"Only one way you could have moved faster." Gallows said, patting the young King on his shoulders. "And I've never been a good catch. Ready?"

"Are we to take horses?"

"No, it is much too thick." Gallows sighed, looking at the Forest. "Besides, no sane beast goes near Tree-Crypt. Let's go, before the guards change."

They began to sneak quietly across the yard. A dog yelped somewhere in the distance. They heard the chatter of the guards playing cards in their hut on the other side of the open yard. Felix felt a nervous excitement rise within him, of danger and death and the purpose those bring. He wondered if he would have made a good thief, if he'd been born amongst the peasantry, sneaking into the palace on crisp autumn nights and stealing away all of the glittering treasures and pale emeralds.

"Did you leave your note?" Gallows asked in a hush whisper.

"I did."

"Might I ask what you wrote?"

"That crazy Ol' Gallows kidnapped me and intends to sell me to the demons of the Forest."

"And quite the price I would demand."

They walked in silence for a moment. "I wrote that I go to seek my fortune and purpose, and that I won't return without it. I said goodbye to my mother, instructed her to rule in my stead. I said the boy that leaves will never return, but the man who returns will do so as their unquestionable King."

"Poetic."

"Do not mock me. It took more courage than I readily have to sign that letter."

Gallows nodded. "Apologies, my King. You are right to have wrote it so assuredly. It will be spoken of. Perhaps you'll become a local legend: The Lost King of Tree-Crypt." Here Gallows took on the tongue of the common folk, slurred and short. "'They say he will return from the Forest, one day. Set things straight, he will.'"

"Legends are dead men never found," Felix said, hiding a smirk. "I would rather serve as King than legend."

"Aye," Gallows said, unwittingly still imitating the common tongue. "But if you become legend, that's not nothing. At least you live on in memory. But me? I'd be dead and forgotten, some dumb fool who followed another man's dream. No, I'll see us leaving Tree-Crypt."

They now stood in front of the Forest. Only the nearest trees were illuminated by the dim moon, clouded over like a glassy eye. The absorbing silence of Tree-Crypt was worse than the unknowing dark. Felix and Gallows stood still, waiting for something to happen.

And there, just out of reach of the bleak moonlight, Felix saw his future self once more. Gallows didn't seem to notice the man in the Forest, grinning mischievously in a friendly sort of way. He wore an emerald in his pommel, stood tall and muscular and commanding of presence. He gestured with his head for Felix to hurry along before he disappeared further into the dark.

The night smelled of winter's nip. The leaves that littered the castle yard curled black with frost. With an assuring glance from Gallows, the two entered Tree-Crypt, whose leaves never fell.

There was an immediate change in both climate and the traveler's mood as they entered the Forest. It was humid and boggy, like a summer day after an afternoon rain. No rainfall reached the Forest's ground, though. It was hard dirt and brittle roots that crunched loudly under their feet. Thorns caught at their clothing, as if Tree-Crypt was actively preventing them from venturing deeper into the wood. It smelled like rotted meat and black smoke. The moonlight ended unnaturally only a few steps in. It was pitch black, the only sound being their labored breath. They stopped and wiped sweat from their brows.

"We need light," Felix said.

"I would have hoped to wait 'til we were further from the castle, but I suppose they can't see us, can they?" Gallows said. Felix could hear him kneel in the dark. "Shit, these thorns," Gallows hissed. He struck flint twice, the spark blinding to Felix, before a flame caught. He held the torch up, careful to keep the flame from the dry kindling the Forest was seemingly built from. "Truth be told, I wanted to avoid a flame altogether, once we were in here. Damned hot for autumn, isn't it?"

Shadows played off Gallows's face. The torch only lit a small area around the pair, like a cocoon. It hardly penetrated the darkness, and it made Felix feel even more frightened than before. The way they had come was already blind to them, the edge of the Forest unknown, and Felix began to feel claustrophobic and lost like a man stranded at sea.

"Easy, now," Gallows said, seeing the fear in the young King's eyes. "You have to search the dark lands of this world if you mean to discover something new. Let's keep on." His voice was all-encompassing, loud like the voice in Felix's head. Felix nodded and the two moved on.

Time passed at a pace neither of the pair could determine. They kept walking into the bleak unknown, stopping occasionally to catch their breath.

"Have you ever seen a night such as this?" Felix asked, looking for the comfort that authority and familiarity could provide. "If indeed it is still night. How can one tell in this dreadful place?"

"I remember our first invasion of the Dunes," Gallows said, smiling bitter-sweetly, "I was serving with your eldest brother, Benji, as you know. That was a hellish land, sun-cursed and parched. Much hotter than this here, during the day anyway." Gallows rubbed stinging sweat from his tired eyes. "But at night," Gallows continued, "it would drop to freezing. We weren't sure what we were going to do. We hadn't prepared for winter in the desert. Just when we thought we'd freeze to death the first night on the Dunes, your brother gets off his horse and digs his shivering hands into the sand." Gallows smiled, not present in Tree-Crypt any longer. "Warm as a maiden's bed. We all buried ourselves in the sand each night to keep warm, after that. It was almost as dark as this, when you were under it. I've never slept better."

They had stopped walking, now, Gallows lost in thought. "Ironic, then, that we buried your brother under those same sands. I hope he rests well. I miss that warmth, in the winter," Gallows said. He sighed, looking down at Felix. "Apologies, my King. I did not mean to—"

"No, it is alright. You two were close. He left for the wars when I was just a toddler. Same with Arkin and Wym. I can hardly remember their faces."

"They looked just like you, at one point or another," Gallows said. "Benji could have been your twin when he first went south."

"Really?" Felix asked. His father, mother and damn near every country man spoke of Benji's natural authority and charisma. How he was born a King, had earned his portrait with his first breath. "Surely you jest."

"He was around your age when we left for the Dunes. More nervous than you, then, truly. Scrawny little thing." Gallows scrunched up his nose in a playful smile, eyes glazed over in memory, as if he'd teased Benji of this before. "But he rose to his calling, same as you, and both times I didn't have the sense to keep away from questful princes." Gallows grinned at Felix. "And he sure as hell would never have stepped foot in Tree-Crypt."

They both laughed. Their spirits lifted in fond memories, and together they pushed through the undergrowth, torches held out defensively against the unknown, and continued into the Forest, which grew darker and drew closer with each step.

*     *     *

Felix wasn't sure how long they'd been marching. Longer than his aching thin legs had ever carried him. It was as dark as it had always been, yet they must have been walking for at least half a day by this point. He was exhausted, having never exerted himself to the point of both his mind and body surrendering in treason against his own will.

"We must halt," Felix croaked.

Gallows stopped, catching his breath before saying, "This is an ill place to make camp, my King. We must go... just a bit further."

Felix was about to scream, to demand they stop by royal decree. But he had already begun to evolve in the dark, and what he had learned now was a little humility. He was not in court, nor in the garden with Queen Mother, picking flowers. He was in a hostile and unexplored wild and must trust in Gallows's guidance if he meant to survive.

"I can keep going," Felix said. It was more of a command to his own body, a royal decree unto himself.

Each step within Tree-Crypt was misery. The ground was covered with serrated, red-tipped grass that grabbed at your boots and pants, making each step feel as if you're walking through water. Sturdy, pulsating red vines ran across the ground and tangled themselves around the grey tree trunks. If you weren't careful with each step, you'd trip over them and into one of the countless thorn bushes. The heat was unbearable, as was the smell of rotting flesh and the complete silence save their own muttered curses, which were painfully loud. The trees deceptively all looked the same, scarred grey bark with a black trunk beneath and inky black sheets of cactus-sharp needles and sappy cones that fell and stuck like tar to your skin, leaving raw skin when ripped away.

"I will paint my portrait in blood," Felix muttered to himself through gritted teeth as he yanked free a boot from the grasping grass. "My own blood or drawn from the bastard that cursed our lands with this damned Forest."

"I'll hold him down," Gallows said, looking half a spectre, but this said with a victorious smirk. "But after we rest."

He lifted his torch, which was his second of the travel thus far; his first had quickly faded, as if there weren't enough oxygen to feed the flame. He'd then made one out of a large, sticky conifer cone and a sturdy dead branch. It had continued to burn for hours and showed no sign of snuffing out anytime soon. The flame revealed a large clearing, where there were no dripping trees, gripping grass or thorn bushes. Even the vines avoided the area, and the ground was covered in a fine layer of undisturbed, ash-like dirt.

They both took a deep breath of cool air; as soon as the clearing had revealed itself to their virgin eyes, the temperature seemed to drop 30 degrees, and the humidity that had dried their pores rolled back, like shifting sands that reveal an oasis.

Felix fell to his knees, his body immediately giving up on him. "I fear I'll never rise again," he said with a chuckle. His hands spread over the powdery dirt that rose like dust, soft as a feathered blanket.

Gallows quickly collected some dead wood and undergrowth and had a roaring fire burning in the middle of the clearing. He purposely did not use any of the sappy cones, as he was not sure how to extinguish their flame and didn't want to burn the whole Forest down. He dug a tight hole and cautiously slid his torch into it, where it continued to burn as if some mystical fuel fed it.

In silence they ate dry bread and tough meat, as there was no beast that they knew of to hunt in Tree-Crypt, not that they had the energy if there were. Felix stretched out, his legs aching from the day's—or night's—exertion. He undid his belt and lay his sword within reach. Gallows stretched as well, though in a much more tense manner than Felix. Now that he had had some rest and had food in his stomach, Gallows was much more wary of the Forest, his eyes scanning the impenetrable dark. Felix looked up, trying to spot a single star in a night sky, but was greeted only by the same black he'd experienced for hours.

"I've never seen so thick a night as this. And it never ends," Gallows said. He drew his sword and laid it across his lap. "I cannot tell if it is night or day. My body tells me to sleep, but to be honest I've felt deathly tired ever since we entered this damned place."

"At least it is cool." Felix took a long swig from his canteen.

"Yes, but it is a stale cool, is it not?" Gallows seemed on the verge of paranoia. "Like the breeze that flows through a catacomb."

Felix did not respond. He suddenly felt much more afraid than he had the entire trip. The darkness surrounding the clearing seemed to pulsate, as if it were attempting to invade their safe space and drag them back into its depth.

"Have you found what you seek, yet, my King?" Gallows asked. He sat back up, looked as if he were about to bolt at that very moment. "Can we return home?"

Felix's soul begged his mouth to say yes, that he had found what he had set out for, and that they can return to the comfort royalty provided. But the fact that his weak being longed to leave was an answer in itself. Felix took a deep breath before saying, "No, I have not found it."

"How can you tell?" Gallows asked. "You've earned a portrait by entering this place as it is."

"I know because I am very afraid. If I had found the king within me, I would not be."

"Fear keeps men alive."

"Men, perhaps." Felix said. "But fearful men kill weak kings. If I don't rid myself of fear, my body will soon be rid of its head."

Gallows bared his teeth and pounded his fist against his knee. The latter action seemed to knock him out of his flight-or-fight trance. The old soldier took a deep breath and sat rigidly straight. "I apologize, my King. This place…it influences me," he said.

"Yes." Felix tried his best not to shiver. "Curious."

They eventually fell into a distrustful sleep, huddling as close to the flames as they could stand.

*     *     *

Felix woke to the sound of a grown man crying.

It wasn't Gallows. He sat alert on the other side of the fire from Felix, listening. It was someone off in the darkness, blubbering and sniffling.

"Is it close?" Felix asked, sitting up frantically.

"Calm yourself, King," Gallows said. He had a white-knuckled grip on the hilt of his sword, a blade much less flashy than Felix's, but honed razor-thin and blessed by enemy blood. Sandstone was placed in the pommel, a rock common to the dunes, polished and grainy. An honor of his standing in the affair. Gallows shook his head uncertainly. "I cannot say. When you speak, it sounds as if you're inside my head. Earshot is not to be trusted."

They sat and listened to the crying for a few minutes. It felt as if they were crying themselves, it was so loud. Felix felt guilty, as if he had caused the woe that tormented this stranger. It was as dark beneath the Forest canopy as it had always been, but the smell of death was much fouler than before. Felix felt rested yet drained, as if the ground leeched all energy from him as he had slept. Dread rose within him that felt more inevitable than the changing of seasons.

"My advice, as before, is that we leave this place," Gallows said. "I believe I could still find the way despite the maze we've been through. But this I know you'll reject, as I suppose you should. I also know that, though I imagine you're afraid, deep down you know that you must face whatever is presented if we are to find what we searched for in the first place. So." Gallows stood, dusting off his rear. He took his undying torch from the ground, sword held defensively in the other. "Let us go take a look."

Felix uneasily rose to his feet. "Perhaps you overestimate my logic," he muttered, drawing his emerald sword. It glittered like freshly minted jewelry and, when wielded by Felix, was about as useful in a fight. "But I suppose I like the sparring image you hold of me. Which way?"

Gallows listened to the sobbing. "Hello, out there!" he called loudly. The crying did not cease. "I said, hello!"

A sappy cone fell free from a tree and thudded into the dirt next to Felix. Felix yelped and, by instinct, stabbed the cone with his blade. Blood-like sap oozed from the wound. Gallows chuckled, took Felix's sword and yanked the cone off the blade.

"Your first kill!" Gallows said with a laugh. He found some kindling and stuck the cone on top, lighting it in their campfire before handing the torch to Felix. "A trophy, from your first battle."

Felix, resentful of Gallows's mockery for a shameful moment, chuckled and took the torch. "Burnt at the stake," he said. "A message to all my enemies."

The two stood staring at the night that surrounded them. The clearing suddenly felt as comfortable as home.

"How are we to find our mourner, if we can't follow his cries? He sounds as if he is right next to us," Gallows said. "This place is cursed. Unnatural. I can hear every word as if it were my own, yet even with a torch, can only see a few steps ahead. And that smell, like a battlefield when the birds set in on the rotting bodies. You'll never forget *that* smell, my King. Shit and vomit and rotten flesh—"

"The smell!" Felix sniffed deeply before gagging. "It is stronger than before, is it not?"

Gallows sniffed, then spat in the fire. He kicked ashy dirt onto the flames. The darkness of the clearing stoked Felix's fears. "So, we follow our noses," Gallows said.

"Unfortunately."

They looked at each other, sighed, and then sniffed. Both gagged before heading straight in the direction the smell seemed to draw from, which they believed was due north, though they were just guessing by this point.

"How many men have you killed?" Felix asked. He couldn't listen to the crying any longer.

"Thirty-eight men, and one woman." Gallows stared straight ahead, stern lipped. "My mother passed in labor. This is an ill topic to speak of in Tree-Crypt, my King."

"You believe, then, that those without honor come here once they've died?"

"Not until I came here, and not until—"

Gallows stopped short as they stumbled into another clearing, much like the one before. The crying man sat on his knees facing away from them. He did not seem to notice their approach. Felix looked up at Gallows, who looked at him, concerned, and gestured for Felix to stay back. Gallows, sword held to strike, walked forward slowly. He had a soldier's stride. Naturally, his weight fell backward on secure footing, and the torch was held in front of him as if it were a shield.

"On your feet," Gallows said to the man.

"Keep the flame away!" the man screamed, and with that, even before seeing him, Felix knew who the crying man was. He had never heard his voice so shrill or afraid, but the man who wept before him was the War-King himself.

"My...my King, is that you?" Gallows asked.

Felix walked forward as the War-King turned to face them. He was in his death garb, black robes and an emerald-green headband. He studied Gallows suspiciously before noticing Felix. He immediately began to cry the harder.

"My boy come to save me!" the War-King said. He had been kneeling over a shriveled sapling that looked to be of the same dark wood as the rest of the Forest. The dirt around the tree was wet and clay-like from the War-King's tears. "I knew someone would...I knew I did not belong in Tree-Crypt! I'm just...I've become very lost."

"Father, I—" Felix felt faint. "How can this be? You are dead."

The War-King's frantic smile disappeared. He nodded, and the tears welled in his eyes. "Yes, I suppose I am. Forgive me, boy. It is so very dark here, and one forgets things," he said. He knelt over the sapling and began to weep once more.

"Father." Felix knelt next to him, placing a hand on the War-King's cold, bent back. The flickering torch illuminated the War-King's waxy features. "Please, tell me the meaning of all this."

The War-King lashed out, pushing Felix away harshly. Felix fell back, hitting his head hard on the dirt. Gallows stepped forward, but did not know what to do, or who to obey.

"Keep the flame away!" The War-King spat, trembling as he waved his hands in a frenzy.

"Forgive him," a stern and capable voice came from behind Felix. Felix slowly turned and saw his future self standing tall and proud before him, looking down upon him with a warm smile, a man Felix had half-expected to be of his own delusions. "The grave does not agree with him."

"You." Felix struggled to his feet. "You were who I came to find."

Gallows walked up behind Felix, eyes on the mysterious man, mouth drooping and eyes wide. "It cannot be," Gallows muttered.

"Yes, Gallows, look! Here is the King I sought," Felix said proudly. He had never accomplished a goal in his life, he realized, not one worth a damn. Not until now.

"Felix," Gallows said. It took the young King off guard, as it was the first time he had addressed him as such since Felix had assumed the throne. "Do you not recognize your brother?"

Felix's heart dropped. He looked up at the man he had thought himself. His eyes began to subtract the years away, shed the beard, and there Benji stood. Gallows walked past Felix and embraced Benji roughly.

"I buried you," Gallows said, laughing. "I thought I'd never see you again." He broke away incredulously, looking Benji in the face, before slapping him on the shoulders with a teary-eyed laugh. "How can this be?"

"Not how I would have liked, I'm afraid" Benji said, chuckling. "It is good to see you, my friend. I have been alone for a very long time."

The War-King sat crying over his sapling during this entire exchange.

Benji looked past Gallows at Felix. "And my brother. I beckoned, and here you are. Braver than I at your age, entering this tomb," Benji said. He walked up and embraced Felix roughly. "And now a King! So much has changed since I left you, a mere babe."

Felix wasn't sure how to react. His first instinct, which he found surprising, was of self-preservation. He wanted to flee from Benji, and the reason for this, he discovered, was that his view of himself as King, the pride he had built since entering the Forest, shrank considerably in Benji's presence. Here was a natural-born leader. Felix was just playing make believe.

He thought back on when he had first heard news of Benji's passing in the Dunes. He had felt dread, not for his dead brother's fate but his own. He was one step closer to the throne he never wanted. Then like felled trees his other brothers were chopped down, and then the War-King grew sick, and finally Felix had been deposited on the throne as a storm leaves debris.

But Felix had for a moment deluded himself into thinking he was almost ready for the throne, that he had earned it by facing his fears and seeking his better self, but instead he found Benji, the person Felix had always been told *was* his better self by the War-King who now sat weeping over little more than a twig.

Felix buried these thoughts and emotions within a shallow grave covered with shame.

"Brother," he said, and the two hugged, much more briefly than when Benji had hugged Gallows; they had been brothers in blood, after all. "I believe I understand, but I do not comprehend. You and father are still dead, yet you lie in Tree-Crypt. You had honor, surely, as did the War-King."

"Yes," Benji said, looking mournfully at their father. "Honor in battle. Our Reed-Priest seems to have misinterpreted the teachings of the Elder Gods."

The War-King looked at the group skeptically, eyeing the torches. "You just keep the flame back, didn't you hear?"

"Why is he afraid of fire, yet you stand so close without a care?" Felix asked.

Benji nodded toward the shriveled sapling. "He only seeks to protect his tree. It is the curse of this place, you see, that those that come here must water their saplings with their own regretful tears."

Suddenly the trees that surrounded them all seemed much larger than before, and more alive. Felix shook his head in fearful astonishment. "All of these, they are..."

"Crypts," Benji finished his thought. "Once it's large enough, I suppose you pass on."

"Can you not leave?" Felix asked.

"Where you saw me, at the edge of the Forest, is the farthest I can go. My spirit is enslaved here."

"You are no ghost," Gallows said. He walked up and patted Benji on the shoulder. "You're as solid as I. Though you are cold for the heat of this place."

"Heat!" Benji laughed. "What an odd place. It is frigid for me."

"Well." Gallows looked at Felix, perhaps the first time since Benji appeared. "I suppose you found what you sought, my King."

"Yes. Why did you call me here, brother?" Felix asked.

Benji looked at Gallows, who took the hint and walked a few paces away. Benji smiled frankly at Felix. "I could sense your troubles, brother," Benji said in a hushed voice. "I've watched you in the garden for quite some time. You do not feel ready to rule. I thought I could help prepare you. Teach you." Benji nodded toward the War-King. "I will not fail this task, as he has. It is not your fault."

"Three sons I've buried," the War-King said. "And countless more that were not mine. How many fathers grieved my rule?"

"We should leave him be," Benji said. "They mourn this way for quite some time."

"Where are our brothers?" Felix asked.

"Both have grown their trees and moved on," Benji said. He led Felix out of the clearing, Gallows behind, and away from the War-King. "I was there for them both. They would watch you, too, at times. Come, my garden isn't far from here."

The Forest was as dark as ever, their torches flickering almost uselessly in front of their faces, but the trees were beginning to thin out, and the forest seemed less old and sparser. The smell of his brother was less so than his father had been, and Tree-Crypt as a whole seemed less hot than before.

"When did you arrive at this place?" Gallows asked.

"As soon as my eyes closed. Though, to be honest, I don't remember how I died exactly," Benji said, keeping a steady pace.

"You buried yourself in the sand and forgot which way was up," Gallows said with a grin.

"Ha! That would explain it. I still find sand in my clothes to this day."

Silence as Benji waited for Gallows to continue. Finally, the latter hastily began, "We were in the city of Gamibra. Capturing the city would all but ensure our hold over the eastern Dunes. Naturally, though I do not mean to criticize—"

"I believe I'm past pride, Gallows."

"Very well. You were persistent, wanting to capture Gamibra quickly, with little loss of life. So, you and I and a group of good men snuck past the walls and broke into the King's estate."

"Yes. I remember this."

"We demanded his surrender on the spot." Gallows was lost in thought. His eyes seemed damp and faded in the flickering light. "And he would have, if not—"

"Yes," Benji said firmly. "I remember it all, now. No need—"

"The boy rushed me from behind. Hardly older than ten, yet when I heard him scream, I turned and deflected the blow and just as quickly cut the boy near in half at the neck," Gallows's lip twitched into a brief snarl. He turned his sword in his hand, looking at it as if it had an evil mind of its own. "With this very blade. An accident, of course, but dead is dead. It was the Dunish Prince. In the distraction, the King drew the knife from your belt and slit your throat."

Benji's blue-tinted lips were pursed between his bushy red beard. "Yes. And then I woke here."

"I slaughtered the King without much a fight. We buried you in the Dunes, where you fell. The city was ours the following morning."

Benji shook his head, pasted a smile on his face. "Ah, such is war. A good lesson for you, Flea. Don't let ghosts hold you back. Tough decisions are always paid for by the bodies of lesser men. That is the cost of leadership."

Felix cleared his throat. "Yes," he croaked.

"Though, slitting a man's throat is a weak thing to do. Face someone you mean to kill. Dishonorable. I wonder if the Dunish King is here, then? Wouldn't that be an awkward thing?" Benji forced a chuckle. "Perhaps Sand-Folk go elsewhere when they pass." He sighed. "I have to admit, I have not taken to death kindly. I felt I had much left to accomplish."

"You would have made a great King, Benji," Gallows said. "And now you have the chance to craft a King out of Felix. Based off my time serving our young King thus far, you have plenty to work with."

"Yes." Benji brushed his fingers across the bark of a cold, dead tree they passed. "Fate is an odd thing."

They walked in silence for a moment.

"What is it you wish to teach me, brother?" Felix asked.

"It must wait until we reach my garden," Benji looked at the darkness that surrounded them on all sides, squinting to see. "We are not the only folk who roam these woods."

"Should we not have asked father to come along?"

"He will not leave his tree. I have tried. He needs more time to accept his fate."

"I still don't understand why he is here, why you and our brothers were here."

Benji stood straight and looked very much like what Felix imagined Benji's portrait would have looked if it had ever been painted. Tall and stern, hand placed on the pommel of his sword. Wrinkles at the corners of his mouth that suggested he was the teasing sort of child growing up, a smirk natural to him. Desert dunes rising in the background like tsunamic waves. Benji shook his head.

"No King dies with honor, Flea. Now, no more talk until we reach my garden. We will be safe there. Hurry."

And they did hurry, as with those words a sense of urgency entered Felix and Gallows as such they had not felt previously. Terror ran through their veins, and the very marrow within their bones felt cold, despite the raging heat of Tree-Crypt. The darkness wanted them more than it ever had, as they ventured deeper into the Forest, and it soaked up their essence like a parasitic worm, feeding off their souls, fueled by their still-beating hearts. They felt its presence rolling through the forest toward them.

"We need to move faster, or you'll never leave this place!" Benji yelled before tugging Felix along with his cold, dead hand. "Tree-Crypt feeds on us wicked souls but craves live blood most of all! Quickly, we are almost there!"

The red-tipped grass snagged at Felix's ankles fiercely, ripping the cloth, and he noticed now that the vines that ran along the ground seemed to pulsate, growing in order to trip them up. The Forest suddenly grew deafeningly loud, roaring like a torrential storm, humid wind tearing at their bodies.

"Hurry, my King!" Gallows hissed. Felix looked over his shoulder and saw a branch whip out and lash Gallows across the face. Bloody welts rose quickly across his cheeks. He pushed Felix faster.

"Almost there!" Benji screamed over the torrent. He had a white-knuckle grip on Felix's sore hand. "Here it is!"

In a bundle of limbs, they burst forth out of the gripping depths and into the quiet safety of Benji's garden. They slid across the dirt and gasped for breath. The silence had resumed, and all seemed as it had before: dreadfully peaceful.

"That was close," Gallows said, chuckling and coughing at the same time. He got up on one knee. "But we are here now, and safe I would hope."

Benji laughed, standing to his feet and dusting himself off. "Tree-Crypt leaves us our gardens, at least. All is well," he said.

Felix laughed along, standing as well. He held his torch up to study Benji's garden. A small, shriveled sapling leaned haggardly in the center, more a twig than a healthy spruce.

"I do not understand," Felix said, his smile replaced by a brow-furrowing frown. "Why is your tree so small? You've been here for years, have you not? Father's tree was larger than yours."

Benji looked at the tree, then at Felix, with no smile upon his face. "Because," he said, drawing his sword, "I refuse to mourn."

Before Felix could respond, Benji knocked him out of the way and thrusted the tip of his emerald-encrusted sword through Gallows forehead. It happened so fast that Gallows hadn't time to respond, his face still holding a grin. Blood dribbled down the blade. Felix sat in shock until Benji pulled his blade free. Gallows dropped to the ground, his head bouncing hard off the dirt.

"What—what have you *done?*" Felix screamed. Gallows continued to grin upwards at him, blood dribbling from the precise hole in his forehead.

"What I must to survive, as any *true* King would," Benji said. He then laughed maniacally, and the façade of royalty melted away. His beard didn't look as regal as it had before; now it looked haggard and dirty and unkempt, like a street urchin. His eyes were wild and suspicious. "*Finally!* I will escape this place." He became deathly serious. "I am sorry what that means for you, brother. But your heart understands what is best for the kingdom if your mind does not. This is why you sought me."

Benji grabbed Felix by the collar and dragged him through the dirt, toward the dying sapling. "They expect me, the rightful king, to just *die* in such a manner? To caste me into this prison and to *weep* like some woman? No. Arkin and Wym's tears didn't work, obviously, should have seen it, because they were dead like me. They had their own trees. But you? You're alive. You can take my place." Benji grabbed Felix by the scalp and held him over the sapling. "You will cry, and I will leave Tree-Crypt to assume my rightful throne."

"No!" Felix said. He struggled limply. Benji drove the tip of his sword into Felix's back, twisting the blade until the young King screamed. "No!"

"Come, Flea. We know why you are here. You saw me in the Forest and knew I was right to rule. You came for selfish reasons, but the reason itself remains the same. I will visit and make this place a grand tomb for your sacrifice. Do what you were destined to do and revive the rightful king!

The light from the discarded torches flickered behind them where they lay in the dirt, casting wicked and fiery shadows on the clearing in front of them. Felix felt his eyes begin to burn as Benji pulled harder on his hair.

"I do not wish to cause you more harm than is necessary, Flea. But I will. I will do anything to leave, because I deserve to. I was *made* to. My burden to bear."

Felix felt tears burning in his eyes. His vision blurred and darkened, and suddenly he wasn't within the dark domain of Tree-Crypt any longer but lost within his mind. A memory that had been lost to childhood, of when Benji first went south. Benji had been just a boy, around the same age as Felix now. And he had been crying in Queen-Mother's arms while the War-King had waited impatiently embarrassed next to the horses. Benji hadn't been a King; he had become one.

"I might not have been born to rule this kingdom," Felix muttered through gritted teeth, "but I would die for it."

Benji pressed the blade deeper, breaking skin, and sighed. "Perhaps your blood will serve just as well," he said.

Just then a huge shadow overtook theirs as someone stepped in front of the scattered torches behind them. Benji noticed it and quickly threw Felix to the side, raising his sword just in time to deflect the heavy blow of Gallows's blade.

"I will not bury another King," Gallows snarled.

Felix looked down at the huddled mass of Gallows's body that lay still in the dirt, and then back up at the woundless form who stood tall before him. Gallows now had his own tree.

Benji roared and pushed back against Gallows, throwing him off balance. "Then I will bury you both!" he yelled before he launched himself.

The clang of metal on metal was so loud within the garden that Felix almost covered his ears. Benji and Gallows were equally skilled, having trained against each other for years, and now for the first time the once-friends met blades in combat, neither able to get the edge over the other. Benji was swift and snuck attacks where you wouldn't think they'd come, while Gallows was strong and ruthless with his articulately planned swipes. Both knew this of the other, and Felix saw that even spirits of the dead can grow weary.

They circled each other, looking for any weakness. Felix stood to draw his blade. Gallows shook a hand at him. "No, my King. Stay there. I'm dead already, got nothin' to lose," he said.

Benji grinned. "Oh, you've plenty to lose. You might match me at swordplay, but you know little of Tree-Crypt." With that a pulsing vein whipped out of the darkness and wrapped itself around Gallows's legs.

Gallows crashed into the ground. He turned and began to frantically hack at the constricting vine. Benji laughed, walking casually up to him. "I'll do you as I did my brothers. Just another flighty spectral who thought he could match me in *my* crypt. This is my realm, Gallows, as all soon will be. Now—" he kicked the blade from Gallows's grip. "Where was I?"

Benji turned to find Felix holding a torch above the sapling. Benji's face went pale as ash.

"Bow." Felix hissed. "Bow before your King."

Benji immediately obeyed, tossing his sword to the dirt before falling on his hands and knees. "Please, brother," he said, shaking his head. "I—I cannot...please." Benji looked up at Felix. A single tear rolled down his cheek and splattered to the thirsty dust. "I'm scared."

Felix's lip quivered, but his resolve did not.

"Return to the dark." Felix held the torch to the parched sapling which immediately burst into flame.

Benji screeched as flames covered his body. He tried to run out of the clearing, but the darkness prevented this, becoming hard as stone, tossing him backward into the dirt, and there in his garden Benji burnt and died and, in a brilliant cloud of ash, was swept away into the depths of Tree-Crypt.

Felix drew his sword and helped hack through the ruptured and gushing vine that held Gallows down.

"How did you know that would happen?" Gallows asked, looking at the smoldering dirt where the sapling had once been.

"My father was very frightened by the flames, remember?" Felix said. He cleaned his blade and sheathed it. "Though, I didn't know *that* would happen."

Gallows stood and hugged Felix tightly. "I was happy to serve you, my King," he said. They both looked down at Gallows's body. "'til the end."

Felix shook his head. "It is not over, Gallows. Not yet. I feel drawn to move deeper into the Forest, and I still need my captain by my side." Felix smiled, wiped a tear from his cheek and flicked it to the ground. "My friend."

Gallows smiled, patted Felix on the shoulders. He sighed and looked down at his own body. He kicked it brusquely. "I suppose Benji's garden is as good a resting place for me as any." He gestured toward the dark. "Come, I'll show you my garden."

They arrived in a short manner. It was close to the War-King's garden, where the trees are shorter and the place smells fiercely of death. Felix hid his disgust of the latter and stood close to his friend as they entered Gallows's Garden.

Felix handed his torch to Gallows before approaching the blooming sapling. He knelt down, took some dirt in his hands and rubbed it between his fingers. "This is solid ground. Your tree will grow well," Felix said.

Gallows nodded. "Yes. I've much to mourn, of a life ill-led at times. My tree will grow strong."

Felix stood, dusted off his hands. "I will visit you as often as I can. I've nothing to fear of this place, not anymore. In fact, I mean to see more of it. Shall we continue on?"

The two left the garden and ventured further north.

*    *    *

The Tree-Crypt was still itself, dark and forbidding and hot, but it seemed less so on all accounts since Benji's demise, as if he had haunted the Forest. Felix wondered where his brother had gone, now that his tree was burnt. He supposed that was what Benji had been afraid of: the unknown and unchangeable future. Wherever it may be, all his brothers would be together now. Felix shook the thought from his head.

"Do you hear that, my King?" Gallows asked.

Felix stopped, taking a deep breath. They had been walking for hours and he welcomed the distraction. He tasted something new on the air, something he had never known. It wasn't the dead flesh of Gallows, or the humid staleness of Tree-Crypt, but salty and fresh. He closed his eyes and listened to the silence, and just faintly could hear—

"Waves?" Felix asked.

Gallows nodded. "Sounds like the Western Sea. I remember that taste of salt in the air, the crisp cool on the face. Hurry!"

"But it could not be the Western Sea," Felix said as he ran along, "There aren't any seas in the—"

Where once there was complete and empty black, now there was endless blue.

They had stumbled out of Tree-Crypt quite unexpectantly, and onto a vast plain of tall yellow grass that sparsely covered red hills. Rolling out from the cliffs was a sea expanding past the horizon and into the unknown. White waves crashed against the rocks far below. Seagulls called from above, unfamiliar with these new arrivals.

"What is..." Felix couldn't find the right words.

"I've never seen anything like it," Gallows said. "Even the Western Sea has an end. This rolls into oblivion."

Felix walked up to the cliff's edge. Gallows stood near Tree-Crypt, not able to leave its dominion. Felix looked down the cliff into the blue depths below, roaring and dangerous and *unknown*.

"No, not to oblivion," Felix said. He smirked, squinting into the unreachable horizon. "To opportunity."

*Five years later...*

Gallows couldn't get his guard up in time. Felix's wooden sword wacked him right in the crook of his neck.

"Son of a bitch!" Gallows said, stumbling backward.

Felix laughed, leaning casually on his practice sword. He was taller, now, but still clean-shaven. His muscles had filled out under Gallows's tough guidance and war play. "Serves you right, after the welt you gave my rear last week," Felix said. "You *do* know it's a crime to strike a King?"

"I didn't strike a *King*," Gallows said. He stood and cracked his neck. "I spanked him, because he misbehaved. Let's go again."

They charged each other before a blaring horn stopped them in their tracks. They both caught their breaths, sweating and staring at one another. Felix had come to Gallows's garden at least once a week to practice and learn, and for comradery.

"I suppose it is time to go, then," Felix said. He tossed the wooden sword to the ground.

"S'pose so." Gallows wiped sweat from his brow. Tree-Crypt still held silence, but not nearly as well as it once had. They both listened to the waves crashing in the distance. "You've already conquered the afterlife, is that not good enough for you?"

"*A King does not serve himself, but the betterment of his people.* You were there when the War-King said this."

"The War-King said a lot of things, and *did* a lot of things, and that's why he was here, crying over his tree." Gallows picked up Felix's sword, placed them on a stand that held their gear. He seemed ashamed of how he was handling this.

"Hey." Felix walked over, patted Gallows on the back. "I'll be alright. I crushed the Lords of the Western Sea, did I not? The Inohmipans hid in their mountains when our new war-machines rolled West. And the Dunes—"

"Was a victory won by a different sword, was it not?" Gallows said.

"Watch your tongue!" Felix said with a chuckle. "I'd have it out if you were anyone else, talking of my queen like that."

"Those were different, Felix," Gallows said, serious once more. He leaned against a tree, avoiding Felix's gaze. "Those were campaigns that I could advise you on, that the War-King could as well. Now it's just me, and I promised him I'd watch after you. How can I do that when you sail into the Unknown?"

"You've trained me well. I'll be alright. You wouldn't have let me go otherwise, right?" Felix punched Gallows on the shoulder, but the large ghost didn't react. Felix sighed, then walked over to

Gallows's tree that now stood as tall as himself. "Your tree grows strong, Gallows, but slowly." Gallows looked over his shoulder, and the two met eyes. "I plan to be here when it blossoms."

Gallows nodded. He turned and hugged Felix tightly, patting him on the back. "You are a good King, Felix. You are the *only* King that I serve, that I've ever truly served," Gallows said.

"And you are the only one who ever believed in me," Felix said.

Both their tears watered Gallows's garden that day.

Gallows escorted Felix as far as they dared, so those outside of Tree-Crypt, which was since renamed The King's Wood, would not see the ghost.

"I will bring you treasures from afar," Felix said.

"Just you will be treasure enough, my King." Gallows put on a smile. "Now go, your people await."

Felix nodded. He looked back at Gallows once more, took a deep breath and walked out of the Forest.

*    *    *

The docks of the new city in the North, named "Gallows" by the King, were built from the oldest trees of Tree-Crypt. The buildings there were made of the same, as were the carts that carried goods all over the kingdom. The port of Gallows was frantic with excitement as the King's Escort galloped into town. A hundred ships that each carried 200 men sat moodily dormant in the choppy bay, sails yearning to be unfurled and to catch the breeze that now flew easily across the entire northern Kingdom, now that most of Tree-Crypt had been used to build the King's Fleet and terrible war-machines.

One corner of Tree-Crypt was kept safe from the loggers: The King's Wood, it was called, but to Felix it would forever be known as Gallows's Garden.

Felix stood on the deck of his flagship, *True North*, and looked back at the few trees left standing at Tree-Crypt. He thought he could distantly feel Gallows watching him from there, waiting for him. His young and pregnant Queen stood crying on the docks next to nearly a thousand cheering citizens. She smiled and blew Felix a kiss, who almost called the whole thing off right then. How he longed to jump off that swaying ship and sweep her up into his arms. But a King must earn his title, and an Empire longs to expand.

"Loose sails and pull oars!" Felix ordered, to great cheers from both the soldiers and the citizens that crowded the docks.

In unison each boat unfurled their sails with a great resounding *woosh*, followed by thirty oars on each ship being released with a splash into the bay. The rowers grunted as they launched into the Unknown Sea, to find new lands to conquer and bring under the Okarish domain. Felix was not scared of death. He grinned at Tree-Crypt before turning to face the horizon.

Whether or not he survived this campaign, he would return to these shores. No King dies with honor.

# PROTECTOR OF THE REALM
## Brett Venter

Queen Amalia marked the faces of her assembled bodyguards. Markus, who bled for her in the east. Piotr, who distinguished himself in the deserts to the south. Cain, the third, who halted an assassination by shielding her with his own body. The three men stood in a row in the high vaulted room. Flame behind an ornamental grate failed to illuminate to the back of the hall. Curtains were drawn against the fading sunlight.

All three knew the honor being bestowed, pride warring with composure on their faces. When the ceremony was over, they would celebrate long and loud enough to wake the dead. In the presence of the queen there was no space for humanity. Only bloody service, to the end and beyond.

Amalia of Vatra nodded to her guard, who filed out and bolted the doors. All twelve once stood before her, and all received the same gift. The trio before her were next, swelling the Immortals to fifteen.

Markus wondered whether the ceremony would be painful. The guard had teased them with tales of irons and potions, unbearable agony in a test of fealty administered by the queen herself. Piotr mentally charted his life-path from this confirmation, his rise in status from minor noble's son to trusted protector, and the benefits for his family. Cain watched his queen, as any former farmhand might in her presence. Though he bathed in her appearance there was no lust in his eyes.

The queen presented a pleasing sight, shoulder-length dark hair framing intelligent brown eyes and cheekbones chiseled from ice. Her forbidding aspect was counterbalanced by a warm smile, a gift to lips that looked haughty at rest. Her slender neck met delicate bones and a tailored neckline over a swelling breast sloping out and back again to a trim waist. The brocade gown reached the ground, leaving her legs enough movement to walk unimpeded. In her hands, fine-boned as a bird, she carried a small silvered mirror.

She held the mirror to her mouth, breathing deeply and misting the bauble. Bidding Markus to recite the oath, she watched the mirror for signs of treachery. The clouding remained unchanged, even as the fire at the queen's back roared hotter. Logs shifted, sending up questing flares of light. Markus completed his words. He breathed on the mirror, the condensation vanishing with his intake of air.

"You are bound to me, Markus. Go now and join your brothers." Amalia waved her hand at the baroque portal sealing the three men in. The newly minted bodyguard hesitated and then hesitantly walked to the door. A succession of thumps opened it from outside. Markus passed through; the door banging shut like a tombstone falling in a storm.

The queen's head cocked, waiting. Her eye was on Piotr and Cain, a kinked smile at the corner of her mouth. Through the door and the velvet-hung walls came an agonized scream, echoed by a collection of voices before diffusing in a gale of laughter. Piotr almost turned to the raucous distraction. Cain's attention didn't waver.

Queen Amalia repeated the ritual with Piotr, peering into the silvered mirror as though it held every secret in existence. The rangy nobleman spoke the words and his life was pledged into service. Breathing on the mirror, he made the walk outside. Again, the shriek splintered the air, shards of noise dashing themselves against the confirmation room's hangings. Cain did not react. His turn came.

Amalia spoke softly.

"Cain, you came to me by killing your own brother in order to protect my life. Already you have done more for me than most who have been given the gift. Will you not take a reward and a trip to your home instead of life-long service in my guard?

The burly farmer-turned-soldier remained steadfast.

"Fate says I stay by your side."

From that she was unable to budge Cain the Silent. The silvered mirror appeared in her hands for the third time, accepting her breath's moisture. Obliged to coach her newest charge through the pledge, her mind recalling the day she had first created it. It was all in play; a stable boy unaware the young girl he played with lived so far above his station that she couldn't see him below her feet. How the ritual worked she had never discovered. What was certain was that it did. They'd both felt the passing of power and one day, weeks later, when the old king's stallion kicked the stable boy in the temple, they discovered what that passing had meant.

Cain plodded through the catechism, enunciating Amalia's invented script while she watched the mirror protectively. There was never any doubt of his loyalty. Cain took in his queen's essence from the silver surface where he swore away his life. She watched him turn, every moment as precise as dedicated effort could make it.

His confident march to the door would end with a sword through his chest, the blade wielded by Justin, the First Immortal. The mark of the stallion's hooves in Justin's skull were barely visible, save for a single line the length of his forehead. Justin hadn't bled, or experienced pain. He simply pressed the fragments of destroyed skull back with his palms and marveled as the edges had knit together. The day Justin failed to die was the day the Immortals were born.

Her bodyguards thought of the first mortal wound as a joke, a way to jar the new inductees while showing them their newly given power. The 'jest' also dispatched those who failed the test in the queen's presence, when the mirror showed darkness in their hearts. But, in truth, the heart-thrust was mandated by the queen. Any aspect of the childhood ritual could be important to the creation of new Immortals— even the first survival of near-death. Once created, her bodyguard could not fall in battle though they aged like normal men.

The door clicked closed behind Cain. Amalia strained her ears at the noises from the other side of the paneling. There was no scream of fear or pain from the farm-boy, only a grunt of effort as his chest accepted Justin's blade. Cain became the first since Justin to complete the ritual without fear.

\*　　　\*　　　\*

Shrieks bounced off the walls enclosing the dying servant. The heated knife wriggled under exposed ribs, flaps of skin hanging in ragged strips. The servant's chest flinched from every motion, arrested at the rear by vertical slats of wood. Zephyr's hands slid in gore running over fingers and wrist, the assassin's eyes a demonic furnace.

They had worked on the footman for months, a trickle of money ensuring eyes inside the palace. The peasant grew greedy, fattened by liberal gifts for inconsequential intelligence.

A blackmail attempt was countered by Zephyr's talented fingers. A family pet paid the price of the informant's greed. Fear replaced coddling. Their information became free, and more accurate for it.

Loyalty in the old boy finally won out, even with his family threatened. The fool moved them out of harm's way and Zephyr's forces were too specialized to go hunting for that particular needle. Instead they pulled the informant into the Lord's home, an isolated embassy outside the main city walls and a fortress in its own right, revealing the hand behind his torment and enslavement.

Impatient questions left unanswered turned the embassy into a charnel house. Zephyr's skill as an assassin was matched by a brutal inventive streak. When he controlled an end completely... then the Wind came out to play. The Wind blew for much of the evening and early morning, his playmate's screams of despair held captive by subterranean walls.

Bits of information were teased out by Zephyr's blade while the onlooker sat passive, watching the reddening scene with a bored expression. Some nuggets proved valuable but the detail they sought remained elusive. Now, in the servant's last moments, Zephyr and his patron awaited answers to the final question, answers to buy an end to suffering.

A blister of blood formed on the hanging man's lips while his eyes pleaded for release.

"A silver... the queen... talisman... the silver and the ritual... please..."

Zephyr's knife slipped between ribs and twisted. The tattered servant expired with a bubbling rasp, hanging limp against the grooved wooden restraints.

Peregrin, Lord of Hawks, lifted hooded eyes at his comrade. Zephyr, the Wind, met the gaze with one of his own. They had enough to put their plans into motion. Conquest was, at most, weeks away. Peregrin dispatched messengers while Zephyr shut the dungeon door, to finish having his fun.

*    *    *

As weeks passed Cain the Silent spent hours with his queen. She took over his instruction, reliving lessons given to Justin when he was a stable boy sworn to her service. Lessons she hoped to one day give her infant daughter. Combat and weapons training the Immortals took in hand. Justin and his compatriots had a secluded area within the palace, cut off from roving eyes, where they would train. The Forge was enclosed on all sides with large bound wooden doors that could rebuff an army.

All around were utilitarian tools of war. Racks of spear, pike, sword, and halberd—the accoutrements of this bloody trade arrayed walls surrounding sawdust-covered floors. The only light came from sconces set in rock pillars. Here, Cain went from a farmer to a competent and, finally, a fine swordsman. Each practice bout was a fight to the death, Immortal against Immortal. The first to sustain what would have been a mortal blow would retire to the bench and a fresh fighter would take his place. Blood was spilled and limbs were wounded but the marks of battle passed in hours. Cain died several times a day.

Away from the secretive sanctuary of death, the queen's lessons progressed. She found that she must teach Cain the simplest of tasks, skills she'd long taken for granted. Cain was unable to do more than write his own name in a rough scrawl. With slate in hand she instructed him in the creation of letters and the reading of them. Lessons continued between meetings with neighboring monarchs and lords, who settled their disputes in the court of Amalia the Wise.

Queen Amalia stood at the nexus of six kingdoms. Her reputation for fairness and honesty were well-founded and even the dissatisfied would admit her rulings were for the good of all concerned. Amalia retained her post of arbitrator through a complex political web pulling Vatra in all directions. Without the queen's hand the kingdom would fall to larger forces and, following that, the surrounding lands on the continent would be embroiled in conflict unseen for generations.

Diplomacy had an ally in armor. The impenetrable ritual of her Immortals gave rise to rumor. A loving population ascribed the induction ceremony to their queen's magic; those of a darker heart spoke of blood sacrifice to powers beyond the knowledge of men. Both views were cultivated, the Immortals rarely put to the test. There were some who didn't believe, who sought to overthrow the Queen. Their failure fueled the Immortal's fire until it shone like a beacon on a mountaintop.

Along a lavish corridor Cain and Amalia were engaged in conversation. Two of her guard followed ahead and another two behind but Cain paced at her side. His lessons on statecraft were concluded and Cain asked questions to fill in the gaps in his knowledge.

"We never needed to know how to bow to one or another of the nobility when I worked on the farm," he said. His skin flushed at the admission of his origins. It was difficult to comprehend his change in station.

"Farmers require knowledge that I and the rest of the nobles in court do not have," replied Amalia. "Yet without the things that your forebears consider common sense, the kingdom would starve, and perish."

Her frank tone put the new soldier at ease enough for him to stammer out a question he had wished to ask since the ceremony.

"Why... why do you need us, my Queen?"

"You know why, Cain. In the scheme of the kingdom, the Immortals are more important than I. By their protection, I am able to protect others."

"That's not what I meant." He flushed again, wishing that he hadn't asked the question. "I don't understand why you couldn't join your Immortals. An undying queen would be formidable."

"Indeed," she smiled. "But it can't be. I give the breath of life to others. I can't breathe new life into myself."

The queen's mind pieced together the sequence of events needed to create an Immortal. The ceremony, with its senseless words spoken in earnest by men blessed with brawn and loyalty. The summary execution taking place at the close of the ritual. Instant death and rebirth followed by the bluster of camaraderie. There was no telling what would happen to her protectors if she attempted the ritual herself.

"I am sorry, Cain."

"Sorry, my Queen? Why are you sorry?"

She sounded as though she were about to cry. "I've condemned you and the others to an eternal life, with no possibility of death until I die myself. If I could stand with you against the flame of death, I would."

Cain the Silent lived up to his name for a time and then said "My Queen, you forget. That is the fate we have chosen for ourselves, would have chosen even without your gift."

Amalia could only stare at her charge. Around them, their footsteps echoing in the gilded passage, the quartet of Immortals smiled at Cain's innocent loyalty.

\*     \*     \*

"So, this is the kingdom that has keeps order."

Lord Andre Peregrin, playing the cultured diplomat, placed an arrogant boot on Vatran soil. He surveyed the tidy city with the air of one perusing a shop front.

"So small a thing to wield such influence. She would fit several times over into my own lands." He addressed his remarks to his guide, an agreeable fellow named Anton who wobbled when he walked. Anton joked that his size was the reason he rode everywhere. 'It makes people sea-sick when I walk,' was his explanation.

"Size is irrelevant here, my Lord Hawk. Vatra exists as a nexus for power. Our queen doesn't hold influence so much as keep the peace and render judgement for other kingdoms. In the, ah, messier disputes." Anton jiggled to a halt. "Queen Amalia serves an ancestral function. She is more a servant than I myself." A proud eyebrow lifted. "She simply serves on a grander scale than others ever will."

Peregrin's lips tightened, dry fingers rubbing over hardened palms.

"A queen who serves? A marvelous notion. Will I meet her on this trip?"

"If her schedule allows, my Lord."

Furrows creased Peregrin's unblemished forehead.

"Schedule?"

"Indeed." Anton began to grudgingly scale the courthouse steps. "Queen Amalia's duties are laid out months in advance, but she is known to halt her duties for the day and talk to petitioners. Royal whim, and one of the reasons she is loved."

Peregrin kept pace with the fast-moving courtier. Who would have thought such blubber could achieve such speed.

"Feared, as well, from what I have heard."

"You've heard of the Immortal Guard, then?"

"I have. They are thought to be a myth."

Anton smiled. "Queen Amalia's bloodline stretches back over a thousand years, to the founding of Vatra. Her ancestors were thought to possess an immortal army that helped maintain control over the region. Our historians have since found that well-disciplined armies were responsible for Vatra's early victories."

Peregrin halted. The courtier hadn't answered his question.

"But her bodyguard? The Immortals? There are tales that her men cannot be killed."

Anton pushed open an ornate door, ushering Andre Peregrin into his first trade meeting for the week.

"Tales, my lord. Tales we've taken pains to nurture, of course. Fewer would-be assassins will face Queen Amalia's guard when they believe the soldiers are immortal."

"I see. So, they are fictions?"

"Is there any doubt, my lord?"

Peregrin, Lord of Hawks, held silent but was unconvinced. He shook hands with trade representatives but behind the grin and banter his mind gnawed at his purpose in Vatra. The old retainer's gasps of secret ritual and blood, and a small item that allowed the creation of the most fearsome beings ever to cross a battlefield — men who would not die. With such a power at his command...

A years-long plan now set in motion by a battery of trade meetings to supply his homeland with enough grain to last through several years. His feints tested Queen Amalia's security time and again, only to fail. But his spies had not confined their activities to assassination. There was news of a new Immortal, a farm-boy elevated for performing a service. Easy prey for the Wind.

"I want all of the grain you can give me," he said to the circle of merchants. "And I will give you more than you deserve in return. Nodgravia has great need of bread and beer."

\*　　\*　　\*

"I know the secret of the queen's power, the secret to creating an Immortal. I alone can reproduce this feat!"

Cain heard the declamation ringing out over the din of the marketplace. His first thought was to acquire this information, to pass it on to his Queen.

This was quickly followed by restraint. He no longer believed every claim made in his presence. Queen Amalia's education had borne fruit. Folding his meal of dried meats and fruits into a square of leather, Cain strode to the gaunt-looking man holding forth to a knot of onlookers.

The preacher ranted in his strange accent. His words were taken lightly, many before him claimed to know where the rumored Immortals originated. A hereditary gift was the most used explanation among the common folk, a belief bolstered by oral tradition. Vatra's lands, built on the backs of warriors who returned from death to do their master's bidding. The palace library held examples of the legend on crumbling parchment.

Cain listened closely to the words. There was a ring to them, a taste he could sense. No sun-addled acolyte this, driven mad by service and too much time outside the city walls. An air of danger hovered around the bloodless lips and the hanging robes couldn't hide the preacher's jerky movements each time one of his audience moved too close.

"I know the source of the queen's power," he cried. "And I will be willing to share the secret with the right man."

The crowd, drawn together for the show, began to disperse. The con was familiar: Forbidden information, a request for money as a show of good faith, and then a disappearing act. Zephyr watched the rubes leaving, an uncontrolled flicker of his eyes in Cain's direction. The young man wore his clothing uncomfortably, as though he were unused to them. The palace spy description of the queen's new pet was accurate. Zephyr made a mental note to thank the betrayer personally when the coup was done.

Zephyr waited until most of the watchers were distracted by the market's wares before directing a low query at Cain.

"And you? Are you the right man to share the secret of the queen's power?" He gave no hint that he knew of Cain's status as an Immortal.

Cain's urge to report whatever this stranger concealed came across as suppressed eagerness. Passers-by interpreted their opposing positions as just another fool being fleeced for knowledge that wasn't knowledge at all.

"I might be the right man," Cain replied. His voice was as steady as he could make it.

"You might be, at that." Zephyr took Cain by the elbow, guiding him to a place where they could converse. A short walk through spices and hanging wares led to a corner surrounded by pillars where there wasn't enough space to set up a stall. The niche, used by those looking to escape the crush of the market, hid a stone bench behind the smooth support columns. Zephyr took the left-hand side and Cain sat on the right, sheltered from the din by a pocket of cool silence.

Zephyr spoke first, revealing that he knew more about his quarry than he might be expected to.

"You're of the palace, aren't you? Don't deny it, the cut of your clothing speaks of the Royal Tailor."

"I am." Cain didn't see any point in denying it.

"Then you are the one to help me. Queen Amalia is said to conduct a ritual with which she creates immortal soldiers." The Wind held up a dry palm to stall any questions. "A part of this ritual is a personal item of the queens. An item of silver."

"And you want me to get it for you." The statement left Cain's lips like lead.

Zephyr licked his own, anxious that he might slip up. "I do. With this item, I can recreate the queen's magic. I can make it better; I can make her guard immune to pain. I can turn their skin to stone. I can make them the most fearsome thing that this kingdom has ever seen..."

The assassin watched Cain considering his words, knowing that Peregrin's schemes teetered on this moment. Only if the simpleton was as simple as they thought would he...

"I will bring the item for you, mage. I serve my queen in all things and she will be glad to loan it if it will increase the power of her soldiers."

"No!" Zephyr composed himself. Some of the merchants had turned towards the noise. In a lower voice he continued. "You must not let Queen Amalia know about this. If my magic were to fail after making such a promise, my life, and probably yours, would be forfeit. But if we are able to deliver an improvement..." His words hung in the air.

Cain seemed to give the words thought.

"What benefit is there for you, mystic? Why would you help my queen?"

Zephyr suppressed the glee that he felt at the other's words. He had Cain.

"I will not lie to you, sir. I hope for glory. To be named as the magician who assisted the Vatran queen... A name like that..." The shrug of his shoulder said he would never want for anything with that reputation. He waited for the young man to swallow the bait.

"I will help you, mystic," Cain said after agonizing minutes of delay. "If my queen can be strengthened then I will risk her wrath." Zephyr was elated, signifying his pleasure with a slight flaring of his nostrils.

"Then you will meet me here, tomorrow, with the queen's silver talisman?"

"I will not."

"I... what do you...?"

Cain, hoping not to be seen as giving offence, followed his statement quickly with "I do not know how long it will take me to find the queen's talisman without being seen. I will meet you here in three days, either with the treasure or to ask for more time."

*     *     *

Cain stood at the base of Amalia's throne; late morning sun cutting through small apertures near the ceiling. His uncertain eyes matched the nervous line his lips had pulled themselves into. The young man swept sweaty palms around behind his back while he waited for his queen's response.

Amalia sat on her throne in court. In evidence were selected members of her guard who stood in the entryways, facing outward. Minor functionaries fussed around drapes and tables, readying the room to receive petitioners that afternoon.

The queen considered what she had learned. That someone knew enough to identify the origin of her bodyguard was concerning. More important was where this marketplace mystic had gathered his information. The specifics of the ritual were tightly confined. Some knew when it would be taking place but none, save her Chosen, had ever been privy to the details.

"You said this mystic asked for the silver talisman, Cain?" Amalia pitched her words so only Cain could hear them.

Cain jumped forward. "Those were his words, my queen. To the syllable."

"And you are sure that he did not ask for the mirror, precisely?"

"Quite sure, my queen." Some of his nervousness ebbed away but something about the mystic troubled his monarch.

"Perhaps, then, he didn't know which item is used for the ritual..." She spoke almost to herself. "Did he take you for one of the Immortals, Cain?"

He told the truth.

"I do not know. He may have known who I am, but he did not show it. My presence in the court hasn't been noted by the usual visitors." Time spent observing courtroom games was not wasted, Amalia saw. "That suggests that he has other avenues of information." Nor were her lessons futile. This son of the soil had a mind more formidable than many of higher status. And then: "I feel that he may not have been completely honest with me."

Cain's almost sly tone caught Amalia's attentions and she saw him suppressing a grin.

"I feel you might be right there," she said, playing along. "So, he might have knowledge of my newest Immortal, after all. But not the mirror. That means his information is incomplete." Queen Amalia clapped her hands together. "Let's complete it for him."

"Your Majesty?"

She smiled at Cain. He was strong and intelligent, though still fresh enough to be innocent of most deception; and deception was needed here. Over time he would learn the baser tools of statecraft. This would serve as his first lesson.

"You will present this mystic with a silver talisman. A personal item, something that he will associate with a magical ritual. A silver goblet from my chambers, perhaps?"

Cain stood to attention, nodding and absorbing.

"You will present it, claiming that it is the item he seeks. Attempt to learn his intentions once you have passed the goblet on but feel no worry if he isn't forthcoming. I will instruct the house spies to follow the servants for a time." She sounded dismayed at the prospect. "He will seek more information about the goblet's magic. Then we will have our leak and, perhaps, our plotter."

Cain, worried about his ability to dissemble in front of the stranger, admitted as much but Amalia reassured him.

"He will be intent on the goblet, not on the one that brings it to him. He thinks you a tool to be used; ignored when your usefulness has ended. Let him."

With Queen Amalia's blessing, Cain departed. First Immortal Justin stood aside to let him pass. Justin had doubted the boy's abilities, but he was quickly proving himself capable. The greying former stable boy reminded himself that Amalia's instincts proved correct more often than not.

*　　*　　*

"I have what you need, mystic."

Cain unwrapped the bauble, eager to be done with deception. His face said he wished he'd never stolen the goblet but was consoling himself that he performed a service for his monarch.

"Not here, fool. Away from eyes," Zephyr hissed the imperative, beckoning the soldier into the semi-darkness.

The noise of the crowd faded like a fleeing storm. Glancing around, Cain made to hand his prize to Zephyr. As the silver flashed Cain noted another presence detach itself from the grey. A crunching impact from behind took the light from Cain's eyes. The last words he heard were "Show it to me" before a white rag clapped over his nostrils and his mind fogged away.

He awoke to a green and grey wall. His shoulders ached. His forehead throbbed. Thin light filtered down from the ceiling, stabbing at his thoughts. He looked blearily around.

His surroundings were small and the brightness above prevented him from seeing into the corners. He stood, arms raised above his head. His knees were useless, as though whatever had knocked him unconscious had sapped his strength.

Cain shook an arm, heard a soft grinding of metal-on-metal above. He could feel the metal cuff rubbing his wrists raw. He was suspended at the end of two lengths of chain. Cognition slowly returned. The light in the cell came from behind, leading him to believe that he was suspended facing away from the doorway.

He twisted his neck as far as it could go before a spike of pain drove him back, gasping desperately. His journey had not been without incident after all.

Waiting for the pain to subside the soldier set about clearing his head. Whichever narcotic had rendered him helpless was wearing off. He was also able to feel, bringing some tension to his arms by pulling against his chains with fists clenched. His legs remained jelly. For the first time since he'd woken, he looked down. His shouts at the sight of splintered bone where once-healthy legs once existed were the prompt his captors waited for.

Zephyr's oily voice preceded the assassin through the captive's cell door.

"The Immortal is awake." A mocking chuckle. "Didn't your mother ever teach you that strangers are dangerous, peasant?"

A more imperious tone cut through the killer's teasing. "Enough, Zephyr. He's going to be in enough pain once the Sorrow wears off and I need to question him thoroughly before this is over."

The burly nobleman stepped into view in front of the hanging man. His look was familiar but Cain, still in shock, could only place

286

him as being around the court. The name that went with the hooked nose, piercing blue eyes and pointed chin eluded him. He could only ask "My legs... what happened to my legs?"

A cold grin was his answer.

"We couldn't have you running away, Cain. Cain the Silent, they call you. We'll test that soon. You will provide the piece I need to take control of this thorny kingdom."

"Control...? What...?"

"Zephyr, explain it to him."

"Gladly." Cain dimly felt his shirt part at the rear, a dagger purring through fabric. A rush of cool air gave way to agony as the knife bit in.

"You will explain to the Hawklord how to control your fellows. You will hand over the secrets of the chalice. Then the pain will cease."

*     *     *

Cain withstood hours of interrogation. Zephyr was delighted. Cain bled like a mortal man and his wounds didn't close rapidly enough for the warlord and his vassal to notice that the prisoner's skin was slowly knitting. Zephyr was a man who liked to retrace his steps.

His gift didn't prevent him from expressing pain, which left his body in a series of grunts forced past his lips by the assassin's skillful knives. But words, about the queen or about his predicament, were stillborn.

"Tell me where the queen's apartments lie."

"What are the movements of the guard?"

"The chalice. Reveal the secrets of the chalice."

Lord Peregrin doggedly rephrased his questions after each of Zephyr's ministrations. Each new indignity was followed by calm-sounding queries. A broken finger, a crushed fingernail, a strip of skin torn off: None of these phased Peregrin, who asked questions without emotion.

Even he grew frustrated. Nightfall departed and they were no nearer to a solution. Zephyr had been careful to leave his captive's mouth unscathed, so that he could answer demands, but the rest of his body was a battlefield of pain. Shards of bone lifted from his ribs and through his skin. The muscles in his forearms hung in shreds and Cain's hands were skinned to a raw, red travesty. Cain the Silent embodied his name like a grim specter. But he listened.

Whispered conversations in the torture-lulls were clear to Cain. There was no roar of blood in his ears and the pinpricks he'd been given were distant calls overridden by their conferences. The moment the pain stopped; his body began to repair. Poorly. Bones knit at unnatural angles, muscle reconnected in the wrong place. A wandering look up at his arms told Cain that he would never be a whole man again. But he listened.

Zephyr had no magic and nor did Lord Peregrin. Only the belief that the Immortal Guard were thralls, slaves controlled by a magical talisman. If Cain could have grinned, he would have. It was as though Peregrin had never heard of loyalty.

On subverting the Guard, Peregrin intended to take the city. His army waited, encamped in a valley. Vatra would become his seat of power and he would control the surrounding kingdoms. He would have his empire. Cain wondered what happened to the farmers occupying the valley while Zephyr resumed his work. At best, the peasants served as slaves. At worst, they were all dead.

As the knife parted flesh again, Cain came to a decision. He would endure a while longer, feigning increasing agony until he confessed to Peregrin. He would tell the beast what he wanted to hear — that a few simple words would turn any of the Guard within earshot to his cause. And then he would tell Peregrin the words.

What Zephyr did after he was no longer useful didn't bear thinking about. Perhaps his usefulness wouldn't end. Lord Peregrin would require a demonstration.

*    *    *

Lord Peregrin of Nodgrav climbed the palace steps. Behind him, footmen cleaned Cain's blood off coach upholstery. The burlap sack he had been wrapped in had been unable to contain Zephyr's ruin. Cain was supported up the stairs by two of his kidnapper's escort.

Peregrin carried the silver goblet in hand, cradling it between his fingers. Thrusting aside courtiers and servants, the lord forced his way into the queen's court. Petitions were in session.

The Hawklord strode to the main entrance, looking the trio of bodyguards in the eye as he loudly declaimed the gibberish that Cain had taught, perfectly. The nonsense went on, involving gestures with the goblet and facial contortions in the direction of his intended victims. He ended with the words "Now your minds are as mine is. Now let me pass!" Peregrin bellowed this last, missing the runnel of blood leaving Cain's downward-facing mouth as a fatigued grin split his lips. The cost of not laughing while teaching the 'incantation' had almost broken him as badly as Zephyr's tools had. In the end the joke had been worth it.

The confused Immortals glanced over their shoulders and, seeing the queen's affirmation, stood aside to let the foreign madman pass.

"My dear queen," Peregrin began as he crossed the hall, shoving petitioners while Zephyr glowered at the ring of guards. "My dear queen. I've come to take your city from you." He brandished the chalice.

The queen was outwardly composed but her eyes went from the flash of silver to the burden supported by two armored soldiers. Her plan had flushed out the spies. She wasn't entirely surprised the ambitious Lord Peregrin was behind it. He probably had bigger designs than just Vatra's little city-state. But her look kept straying to the dripping bundle behind the lord. The longer she looked, the more her stomach shrank.

Amalia forced her stare to the strutting nobleman, who took frequent chances to wave the chalice in front of the unreacting Guard. She was puzzled for a moment before recalling his eccentric performance at the entryway. Doubtless Cain's work.

"You will take my kingdom from me, are you? How?" The room fell silent at Amalia's words.

"With this!" was the gleeful reply. Peregrin was almost dancing with excitement. "Now I am the one who commands your Guard!"

Audible gasps slivered through the air. All knew the rumors surrounding the queen's Immortals. If this interloper took those warriors for himself the effects would be disastrous.

Cain stumbled forward with his last reserves of energy. He was slowly healing but his fatigue was terribly real. The recruit had forced his body through agonizing postures at the behest of Lord Peregrin in an effort to convince the rebel the chalice was real. Each act, no matter how ridiculous or painful, was performed without hesitation or complaint. His efforts paid off in the overconfident lord prancing around the throne, but they had cost dearly. Splinters of bone were driven out through the soles of his feet and his legs were warped and broken. He wheezed when he breathed, shattered ribs pressing into organs, and his skull had changed shape. The remains of Peregrin's dagger protruded from his spine, wedged between unforgiving bone. The soldier fell to the ground in front of Amalia's throne.

Fully seeing Cain's body, shredded after Zephyr's play and sporting the Hawklord's signature, narrowed Amalia's eyes into points, sending her into a shrieking frenzy. The first sonic blast wiped the smirk from Peregrin's face. The second brought the demon wanderer Zephyr to his knees, palms clapping uselessly over bleeding ear drums.

The chalice vibrated in Peregrin's grasp, heating until he snatched his hand away. Gawping at white blisters, he kicked the vessel across the throne room's flagstones. It came to rest against a pillar which started smoking. Stone glowed red and ran like water. On the floor the travesty that was Cain formed a fragmentary smile through the crusted blood on his face.

Another scream, pitched beyond the limits of human hearing, summoned all of Amalia's guard. Armored and unstoppable, they crashed through doors and windows. Justin, her First Protector, plunged through white marble to stand at his queen's side.

Lord Peregrin turned to run only to find the way barred by flesh and steel he did not control. His own soldiers waited, an entire army covering the plains in front of the fortress, but they served no purpose while he stood on the point of the queen's knife. He turned a pleading face in the still-shrieking monarch's direction.

Amalia's agonized eyes fixed on her guardian's dripping form. His eyes had been gouged from his skull with ragged, uncaring cuts. Ribbons of cloth masked ribbons of flesh and broken bone. The queen's torment built in a titanic thunderstorm, clouding the court with red streamers of pain.

Zephyr glanced quickly at Lord Peregrin, understanding his handiwork was to blame but too absorbed in watching the threat of the Guard to care. Peregrin's soul dropped through his chest where it withered in the monarch's awesome presence. Conquest and rule were forgotten, and a frozen panic had set in. He would have run if he could, but the imposing wall of soldiery fanned out in front of

Queen Amalia, poised like dogs on a chain. The first sign of weakness... His fingers creaked as he closed his hands into fists, debating whether to run or fight or fall prostrate in front of the devastated ruler.

Zephyr, in his turn, focused on the threat in front. There were, as ever, no thoughts of the future. He would run, and he would kill every courtier and page and nobleman he could in his flight. His end was already written. He just wanted to scratch out a few more lines before being hewn to pieces.

Amalia unthinkingly held her men in check while grief vented from her like steam. The screams built to a crescendo, the walls vibrating in sympathy. A red and grey fog filled the ceiling with each vocal outpouring. A final throat-ripping cry wrenched through her chest, continuing far beyond the limits of a human lung capacity. The queen flopped forward onto her hands and knees, vomiting blood and broken membrane onto the marble flagstones. For long seconds all that could be heard was her pitiful retching. Then she looked up at Cain's torturers.

For the first time in his twisted life Zephyr felt fear. Pinned by the queen's gaze, he lost his head and hurled himself at her phalanx. Lord Peregrin's nerve broke on the iceberg of Amalia's stare. He dashed through the rear of the room, consumed by the need to escape. The fog billowed in his wake.

The Wind's twirling leap carried him onto the points of the Immortal's swords. Amalia remained where she had fallen. Watching Justin and his fellows destroy the trickster brought no solace from the agony she felt at Cain's plight.

Peregrin charged through the castle, screaming in fright at cowering groups of servants. Catching his own reflection drove him to more frantic motion. Outside his carriage waited, with a retinue of bodyguard he could throw at her monsters to buy enough time to join his army. And then... then...

He burst through an ornamental door and into the light, cascading down the wide stairs and into his manservant's arms. His chest heaved.

"Run... drive... go...!"

The panic on his face was sufficient to create motion without questions. Following were his lancers, who stayed close in anticipation of violence. No pursuit followed. The court was watching Zephyr's execution. The madman gibbered and raved. He took an age to die, cursing the queen and his employer, spitting details of the plot to overthrow Amalia's kingdom. At no point did he stop fighting, using his final breath to heave himself upwards and draw a dagger from an unguarded belt. The blade plunged into an Immortal's chest. At the back of the room, the last of the fog leaked outside.

Only once the assassin had stopped breathing did Amalia come close enough to touch him. She cupped Zephyr's cheek, staring into his dead eyes. Turning away, she murmured to her Immortals to convey Cain's tortured body away. Soft commands saw warm water and rags sent to the room her bodyguard's body was taken to. Dead-eyed, she ripped the sleeves from her gown. She dipped clean rags into water and set to work, staining cloth and liquid pink as she wiped away what damage she could. Her soldiers covered every entrance to the makeshift infirmary. She lost the capacity for speech. Nerveless fingers dug out the splinters of steel in Cain's back.

*     *     *

Peregrin's army were apprised of events by the slowly calming lord. A council of war convened in the main tent. Generals and attendants stood clustered around a table, planning their conquest of the kingdom. The bloodless coup had failed. The Lord of Hawks could no more march his troops from the field than he could upend the skies. His own people would crucify him for the humiliation.

Peregrin, nursing injuries sustained in his flight, addressed his commanders.

"Capture of the city should be a simple task, except for the palace. We will be marching into a grinder. I would counsel taking the city proper and surrounding the royal dwelling with soldiers before making an advance. One of Amalia's Immortals will be enough to hold a gate against entry. We will have to overwhelm them, like ants streaming over a dying beetle."

"You mean, if the rumors are true, my Lord? Don't you?" The minor noble fielded his own troops, bought with promise of a prime place in court. "The Immortals are just men, surely?"

Peregrin pivoted on a heel, pacing up and down.

"Not just men," he said, to himself and to general consternation. "If we do not throw everything into a single attack the soldiery will break before the palace does. The number of men that will die today will be fantastic—better it happens all at once, before it breaks morale."

Peregrin's brow furrowed and he flexed his blistered hand.

"I had it in my grasp. I could have turned the tide alone."

He regarded the shape of gems molded into skin, burnt black.

"Lord, what orders will we give the men?"

Peregrin opened his mouth to issue official battle commands when a clattering of cups came from the edge of the tent, followed by a perceptible shaking of the ground. Officers turned to each other in confusion, but the tremor passed before anyone could remark on it. His mouth snapped shut.

"Tell the men that the attack goes soon. They take the city but treat the palace as the final target. Any scouts or looters who attempt to enter before I give the command will be executed."

\*　　　\*　　　\*

The ground shook under marching soldiers, stepping in time towards an unprepared foe. Metal clanked, armor rustled and bounced, and dust lifted into flexing nostrils. Peregrin's forces closed over the plain, towards the walls where the gates stood open. Even if closure was considered, the hinges had long since rusted open.

Nervous citizens fled the scene, the normally busy market district that ringed Amalia's little city-state deserted of all but flies. Clumps of people watched the army advance on their homes.

Worried conversations died and heads turned towards the palace as citizen after citizen fell to their knees. Amalia, stripped almost bare and covered in Cain's blood, walked from the ornate building towards the gates. In her hands she carried the fragments of the knife shattered on Cain's spine. The knife which wounded her vassal beyond repair. She ferried it like an offering, the slivers of metal held chest-high on her upturned palms. At a respectful distance came her guard, led by Justin.

The silent party cleared the crowd. Justin spread their number with a gesture, and they remained in step behind the queen. The barefoot royal closed the distance toward the advancing army without acknowledging its presence.

Peregrin's soldiers took up position in front of the main gates, companies preparing to march or ride for other entry points when a scout brought word to the field command that a nearly naked queen stood before the city.

"Her mind's broken. She's come to die."

"Could it be surrender?"

"Why is she naked? I've never seen a naked queen before..."

"Her bodyguard? Why aren't the Immortals attacking?"

Speculation among the soldiers was rife. A messenger was dispatched to Peregrin, who rode to the front himself to see the queen.

He stood on a slope, peering at the bloody monarch through a telescope.

"She's carrying something. Can any of you see what it is?"

A chorus of negatives lapped around his knees.

"Her guard are present. I'm not about to risk a meeting with her. Tell the men to wait... what are those idiots doing?"

The ground shook, tiny pebbles dislodging underfoot. Peregrin looked around for the source of the rumble without seeing it.

A small party, thirty men hoping to boast of having seen a naked queen, presented themselves. A handful harbored thoughts of *taking* a naked queen as they wheeled their mounts in the direction of the city. At the first sign of hostile action the Immortal guard moved forward in a defensive wall in front of the queen. She stopped and stared ahead, as though a statue.

Horses flew at the solitary knot of flesh and armor. The watching army held its breath. Justin, as silent as Cain ever was, placed himself at the brunt, swinging his sword at the lead horse. The rest of the Immortals lashed out with spear and shield. The sortie split like cheesecloth on a razor, a lone living horse barreling into the city walls and leaving the remains of its rider on the plaster like a squashed bug. Amalia's bodyguard settled back into their watchful post behind the queen. She hadn't moved.

Watching through his telescope, Peregrin gulped around a knot in his throat. Conscious of his men's eyes at his back, Peregrin lowered the tube and called for his jacket.

"I think she is waiting for me. Summon my horses and attendants." A quick eye flicked over the officers. "You, you, you, and you. Saddle your horses. Leave your weapons behind." He picked the most frightened of the lot, to give himself an excuse if Amalia's men menaced their approach.

He caught the look he was given.

"What good will they do? There are only ten of us." His own weapon thumped into the dirt.

As the retinue rode the Immortals were kept under observation. Corpses had proved livelier. Peregrin's party halted at a distance, out of respect for the Immortal's skills. They left enough space to turn and scatter, should the need arise. Peregrin attempted to brazen it out.

"Your Majesty?"

The young queen's features sparked with life. First a faltering step, then a second. Amalia almost slid in the blood-soaked mud, but she carried her burden forward, lifting it to Lord Peregrin.

"Your knife, my Lord." The queen stared through her foe. "Please." A small gesture and Peregrin gathered the fragments, slipping them into a saddlebag. When he looked up, Amalia was already retreating without turning her back on him.

"Your army dies today, my Lord."

A serene smile split her lips, exposing neat, square little teeth.

"All of it. Back to your wolves. The sheep attack soon."

A wave of her hand dismissed them. Justin took a pace and the enemy party bolted as though pursued by death. Hurtling to the comparative safety of his army Peregrin countermanded instructions, overriding all of the objections his advisers hoped to raise.

"All of the men. Now. We have an opportunity. We cannot waste it. Her bodyguard are outside, without benefit of walls. They must be dismembered, the pieces carried apart as soon as they are severed."

A ring of shocked faces stared at his wild features. Calmer minds searched frantically for faults in the plan.

"I'm sick of waiting. Sound the attack or I start claiming heads."

Peregrin pointed his fatigued features at the queen, already savoring her end. The Nodgrav army commenced its attack, neat ranks advancing on the queen's position. Queen Amalia stood firm, her stare of devastation boring into advancing soldiery. Her bodyguard formed into a relaxed semicircle, wasting no effort for the coming fight.

Horse and footman marched in time. The ground shook, pebbles dislodged and sent rolling across the ground by the beat of war. A shiver of discomfort rippled through the ranks; driven by the size of the force they were facing. The Hawklord's men felt like butchers rather than warriors, but their training provided anger instead of guilt. The beat quickened. Horses cantered; men broke into a jog. Clashing metal splintered the air. Still Amalia stood.

Like an ocean wave breaking around volcanic rock, Peregrin's charge hammered into the handful and split around it, unable to pierce the circumference of shield and spear. The nearest horsemen were cut to ribbons as they passed, their armored steeds left to clatter into the city itself. The horse charge wheeled and struck from behind as infantry smashed against the Immortal's shields in an aftershock. An audible crack pierced the air a moment later, distracting the attackers for a brief second. That was enough for Justin's company to add more soldiers to their tally. The Immortals were unscathed, shallow wounds already closing on their own, but the volume of humanity surrounding their queen would eventually wear them down through attrition. The melee closed on Amalia's island.

Queen Amalia stared through clashing warriors as they became worriers. Though unable to directly see him, her head turned to keep Peregrin, Lord of Hawks, in front of her eyes. Behind those eyes, something broken and angry capered and laughed. The queen could feel the shuffling advance of Cain, her Silent Cain, from behind as he dragged his wrecked and tattered form out of the palace and onto the battlefield. The creature behind her eyes broke further in response to his pain.

*     *     *

A final great rumble, owing nothing to the charging horse or the horde of infantry screaming in the wake of horse flatulence and terrified piss, shook the field. A spreading red mist escaped the city gates, sending tendrils along the walls. Peregrin's spotters discarded the phenomenon, focusing on the formations and the charge. Crimson vapor settled into the ground and through the city walls, outlining indentations of venerable graves.

Cracks appeared. Skeletal warriors, scraps of rotting flesh dragging at their bones, clawed their way up from the dirt. The rusted remains of mail rustled and shook. Bony fingers closed around ancient hilts set over ancient breasts. Tattered eyelids on gaunt corpses flew open, revealing black eye sockets.

The Company of Immortals came to attention.

The flailing combatants failed to see shedding dust sprouting swords along the length of the city walls. Generations of Immortals past, called to action by the queen's grief, awoke as one. A parade of uniforms stretching back a thousand years shone through the dust of years. Vatra's standing army closed on the queen's position, ripping into the circle around her living protectors.

Fury met the undead charge, replaced by unreasoning fear. Swords clanged against bared bone, hardly shifting wasted bodies. Peregrin's troops launched away from the battle in panic, colliding with advancing men who hadn't yet learned what fear looked like.

The army took ineffectual swipes at Amalia's position. Her living guard ringed her in, bared teeth defying any normal warrior to leap within their reach. Charges on the flanks were turned by the dead. Soldiers streamed from the field like water-soaked ants, avoiding reaching arms set into burst brickwork. Mutiny proved infectious and more peeled off without ever seeing what would give their countrymen nightmares for the rest of their lives.

Lord Peregrin watched in horror as his forces threw themselves against an immovable rock of immortal men and supernatural soldiers. With time and enough men... but he didn't have either luxury. His burned hand flexed and twitched, seared nerve endings sparking against the trauma.

Queen Amalia's eyes opened; her serene smile unchanged. A delicate step forward moved her protective circle deeper into the press of bodies and steel. Methodical, untiring attacks drove off opportunists. Some of Peregrin's soldiery struck at the circle. The Immortals, fueled by her ferocious anger, no longer even bled.

The tattered queen walked faster, her mental command keeping the Immortals around her even as her pace increased. Her bodyguard advanced through the army as though it weren't there. Her opponents were distracted by an advancing line of antique soldiers.

Clasped loosely in her hand was the ritual mirror, the toy she had been given as a child. Her mind was somewhere within its depths. Amalia, her gaze fixed on a silent point in the past, picked up speed until she was sprinting towards Peregrin's command tents. Her living and undead phalanx kept the mortal queen unscathed, though she wore more enemy blood than clothing. Her fingers reflexively brushed dried matter from the silvered surface in her hands.

The shocking advance threw Peregrin's commanders into a panic. There were no reserves left to cast at the Immortal's advance, if there even was a hope of slowing it. Common soldiers stepped aside for the racing company. Only the foolhardy or suicidal braved the onrushing attack. Chaos spilled everywhere, lighting up the battlefield with conflagrations of pain.

Horses were summoned but before Peregrin could mount and retreat, the Immortals collided with their position. A controlled frenzy of slaughter beheaded the army's command, two of the Immortals leaving the safely of the ring to dispatch the trumpeters and complete the task of throwing the attackers into disarray.

Immortals split and closed, trapping a frantic Lord Peregrin inside their circumference. He flinched like a turtle, expected a killing stroke to come at any instant. Instead he felt a hand on his shoulder. Peregrin extended his head and looked to see the queen holding the mirror out towards him. It was misted over as though it had been submerged in ice.

"Breathe," she commanded. Lord Peregrin, fighting to hold onto his bravura, obeyed. His breath washed over the mirror, staining its silver surface black.

Amalia smiled again, dropping the mirror into the dirt. At an unspoken command her Immortals stood away, taking up guard positions in the enemy encampment.

The noises of battle had ceased. Peregrin's troops had halted in stunned silence to watch the queen's impossible strike. Movement returned to the field like a wind descending from the overworld. Skeletal soldiers destroyed their immediate opponents, a line of death scything through enemies as though through chaff. Each corpse travelled towards the shocked and unblinking lord, jagged sword edges extending to put an end to his ambitions. Each rotting combatant took on a more spectral character the further they got from Vatra's boundary until they floated above the ground, little more than vengeance and a blade. They met in a hurricane of iron and steel which lifted Peregrin into view of his surviving men. His last moments ended in a flurry of red haze and splintered bone.

The rotation of death ended with Peregrin's dismemberment, the surviving members of the Nodgrav army throwing down their arms in horror at their leader's execution. His threat ended; Amalia's vitality burnt away. She crumpled to the ground, breathless. Ghastly warriors arrayed themselves in ranks next to the fallen queen. Amalia lay motionless. The limping ruin of Cain arrived at her head, sorrow distorting already twisted features. The Immortals came, one by one, to take position by their commander.

The queen's end, preceded by her charge into the thick of battle, could not be ignored. The people must know how Amalia perished, in service to her kingdom. Justin called for the construction of a pyre in view of the city. Tents, cabinets, and siege weapons were reduced to kindling and stacked into a monstrous wooden grave. The army of death took on physical form, returning to the city to carry out the First Immortal's commands.

*    *    *

The pyre took shape, erecting from still-dripping wood. Antique battle axes and modern swords smeared Nodgrav blood against uncaring trees. Tireless arms ferried splintered beams into the pile growing over the blood-soaked battlefield. As the pyre neared its height, the Immortal Guard ceased its labors, lying down to rest or sitting against the city wall and not getting up again. Wasted flesh pressed against bared bone through which crept grasses and weeds.

A croaking command burst from Cain's throat, echoing around the city walls that had entombed the old guards. The noise tugged every fallen eye open. Tattered rags stirred as the Immortals stood to attention once more.

The broken sons of Amalia received their instructions. The still-living Immortals lined up in an honor guard next to the structure, all staring into an emotionless distance while they waited for their queen's final journey. They were joined by a line of the past stretching from the dormant mountain of flame to Cain's wracked form as he held Amalia in his arms. The army stood in silence echoed by the watching Vatran residents. Sobbing faces filled the wide city gates and lined the ramparts and the outer edges of the city walls. None of them would move any closer.

Night fell on the Immortals for the last time. The dissipating mist settled on the green and brown mass, the last of Amalia's sputtering rage igniting the material with a subdued cough that ate at spitting sap and varnish. The glow from the flames reached the center of the city, drawing more spectators abroad. They were greeted by the skeletal march. Polished steel shone in the firelight. The honor guard stood immobile, as if on a parade ground. Behind came the queen, borne by Cain, his face as emotionless as a sharpened knife.

Metal clashed and weapons were presented in the wake of Amalia's passage. No other murmurs of sounds were taken on the rising wind. The plains were lit as though a flaming dervish danced there, contorting like a living thing waiting to be sated on flesh.

Cain, bearing the burden of his queen, hobbled into the flames. He was watched by the unfeeling shapes of the Immortal Guard, their wounds starting to flame as the fire ate at Amalia's form. The living and the dead stood in silhouette before the city's eyes. The queen's fourteen silently hoped their remains would be laid to rest within the city walls, as their companions in battle were.

Justin, the First Immortal, was struck with a strange fatigue at the passing of the queen. He picked up the silvered mirror that had fallen to the ground at Peregrin's end. He slid it into a pocket, as a keepsake and talisman for his daughter, while he watched the flames a while longer. She would need her own army of Immortals soon. Justin believed that Princess Chloe would measure up to her mother's example.

# ABOUT THE AUTHORS

Emory Glass is a dark fantasy author, artist, and worldbuilder. A lifelong owner of a vivid imagination, Emory's first literary love was epic fantasy. At age thirteen, she discovered stories of the gloomier variety and resolved to write her own dark fantasy series: THE CHROMA BOOKS. Alongside writing, Emory loves tea, learning Scottish Gaelic, and creating videos for her YouTube channel WriterPunk. She is pursuing an A.S. in Business Administration to further her goal of opening a book shop. You can read her stories FALL, SACRED APPLE in Kyanite Publishing's Visions of Darkness anthology and THIRTY-THREE TALES OF WAR in Worldbuilding Magazine.

Alan G. Provance grew up in southern New Hampshire, and has been reading fantasy and science fiction books from a young age. Also an avid tabletop gamer, he's been writing for campaigns and characters since his teen years, and developed a passion for reading and writing that lasted throughout his life. After a few years in the military, Alan finished school to become a history teacher. He still lives in southern New Hampshire with his family.

Crystal L. Kirkham resides in a small hamlet west of Red Deer, Alberta. She is an avid outdoors person, unrepentant coffee addict, part-time foodie, servant to a wonderful feline, and companion to several delightfully hilarious canines – Treble and Freddie, the Standard Poodles, and Nahni, the Australian Shepherd. Crystal has published novels across several genres and is a contributing author to multiple best-selling anthologies. She will neither confirm nor deny the rumours regarding the heart in a jar on her desk or the bottle of readers' tears right next to it. However, she will confirm that she once broke the metal handle to a 4-tonne car jack with her bare hands.

Melissa Matos is a creator of stories in many forms, including novels, games, art and music. Her love of fantasy began with Disney and The Last Unicorn. Since then fantasy stories have expanded her world with the likes of the Dresden Files and Name of the Wind. She enjoys creating complex characters having exciting adventures, usually with a bit of mystery thrown in. She lives in Philadelphia with her family and two grumpy cockatiels.

Born in the usual way, Michael D. Nadeau found fantasy at the age of 8 with Dungeons and Dragons. He loved being different people and casting magic. By the late 90's he discovered his love for reading. His favorite teacher gave him her personal books to bring home, and he couldn't get enough. He had even more ways to explore the great worlds out there, and it was harder and harder to come back. When he was much older, and had created and destroyed more worlds than he could count, he decided to delve into the literary world. He created Lythinall, a place where he could tell epic stories and invite his readers on the journey with his characters. The Darkness Returns is the start of the journey, but certainly not the end.

Elizabeth Carlyon is a newly emerging writer, researcher and director with a passion for the fantasy genre. Her mission is to tell creative tales that take real world individual and social issues into new, evocative settings. She has written and directed an array of short films that have received screenings at international festivals.

Sam Claussen is a writer from Des Moines, Iowa. He's taken a swing at multiple genres and has even succeeded a few times. His work rarely features happy endings. "Bittersweet is my beat," he's been known to drunkenly shout at cornered and concerned family members on holidays. He wore all black in high school, listened to emo music and imagines that had some sort of influence on his work.

Brett Venter is a South African writer and magazine editor with an interest in horror, fantasy and science fiction, both as reading and written genres. He has a special fondness for Ray Bradbury and Philip K. Dick and writes cyberpunk when he thinks no-one is looking. If all goes very well, by the end of 2021 someone other than himself will wind up reading his second novel. Brett has previously published horror and science fiction in South African anthology magazine Something Wicked.

# MORE TALES OF DARK FANTASY CHILLS
## FROM KYANITE PUBLISHING

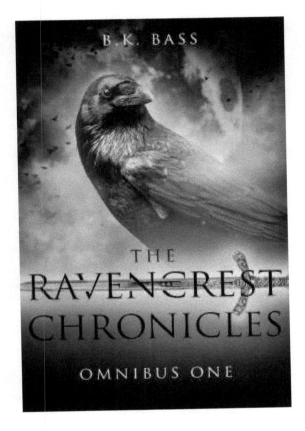

In the city of Seahaven, dark threats loom around every corner. In such a desperate place, it falls upon the shoulders of thieves, pirates, scoundrels, and even orphans to fight to protect the people from things lurking in the shadows.

The Ravencrest Chronicles Omnibus One includes the first four books of the series: *Seahaven, The Hunter's Apprentice, The Giant and the Fishes,* and *Tales from the Lusty Mermaid.*

# THE DEAD TRILOGY
## by ANTHONY D. REDDEN

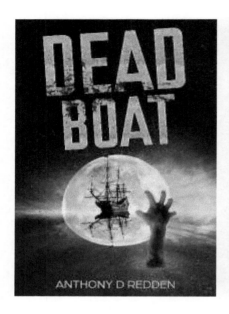

## DEAD BOAT
Given a choice between the noose and a deadly voyage, six men set sail on a ship full of corpses. They expect their passengers to be a quiet crowd, but were they wrong?

## DEAD TOWN
When a blood-soaked lifeboat reached the coast of England, nobody could have realized the horrors it brought with it; for when the dead take to the streets of this thriving metropolis of sin, nobody will be safe.

*BOOK THREE COMING SOON!*

Lightning Source UK Ltd.
Milton Keynes UK
UKHW022016261120
374146UK00014B/1123

9 781952 152535